Currents of Vengeance

Currents of Vengeance

A Darcy Farthing Novel

Arleen Alleman

Praise for Currents of Vengeance

"A visually- and emotionally-rich story of personal greed and desperation . . . set on a cruise ship and in historic South American sea ports. Plots and subplots abound in a delicious blend of fiction and fact with vivid descriptions and compelling characters . . . exciting can't-put-it-down novel tackling the timely issues of crime and justice in international waters."

"Alleman's prose flows effortlessly as she combines mystery, murder, travel, history, and science into a fast moving plot that is totally engaging. One of those books that I was excited to get back to for the unraveling of more suspense . . . and, a "must read" for cruise ship lovers!"

"Alleman's characters add an interesting element that provides suspense and curiosity from multiple angles. Their antics are so well described I can easily see them in my mind's eye."

"Alleman's story-telling is brilliant, as is her captivating use of the English language."

Currents Deep and Deadly

Darcy Farthing Adventures: Book One

"Find adventure, romance, mystery, bizarre interconnected coincidences, brutal murders and a journey of self-discovery on a luxury cruise ship . . . Alleman has done her homework. . . with well-researched details . . . [she] successfully keeps the reader guessing who-dun-it . . . and wraps up the loose ends while nicely setting up the sequel."

--Readers Choice

"Great read . . . the story will not disappoint . . . Alleman's character development is superb and her writing style is captivating . . . Travel lovers will enjoy the travel side . . . and mystery lovers will enjoy the suspense . . ."

--Bookbuzz

Alleman's ability to tell a story is incredible . . . and her writing ability in developing such an intricate plot and pulling it off is superb . . . I'll be reading the sequel and highly recommend this one first.

--Mary Deal, author

To Tim, for a lifetime of love and gratitude.

Acknowledgments

I want to thank Dr. DiAnn Ellis, Roxanne Lindeman, Margrit Mackey, Mildred Simmons, and Marilyn and Bob Tribou, for their thoughtful reviews of my early manuscript. Their ideas and suggestions greatly improved this book. I want to especially thank Sue Ellen Naiberk, a former Government Accountability Office manager for her suggestions and insightful critique. I am genuinely grateful to the real world cruise lines and their employees who have provided so many days and weeks of pleasurable travel. I am an avid cruiser, and you might find me on board a ship one day signing copies of my books. Cruising is a fine way to vacation and see the world.

Unfortunately, crime does happen on cruise ships from time-to-time as it does in any environment where thousands of people congregate. However, in creating the fictional World of Seas Cruise Line and the *Sea Nymph*, I have embellished with an overabundance of drama and treachery for your reading enjoyment.

With that said, in 2010 President Barack Obama signed the Cruise Vessel Security and Safety Act, enacting a law with similarities to the one proposed in this novel. The real law, sponsored by Senator John Kerry and Representative Doris Matsui—without the assistance of the GAO to my knowledge—was designed to enhance the personal security of American passengers aboard cruise ships.

This edition is an updated and reedited version of the original. Like all authors, I greatly value customer feedback and reviews posted on booksellers' Websites. I hope you enjoy this second installment of the Darcy Farthing Adventures and that you will read the other five books in the series as well. Because the first book in the series, *Currents Deep and Deadly*, introduced many characters, I've included a list at the beginning of this book. I hope you find it helpful. I welcome you to contact me through my Website at www.arleenalleman.com. You can also find me on my Facebook page, Currents Deep and Deadly, or on Twitter @aallemanwrites.

The Main Characters

Marianne Alosa	Rachael's adoptive mother
Rachael Alosa	Darcy's nineteen- year-old biological daughter
Ray Alosa	Rachael's adoptive father who works at the U.S. consulate in Buenos Aires
Eve Benton	A member of Mick's GAO team
Dolf Bentzer	The Swedish master captain on the *Sea Nymph*
Michelangelo (Mick) Clayton	Darcy's boyfriend and a GAO manager
Manuel Delgado	A bartender on the *Sea Nymph*
Paul Denezza	The wealthy and ruthless owner of Athens Olympia Hotel and Casino in Las Vegas and Sidney's ex-husband
Sidney Denezza	Darcy's best friend and Paul Denezza's ex-wife
James Early	Staff captain and second in command on the *Sea Nymph*
Don Freeburg	Darcy and Mick's friend from the previous *Sea Nymph* cruise and Charlie Scott's partner
Brooks Larkin	Darcy's ex-husband, Rachael's biological father, And CEO of American Travel Corporation
Suzanne Moretti	The prior hotel manager on the *Sea Nymph*, now deceased

Plato	A former stateroom attendant on the *Sea Nymph*, now deceased
Roger Ramirez	The security chief on the *Sea Nymph*
Bill Sawyer	A U.S. senator from New York and friend to Mick Clayton and the Alosas
Charlie Scott	Darcy and Mick's friend from the previous *Sea Nymph* cruise, and Don Freeburg's partner
Lilith Schrom	A researcher at Wilmore Laboratories and a compulsive gambler
Danny Silva	A member of Mick's GAO team
Tom Smythe	The former chief of security on the *Sea Nymph*
Isabel Trindade	A stateroom attendant on the *Sea Nymph* and Plato's former girlfriend
Ken Worthford	A U.S. Assistant Comptroller General and Mick's boss at the GAO

Introduction

To keep your sanity when it seems everything in your life has gone over-the-top crazy, you can step back from the action and try to gain an astronaut's perspective of the world. But when you find yourself getting lost in the tranquility of that detached view, it's time to dive into a current and get back in the flow.

My name is Darcy Farthing, and I learned this lesson while trying to cope with the emotional upheaval that began in February 2008 when I returned from my now famous and ill-fated South American voyage. As I tried to sort out all the unbelievable events of that four-week cruise, I wanted to believe my life would be much better than before it all happened. After all, my beautiful daughter, Rachael was back in my life, and I had left a lot of pain behind—pain that was locked in a psychological prison for years.

I had also found my old best friend, Sidney, and of course, I had met my Mick. Sure, he and I had many things to resolve before we could get on with our relationship since he lived in DC and I was in Colorado. But those problems just seemed like logistics. Well, as we were soon to discover, they were a little more than that and geography turned out to be the least of our worries.

The media attention heaped on all of us when we arrived home from Valparaiso, Chile was at first unexpected and unwelcome. The world press played up the story because of the human-interest aspect, and the involvement of cruise line employees in murders on board the ship. Before long, everyone seemed to know about me and being an instant minor celebrity created a whole new level of stress.

I still needed personal time to work out my feelings and analyze how my beliefs . . . or lack thereof . . . had been affected by it all. Suddenly, however, there didn't seem to be any privacy. I suppose the upside was that I became accustomed to everyone knowing about me and my past. In retrospect, I believe that enabled me to write candidly about the experience.

As everyone with a TV, computer, cell phone, or radio now knows I am a skeptic about anything that is not tangible or at least potentially knowable in the physical world. For quite a while now I have believed there is an elegant simplicity to everything that does not require the added layer of supernatural intervention. So I was still clinging to the hope that many of the unlikely connections I experienced on the cruise were the result of real coincidences— happening just by chance. But that didn't mean I wasn't bewildered by all the layers of impossibly related events.

In the end, writing the book was cathartic, and it helped me sort out my feelings, but because the public continues to be fascinated with the story of what happened on the *Sea Nymph*, it has naturally brought even more attention to all of us. Ultimately, the moderate success of the book completely changed my life, both personally and financially.

I am amazed at how far the currents flowing through my life have carried me from where I thought I was headed just over a year ago. After the cruise, we all wanted to leave the trauma behind. It was just that we were not willing to let Paul Denezza, my friend Sidney's ex-husband, get away with hiring people to kill her.

Amazingly, the desire to see Paul pay for his crimes led us to embark on a second cruise. This one started with a very business-like agenda, but the mysterious underlying currents that carried us through the first cruise were still lurking below the surface waiting to drag us under. This time, however, nothing happened by chance or coincidence. I guess you could say that multiple manifestations of revenge sailed along with us, and as a result, we are now intimately familiar with the physical and psychological damage wrought by vengeance.

Along the way, we encountered more than our share of deeply flawed individuals, and in telling this second story, I hope to deepen my understanding of human nature and regain a comfort level with my personal philosophy. More than anything else, I am hopeful that our saga is finally at an end along with all the personal suffering and public attention of the past year.

Part One

The Death Stalker

1

February 17, 2008 – Washington, DC

Michelangelo Clayton turned carefully onto his side to check the clock on the bedside table. With some relief, he noted that this simple maneuver was a little easier to accomplish than it had been a few days ago. He raised his head and squinted at the digits in the dimly lit room; Sunday, 11:14 a.m. Mick sighed and fell back against the pillow. For the past two weeks, he had spent most of his time in this charming blue and brown reproduction colonial-style bedroom. Now that he was feeling better, boredom was setting in, and he was looking forward to having Bill around for some company at least for part of the day.

A door had closed quietly at the other end of the house, and Mick was waiting to see whether it was Bill or the nurse who was supposed to visit two days a week to check his stitches and help him with his personal care. He never knew exactly which day she would show up and assumed that Aetna would soon curtail the visits, which was fine with him because he didn't think he needed her minimal efforts anyway.

Senator Bill Sawyer stepped into the bedroom with briefcase in hand. He wore a dark grey suit and a black and red striped tie over a dazzling white shirt, indicating that he had come from work. He glanced at Mick and walked directly to the window to raise the black-out pleated shade. Bright sunlight immediately penetrated the gloom, significantly improving the room's overall ambiance. Then he returned to the foot of the bed and peered down at Mick.

Mick thought that his friend was still in decent shape for a guy who had little time to take care of himself. For some reason, at that moment he noticed for the first time that his sandy hair was beginning to thin a little in front. Otherwise, he still had the same freckled boyish look as when they met at Cornell more than twenty years ago. The two had been best friends since then, and after the events of the past seven weeks, their friendship had deepened.

"Hey buddy," Bill was saying, "is there anything I can get you or are you going to get out of that bed? It's almost noon, and I'm taking the rest of the day off so I'm thinking we should get you out on the terrace. It's a beautiful day and not really that cold . . . anyway, we can sit in the sun."

"Yeah, good idea. I've been thinking that I want to talk to you again about some of the stuff that happened on the cruise and ideas I have about Paul Denezza." He pulled himself up as he spoke and managed a sitting position on the side of the bed. Bill stepped up and bent over to take his elbow. After helping him up, Bill let go and started for the door. Mick said to his back, "I'm so much better now. I don't know how I can ever repay you for letting me stay here and for nursing me back to health."

Bill turned around to see Mick struggling with his bathrobe and returned to help him put it on. The deep chest wound had made his left shoulder stiff and reaching behind him was still a chore. He answered with a chuckle, "I think if I had a big hole in my chest and had lost half my blood supply you would do the same for me, right?"

"Let's hope you never go through anything like this, but yeah, I guess you could count on me," He tried to laugh without taking too deep a breath.

Mick proceeded slowly down the hallway and across the polished oak-planked living room floor to a set of French doors. Out on the grey and black flagstone terrace, he sat opposite Bill at a glass-topped iron filigree table. Before they became involved in a conversation, though, Bill suddenly excused himself and went to change into jeans and to get them both a beer.

Mick breathed deeply and looked at his surroundings, grateful that the pain in his chest was greatly diminishing. He gazed at the remaining red and gold leaves of the winter garden surrounding the perimeter of Bill's back yard. The $3 million two-story brick row house on North Carolina Avenue had been beautifully restored, but only had seventeen hundred square feet. Bill had said it was plenty big enough for him, and besides, it was only about six blocks from the Russell Senate Office Building at First and Constitution where he spent much of his time.

Bill soon returned to his seat and held out an icy bottle. "Here, try this, from the Blue and Gray Brewing Company in Fredericksburg. Lately, I've been trying to sample some beers from our great local micros." They both chugged and leaned back stretching their legs out in front of them.

Mick held the bubbling amber liquid up to the light and studied the carbonation. Turning the bottle, he read the label—Blue and Gray Classic Lager—then took another sip and savored the smooth malty flavor. "This is pretty good and fairly light, which is probably a good thing for me right now since I'm out of training."

He tried to draw a deep breath and leaned forward in his seat with his elbows resting on the table. With a subdued tone, he said, "You know, I've been thinking a lot about what I can do to make sure Denezza pays for at least part of what happened on the ship. There is no doubt that he hired those two crew members to get rid of his wife and now they're both dead." Bill swallowed and waved his bottle for him to continue.

Mick nodded. "His involvement will be hard to prove with no one left to give direct testimony. It's all so damned complicated because Sidney Denezza is still alive and four others are dead . . . I don't know, maybe there's no one left who knew about Paul's plan." He shook his head and sipped his beer.

"So what do you think you'd like to do about it?"

Mick seemed to perk up a little. "OK, Tom Smythe, the security chief on the *Sea Nymph* was fired by World of Seas Cruise Line because of everything he supposedly allowed to happen on the cruise. Well, he tells me he intends to continue working with the Vegas FBI to try and prosecute Paul."

Finally, Bill set his bottle down and leaned toward Mick. "Really? That is a little surprising under the circumstances."

"I thought so too, but I mailed him the keys to the Range Rover, still parked where I left it at the Miami Marriott, and he's driving up here to talk to me."

Bill pursed his lips and pulled his legs under him. "Sounds like the two of you already have a plan in mind."

"Well, one of the things we're thinking is that someone needs to go back to the ship and talk to members of the crew to see if anyone else knew about Paul's scheme. That's the only way we're going to get evidence to prove what he was doing if evidence even exists."

Bill stared across at his friend as he took another swallow of beer. Then he shook the empty bottle, pushed himself from the table and jumped to his feet. "Want another one?"

"Sure, but that had better be it for me."

A minute later Bill returned and lowered himself into his chair. "I get the feeling there is something you think I can do to help, but I can't begin to imagine what it would be."

"You've already done so much for us by making that arrangement with your friend, Ray Alosa. If he hadn't delayed Denezza at the Buenos Aires consulate causing him to miss the sailing, things would probably have been much worse." Mick felt guilty about involving his friend even further, but he was desperate to make sure Denezza paid for his crimes. "And now you've done so much for me personally, I wouldn't ask for anything else . . . only a little question and some advice."

"Oh, oh, that even worries me." Bill grinned and shook his head. "OK, what do you have in mind?"

"What Smythe and I have in mind is something I already tried to initiate with Ken, but I didn't get very far over the phone. He's sympathetic to my situation, but in a way, I think this is the last straw for him. Let's face it, I haven't been putting my full effort into the job for a couple of years and now living here with you is making it even worse." Ken Worthford was the U.S. Assistant Comptroller General for Law and Justice at the Government Accountability Office, and Mick's boss. As Director of State Law Enforcement Issues, Mick was responsible for the work of twenty analysts who conducted audits of federally funded law enforcement agencies. Even before his recent injury, he hadn't been in a healthy emotional state and hadn't been carrying the full weight of his position.

"We know Ken has always had a problem with our friendship. He thinks it's a conflict of interest that I'm a member of Congress and you work for the GAO, and it doesn't matter to him that we've been friends since college. In his mind, we should not have a personal relationship at all . . . but what did you say to Ken about Denezza?"

"Nothing directly about him; just that I want to lead a review of crimes on cruise ships and use that opportunity to go back to the *Sea Nymph* to interview crew members about the death plot."

"Wow, that's huge—you would really get back on that boat?"

"Like I've said before, you wouldn't have believed the situation on that ship, Bill. People were dying and all the cruise line seemed to focus on was making sure there was no inconvenience to passengers. Even if I had not been stabbed and the rest of the shit hadn't happened, I would still think we should do some kind of study of the situation."

"Yeah, I know all about that. Lots of Americans are on those ships, and more passengers are assaulted or disappear on cruises than most people realize. What did Ken say when you suggested the job?"

"He said no. He said that because GAO is not an enforcement agency and we don't have much extra money in the budget for self-initiated work, it just isn't feasible to go sailing off on a cruise ship . . . in his words." Mick paused as if assessing whether he should say what he was thinking. He ran his hand through his dark wavy bangs and smiled at his friend.

"But Bill, I've been wondering, what if you or your International Relations Committee requests the assignment?" Mick knew that GAO usually accepts Congressional requests and when he first came back to DC after the cruise, Bill told him about Congressional hearings where victims and family members told stories about crimes committed against them on cruise ships. "Remember the

16

hearings you talked about? Wouldn't it make sense if you were interested in determining how widespread these problems are?"

Before Bill could answer, Mick rushed to finish his proposal. "And one more thing; I want to bring Tom on board—so to speak—as a consultant. He used to be an L.A. cop, and he worked on the *Sea Nymph* for ten years. Maybe the committee could request his assistance as well." He sat back with a sheepish expression and waited for Bill's reaction.

"So you just want a little advice, ha? OK, that is an interesting idea. Those hearings were held several years ago, and now it's 2008, and we haven't done a damn thing about it. My committee and others have talked about drafting some kind of legislation related to passenger safety on cruise ships, but it's one of those issues that just gets pushed down the list of priorities, mainly because there's a big problem due to the lack of jurisdiction in international waters." He paused and looked away for a few moments. Then he drew his long legs under him and leaned forward with an earnest expression.

"Maybe this could be a way to get some information to help us formulate something." Another thoughtful pause ensued while he stared across the yard. Finally he nodded apparently having made a decision. "OK, tell you what, I'll speak to Ken next week." He saw Mick flinch and added, "I won't tell him we talked about it. I'll give him the history we already have on the hill, and try to get him to see that it's only natural for my interest to be revived after all the press coverage of the *Sea Nymph* nightmare and your involvement in it."

Mick smiled and leaned back in his chair. "Thanks, Buddy, you're coming to the rescue again. I can't wait to hear what comes of that conversation."

They chatted amiably about other current events, but after about twenty minutes Mick was obviously becoming restless. "I'm getting a little tired. I think I'll go back inside and I really should call Darcy, anyway." His brow furrowed as he stared sadly at the flagstone floor—then seemed to catch himself. "I haven't talked to her much since we got back."

"OK, say hi to Darcy for me. I'm hoping to actually meet her before long. Has Rachael flown up from Buenos Aires to see her yet?"

"No, but apparently she has a break from college in about a week and plans to visit Darcy in Colorado Springs. Bill, can you imagine what it must be like for a mother and daughter to be meeting each other after almost twenty years apart?"

"I know it all seems amazing."

"I still can't believe how the cruise brought them together like that . . . and our role in it. Darcy is really working hard to overcome the guilt she was carrying all those years."

Bill's face lit with a spontaneous thought. "Hey, I have an idea. Maybe Darcy and Rachael can fly out here during her visit. Rachael can stay in my other guest room, and it's about time you and Darcy got to spend some time together."

"Thanks, that really is a great idea, but I don't know how she would feel about it. Part of me thinks I should back off a little, for now, just to give her time to build a relationship with Rachael. But I'll tell her about your offer when I call."

Bill squinted into the bright sun behind Mick's chair for a few moments. "Good enough, but you know, I should think Darcy would want both you and Rachael in her life now."

When he did not get a response, Bill changed the subject. "Oh, I almost forgot. I'm making us a dinner reservation at Sam and Harry's for Tuesday. It's time you got out of the house, and I've really missed our happy hours. It's been since before you went down to your place on Marco Island, which was way before you went on the cruise."

Mick felt a jolt of anxiety. "I'm a little anxious about how I'll feel getting out in public, but I know I have to do it soon." He sighed and pushed away from the table. "Thanks, I'll be looking forward to one of those rare NY strips not to mention the great wine selection." Mick sincerely wished he felt as enthusiastic as he tried to sound.

2

On Tuesday evening, Bill and Mick were sitting at Sam and Harry's bar sipping champagne and munching baked spinach and Gouda with crab on baguettes. They were chatting about the approach Bill planned to take when he talked with Mick's boss, Ken. They had already decided it would help their case if the FBI had a stake in the GAO request. So, Mick had called Special Agent Grant Murray in the Vegas field office to request his cooperation.

"Murray really wants to get Paul Denezza," Mick was explaining without much enthusiasm. "It seems the bureau has had suspicions about his business operations for a long time or maybe something in his past, but they evidently haven't been able to put enough evidence together to prosecute him. I'm thinking it might be a tax thing or maybe even a mob connection." He paused to sip his drink and audibly sighed. "Anyway, Murray was delighted to sign on to our review and actually said that whatever methodology we come up with he wants us to include the *Sea Nymph* in our study."

"Well, I can't imagine Ken rejecting a request that has the interest of both the Congress and the bureau. I'll try to talk with him tomorrow."

Mick looked around at the familiar jazz motif. He couldn't count the number of times he'd sat in this same spot after work with Bill, while Congressional staffers and occasionally other members passed by, often stopping to greet the popular senator on their way to the dining room. The environment had always been comfortable and stimulating, yet this time he felt nervous and jumpy in a way he could not recall feeling before. *It must be something to do with the stress of my recovery.* After all, he had come very close to dying on the deck of the *Sea Nymph* and then again in the Valparaiso hospital.

The hostess came to tell them their table was ready. Bill stood and waited while Mick eased off his stool. As he watched his friend, he worried. Mick was not himself at all, and the change didn't really seem related to his physical injury. Knowing him as he did, he noticed that his mannerisms—and seemingly his personality—had somehow dampened. He appeared emotionally flat despite his supposed new love relationship with Darcy.

They slowly made their way to the table and were soon enjoying their meal of rare steaks, baked potato heaped with sour cream, and lightly grilled asparagus topped off by a bottle of 1998 Napa Valley Mount Veeder Cabernet. As Mick slowly chewed, he leaned back and tried to relax. *I can't wait to get back to feeling normal. This uneasiness sucks.*

3

May 12, 2008 – Las Vegas

Paul Denezza sat rigid, keeping his eyes pointed straight ahead, as he made his way down Martin Luther King to the John Lawrence Bailey Memorial Building. He really hated this part of town and totally resented having to be here for the second time in three months no less. The neighborhood really didn't look that bad now, but when he was a teenager this area had been the territory of predominantly black gangs, and he and his friends had risked serious injury to their souped-up Furies and GTOs, and to themselves, just by driving down the street. Of course, that had not stopped them from many Saturday nights of exhibition speed racing down Lake Mead Boulevard just to taunt the locals.

He turned left onto a Lake Mead that was much busier these days and made another quick left on Stella Lake. He caught himself absentmindedly thinking about John Bailey, the 48-year-old veteran FBI agent killed by a bank robber in 1990. Paul mused with characteristic meanness and hostility, *the dumb ass stumbled onto the crime while he was off duty and somehow managed to botch his arrest of the gunman.*

Opting for a parking place on the street behind the building rather than dealing with the FBI parking lot, he noted that he was about twenty minutes early for his appointment. He got out and stretched. Adjusting his three hundred dollar hand-painted tie, he swaggered across the street.

A little way up the sidewalk he decided he could use some coffee, so he stepped under the green awning of Gritz Café. Once inside and seated at one of the six metal tables in the tiny restaurant—little more than a takeout place—he stared out the window at the vast modern beige block and glass structure directly across the street.

A smiling waitress approached optimistically but was met with Paul's surly expression. In his opinion, she was a typical bleached blond sun-dried sixty, wearing a short skirt above too-fat knees and a too-small tank top with flabby cleavage bulging out of the top. Mutton in lambs clothing is what his dad used to say.

She took his order, still smiling, and after a minute returned and set down his coffee and a glazed donut. He mumbled his thanks and took a bite as he looked around. Suddenly he realized that everyone in the place looked like a cop. He looked down at his donut and almost laughed out loud. *Shit! Of course, this is just a bureau hangout. What the hell am I doing in here?*

He tried to relax, telling himself he had nothing to worry about. His first interview with agent Murray back in February had not resulted in anything detrimental as far as he could tell. Murray had asked him to describe his whereabouts during the time of the cruise and then asked for a detailed account of why he had taken a month-long journey around South America in the first place. He had answered easily enough that he was under a lot of stress from his business and had needed a rest, and he had also thought it would be good for his marriage. Paul chuckled to himself. That last point sure had been a nice touch.

He knew nothing would come of today's interview either. He didn't see how anyone could connect him to Suzanne Moretti's madness and murderous rampage on the ship, and all he had to do was remain calm and adamant about their friendship. It would probably look better for him if he were still married to Sidney, but divorce certainly wasn't unusual these days. Anyway, he thought he could convincingly play the sad ex-husband who had planned the romantic get-away to try to save the marriage.

As he sipped his coffee and watched the building, taking care to avoid eye contact with the other patrons, his mood quickly deteriorated. He was barely able to contain his anger as he thought about how he would eventually exact revenge on Darcy Farthing and Mick Clayton, but especially on Tom Smythe. No matter what he may have done and how it had turned out, those assholes had interfered with his plans, and that was unacceptable. He truly believed that without their meddling he would have accomplished his goal...even if he had ended up alone anyway.

He ruled his world with an iron hand. That is simply how he lived and had known no other way ever since he learned from the pros about the importance of maintaining control in order to get what he wanted from life.

His middle-class childhood in the old Huntridge neighborhood just off the Maryland Parkway circle had been relatively normal except that his mom was a part-time hooker. He laughed to himself when he thought about his den mother mom, enthusiastically entertaining cub scouts with homemade brownies, still dressed in her short low cut black sheath and spike heels, having just returned from work. The thing was, in those days no one seemed to have any problem with it—seemingly not even her husband.

His dad worked as a pit boss at the old Aladdin Casino and as a fringe member of the mob. At the age of sixteen, things had started changing rapidly for Paul when his dad helped him get his first job. He started out as a busboy and room service waiter at the old Sands, and he knew that having an Italian heritage and *the look* had helped him fit into the casino environment back in the early seventies. He had paid close attention to the subtleties of what went on around him and had been more than willing to do odd jobs for the bosses; running messages, money, and suspect packages up and down the strip.

These errands gradually became more frequent and increased in importance. As a sort of compensation, he had asked Mario, the daytime pit boss, to teach him how to play poker. By the time he turned twenty-one he was so proficient at the game that Mario hired him as a shill to play for the house.

Quite simply, he became a world-class gambler. After a couple of years, he found himself playing for high stakes sponsors who flew into town with far more money than ability. He played with their cash, and they paid him twenty percent of his winnings. It quickly added up, and he knew how to save.

One evening, when he had finished raking in his winnings and was heading for the casino cage to cash in, a pudgy middle-aged guy sauntered over and struck up a conversation. The guy was Byron Cangey, the owner of the Athens Olympia, a small hotel and casino just off the sparsely populated south end of the strip. Cangey, what a puss, Paul remembered. After a little small talk, the man offered Paul a job. He was to play and cheat with Athens Olympia house money, duping customers and sending the winnings back into the casino. This was one of the mob's infamous skimming techniques, but the bit-player Cangey was operating entirely on his own. Paul quickly assessed the situation and barely hesitated before accepting the position.

Paul had been developing his Vegas contacts for ten years by then, and he knew the ropes. He played along with the illegal scheme for six months, gambling with high rollers and amassing a million dollars for his boss. One early morning after a particularly lucrative night, he presented Cangey with taped evidence of the fraud along with a threat to send it anonymously to the police and gaming commission. With several of his mob-wannabe friends lurking menacingly beside him, Paul had little difficulty persuading the owner to sign over his share in the business.

As it turned out, Cangey met with an unfortunate accident several months later. His brakes failed as he drove at an unsafe speed on a twisty road with no guardrail near Mount Charleston, not far from town. His lesser partners fell by the wayside as well when they realized the new owner had wise guy ties. That is how Paul acquired the Athens Olympia, which he subsequently expanded into the major hotel and casino complex it is today.

Since then, Vegas had dramatically changed and the mob's role in casino skimming operations greatly diminished, especially after Anthony Spilotro's downfall and eventual demise in the 1980s. In the new Vegas family environment, Paul had engaged in only minor infractions of the law, that is, until he conceived of his failed plan to rid himself of Sidney.

He shook his head as he thought about how lucky he'd been to dodge the bullet coming straight for him. His friend Suzanne Moretti's murderous insanity was now legend in the press, and he was glad he left the cruise early and returned to his business before things got entirely out of hand. After returning home he followed all the media accounts of the cruise and the aftermath, and the relief he felt when he heard that Suzanne was gone was liberating

He had little contact with Sidney now that the divorce was just about final, and he knew his best bet for determining what was going on with Darcy Farthing and Mick Clayton was to cultivate his relationship with Brooks Larkin. He was pissed at Larkin too but knew it was more important—for now—to use the Vegas businessman rather than harm him. Larkin was Paul's acquaintance and had provided travel services for many years, including arranging Sidney's and his bookings on the Sea Nymph. He now understood that Larkin had manipulated those reservations to orchestrate a shipboard reunion between Darcy and Sidney.

He still could not get over the revelation that Larkin was also Darcy Farthing's ex-husband and the father of her daughter, whom she had somehow found in Buenos Aires. Paul did not believe in coincidence, and he suspected Larkin had something to do with that reunion as well.

Paul also learned that the ship's security chief, Tom Smythe, was canned by World of Seas following the disastrous cruise. That revelation had made his day. He hated the guy for meddling in his affairs, but more than that for making him feel vulnerable and weak in a way he'd never before experienced. He promised himself that one way or another he would find out where Smythe was and make him pay in a big way. He would have to come up with something brilliant and untraceable to deal with him, and he was already working on that.

4

Paul abruptly stood, threw a $5 bill on the table and hurried outside into the already parching midday sun. He tried to put a bounce in his step and suppress his nervousness as he crossed the narrow deserted street, but he felt himself beginning to sweat under his expensive silk jacket, and that pissed him off.

He entered the grounds through a gate in the low fencing, apparently fashioned to resemble stylized white pickets. Once inside, he proceeded through security and then rode the elevator to the second floor. He was disconcertingly familiar with the layout of the place and the location of Murray's office, and this fueled his anger. By the time he approached the door, he was so worked up that he had to stop and take several deep breaths to release some tension. Finally feeling more in control, he stepped inside.

The receptionist made a call, and within three minutes, agent Murray strode out of his office dressed in the cheap dark-suit uniform of the FBI and offered his hand. Paul shook it and looked into Murray's grey-green eyes, slightly magnified behind rimless glasses. The now presbyopic ex-Navy seal was in his mid-forties, trim, with short dark hair and erect posture. He escorted Paul back to one of the interview—or interrogation—rooms, depending on perspective.

After they seated themselves opposite each other at a small rectangular table in the scantily furnished government-green room, Murray stared silently at Paul for a full minute. Paul thought the agent probably just wanted to add to his anxiety, but Murray was actually noting Paul's arrogant demeanor and trying to subdue his own anger, which was threatening to bubble to the surface. He hated this guy but didn't want to show that particular emotion.

Paul was about five feet nine, a little stocky, but in pretty good shape. He looked fifty, but Murray knew he was actually fifty-eight. Olive skin, dark eyes, and wavy black hair befitted his Mediterranean features. What Murray noted most was the difficulty Paul was having hiding his supercilious expression, right down to the involuntary lip curl. *Man, I want a piece of you so bad!* Finally, Murray leaned forward on his elbows and calmly began the interview.

"All right Mr. Denezza, we are here to follow up on our last conversation regarding the cruise you took on the World of Seas Cruise Line's ship, the *Sea Nymph*, this past January 2008. I will be taping this conversation. First, please describe exactly your relationship with Suzanne Moretti, the ship's hotel manager."

"As I have said repeatedly, I met Suzanne here in Vegas at my hotel about a year ago when she was on vacation with her husband. She became a friend, nothing more."

"What was your relationship with the crew members Ronaldo Ruiz and Plato Des Rameaux?"

"I had none. I knew that Ruiz was the cruise director in charge of entertainment on the ship, but I did not know Plato. I only know from all the press coverage that he was a cabin attendant and worked for Suzanne."

"Do you understand that you were seen having conversations with this Plato?"

"Yes, that is what Officer Smythe told me on the ship, but at the time I did not know who he was. I was just being friendly to a crew member who happened to be in my vicinity."

"Did you solicit these crew members and Ms. Moretti to kill your wife for money while you were on the cruise?"

"Absolutely not. As it turns out, Suzanne was apparently quite insane, and I have no idea what arrangement she might have had with other crew members, but I had nothing to do with it."

"What information can you provide about the deaths on board the *Sea Nymph*?"

"I have no personal knowledge about them. All I know is what the media has repeatedly reported. That is, Suzanne Moretti and possibly her husband committed the murders. I don't know anything more."

"What knowledge do you have about Ms. Moretti's possible motive for her actions?"

"Once again, I have no idea about any of that. The woman was crazy."

"Why did you abandon the cruise and your wife in Buenos Aires?"

"Someone stole my passport from my stateroom, and I had to go to the U.S. consulate to get a replacement. There was a delay in getting it done, and I could not make it back to the ship in time for the departure. You can verify that with Ray Alosa, a big shot at the consulate."

"Why didn't you fly to the next port and resume the cruise?"

Denezza hesitated. He thought he was doing well so far, but he had to be careful to sound logical. "I thought about it, but Sidney and I weren't getting along all that well in the close confines of the ship. And anyway, I was getting nervous about being gone from the hotel for so long, so I made a quick decision to fly home. Actually, when I was on the plane, I had second thoughts about leaving Sidney behind, but in the end, I believed she would be fine, and she had her plane ticket to fly home from Valparaiso."

The interview progressed in this fashion with Paul presenting a somewhat plausible explanation for everything he'd done—or not done. Finally, Murray said, "Mr. Denezza, this concludes the interview for today. Please understand that we might call you back at a later time with additional questions."

Paul was seething with frustration and anger, but he tried to come across amiably. "Whatever you say, but this is a waste of your time and, *more importantly*, mine."

Murray escorted him out into the lobby area, and he unceremoniously left the building. Jogging back to his car, he thought he'd performed well again, but made a mental note that if Murray had him back a third time, he would bring his lawyer along.

5

June 14, 2008 – Colorado Springs

"But Darcy, I still don't see why you won't come to Vegas with me this time. I thought we had fun there before." Rachael shifted uneasily in her seat and looked away from me to study towering Pike's Peak while she waited for my response. If I didn't know better, I would think she was pouting a little. I knew my daughter loved being here on my deck so close to the mountain, but she was becoming more anxious the longer we talked about her upcoming trip.

"Rachael, it's tough for me to describe how I feel. You know that Brooks Larkin and I had no contact at all for eighteen years—from the time we were divorced until you and I went to see him in March. I absolutely don't want to get into any relationship with him. Can you understand that?"

Having only recently been reunited with her myself, I didn't want to say how uncomfortable I had been with my ex—her father. He had acted far too familiar under the circumstances, and I was still upset that he had interfered with my life and manipulated my travel reservations—even though it had turned out amazingly well for Rachael and me. I still didn't understand what he was trying to do. I only wanted to focus on Mick and our budding relationship, and I just didn't want to visit Brooks again. I watched her face—it was my face minus about twenty years, as she turned from the mountain, tossed her long blonde hair and looked back at me with those enormous cornflower blue eyes.

"Yes, I guess I can understand that. But isn't it more important for me to get to know my birth father and any other relatives I have that I never knew about?"

"Oh, Rachael, please don't go there again now. I've tried to explain that I never got along with my parents and haven't spoken to them for over twenty years either. I know it's hard for you to accept because you had such a great childhood with Ray and Marianne . . . I mean your mom and dad. But we weren't all lucky enough to have that kind of experience. I can't just call my parents and start trying to explain everything even if I wanted to. If they have any smarts, they already know about all of this from the publicity about the cruise, but they have not tried to contact me.

"Besides, you did get to talk with Granny Elizabeth on the phone and I know you enjoyed that. Even though she lives in Liverpool, she's in good shape for being eighty-four, and maybe we can get her over here on a trip or go there ourselves. I've told you she's the only member of my family I ever got along with." *And that is ironic since she is my dad's mother and he is even more of an asshole than Brooks was.*

Rachael looked at me with a sad expression and shrugged in a manner that left no doubt that my sad family situation was a huge disappointment to my new daughter. "All right, Darcy, I'll go to Vegas to see Brooks by myself and then fly home to Argentina from there."

She paused and glanced back at Pike's Peak with its tiny remaining patch of snow shimmering in the sunlight, and then turned her eyes to me with a small smile. "I still have to figure out what I'm going to do when dad gets reassigned to the embassy in Africa next year. I don't want to go to Kenya, mainly because of school and I still want to get on a rowing crew you know."

"I know, and there are many schools here in the States where you could transfer and do that. Some are in the northwest and some back east. It would be wonderful for me if you came here to Colorado Springs or Denver, but I know those wouldn't be the best bet for the rowing, especially if you still have Olympic aspirations."

"Oh I do, and my parents have said they support whatever I decide, but I know they would feel better if I move near you or Brooks so I wouldn't be all alone."

"Ray and Marianne are amazing people, and I am so happy that they are the ones who adopted you, Rachael." I paused for a moment, wondering if I should say what I was thinking, then forged ahead.

"There might be another option as far as your moving near to me is concerned. I wasn't going to mention this yet but I might as well. Mick has asked me if I would consider trying to transfer or even quit Shrinden Pharmaceuticals to move to DC." Rachael looked startled. "I'm thinking about it and please understand I haven't decided yet, but Georgetown University and George Washington University both have excellent rowing programs. You couldn't ask for a better school than Georgetown if you can get in and I bet you can. Bill Sawyer might be able to help with that."

"Oh, I had no idea you were thinking of moving. It would be great for you and Mick." She hesitated and looked as if she wasn't sure she should say whatever was on her mind.

"What is it, honey?"

"Well, it's just that I thought maybe I could be close to both you and Brooks somehow. I think Mick is great, but . . . that is just what I was thinking."

So straightforward, just like me, even though I was out of her life from the time she was eighteen months old. "Rachael, I'm not going to have a relationship with Brooks. You simply have to accept that."

"I know, but it just seems like it could be so perfect."

Perfect, huh? *If she only knew the nightmare I lived with him.* I had explained it to her the best I could without making her father sound like a monster, but she had no way of understanding how horrible my time with him was. I had to admit, though, that something else was going on now. I didn't completely understand my confused feelings, and that was the real problem.

When I took Rachael to meet Brooks, I confronted him and told him I knew he had used his business, American Travel Corporation, to manipulate Sidney and me so that we'd be on the same cruise. Before that, Sidney and I had not spoken since shortly after my divorce from Brooks. I demanded to know why he had done it. His response was that it was to get us back together and basically just because he could. But I couldn't have been more shocked when he admitted he'd been keeping track of Rachael and me for fifteen years and that he only wanted to make amends for his behavior during our marriage. I couldn't make myself believe him.

The next day when we met him for lunch, I have to admit we spent a strange and surprisingly pleasant couple of hours chatting. He appeared to be a completely changed man from the out-of-control alcoholic I married. I had some weird and unwelcome thoughts—I felt drawn to him somehow—and that was bizarre and wrong.

6

That night, long after Rachael had gone to bed, sleep just would not come to me. I thought of getting up to take a Tylenol PM but decided maybe it would be better to let my thoughts flow and see where they led me. I hated that there was tension between us for the first time since we found each other. Her talk of moving to Colorado or Vegas to finish college when Ray and Marianne moved to their new post in Africa was great and totally understandable, but the whole business of her wanting to meet my parents and her notion that somehow she and Brooks and I could be some sort of family unit was distressing, to say the least. I just couldn't believe how naïve I had been to think that I could isolate her with Mick and me and somehow pretend that her other blood relatives didn't exist.

I thought about how Rachael had not really gotten to know Mick, and now she had so much more experience with Brooks. I wondered if Brooks would introduce her to his parents. During our short-lived marriage, I never got to know them and had no idea whether he even had a relationship with them. *It couldn't be worse than the one I don't have with mine.* I didn't know much about Brooks either, and that was disconcerting now that Rachael was back in our lives. I knew I should be talking to him about our daughter, but I was just too uncomfortable around him.

Then there was Mick, another source of stress and confusion. It was nice that he asked me to live with him, but something was nagging at me that would not let go. Traditionally, I have good intuition and perceptions, and lately, they were screaming that something was not right with Mick. He seemed distant and certainly wasn't calling me as much as I thought he should.

For about the hundredth time, I thought about my visit to DC at the end of April, after Mick moved from Bill's house back to his own condo. Bill had invited Rachael and me to stay at his place back in March, but Mick had not seemed very enthusiastic about it over the phone, so I waited another month and then made the trip alone.

Mick's condo was located just inside the Northwest quadrant of DC in Tenleytown, originally named for John Tennally, the owner of a roadside tavern. I was surprised to learn that during the Civil War the area hosted Fort Reno, the largest and strongest of a string of protective forts encircling Washington. When the war ended, the area became a home for freed slaves and slum-like conditions until the district razed much of the neighborhood in an early attempt at urban renewal. These days, Tenleytown is an affluent area of trendy shops and cafes along Wisconsin Avenue near the American University campus and the red line metro station.

The week I spent there was wonderful because all I wanted was to be with Mick. But even though I saw that physically he had healed rapidly, he was very different from the man I met and fell hopelessly in love with on the ship. We shared a romance that was unprecedented for me. I had never been with a man who was so . . . well, so normal. Everything about him fit me perfectly not the least of which was his finely toned body and the passion he always brought to our lovemaking. No matter what, just being near him still made me hot, but in a way, I felt as if I had to get to know him all over again.

The worst of it was that he did not seem to have much enthusiasm for sex and that was completely unexpected. He just lacked his previous intensity and passion. Of course, I realized the intensely romantic environment on the ship was not like everyday life, and I told myself he just needed more time to get over the trauma he had suffered several months earlier. After all, I had the wonderful memories of the old Mick and wasn't about to give up on him yet.

Mick had returned to his work at GAO, so I had a lot of free time during the day. I enjoyed my first trip to DC as a tourist and visited all the major attractions, including the National Gallery and the Smithsonian. Typically, I slept in until around 9:00 a.m. and ate a light breakfast. Then I left the Cityline at Tenley Condominiums and walked up Albemarle Street to Tenley Circle at Nebraska and Wisconsin to hop onto the train. As an added bonus, cherry blossoms were in full bloom virtually everywhere, and the sight and scent of them helped soothe my stress and uneasiness.

The National Zoo at Woodley Park is only three metro stops from the condo, and I visited there several times. I loved strolling aimlessly through the park, stopping to look at whatever animals presented themselves for viewing along the way.

By far my favorite excursions were the tours of the Capital and the White House. During that first trip to DC, I finally met Bill Sawyer, whom I already considered a close friend because of his role in bringing Rachael and me together. Actually, it was his friendship with both Mick and Rachael's father, Ray that enabled our meeting. One day he gave me a personal tour of the Congressional offices, including some areas that are not ordinarily open to the public—backrooms where the staffers work in unbelievably cramped spaces and where the real work of the Congress happens.

As we strolled around the quiet halls, I gently asked how he thought Mick was doing. It was apparent he had some of the same concerns as I did. Bill thought Mick was experiencing some turmoil that he was unwilling or unable to discuss. "I've been wondering if maybe it's a reawakening of the depression he suffered following the deaths of his wife and parents. That horrible sequence of events a few years ago really knocked him out. I can't think of any other reason for his behavior."

Bill has known Mick very well for many years, so I trusted his judgment. There just didn't seem to be anything either of us could do about it then. I was so impressed with Bill, not only because of his stature and position as a U.S. Senator but because I could tell that he was a genuinely good person and a great friend to have in any circumstance. I couldn't help but wonder what had happened to his marriage, which had apparently dissolved shortly after his first election to the New York Senate seat. Even I realized it would not be appropriate to ask him about it.

He marveled over my resemblance to Rachael, whom he had known for almost her entire life. How bizarre that he knew my daughter during all those years when I had no idea where she was. Ray and Marianne Alosa have been his good friends since shortly after they adopted Rachael in Albuquerque and then moved to DC. It was coincidental and shocking that his friendship with them and with Mick indirectly brought Rachael back to me.

 Forcing myself to return to the present, I tried to stop thinking about Brooks and Mick. I really wanted to sleep, but instead, my mind turned to my employer, Shrinden Pharmaceuticals. To make things a little worse, my managers had finally had enough of my personal problems. I had to admit that everything that had happened was having a detrimental impact on my work. I had never felt so ambivalent about my responsibilities. Several times I found myself daydreaming, and craving my laptop and my expanding manuscript, rather than tending to business—studying new drug protocols and setting up appointments with new clients. My boss had pretty much demanded that I get my head back on straight, and he made it clear that the company did not need any more publicity spilling over onto it.

As a result, I now had a two-week trip to North and South Dakota scheduled in the middle of July, ostensibly to supervise new sales representatives on their calls to doctors' offices in ten towns. This was not the sort of assignment I typically was handed at this stage in my career, and it was apparent to me that I was being punished.

After I'd exhausted my ruminations on all the topics that were keeping me awake, I was finally able to tuck my negative thoughts away and with a few cleansing breaths and pleasant thoughts about my good times with Mick on the *Sea Nymph*, I drifted off into a less than restful sleep.

7

August 5, 2008 – Washington, DC

Juggling his Starbucks and briefcase, Mick extracted his ID card and proceeded through GAO security at 441 G Street NW. He smiled at Verna, the security guard and crossed the wide corridor to join the surge of employees swarming toward the elevators. Up on 6, on autopilot, he wound his way through the maze of narrow aisles, taking a short cut to his office on the opposite side of the building. As he rounded the corner, he was a little dismayed to see two of the analysts on his team already sitting on the small sofa in the waiting area outside his office.

"Good morning, Mick." Quickly jumping up, Eve Benton smiled at her boss as he turned the key and opened his door. She pushed past her coworker, Danny Silva, to enter the office right behind Mick and commandeered the seat directly across from his desk. Mick noted this aggressive display and sighed as he hoisted his briefcase onto the credenza next to his L-shaped work station. "Good morning to you, Eve and Danny." He nodded at the two senior analysts, as he took a sip of coffee and sat down. "You're at it early, I see. What's going on?"

"Sorry to bother you before you get settled," Danny apologized quickly, glancing at Eve before she got a chance to take over. "We have put together a tentative plan for the cruise-crimes job, and we're hoping you can take a look before we finalize it."

Eve leaned forward not quite into Mick's space, only because the width of the desk hindered her progress. She tossed her straight brown hair away from her face and favored him with a bright white smile. "Yes Mick, we think what we have is pretty good. Also, I wanted to talk to you about the possibility of putting a team together for the case study."

Danny rolled his eyes before he could stop himself and Mick almost laughed out loud. What a competitive pair these two were. They were good at their jobs, but the political undertones of everything they did together were wearing thin on his already fragile psyche. He wished he hadn't started working with them directly and had left his assistant director to interact with them.

He decided to take over direct supervision this time because the *Sea Nymph* was scheduled to leave port in January—and of course, the job was very personal. Planning a project like this always required a lot of time, but they had to be ready to go when the ship was. Well, technically he and Tom Smythe had to be ready.

"Sorry, Eve, we won't have a budget for a team to do the case study. I'm going myself and taking Tom Smythe, the previous chief of security on the ship, with me. You know why, right?"

The twenty-eight-year-old woman actually stuck out her bottom lip for a moment. Her hair half covered her so-so features as she looked down in her lap then over at Danny's smirk. "Oh yes, of course, I understand." She suddenly sat upright, folded her hands on top of the notebook in her lap and looked at Mick expectantly.

Danny pulled a copy of their audit plan from his folder and handed it to Mick. "I thought you might like a hard copy rather than just looking at it on the screen."

Mick liked Danny. In his mid-thirties, he was bright, energetic, and always looked professional, which was no longer the case for many of the office's employees. Danny might never get promoted here, but he was an outstanding project manager and probably would leave GAO for a better offer with another agency before long.

"Thanks, Danny. I'm anxious to get going on this so I'll try to review your work today and tomorrow. I have to meet with Ken this morning, and I'm sure he'll be happy to hear that we have a tentative plan. Will you two be around here for the next couple of days if I have questions?

Eve piped up. "Oh, of course, we'll be here if you need us. Meanwhile, we're looking at some early data coming in from our preliminary test locations and working on a pro forma we'll use to extract the items we're interested in. We've left a blank for that in the plan, but we'll have it completed before the week is out.

Right, if you don't kill each other before then. "Fine, go on now and let me get my bearings here. I'll talk to you both later." Mick was relieved to see the pair leave his office and close the door behind them. *Why is it so hard to concentrate?* He was still waiting for a full recovery to set in and although he was going through the motions pretty well, he was only sleeping a few hours a night, and he had lost weight.

Ordinarily, he would blame the GAO cafeteria for his lack of appetite, but he knew it was something else. Somehow he just didn't feel like eating a lot of the time, and he hadn't been working out or running as much as his doctor said he could and should. He just seemed to feel bad about everything.

He understood that he was still avoiding Darcy to some extent. He hadn't called her nearly enough times since her visit in April. He told himself he was just too busy, and the truth was, he felt exhausted much of the time. He wouldn't allow himself to wonder a great deal about the validity of these excuses and lacked the energy to ponder the cause of his depression. He just kept going through the motions and told himself he would feel a whole lot better once they nailed Denezza.

He picked up the document Danny had left with him and riffled through it. The plan included a questionnaire to be mailed electronically to several cruise lines. The responses would provide data on the number of incidents of shipboard crime reported by victims or their families during 2008. This included complaints the passengers made to local law enforcement agencies when the ship returned to port. An electronic form would also be sent to the Florida, Texas, and California jurisdictions with cruise ship terminals, to request data from the law enforcement agencies. Once analyzed, these data would provide the meat of their findings on type and severity of crimes on cruise ships.

The *Sea Nymph* would serve as a case study, which would require Mick to collect information from the crew and the ship's log about complaints by passengers who had sailed on the ship during 2008. Of course, the real reason for selecting the ship was obvious. The case study would be as much about interviewing members of the crew to find out about Paul Denezza's previous shipboard relationships as it would be to benefit the GAO project. It was not entirely orthodox for Mick to be the only GAO official going on the trip, but they had to minimize expenses. Ken knew the FBI was involved and he was willing to go along with the plan to use the audit for a dual purpose, since receiving a formal request to do just that from Senator Sawyer. The ship would sail a six-week west to east route from Los Angeles around Cape Horn to Miami at the beginning of January. Mick and Tom would ride along for the first four weeks and fly home from Rio.

Mick knew the *Sea Nymph* had many of the same fifteen-hundred crew members as on their previous trip. He planned to talk with every one of them who could have any knowledge of the incidents and the deaths of their colleagues on that sailing.

As he left his office to meet with Ken, Mick reminded himself to mention the meeting Grant Murray had set up for later in the month at the Vegas FBI field office. Murray planned to take depositions from Mick, Darcy, Sidney, and other witnesses regarding the events on their previous cruise.

8

August 24, 2008 – Las Vegas

The trip to Vegas was like a cruise reunion with all the members present except for Paul. We were there to describe what happened on the evening of Suzanne's final meltdown and to provide formal eyewitness testimony to agent Murray. Mick and I met Sidney in the lobby of the Bailey building and rode the elevator up to Murray's office.

We were joined almost immediately by our new friends—our heroes—Don Freeburg and Charlie Scott who had just flown in from Seattle. It was good to see the guys looking healthy, and there was a tearful moment of greeting since it was the first time we'd seen them since parting under those awful circumstances in Valparaiso back in January. Sidney was a little overwhelmed. They were so instrumental and courageous in literally saving her life.

I had just returned from the Dakotas and had spoken to Mick by phone only twice during that three-week trip. I could not understand why he was acting so strangely and couldn't help but wonder what the hell had happened to our beautiful romance. Now there was an uncomfortable awkwardness between us. We were sharing a hotel room because we were ostensibly a couple, but it just didn't feel that way. Rachael was in town with us and also had a room at the MGM Grand. At this moment, however, she was visiting Brooks at his luxury suite high atop the Stratosphere.

Agent Murray called the meeting to order, and we all sat around his conference table. A pitcher of water and glasses sat on a tray in the middle, and that was all. He began to speak, and ten minutes later he'd thoroughly briefed us on what had happened so far with Paul and what he intended to get from this meeting with our little group.

Towards the end, he looked across at Tom and said, "Let me just say that Tom here has provided some physical evidence that he collected at the crime scenes on the ship. Some blood evidence helps, but fingerprints were not helpful due to the number of people who touch the railings."

"The bottom line? If we're going to nail Denezza for hiring crew members to kill Sidney, we have to find someone else who knew about the plot. We know that Suzanne was insane and what she did cannot be linked directly to Paul. But, if he hired people to kill Sidney, he is equally guilty. Let's take a short break and then we'll begin taking the statements."

*　　*　　*

"OK, Darcy. I feel like we're back on the ship trying to decipher your mood. What is going on with you and Mick? Neither of you is acting normally. At least not the normal we came to know on the cruise."

It was déjà vu all right, and I knew just what Don meant. I was standing with him and Charlie in front of a bank of snack vending machines contemplating an Orange Crush, my favorite drink—when a martini is not appropriate. I couldn't help but smile at the two of them with their almost matching outfits: similar jeans and wildly patterned shirts.

I looked into Don's grey-blue eyes staring out from his perfect face and felt the familiar sensation of being probed. I glanced briefly at his gym-carved body and thought fleetingly about how much fun I had with them on the cruise and how I still coveted Don's long blond waves. Then I turned my back to him and inserted quarters into the machine. The can fell to the bottom, and I grabbed it. Then I moved on to stare at the candy bars and tried to decide between Snickers and M&Ms. I could feel their eyes drilling into my back as they waited for an answer.

"Look, Guys, give me a break," I managed as I tried to swallow the first icy mouthful of fizzy orange heaven without choking. "As usual, you are perceptive to the point of irritation. I don't know what is wrong with Mick. He isn't the same at all. He wants our relationship to continue, I do not doubt that, but he seems emotionally flat and not interested in much of anything . . . except getting Paul the justice he deserves."

Charlie glanced at his partner then lowered his chin and peered slightly up at me through his dark wavy bangs, a mannerism that was very familiar to me. "Darcy, here we go again. Have you even tried to talk to him? You know, asked him what is wrong? What happened to your usual direct approach and why are we having this type of conversation with you again when we only just got back together?" Charlie's cherubic face twisted into a look of distaste. "And how can you drink that awful stuff?"

"Charlie is right," Don said. I thought maybe he meant about the soft drink. "We didn't go through all that hell on the ship and almost leave our little Penelope fatherless only to end up seeing you and Mick miserable. He is lucky to be alive, and you deserve happiness together. You are too smart to let this go on. There has to be an explanation for his behavior. Find out what it is!"

"I understand how you guys feel and what you are saying, but he won't talk about it. I can't explain it very well, but it's as if the topic is off limits somehow and I guess now that I'm saying it out loud, that is what is tainting our whole relationship. He was always so open with me when we were on the ship, and we could talk about anything."

Our little parlay ended abruptly when agent Murray's assistant called us back into the meeting. My conversation with the guys upset me even though I knew they meant well and were right, as usual. I sat down at the conference table beside Mick and rested my hand on his thigh. He smiled at me and lightly patted it. I loved him so much and knew I wanted to be with him forever. *I need you to reciprocate and get back to your old self.*

Don and Charlie gave great dramatic performances as they explained in an animated fashion what they witnessed and experienced the night we were attacked out on the deck. They responded eloquently to all Agent Murray's questions, and their eyewitness account left no doubt about Suzanne's rampage. Ditto for Tom's and Mick's reports of the incident.

Then Mick, Tom, and I gave depositions about what we saw and heard on the cruise regarding the dead crew members, and Mick spoke at length about his prior knowledge of Paul and his informal surveillance of him during the cruise. Everything that happened—all the unlikely coincidences and especially the violence—came rushing back and it was all I could do to stay in the room while we rehashed the events. I sensed Mick was feeling the same way and at one point I could feel his body quivering with the effort to remain calm.

All the testimony went well, but Murray recapped by saying that so far there was not enough evidence to arrest Paul for any involvement in the crimes that took place in his wake. Suzanne might have been the only person who knew what he was up to and she was dead. Tom's conversations with her in the ship's lock-up with no witnesses present, and considering her insanity, were not enough to link Paul to the crew deaths or the plot against Sidney.

Murray looked at Sidney, who had been sitting quietly beside me. "Paul continues to run his hotel as usual and is acting as if nothing is wrong. He has not provided any useful information, but I am determined to find a way to link him to the murder for hire plot against you, Sidney."

She had been strong throughout this ordeal, but overall she looked a little frail and had an air of vulnerability about her. As she listened, she looked down at her lap. Her shiny auburn hair, cut in a perfect jaw-length wedge, fell forward framing her pretty freckled face.

Suddenly she raised her head, and we all saw the angry flash in her green eyes as she looked around the table. "I know without a doubt that Paul wanted me dead and almost succeeded through Suzanne. I don't care how crazy she was; it was all his doing from the beginning. If I had not minimized my take in our divorce settlement, he may well have come after me again and succeeded in killing me. He is also crazy in his own way."

I grasped her hand, and she fell slightly toward me resting her head on my shoulder for a moment. "I guess we are finished here, right, agent Murray?" I asked.

"Yes, we are finished, but I want to talk with Mick and Tom about the GAO job. Will you two guys stay for a few minutes?"

"Sure," Mick answered and moved around the table to sit closer to Tom and Murray.

I said, "We'll all go on to the restaurant for lunch and wait for you. See you in a little while."

Sidney and I drove together in Mick's rental car with Don and Charlie following in theirs. On the way, Sidney talked more about how her life had changed. She was understandably very emotional as she explained how she felt about Paul's betrayal. Wiping away a few stray tears, she told me again how he forced her to accompany him on the cruise and then ignored her. She now knew that he planned to return to Athens Olympia alone.

She also described the $5 million settlement with Paul with an agreement to leave all his other assets alone. Eventually, she would be able to do anything she wanted, but for now, she was living in a condominium just off the strip. She said she hoped she could eventually leave Vegas for good.

I didn't hesitate before asking, "Why don't you come and stay with me in Colorado Springs for a while? I have a spare room for you, and it would be fun. Of course, I'll be traveling a lot, but you would enjoy the fresh mountain air and relative quiet there."

"Thanks, that is so nice of you. I might take you up on it. Something is keeping me here, though." She looked over at me sort of shyly.

"Have you met someone, Sidney?"

"Well, sort of. I don't want to say too much about it yet, but yes, I've found a man I think I care deeply for. I'm just not sure yet that the feeling is mutual."

"Well, I'm happy for you anyway, and I hope it works out for you." I didn't let on, but I had an odd feeling about what she'd revealed . . . or hadn't. Her comment seemed a bit formal, and it wasn't like her to hold back. Ever since renewing our friendship we'd talked about our lives like a couple of teenagers. *Why isn't she telling me more about a man she is obviously interested in*? I decided not to push it and changed the subject.

9

Later that afternoon Brooks Larkin sat in his office on Main Street near downtown and not far from Las Vegas Boulevard. He was thinking about Rachael and their earlier lunch date. He could not believe how life had offered up this tremendous gift. Having his daughter back in his life just as he had always hoped he would was a blessing. Now, if he could just convince Darcy to give him another chance . . . his thoughts were interrupted by a knock on the door. It had to be Tom Smythe. Brooks felt a surge of excitement as he stood and stepped from behind his desk.

He'd been waiting for Tom, and now he greeted him with a warm handshake and a squeeze to the shoulder. They sat down in chairs beside each other in a little seating area across from Brooks's desk. The talk centered on how they'd known each other for five years only through many phone conversations, and how happy they were to finally meet in person. A few minutes of pleasant conversation followed as they caught up on their lives over the past few months.

During a lull, Tom said, "By the way, I want to thank you for handling my reservations for this trip."

"No problem. I wish you'd let me put you up at the Stratosphere or some other strip hotel, though."

"That's OK. The downtown joint is just fine, and I have to be careful with money until I find a new job. That reminds me, I have a question for you, Brooks. I'm wondering what kind of rapport you have with the new security chief on the *Sea Nymph*?"

"Since you ask, it's just not the same as when you had the job. I know things change and I probably can't expect a collegial relationship like the one you and I developed, but the new guy seems unnecessarily standoffish and not very helpful when I have questions about my tour groups. Why do you ask?"

"I know the fellow, Roger Ramirez, and I understand that he is not as personable as he might be with the crew and passengers. I'm sorry you're not getting the cooperation you would like." Tom paused and measured his next words carefully. "I'm going to need his cooperation myself. I'm going to tell you something that will surprise you. Mick Clayton and I are going back to South America on the *Sea Nymph* in January. We're going in connection with a project of Mick's for the GAO and the FBI, but we'll also be trying to get information about whatever it was Paul Denezza was doing on the ship. You know the FBI here wants to build a case to prosecute him and going back there appears to be the only way we have of doing it."

"Yeah, I know about the FBI investigation from Darcy and Rachael, but I'm surprised you would go under the circumstances. I have known Paul for many years, and although we're close acquaintances, I guess you'd say, I don't trust him, and I can understand why the FBI is after him. He's about as sleazy as they come and has a reputation here in town for having a suspicious history regarding how he got his hotel and money."

Tom's interest was obvious. "I'm sure Grant Murray would be interested in those suspicions."

"Oh, I'm sure he is aware of the Vegas lore, at least I hope he is." Brooks gazed out his window at the strip shimmering in the distance. "Coincidentally, I've been getting reacquainted with Sidney since she divorced Paul and we've gone out to eat a couple of times. You know I knew her back when I was married to Darcy because they were good friends then, like now. Anyway, it is beyond me how such a great girl could have been married to Paul. What a mismatch!"

"I know what you mean. I got to know Sidney during the cruise, and she certainly deserves better." Suddenly, Tom no longer felt in the mood for small talk, especially about the cruise. He was exhausted after his early morning flight and the deposition. After about ten more minutes, he told Brooks he wanted to go back to his hotel to take a nap. "Do you want to meet me later for dinner?" he asked.

"Great idea! In fact, I'll pick you up, and we'll go to an old local landmark restaurant, Battista's Hole in The Wall, near the strip just off Flamingo. The place has a lot of local color complete with walls papered with celebrity pictures, and a full Italian menu with all the table wine you can drink. I know you'll enjoy it. I'll call you from your hotel lobby when I get there."

10

Mick and I were enjoying ourselves at the award-winning Craftsteak restaurant in the MGM Grand. Chef Tom Colicchio was indeed living up to his reputation, in our opinions, as we savored the signature lobster bisque and Kobe skirt steak. My Ketel One martini made just the way I like it; icy, extra dry and slightly dirty was marvelous. Mick, who was usually a beer man, had ordered a Glenlivet single malt. This was something I had not seen him do before and I wondered if it was Bill Sawyer's influence.

The restaurant had a business casual dress code, which is something almost unheard of back home in casual Colorado. In compliance, Mick looked handsome and very hip in a lightweight beige sport coat with an open-neck shirt in a subtle brown, beige, and blue paisley pattern. I thought I looked pretty good myself in my pale yellow—still my favorite color—sundress and fabulous Roberto Cavalli platform sandals with a 4-inch clear plastic heel. These brought me eye-to-eye with Mick, which I like. For some reason, even though I'm already five feet ten, high heels are one of my weaknesses.

I gazed around the spacious contemporary room warmed by red walls that melded seamlessly into the gently curved ceiling, then looked across at Mick. I suddenly had the feeling that everything would be all right now and I was thinking a little guiltily that it was a good thing we were alone. Rachael had not joined us, saying she was tired and wanted to stay in her room. Tom had also opted out in order to visit Brooks. The idea had taken me aback at first, but then I remembered about their connection through Brooks's travel agency and Tom's previous job with World of Seas. This was another of those weird coincidences.

Surprisingly, Mick and I were discussing our relationship and remembering the excitement we both felt when we first met. *This is very good.* Mick smiled at me and reached across the table to pick up my hand.

"Darcy, I want to ask you something important. But judging by the way I feel myself, it might be upsetting to you, and I want you to think about it before you answer."

"If this is about me moving to DC I do need more time to think about it. I have to consider Rachael's plans as well." I was not prepared to discuss that subject right then.

"No, it isn't about that although I'm hoping you'll decide to come live with me. I'm going to do something I haven't told you about yet."

I watched him shift in his seat and take a deep breath. Oh oh, something is coming that can't be good. *Why do we always seem to have drama in our lives?* I sighed back at him and squeezed his hand.

"OK, Mick. Spit it out, as Don would say. I can see that whatever this is it's a big deal."

"I've agreed—or rather decided—to go back to the *Sea Nymph* and do the case study for our cruise crimes job myself. Tom is going with me, and we plan to interview crew members to try to find out what Paul was doing."

That was the farthest thing from my mind, and it left me speechless. I know I must have looked dumbfounded staring across the table at him while he went on talking. "Anyway, that is a done deal. What I wanted to ask you is . . . well, will you go with me on the cruise?"

"What? No, I couldn't go back to that ship after everything that happened to us. How can you be doing it?"

"Honestly, Darcy, I know how you feel. It took me a while to get over my repulsion at the thought of being back on that ship. But there is nothing more important to me than finding evidence against Paul."

"Wow, I don't know what to say."

"Sidney is a friend to both of us, right? And I still feel some obligation to her. I hope you understand how I mean that. I would never have met you if I hadn't taken the cruise to watch out for her. So in a way, she brought us together, right?"

"I guess so when you say it that way. Oh, Mick, I do want to be with you and if it could be the way it was between us before on the ship I would probably say yes." I should have stopped there. "Do you think it could be?"

Mick's face clouded over, and I knew I had touched on that nerve, that off-limits topic for him. I could feel myself getting angry and knew it would not help, so I tried to relax and wait for his response. I waited more than a minute. Then I sat back in my chair and brought my hand over to my side of the table.

"Mick, can't you describe to me what is wrong with you . . . what you're thinking or feeling?"

"I love you. That's all I know. I guess I'm just taking a long time to get over my injuries, and maybe almost dying myself stirred up the anxiety about losing Beth and my folks. But it isn't about you, Darcy. Please believe me. I so want you to be with me on the ship."

It was my turn to sit there in silence while Mick watched me and chewed his bottom lip. I knew I wanted to go with him, but I didn't want to go back to the place where people died, and Mick and I almost joined them.

Finally, I gave in. I guess I didn't want to be left out of another important part of my own life. "All right, I'll see if I can arrange to get off work, but I have to say that Shrinden is not happy with me right now and they might just fire me if I ask for a month off." Then I had a brainstorm. "What if Rachael could go along too? She would have to take time off school, but it would be a good time for us to spend together while you're working. It will be scary to be back on the ship, but maybe it would be good for us to confront it."

"That's great. I don't see any problem with Rachael coming along. After all, this will be an uneventful enjoyable cruise, not the nightmare we lived through before."

I thought maybe I was going a little crazy then because I felt a distinct shiver move down my spine and I know from experience that is never good. As I reached for Mick again and tried to recapture our previous mood, another thought kept trying to push its way forward, and I kept trying to push it back. It was something about Brooks. I understood that part of the reason I acquiesced about going on the cruise was that being out of the country seemed like a good way to avoid the confusing feelings I had about him.

11

Lilith Schrom unwound her long tanned legs from her new black BMW 3 Series convertible and stood up. Smoothing lap wrinkles from her tight brown silk wrap-around skirt, she slowly gazed around the parking garage. Glancing down at the car, she ran her hand lovingly over the soft top. After another quick survey of the area, and not seeing anyone about, she bent down and dragged her purple sequined duffel bag out of the back seat. Stretching her back up straight and hoisting the strap over her shoulder, with one more look around, she strode to the entrance of Players Paradise.

During the elevator ride down two levels, she tried to ignore the disgusting smudges on the walls surrounding her, but upon exiting her nose wrinkled involuntarily. This was not the sort of hotel she was accustomed to, and it seemed small and drab compared to the glittery strip establishments she frequented during the past several years.

Turning right into the casino, she followed the directions she'd been given. *Thank God I will soon be back home, and I swear I will never come to his horrible city again.* The gaming tables commanded her attention as she passed, but because of her tight schedule, she quickly looked away and did not hesitate. She hurried along to another set of elevators at the far back corner of the casino, opening the side zipper pocket of her bag as she approached. After stepping into the open car and inserting a room key into the security slot, she quickly pressed the button for the eighth floor before any other guests could enter.

Lilith was thrilled to be living and working in the United States, and for the first couple of years after her arrival, she had traveled around the astonishing country whenever her schedule permitted. She loved everything about it, but her favorite spots had turned out to be Atlantic City and Las Vegas, especially the latter, for a while at least. Lilith found Vegas to be the more glamorous of the two, and the larger city offered complete anonymity. Not having anyone know about her visits was extremely important because when she was in town, she assumed an utterly different persona, that of a beautiful sexy player—far different from her normal dowdy life.

Sadly, she discovered way too late that her personality was far more addictive than she would ever have dreamed. Somehow over the past year, she amassed a debt of $200,000 at her favorite casino and could see no way to repay it. Worse, she could not seem to stop herself from playing blackjack and poker, even though her current losing streak extended back several months.

Her job at the Wilmore Neuroscience Laboratory near Boston did not exactly pay minimum wage, but still, her lucrative salary was not nearly enough to cover her mounting gambling debts. Thankfully, several months ago she was offered an opportunity to wipe the slate clean by carrying out this assignment. It was so dangerous that a month passed before she could agree to the scheme. During that period her debt substantially increased. In the end, the new $50,000 car sweetened the deal considerably, and she reluctantly made the decision.

She knew very well that if she failed—or worse, was apprehended—her career and everything she'd worked so hard to achieve would vaporize overnight. No, she definitely did not want to return to Israel in disgrace, and so she must be cautious with what she was about to do.

She understood how fortunate she was to land her current position at the lab shortly after publishing her doctoral thesis in biochemistry at Tel Aviv University. Her work at The Adams Super Center for Brain Studies focused on deciphering brain activity related to devastating diseases. Amazingly, the results of her research there relating to potential cancer treatments or cures brought her instant recognition in Israel and later in the United States.

For ten years now, she'd dedicated her life to running her experiments associated with treatments for cancer and diabetes in her narrow area of study, partially funded with grants from the National Institutes of Health. The fact that applied research teams were already using her basic research to develop methods of treatment and diagnosis for several cancers was a source of great pride.

She stepped out of the elevator and stood in the foyer for a few moments to get her bearings. At this time of the evening, virtually everyone would be either gambling or at dinner. Seeing no one in the immediate area, she consulted the sign that provided directions to the rooms. A short way down the hallway she stopped in front of a door.

Holding her breath, she rapped loudly and as expected received no response. Letting herself in using a housekeeping key, she went straight to the bed. A moment of intense anxiety came and quickly passed. Drawing in a deep breath and exhaling slowly, she gently placed her bag on the bed and carefully began to unzip it.

In under three minutes, she completed her task and returned to the elevators. As she nervously waited for the car to arrive, she could hardly stand still. When the doors opened, a rather unremarkable middle-aged man stepped out. He nodded and smiled at her, then walked down the hall in the direction from which she had just come. She had an urge to follow him just to see which room he entered but decided her scientist's curiosity would not serve her well in this case.

Following an anxiety-filled ride down to the casino, Lilith quickly retraced her steps to the parking garage and was soon driving down the exit ramp. The right thing to do was to continue straight to Interstate 15 and head east toward home, but before reaching the highway entrance ramp just two blocks away, she convinced herself that it would not hurt to spend one more hour trying to win back some losses. She'd just completed a scary job and felt lucky but wasn't about to stop at one of these shabby downtown casinos. Instead, she turned around, found Las Vegas Boulevard, and headed south toward the familiarity of the strip.

12

Tom Smythe entered his room, threw his briefcase on a chair, and immediately undressed down to his underwear. He turned down the bed covers and set the alarm so that he could catch an hour's nap before meeting Brooks for dinner, then slid between the sheets. Drifting into sleep, Tom thought about his earlier meeting with Brooks and about the deposition he gave to Agent Murray earlier in the day.

Only half awake, he rolled over to achieve a more comfortable position, but instead, was jolted wide-awake by an intense stinging sensation in his leg. Yelping involuntarily, he jumped from the bed. Obviously something had bitten him, and he threw back the covers expecting to see a spider of some sort. Instead, what he saw near the bottom of the bed boggled his mind, and caused his stomach to flutter.

Two very strange looking scorpions, each about four inches long, were curled into a sort of fetal position with their pointed tails wrapped loosely around their bodies. That they were scorpions was evident, but these were not the normal whitish arachnids he'd seen in the southwest desert. Their front claws were extremely thin, and the tails seemed fat in comparison to their bodies. But it was their color—a sickening pale greenish yellow—that made Tom's skin crawl. No, this pair did not find their way into the hotel from the nearby open space.

Even as he thought about grabbing a towel from the bathroom to capture them, the pain in his right ankle and calf was fast becoming excruciating. Staggering the few feet to the bathroom, he yanked a bath towel off the rack. As he returned to the bed and threw it over the pair, gathering it up in a ball, his vision blurred and he began to wheeze. This was an unbelievably fast reaction, and a wave of panic suddenly overtook him. Attempting to clear his thoughts, he examined his leg and grew even more alarmed to see rapidly growing areas of swelling around two bright red sting marks. He was having an allergic reaction to venom and didn't have a lot of time to waste thinking about it. His leg would not support him any longer, and he sprawled across the bed. Now panic did not begin to describe the feeling, as he grabbed for the phone.

He realized he was going to vomit and his throat was rapidly swelling shut. Gasping for air, he willed himself not to throw up. By the time he reached the hotel operator, his chest was pounding, and his airway was almost completely blocked. The room closed in around him, and the last thing he remembered was the operator's voice urgently asking him what was wrong.

Brooks arrived at Players Paradise early. He did not want to wake Tom from his nap prematurely, so he was hanging around the casino playing some dollar poker machines. Suddenly, paramedics rushed through the front doors and flew into the elevator. He didn't think much about it until they came back down about five minutes later. He walked over along with other curious patrons to watch them wheel the sick person out of the elevator.

Brooks couldn't believe his eyes when he saw Tom on the gurney, pasty white with an oxygen mask over his face and pink foamy drool running down his chin from under the mask. A drip line hung from his arm, and one of the medics was holding the plastic bag in the air as they rushed through the casino. Brooks darted forward and grabbed for Tom's hand.

"What the hell happened?" he asked, jogging to keep up with the medics as they continued toward the front door.

"Apparently the gentleman was stung by whatever is in that towel," one of them answered as he pointed gingerly at the rolled up white ball riding along next to Tom's covered legs. "Are you a relative?"

"No, I'm a friend. What's in the towel?"

"We didn't look, but we think he said they are weird-looking scorpions. It was hard to understand him. He's in shock, but this looks like a serious envenomation."

"I just arrived to pick him up to go to dinner," Brooks said breathlessly. "Where are you taking him? I'll follow you."

"UMC, that's University Medical Center on West Charleston. It's the only level one trauma center we have, and by the looks of him he's going to need it," he called over his shoulder as they wheeled Tom out the door to the waiting ambulance.

Brooks was in a state of bewildered shock himself, and as he followed them outside, he was trying to think of what he should do. Then he remembered that Mick and Darcy were also in town for the FBI meeting. While running to his car, Brooks called Darcy's cell phone, glad he'd programmed her number into it as soon as he learned it. He caught her just as she and Mick were finishing dinner.

13

Brooks seemed frantic to explain something to me, but he wasn't making sense. The thought leaped into my mind that something had happened to Rachael. "Is Rachael all right?"

"No, not Rachael. It's Tom . . . a scorp . . . on my way . . ." he yelled.

I could hear traffic noises in the background, and we obviously had a bad connection. "No, I know it's you, Brooks. What do you want and why are you calling me now?"

Getting a call from him was so bizarre that I really thought he was making something up to try to get me to see him. He had caught me off guard, and I was flustered and embarrassed that he was calling while I was with Mick. "What are you trying to do, Brooks? Why are you calling me?" I was talking way too loud, and Mick was shushing me.

I looked at Mick helplessly, and he could readily see that I was stymied. Gently, he took the phone from me and asked Brooks what was going on. I was mortified, but when Mick finally made sense of what he was saying, we ran from the restaurant, caught a taxi in front of the hotel and told the driver to fly to the hospital.

We found Brooks in the emergency room waiting area, and I introduced him to Mick trying for a light tone that didn't do much to hide my confusion and discomfort. The two men in my life shook hands with a friendly greeting. I tried to shift my entire focus to Tom's situation. I leaned toward Mick and asked Brooks, "What do you know about his condition?"

"Nothing yet, no one has come out since they took him in there," he said, pointing toward the double doors just down a short hallway. "He was somewhat lucid for a few minutes, and they asked him who they should call. He said there was no one. Do you think that's true? I've known Tom for five years, and I just realized I've never heard him mention any family."

I thought about it and realized I had never heard him mention family either. I told myself I would learn more about the man who had helped save Mick's life, had lost his job for his trouble, and had dedicated himself to bringing Paul to justice. I looked at Mick and saw his frown. "What is it?" I asked.

"I just can't believe this is happening. We have to find out whether this was an accident or someone put those scorpions if that is what they were, in Tom's room."

"What do you mean?" Brooks asked, "that someone could deliberately use them as a weapon? I didn't think a scorpion sting was that big a deal."

"I can't imagine how, but doesn't it seem odd that something this bizarre would happen when Tom is here to talk to the FBI? I . . ." A tall very slender doctor with thinning grey hair wearing a traditional white coat had suddenly appeared from around a corner about twenty feet from us. He was striding directly our way.

"Are you folks with Tom Smythe?" he asked before he even arrived.

"Yes, we're his friends," Mick answered. "What is going on?"

"I am Dr. Ed Milner, how do you do?" He offered his hand to each of us, and I couldn't help but fixate on his serious demeanor and the piercing pale grey eyes scrutinizing us from a rather hawkish face.

"Since Mr. Smythe has no family, we will treat you as next of kin at his request. There is some paperwork that needs to be completed when we are finished talking if you would not mind. He is conscious but in extreme discomfort. He has suffered two stings from an unusual species of scorpion, which we have just now identified."

Mick started to say something, but the doctor impatiently waved him off and continued. "Thankfully, he had the presence of mind to capture them. This is important for the identification, and so they cannot harm anyone else. We have anti-scorpion venom serum on hand, and it normally works quite well. However, in this case, he has two stings from a very dangerous species, and we estimate he has received nearly one milligram of venom, which is quite a lot."

I wanted to interrupt his presentation with a few questions, but he obviously wasn't finished, and he struck me as the type of person you probably should not interrupt.

"One positive thing is the stings were on his lower leg, which allowed for slower absorption into the bloodstream. But he has suffered anaphylaxis, an extreme allergic reaction, which can cause paralysis and pulmonary edema. We'll keep him for at least several days, and we cautiously predict that he will recover. He is very lucky he managed to get help quickly."

Dr. Milner finally took a breath but held up his hand to forestall the question Mick was trying to ask. "I'm almost finished. We'll let you know when you can go in to see him. It should be within the next hour. By the way, the Las Vegas police are sending over a detective to look at this situation, and I believe he will want to talk with you." He looked at all three of us in turn, in what I thought was a very disconcerting way.

I glanced at Mick and suddenly felt clammy all over as I realized what Dr. Milner was talking about. I cleared my throat and managed to ask the doctor, "Why would the police be involved in a scorpion sting?"

That set him off again. "It turns out that this is a fascinating and unique situation. You see, our normal southwest desert scorpions have a sting that is rarely lethal, but the pair Mr. Smythe encountered are definitely not native scorpions. I'd say there are about twelve hundred known species on the planet. Most are not very dangerous, but these two are specimens of the species, *Leiurus quinquestriatus*, the Israeli desert scorpion, also known as the Death Stalker. This is one of the deadliest scorpions on earth, and they absolutely came from the Middle East, not the Nevada desert. So, as an added precaution we have ordered an emergency shipment of anti-venom specifically made for Death Stalker envenomations, from Twyford, a German pharmaceutical company. It should be here by morning."

Seeing our awestruck reactions to his lecture and perhaps feeling that he had found his audience, Dr. Milner was on a roll. "We have placed a call and sent pictures to an entomologist over at the University, and we are quite sure about the species. Also, we are familiar with the Death Stalker because it is actually medically famous for its venom properties. You see, all scorpions paralyze their prey by injecting a potent mix of peptide toxins, which are relatively short chains of amino acids. That is what is wreaking havoc with Mr. Smythe's nervous system as we speak.

One of the polypeptides found in the venom of the Death Stalker, chlorotoxin, is used to treat cancer, specifically gliomas—that is to say, brain tumors. Basically, the chemical binds with and inhibits cancer cells while bypassing healthy cells."

"There are several places in the U.S. carrying out research with chlorotoxin, including the University of Alabama, and only a research facility should have these scorpions. No one in their right mind would travel with them, and of course, it would be quite illegal to do so, but people do foolish things these days." He shook his head and finally paused to see if we had any questions.

All three of us stared at him, and I'm sure we were all thinking the same thing at that instant. Mick had been right. This can't be a coincidence, it just seems too diabolical. Mick shook hands with Dr. Milner and said, "Thank you for your explanation. We certainly would like to talk to the detective when he arrives. Please point us in the direction where the paperwork is required."

At the hospital's administration desk it quickly became apparent that Tom probably had no health insurance. Of course, he would have been insured with World of Seas, and that coverage disappeared with his job. Brooks immediately offered to pay Tom's bill and signed as the responsible party.

After we walked away from the desk, he explained to us how well he had come to know Tom over the years. It made sense that he had numerous occasions to talk with Tom about the problems and mishaps of *Sea Nymph* passengers who were members of American Travel's tour groups.

"We hit it off and became friends, but only met in person for the first time a few hours ago. We were planning to have a late dinner together." Brooks looked as if he was going to cry and that shocked me. "I can't believe this is happening, but I'll take care of whatever he needs," he said, then turned his back on us to gaze out the window.

The connections among people and events just keep getting more and more complex, I thought, as I moved away from the two men and went to stand at another window overlooking the parking lot. Brooks's sensitivity and generosity impressed and touched me, and I was fighting back the tears without understanding exactly where they were coming from. I glanced over my shoulder at Brooks. He looked good in perfectly fitted chinos and a form fitted polo shirt. *Oh, oh, this isn't a good time to feel drawn to him.*

As I tried to reset my mind to think about Tom rather than Mick and Brooks, who were disconcertingly standing next to each other only a few feet away, I let my mind wander to the few facts I knew about the Death Stalker.

Dr. Milner had jogged my memory about this fascinating line of medical research. Shrinden does not sell a chlorotoxin-related medication, but I knew about clinical trials of TM-601, a synthetic version of the chemical used to treat malignant brain tumors. I had also heard about a combination of chlorotoxin and a fluorescent material that researchers at Seattle Children's Hospital Research Institute have used to demarcate cancer cells from healthy surrounding tissue.

I also understood that only the most basic research would involve actual scorpions and as I tried to concentrate on what I had read about such efforts, I vowed to do a little digging of my own to find out as much as I could about where the Death Stalker specimens might have come from.

14

September 8, 2008 – Las Vegas

Paul's anger escalated as he studied his eye-in-the-sky security screen. He had dismissed the technician on duty so he could conduct his surveillance in private, and now he watched in disbelief as Lilith strode through the casino and perched on a stool at her favorite blackjack table. She looked as glamorous as ever, with her lithe subtly curved body wrapped in metallic gold that barely covered her butt. The dealer, Lance MeKenna, nodded to her as she approached and then glanced up at the camera unobtrusively placed above his table.

Paul shook his head. *The woman must be crazy to come back here. Can she possibly think I wouldn't find out?* Paul knew all about addictions and had known many hotel patrons over the years who were driven to lose any money that came across their palms. Worse, they were unable to curb their borrowing habit, even in the face of near-violent censure by casino bosses. Lilith Schrom was one of the worst gambling addicts he'd ever encountered.

Of course, her illness played directly into his hands when he needed someone to take care of Smythe. But her failure to follow through with that little job, and her apparent overestimation of the power of her weapon, plus her subsequent return visits to Athens Olympia, were becoming very problematic.

Paul reached over the console and pushed a button. In response, down at the table, Lance immediately beckoned to the nearest security guard. The burly man stretched, pulled his shoulders back and tried to pull in his gut. Then he pasted an intimidating scowl onto his already repulsive face as he approached and leaned down to hear what Lance had to say. He straightened up with a smirk and slowly swaggered to the opposite side of the table, where he took a position directly behind Lilith. With a firm, meaty hand under her elbow he bent down and whispered in her ear, "Mr. Denezza requests your presence."

Lilith nearly jumped off her seat. She frantically glanced about the casino with a frightened expression that was almost comical. Lance smiled over at her and thought that the woman was probably in for a long night. He shrugged and began to deal the next round as Lilith slid off the stool and allowed the guard to escort her across the expansive ornate casino, past the cocktail lounge, and into the elevator.

Paul was waiting in the hallway outside his office when Lilith was delivered to him like the cheap package she was. He dismissed the guard, opened his door, and pushed her inside. "Sit down," he commanded as he walked behind his desk but remained standing.

Lilith tentatively sat on the edge of the chair facing his desk. She tried to control her shaking hands by grasping the wooden arms as she looked up into his angry face. Several seconds went by before Paul spoke and this raised her anxiety to an almost intolerable level. She jerked back in her seat when he finally spoke.

"You just don't get it, do you? Where do you think you are and who do you think you are dealing with? What part of don't ever come back here did you not understand, Lilith?" Paul breathed deeply and willed himself to remain relatively calm. What he really wanted was to reach across the desk and backhand her across the room.

"I'm so sorry, Paul. I thought enough time had gone by that it would be all right for me to come back. I drove again, and no one knows I'm here. My coworkers believe I took a long weekend to rest and do some reading."

"Lilith, you are such a stupid cunt for a bitch who is supposed to be so smart. LVPD and the crime lab are still investigating the scorpion attacks. It's still all over the news and only a matter of time before they connect you with your research and Wilmore Lab. It isn't as if there are that many places doing work like yours. I erased the record of your stay at the hotel during that time, but you can't keep coming back here." Paul's voice was increasing in volume as he spoke, and finally, he leaned toward her and yelled, "Do you understand me, bitch?" Spittle flew from his mouth across the desk and landed on her cheek.

Lilith flinched and looked away toward the door as she wiped her face with the back of her hand. "Yes, Paul," she whimpered, "I really do understand, and I won't come back until you tell me it is safe."

Paul looked as if he would pop a carotid artery as his face reddened alarmingly. He flew around the desk in a rage and yanked her up out of the chair by her thick dark curls. "I ought to eliminate you once and for all, you worthless slut." He pushed her away, and she staggered to the far wall, sobbing with her hands covering her face as she slid down to the floor.

Looking at her with a belly full of disgust, he knew there had to be a final solution to this little problem. With a deep sigh, he slumped back onto his chair. While waiting for Lilith to regain her composure, he weighed his options. When she finally pushed herself to a standing position and glanced sideways at him with mascara streaming down both cheeks, he gestured for her to return to her seat.

"I'm sorry I lost my temper," he said, with no apparent sincerity. "Look, Lilith, I have an idea how you can redeem yourself and still erase your remaining casino debt. The venture with your little Israeli pets did not work out as planned but there might be a better way. First, I want you to explain some additional technical things about your work, all right?"

With relief, Lilith sagged and slumped in her chair. She was scared to death of Paul, but even more so of losing her job and reputation. She knew her life had spiraled way out of control and she was at a loss as to how to get it back on track. When she was at work in her lab in Watertown, just west of Cambridge, everything was fine. That is, until that urge rose from the depths, first tickling her spine like tiny air bubbles, but soon enough, chomping at her guts as it emerged to the surface, a full-blown obsession—and it always did— and then she had no will power to resist it. "Yes, Paul, anything you want. I will tell you whatever you want to know."

15

September 15, 2008 – Las Vegas

Brooks felt as if his life was settling back into its normal routine. He'd taken care of Tom at his penthouse suite atop the Stratosphere for over a week, following his release from the hospital. He was still worried about his friend, but Tom insisted he was well enough to travel to his own apartment in Ventura.

How cool it would be if this were my normal life routine, he thought, as he gazed across his dining table at Rachael. He was listening to her talk about her tentative plans and the decisions she needed to make about her future. Still overwhelmed and overjoyed at having her back in his life, he found himself memorizing every word she spoke to him. Despite how out of control and hurtful he had been to her mother early on, for the past fifteen years he'd tried indirectly to make amends for his neglect, and it was finally paying off.

Rachael had been staying at Darcy's house in Colorado for several weeks before coming to Vegas and would fly home to Buenos Aires tomorrow. He was overjoyed when she called to say she planned to visit him for a couple of days before heading south. Then she informed him that Darcy had just left Colorado to live with Mick in DC for a while, and this news dampened his mood considerably.

She looked at him with an intense expression that seemed out of character for the lovely somewhat naive girl he'd come to know. "What do you think, Brooks, should I go on the cruise with Darcy? I guess I would really like to even if I have to miss some school. Actually, I'm really more concerned about missing a sculling crew that's scheduled during that time."

Brooks did not want her to see the mixed emotions he was feeling. It was a fine idea for her to spend time with Darcy so they could continue to bond, but the thought of them being with Mick in a quasi-family setting was extremely troubling. What he really wished he could do was undermine Mick's hold on

Darcy so he could get his family back together. He was experiencing an intense bout of jealousy at the thought of Darcy and Mick spending that time together with Rachael, but at least he would be able to use his daughter as an excuse to stay in touch while they were on the ship.

"I think you should go on the trip if you want to. It seems to me that the relatively few things you would miss at school would be outweighed by the opportunity for you to be with your mother. . . I mean Darcy."

Rachael nodded and looked out the window at the colorful view of the strip to the south. She felt good—really good—being with Brooks in his home. Despite Darcy's warnings about her birth father, he'd been nothing but loving and charming towards her each time she visited, and she already thought the world of him. She still could not quite believe he could be her father, given that he and his life seemed so glamorous.

As she looked back at his movie-star-handsome face, she felt a familiar longing. She knew she should be grateful for all the recent changes in her life, and nothing could diminish the love and respect she would always feel for her parents, Ray and Marianne. But she just could not stop herself from wishing that Darcy and Brooks would get together and that she could spend time with both of them as a family.

Darcy had been clear that such a scenario was not possible, but after the amazing events of the past few months, Rachael now believed that anything was possible if you wanted it enough. She did not realize how much like her birth father she was in that regard.

After Rachael returned to her hotel, Brooks sat at the window staring down the strip and spent some productive time planning and scheming about the future. He was so close to having what he craved for so many years. He just had to come up with a way to get Darcy to come back to him . . . and Rachael. Fortunately, there would be an American Travel tour group on the ship, and as he knew from the previous cruise, that could be a real asset for him personally.

Meanwhile, the evening was young, and he had taken the entire day off—an unusual occurrence. He did not want to be tempted to work at home, as he often did. A nice relaxing dinner and some music sounded much better. He picked up the phone to call his assistant, one of his travel agents, who had also been a part-time lover for several years. For some reason, without thinking much about it, he dialed Sidney's cell instead.

16

October 9, 2008 – Washington, DC

Rain, perhaps carrying a softening salty payload from the nearby ocean, formed a perfect sheet on the picture window overlooking Albemarle Street in Tenleytown. Unlike the sometimes muddy downpours we get in the Colorado high desert, maybe this east coast rain actually washes your windows for you, I thought. After returning from the gym in the condominium complex, I showered and gave significant thought to my attire. I settled on low-riding jeans, a turquoise long-sleeved T-shirt, and a wide silver studded belt—a more western look than one typically sees in DC.

Leaning back on the couch, I watched the storm exhaust itself, shifting from a driving torrent to a drizzle. Stretching my legs out and taking care to keep the three-inch heels of my palomino Fry boots off Mick's seat cushion, I used the rare moment of total relaxation to gather my thoughts while I waited for Tom to arrive from the airport.

We hadn't seen him since his release from the hospital and subsequent stay at Brooks's suite in Vegas. In a week, Tom had recovered enough to fly to his apartment in Ventura, California saying that he had to decide whether to live in it or move somewhere else. Apparently, he had spent very little time there during the years he worked on the ship, and it was nothing more than an address and a place to keep his few belongings. Life had changed for all of us, but Tom might have suffered the greatest upheaval.

At this point, my initial book sales far exceeded my expectations, although my publisher told me it was a no-brainer, given the advance (and free) publicity we endured. I would soon have an infusion of money from royalty payments, so I decided to take Mick up on his offer to move in with him—at least for a little while.

I took a leave of absence from Shrinden partly because I wanted this move, but also because the company refused to grant the month off I requested for the January cruise. *So screw them, it is probably time to move on career-wise anyway.*

In reality, I appeared to have a new career of sorts. I'd been keeping busy with travel to events and signings arranged by my publisher following the book's July release. I suppose I should feel like a real author, but it was happening way too fast for me to settle into that persona quite yet.

The media was hounding me, and that was another reason to leave Colorado and hide out at Mick's condo. Before I left home, an ABC network producer called asking if I would consent to an interview with Barbara Walters. The situation had gained sufficient critical mass that it was threatening to crush me, and I couldn't bring myself to go that far into the limelight. I told him no and have wondered ever since whether it was a mistake.

My relationship with Mick seemed to be progressing in some direction, but I wasn't sure it was the way I wanted to go. He was acting more like his old shipboard self, which I hoped was his real self. Over the past couple of weeks, we made love several times, and his gentle, sweet attention to my needs was almost more than I could bear. Despite my lingering unease about Mick's behavior, we both said we were relieved to be getting back the relationship—and some of the romance—we hoped for.

Amazingly, we were starting to look forward to revisiting the *Sea Nymph*, where it all began--and almost ended. We were practical enough to realize that our previous cruise was a huge anomaly, and this one would be perfectly normal.

I was also enjoying an entirely new kind of social life and was thrilled with the excitement of frequent dinners at Sam and Harry's with Bill and Mick, where at least once an evening, Bill would point out some famous political figure to me. They made me feel a part of their camaraderie, and I was very grateful to Bill for his friendship and his dedication to Mick.

Mick was keeping busy with the final arrangements for the GAO cruise crimes job, as he dubbed it. World of Seas Cruise Line reluctantly agreed to participate in the study after quite a bit of back and forth discussion. Actually, the cruise line did not acquiesce until Bill called the CEO for a friendly chat. Truth be told, between Mick and Tom planning to conduct sensitive interviews with crew members, and my having written a book about the cruise from hell, we weren't sure what kind of reception awaited us on the ship.

I continued to visit the Smithsonian museums and toured federal buildings whenever possible always feeling like a tourist, and learning a lot of U.S. history. I hadn't spent any time thinking about what I would do about my job at Shrinden, but that luxury would have to end soon. Rachael came to visit for a week in September, and we had great fun touring museums and galleries together. I especially enjoyed seeing her interact with Bill who was like an uncle to her. Seeing their mutual affection made me feel as if I was part of a functional, loving family and that was so ironic.

The security buzzer jolted me into the present, and I leaped up to unlock the door. I held it open and waited for the elevator to arrive. When Tom stepped out, I was shocked at how much weight he had lost but other than that he seemed fit. In fact, he looked younger due to the weight loss around his middle and the tight jeans, well-tailored Chambray shirt, and camel wool sport coat. Unfortunately, he was umbrella-less and quite wet.

"Darcy, I'm so happy to see you, but then I'm happy to see anyone these days," he quipped, as he brushed at his jacket lapels.

"Tom, you look fine," I laughed as I pulled him into an embrace despite the wetness. "Come on in and tell me what is going on with you and the investigation. Mick will be here in about an hour, and we hope you will join us with Bill Sawyer for dinner at Sam and Harry's. Can I get you something to drink or eat now?"

"Just some water would be good, and Sam and Harry's sounds great. Mick talks about the place so much, I feel as if I've been there." He kicked off his loafers just inside the door and removed his damp jacket, placing it over the back of a dining chair. Then he crossed the living space to the black leather sofa and sat down, putting his feet up on the ottoman and leaning back against the cushion.

I filled a glass with crushed ice and water and returned to the living room. "So tell me how you're really feeling and what is going on," I said, settling down beside him.

"Honestly, I feel pretty good, and my leg hurts less all the time. I have to gain some more strength in it and get back some of the weight, but not necessarily all of it," he chuckled. "I'm pretty pissed, though. There is no doubt in my mind that Paul is somehow responsible for what happened to me and that he did it to get revenge for my investigation on the ship. That guy is so dangerous we have to take him out one way or the other."

"You know, I sent some information to Detective Sandoval, the LVPD cop who originally interviewed us at the hospital. My biochemistry background and pharmaceutical work paid off because I had collected a few papers on basic chlorotoxin cancer research. There were some good experiments by an Israeli graduate student who worked directly with the Death Stalker. I noticed that her bio indicated she moved to the U.S. to work on brain cancer remedies with the NIH. I hope they talk to her to see if she has any ideas. I assume they haven't been able to find anything linking Paul to the attack?"

"Not yet, but I believe they will. Paul screwed up big time because let's face it, not that many people have access to those research scorpions and it's just a matter of time before they find the person who helped him. Anyway, Grant Murray is working with the police, and as determined as he is to get Paul, it will happen. I'm sure of it."

"I hope you're right, Tom." I'll never be at ease as long as that jerk is free to spend his considerable resources on ways to get revenge on you, Sidney, or any of us he thinks are responsible for spoiling his little plot. You guys have to find something helpful on the ship. It might be the only way."

17

November 24, 2008 – Las Vegas

Grant Murray shifted the phone under his chin as he reached across the desk to retrieve a report written by LVPD detective Sandoval. "So you're feeling pretty good, Tom? That's great news. Yeah, I have it right here. Darcy might be on to something with the information she sent to Sandoval. Apparently, there is a woman from Israel working at Wilmore Laboratories near Watertown, Mass. It might be worth talking to her about how someone could get their hands on the scorpions. There doesn't appear to be a connection between her and Paul, or even Las Vegas.

"Even so, Sandoval is trying to get some shred of evidence that would allow them to subpoena Athens Olympia records to match with people in the U.S. who work with the scorpions, including the woman Darcy found—Doctor Lilith Schrom. It's a stretch, but it might turn up something of interest."

Tom sighed audibly. "Part of me wants to go to the hotel and wring the information out of Paul, but I know that would only complicate matters, and he undoubtedly has an army of security shielding him."

"Right, and interviews we did with a couple of Athens Olympia employees were not fruitful. The local car rental agencies and the airlines have cooperated, but it's tough when you don't know precisely what you're looking for. A cursory search of their records for the days surrounding your attack didn't produce any names matching the lists of employees at the chlorotoxin research labs.

"I guess the person could have come from another country or even driven to Vegas, Murray continued, "and it's hard to see how they could have gotten the scorpions onto a plane in any event." He paused to think about that for a moment. "I wonder if something like them would show up on the X-Ray if they were in a carry-on? I'll have to check with TSA on that."

"Good idea, but I can't imagine you could get through security with those things in a bag. I mean wouldn't they have to be in a cage or container of some sort? Anyway, I hope not, for all our sakes."

"Tom, another problem is that Paul was with about fifty other people at a fundraising event the afternoon and evening of the attack on you, and since he has no connection to scorpion research, there's no reason to question him. But I still believe as you do, that there's a tie to Paul."

"Thanks for the update. There is a connection somewhere, and we'll find it. Speaking of that, we're good to go on the January cruise. World of Seas has agreed to provide access to the crew for interviews, with the assurance that there will be no publicity about the study before GAO delivers its report to Congress. As you can imagine, World of Seas management is not happy about all the press regarding their former captain and his wife's involvement in murders, and they still deny that the captain did anything wrong."

"I hope that doesn't interfere with your ability to get information on the ship."

"Me too. Suzanne's confession to me before we left her in Valparaiso, and her insistence that the captain killed the cruise director were completely believable. I still can't get over her death in that jail.

After a thoughtful pause, Tom said, "By the way, Grant, did you know that Darcy and her daughter, Rachael, are also coming along on the trip? I think they are very brave to go back there, and their presence will certainly make it more enjoyable. I have to admit, though, I'm still ambivalent about going back, including the fact that they fired me. I'll handle it, though, because my main interest is in getting Paul to pay for his crimes, and I can't see any other way."

Part Two

A Saboteur and More

18

January 2, 2009 – The *Sea Nymph*

The same, yet so different! That thought careened around in my head as I stepped onto the *Sea Nymph* and looked around. I hesitantly crossed the eight-foot-wide deck and approached the double glass doors leading into the ship. A powerful disorientation swept me to one side, and I grabbed for the outside wall next to the doors. Taking a moment to recover my cool, I bent over as if looking for something I had lost. After an embarrassing moment, I regained my composure and stepped to the side and back into the flow of excited passengers jostling to enter the ship.

I didn't even have to look around to recall the opulent surroundings. The floors and walls covered with granite and marble slabs, the brass and teak wood trim, and the modern art décor were imprinted on my brain as if this was a home away from home. Disconcertingly, the familiar surroundings provided some sense of safety. At the same time, flashes of Suzanne's horrific attack on us—like out-of-context bits of video—pricked at the edge of my consciousness like tiny lightning bolts. *What am I doing back here?*

I had to keep walking to prevent my fellow cruisers from stepping on my heels. At the first opportunity to turn away from the crowd, I darted onto the beautiful and achingly familiar star-patterned mosaic wood dance floor and headed for the Center Bar. This is the place where I met Mick, and it became our favorite hangout . . . despite the cruise director Ronaldo's horrific death that took place here.

I had just flown in from Colorado where I spent the past two weeks. Rachael was flying up from Buenos Aires and should be on the ship by now, and Mick and Tom were flying in from DC. They were supposed to meet us here at the bar before 5:30 when the ship was scheduled to leave port. It was

4:00 and I was deciding to find our stateroom and unpack some of my things while I waited. But suddenly, Manuel Delgado was standing behind his bar as if he, or rather I, had never left.

Quickly revising my plan, I stepped up to one of the nine teal and brown patterned bar stools arranged in front of the pleasingly curved light wood bar. Manuel looked up, and it took only an instant for his dark features to light with recognition. That smoldering Latin face, which I found so romantic and appealing, brightened with a wide grin.

"Darcy, you are back!" I cannot believe you are here after all the terrible things that happened to you on this ship. Is Mick with you?" He glanced over my shoulder.

Manuel still took my breath away a little, and I laughed, more at myself than anything. It just seemed so strange to be back. "Coming back here is something I would never have believed," I said, as I dropped my carry-on bag onto the stool beside me. "Believe it or not, Mick and Tom Smythe will both be here to do a little work for the government and I'm along for the ride."

His expression drooped a little and took on a look of bewilderment. "Tom Smythe, the former security chief, will be on this cruise? I know he lost his position and many crew members are very angry with him for making accusations against poor Captain Oldervoll."

"Oh, is that right, Manuel? They blame Tom for what happened? I am so sorry to hear that. He's a wonderful man and has only tried to determine the truth about the murders. You know about that last night, right, including Suzanne's attack on us?"

"Of course, we all heard about Suzanne, and it was hard to imagine how mentally ill she must have been. But no one wants to believe the captain killed anyone. They wish Tom would keep quiet about it."

"That is not good to hear, Manuel because Mick and Tom are going to be asking members of the crew about some details related to the crimes. Now you are worrying me about how that will go."

I tried to enjoy the remainder of my conversation with Manuel and stayed away from the events of the earlier cruise. I explained that Rachael would also be joining us, and he said he would be delighted to meet her. While we talked, I began to relax with the realization that even if Tom and Mick met resistance from the crew, this could be a peaceful, pleasant vacation for Rachael and me. I stared around the familiar lounge and lectured myself. We are fortunate to be traveling on this luxury cruise ship with the opportunity to visit so many exotic seaports along the way. The thought occurred that I just needed to keep telling myself that.

19

Time flew as I enjoyed an update on Manuel's family in Cartagena. I almost felt as if I knew his wife, Juliana, and their two children from our past conversations. Next to Tom, Manuel was the crew member Mick, and I had gotten to know the best, and we both considered him a friend.

When five o'clock came and went, and no one had joined me, Manuel could tell that I was getting a little anxious. After declaring the bar open, he grinned at me and said, "Darcy, would you like your first Ketel One martini of the cruise, extra dry and slightly dirty with olives?"

"Wow, you even remember my favorite drink. Yes, why not? I'm sure Mick and Tom will be here any minute since the ship is about to sail." I hoped I was right.

At that moment, I saw Manuel's expression change to surprise and something like amusement. I followed his stare to see Rachael struggling with a large rolling duffle as she made her way across the dance floor. She looked terrific in a simple long-sleeved hot pink cotton dress that draped her lithe body beautifully, ending about six inches above her knees. Three-inch platform sandals, brought her to over six feet tall. She straightened up when she saw me, smiling broadly as she quickened her pace.

I had not seen her for nearly three months, and I stood to receive her into my arms, lightly kissing her cheek. This simple gesture held a world of meaning for me. For so many years I had no reasonable hope of ever seeing my daughter again, much less holding her against my body. I loved her so profoundly that losing her at eighteen months almost killed me, even though it had been my decision. But that is another story. Then I turned to Manuel. "This is Rachael. You know the story of how we got reunited during the last cruise."

Manuel gaped at me and then at Rachael. He caught himself and laughed. "I am happy to meet you, Rachael. Darcy told me all about you during the last cruise. I'm sure I am not the first to be amazed at how much the two of you look alike." Then he favored me with a familiar impudent grin. "Darcy, you know you do not really look like Rachael's mother . . . more like an older sister."

"You are very kind, Manuel. I was quite young when she was born," I began to giggle, and then got hold of myself. Manuel had that effect on me.

Rachael seated herself on the stool beside me and asked Manuel for a glass of water. "Where is Mick?" she asked, swiveling toward me.

"I'm sure he will be here any minute . . ."

"Yeah, any minute now," Mick announced from behind us.

I jumped down and threw my arms around his neck as I nodded to Tom who was coming up behind him. "I was beginning to wonder if you two missed your flight or something. I'm so glad you're here."

"No, we just cut it a little close, I guess." Mick turned to Rachael and kissed her cheek. "How was your flight from Buenos Aires, Rachael?"

"It was long but uneventful. Thanks for asking, Mick. How are you Tom?" she asked over Mick's shoulder.

"Better all the time, thanks. I feel almost back to normal."

Manuel now held out his hand. "Hello, Mr. Smythe. It is good to see you again. Have you been ill?"

"It's Manuel, right?" Tom shook his hand enthusiastically. "Yes, it is good to see you. So, you are still here with World of Seas. Good for you. I have mixed feelings about being back here myself, but it is good to see a familiar face. As to your question about my health, I'm afraid I had a little mishap, but I'm fine now."

Mick also reached out to shake Manuel's hand. "Good to see you again, man. We sure spent some long hours sitting here working on fixing the world's problems, didn't we?"

"I guess that is true. Now and then some guests become much more than fleeting passengers. I have enjoyed knowing you both, and I am so happy that you have returned." He nodded to Mick and me.

We all sat at the bar then and caught up on the events of our lives over the past couple of weeks. Everyone was surprised and pleased at how well my book was doing. I had just completed a tour of signings at three Colorado Barnes and Noble stores, where I sold hundreds of books.

Rachael had just competed in a rowing event at the University of Buenos Aires and placed second out of forty in a singles two-oar scull. She was still clinging to her dream of joining an Olympic crew. I had a moment of sadness as I tried to reconcile that goal with her plan to move to the U.S. She was going to have to make some difficult decisions when her folks moved to their new post in Africa.

76

Of course, Mick and Tom had been fully engaged in planning their role in the GAO assignment and hadn't had time for much else. That was pretty much all Mick had on his mind, and just as we were enjoying a friendly discussion, he leaned over the bar toward Manuel and lowered his voice to a loud whisper.

"So, Manuel, we are wondering if you have any knowledge about what happened on the cruise last year. I mean, for example, did you hear about any crew members having an arrangement with the passenger named Paul Denezza that might have led to the deaths?"

This abrupt questioning seemed very inappropriate, and it annoyed me. Manuel was obviously and understandably distressed, but he tried to maintain his practiced friendly demeanor.

"No Mick, I have heard nothing except that Suzanne attacked Mr. Denezza's wife and you two, and Tom arrested her. I have not heard anyone say they know anymore." He squared up a stack of cocktail napkins then looked back up at Mick. "The only thing is, some American police—maybe the FBI—came on board in Miami and questioned a few crew members, but I don't know anything about that. Nothing bad has happened on any cruises over the past year, and mostly, we'd like to forget all of it."

At least Mick recognized Manuel's discomfort since he is not a completely insensitive guy. "I'm sorry, Manuel, I shouldn't have asked you that way. We've come back to find out once and for all how the crew members' deaths relate to what happened with Suzanne."

"No problem," Manuel said with one of his ready smiles. Just keep in mind that I, for one, know nothing about nothing, OK? You want another Corona, Mick?"

20

Much later that night, Mick lay beside Darcy willing himself to be still so as not to wake her. He and Tom had an important meeting in the morning with the captain and security chief, and he needed to sleep. Unfortunately, his level of anxiety and humiliation seemed to be increasing with each sleepless minute. The failed attempt to make love to Darcy a few hours earlier brought on another wave of embarrassment.

They had been so close to each other by the end of the first cruise and had been having sex virtually every day. Something like this would not have happened back then, or if it had, they would have taken it in stride . . . no big deal. But this was now, and try as he had been since he supposedly recovered from his injury, Mick simply could not understand what was wrong with him.

For almost a year, Darcy had been very understanding, sympathetic actually, and that seemed to make him feel worse. *How much longer can I expect her to go on like this?* He had to admit that he was surprised she was still with him. There had been weeks at a time when he didn't even call her. Worse, when they were together, days went by when he did not even attempt to have sex with her. Why? He did love her and wanted nothing more than to be with her in a healthy happy relationship. Trying to think about the situation rationally always seemed to exhaust him.

Intellectually, he understood that something had gone very wrong with his emotions or psychology or something. Even when Beth, his wife of fifteen years, had been days away from succumbing to her brain tumor and even after she was gone, he had never experienced the type of confusion and depression that was now routine.

The only thing he could discern through his mostly futile self-analysis was that it seemed as if just when he was getting back on track, his encounters with Darcy seemed to renew his anxiety. He understood that he wanted to avoid her on some level. It made absolutely no sense. It was as if he were two men . . . the one who loved Darcy and wanted nothing more than to be with her, and the one who was horribly uncomfortable being with her.

He turned his body and sucked in his breath at the sight of her beautiful face turned toward him almost aglow in the dim night light and partly hidden by her thick blond hair. He placed his hand gently on her arm and was rewarded with a contented sigh. *Maybe she's dreaming about the way we used to be.* He closed his eyes and breathed deeply. Her scent, like fresh flowers, was once all that was needed to arouse him. He waited a moment to see if anything was going to happen to his body. Finally, he let go and allowed himself to float on the fragrance and the memory all the way to slumber.

21

Day 1 – at sea

Promptly at 9:00 a.m., Mick and Tom arrived at Merida, the conference center room where they were to meet with Master Captain Dolf Bentzer and Chief of Security Roger Ramirez. In the space next door a class or lecture was already underway. An odd sound filtered through the folding wall, which resonated like some sort of strange musical instrument. Mick and Tom looked at each other and laughed despite their tension. You never knew what type of activity you might encounter on this floating village.

They proceeded to the end of the conference table farthest away from the noise of laughter and applause mixed with loud and eerie bass notes. They began comparing their notes while they waited for their hosts to arrive.

At 9:20 Captain Bentzer and Ramirez finally came through the door. They were very rushed or perhaps they were trying to appear so, as they sat down across from Mick and Tom. The captain immediately took charge of the meeting.

"I apologize for the whale watch and singing lecture, ya?" he began as he tilted his head toward the sound. His heavy Swedish accent was difficult to understand, and he had completed half his remarks before Tom and Mick got used to his off-beat cadence and miss-accented syllables. They could, however, understand perfectly well where he was coming from. His manner and tone left little doubt that he was annoyed with them being on board. He didn't exactly appear to be angry, just impatient and concerned about how much of the crew's time they would require. Then he tried to express what was really bothering him. "I am not wanting the crew to be upsetted, ya? They have gone around this thing and nothing good to bring out bad memories, ya?"

Mercifully in a sense, Ramirez took over from the captain, and his speech and meaning were crystal clear. He began in a booming voice that completely drowned out the whales. "Look, the main thing is that you are on your own with these interviews as you call them. Out here in international waters, the captain is the sole authority over whether you are allowed to continue your discussions with the crew." He pointed a finger in Tom's direction. "The crew can't escort you or assist you in gathering information." He glanced toward the captain who was looking off to the side. "The ship is just getting back to normal after the events of last January, and we don't need a constant reminder of it."

He looked at Tom with an openly hostile expression. "You also should know that many of us believe you are largely responsible for what happened. If you had not dropped the ball, Suzanne Moretti would not have carried out her murderous plans . . ."

The captain interrupted his tirade. "Ya, the official position of World of Seas is with the mental illness, she is only responsible for crew members' deaths. You complicate more with implicating passengers or other crew members."

"Besides," Roger added, "the FBI spent two days on the ship when we docked in Miami, and their investigation found nothing to indicate there was any conspiracy."

Mick saw Tom experiencing a slow burn and was mightily impressed with his friend's ability to maintain his composure. He decided to let Tom respond rather than coming to his defense. After a few moments of silence, Tom spoke very quietly and firmly.

"You have made your positions and that of the cruise line very clear. We will do everything possible to make sure there is minimum disruption as we talk to crew members." He glanced over at Mick before continuing. "Just so you are fully informed, you should be aware that the FBI is involved in our effort—a continuing investigation by their Las Vegas office in conjunction with the GAO."

Finally and begrudgingly, Ramirez handed them the list of crew members who worked for both housekeeping and the cruise director during the previous cruise. These names would constitute the starting point for finding at least one person who knew about Paul Denezza's plot to kill his wife using the crew as his weapons.

Another booming note from the next room proved to be almost as irritating as Ramirez and seemed to signal the end of the meeting. Mick and Tom hurried out of the conference center and rode the elevator to the top of the ship. They needed some fresh air and a meeting of their own to decide where to begin.

22

Day 2 – at sea

Joe pulled the folding wrench he had brought on board—along with numerous other tools—from the pocket of his white coveralls. He looked around to determine who might be nearby and then began tightening screws in the four-inch brass tubing that surrounded the foyer just outside the Center Bar. He was still a little hung over—drunk actually—but he was used to operating in that condition. As he pretended to care about the sturdiness of the useless decorative railing, he looked around at the other passengers and wondered how long he would be able to keep up this charade.

He was determined to complete his mission and had decided that nothing was going to stop him. However, he was realizing he might have to act more quickly than he had planned. For the better part of a year, he spent every spare moment working on his schemes, usually in a drunken stupor. He spent many confusing hours at his computer blearily studying mechanical drawings and layouts of cruise ships. The information he found on the World of Seas website describing various onboard systems was also beneficial.

For most of his adult life, ever since his discharge from the Army following service in Vietnam, he had been a *functioning* alcoholic. For many years he consumed several six-packs every day, but recently he increased his daily alcohol consumption by at least a pint of Jim Beam. Since the day he received the notification of his daughter's death at the hands of the cruise line—that is how he saw it—he dedicated his life to seeking revenge, a life now spiraling out of his control.

First, he received a phone call from World of Seas headquarters telling him she had suffered a mental breakdown and was under arrest for murder. Then, the official-sounding letter from the State Department arrived, explaining how she died. His outrage and incredulity overwhelmed him and pushed him over the brink on which he had been teetering for years. At some point during Joe's tenth reading of the letter, something broke deep inside him that he could never repair.

In 1970, shortly after returning home to Kansas with his South African bride, Joe found Jesus and was born again. For many years before his rebirth, he was estranged from his family and their meat packing business. Nonetheless, they welcomed him home, even paying for his education in electrical engineering. Joe turned out to be a very handy guy, showing a surprising aptitude for the field.

Although he gave up on formal schooling in less than two years, he continued to teach himself and eventually took over all the maintenance and upgrades of the company's meat processing, packaging, and conveyor systems. For the past twenty years, he had been running the family business despite his steadily increasing alcohol consumption.

His relationship with Jesus become increasingly intimate over time. He jumped wholeheartedly onto the *What would Jesus do?* mantra the first time he ever heard it. Now he knew without a doubt that Jesus would clearly be in favor of avenging his daughter. Joe was a member of the *eye-for-an-eye* persuasion, even if that punishment predated—and contradicted—his savior by a couple of millennia.

Now it was time for all his research and preparation to pay off. Here he was on the ship and had already implemented the first part of his plan. He was not so far gone as to believe he could destroy the *Sea Nymph* or the cruise line for that matter, but he was determined to cause significant damage and wreak plenty of havoc. If World of Seas managers thought they had suffered their worst adverse publicity, they were in for a shock. Up to this point, Joe had not the clarity of mind to think about what he would do if someone interfered with his plans. Was he prepared to implement a violent solution? Maybe Jesus knew what he would do, but Joe did not.

He reached down, pretending to address the bolts in a lower railing and nearly fell on his face in front of an elderly couple who were strolling past trying to utilize it to remain on their feet. Oops, maybe I should go back to my cabin for a nap, he thought . . . and a few sips from one of the Jim Beam bottles he smuggled aboard in his suitcase.

Heading for the stairs, he almost laughed out loud as he congratulated himself once again for his stealth and cunning in procuring his maintenance uniform. The supposedly crew-only laundry area was just down a passageway and around a corner from his cabin, which bordered an area of crew activity down on deck 2. He knew he'd been especially cunning in requesting his particular stateroom after studying a plan of the ship.

So very early yesterday morning, dressed casually in faded jeans and a white T-shirt, he easily slipped into the laundry and picked up a pair of coveralls from a pile of clothes still warm from the massive dryer. He rolled them under his arm and quickly returned to his cabin.

He tried on the coveralls with his tool belt, and as he stood in front of the full-length mirror on the bathroom door running his hand across his grey two-day stubble, it occurred to him that he should shave. Peering closely at his reflection, he was glad he had thought to dye his hair blond, which was very different from its original dark color. At least he wasn't bald, although time—and alcohol and tobacco—were taking their toll. While his body remained in decent shape, a map-like record of nearly life-long abuse etched his once handsome features.

Fortunately for Joe, each time the ship sailed-a number of new crew members came on board, and today he found that it was not difficult to blend in with the other deckhands. So far he had avoided any meaningful conversation with the legitimate workers and had found places where he could assume a confident demeanor as he tinkered with minor elements of the ship's accouterments.

The problem would come at night when he had to return to his passenger state room. He knew that sooner or later his coworkers would realize they did not know him and that he was not living with them in the crew lodgings on decks 1 and 2.

As he approached his cabin, Joe discreetly looked around but saw only passengers. It would not do for any of the workers to see him here. Yes, he would have to implement his plan quickly. The good news was that despite the ship's considerable security measures, he was carrying out his mission perfectly so far. Who would ever expect a passenger to want to pose as a deckhand on a luxury cruise ship?

23

Day 3 – Cabo San Lucas, Mexico

We anchored just offshore at Cabo, located at the tip of the Baja Peninsula on Mexico's west coast. We were visiting for the first time, but other passengers assured us that the port area offered great opportunities to sightsee on foot. So, Mick and I climbed onto the tender—an enclosed boat supplied by a local contractor—along with Rachael, Tom, and about fifty of our fellow passengers for a short ride to the pier.

With the sun high and bright, we slathered ourselves with sunblock, packed water bottles, and anticipated a fun, relaxing day. It was one of the few times during the cruise that Mick and Tom would be able to go ashore because they would be busy conducting their one-on-one crew interviews.

As we hurried down the short gangplank onto the dock I glanced at Rachael striding alongside me. She seemed happy to be on this trip with Mick and me. Even though she had lived in many exotic cities around the world with her parents in the Foreign Service, she was eager to explore another new locale. She was so much more confident than I was at her age—and so gorgeous. I saw that she was already drawing stares from men and women alike as she strode out ahead of us down the covered walkway.

Rachael and I were getting used to the looks people tended to give us everywhere we went, apparently due to our similar looks combined with our tallness and, well, I guess for my age, I didn't look too bad either. I caught up and grabbed her hand for a moment. Tears welled as I looked into her extraordinary blue eyes and felt her squeeze my hand. She gave me a radiant smile. "I love you, Darcy. Thanks so much for this trip."

"My pleasure, Hon. I'm so glad you decided to come along."

Mick and Tom caught up with us, and we started strolling down the boardwalk, which gently curved around the small harbor. Street vendors peddled their supposed handmade goods on the shore side across from all sizes of recreational motorized craft and sailboats sitting along the pier with local fishing boats. We stopped a few times to look at handcrafts and chatted about what we wanted to do while on shore.

We reached a consensus that after walking into the town for a look around, a Mexican lunch with Margaritas would be perfect. Mick was game at that point, and I could tell he was trying to be upbeat. Unfortunately, he wasn't able to sustain his carefree mood for very long.

The first sign of trouble came when we left the boardwalk and cut through an alley that connected to a bustling downtown street. We proceeded at a leisurely pace looking into the many shops and restaurants. Proprietors of jewelry and souvenir shops hawking their wares mildly accosted us as they tried to entice us to step inside. At one establishment a couple of local guys hanging around the entrance made mock attempts to grab Rachael and yelled comments that we knew had to be lewd even with our poor Spanish. I figured this was par for the course and Rachael just shook her head, laughed, and kept walking.

Mick immediately jumped on the incident as an excuse to return to the ship. "This is obviously no place for you and Rachael," he said, as he pulled me toward the curb and away from the buildings.

"For heaven's sake, Mick, that sort of thing can happen anywhere—trust me, I know from experience."

"I'm sure you do since you're always putting yourself out there, but don't you care about Rachael's safety?"

The disrespectful comment was not like Mick at all, it was embarrassing, and it really hurt my feelings. I swallowed hard and tried to answer with a light tone. "With all these people around and you and Tom beside us? No, Mick, I'm not the least bit worried."

Rachael heard this exchange and stepped up behind Mick placing her hand on his shoulder. "Don't worry about me, Mick. I can take care of myself. I'm big and strong and a world traveler," she teased good-naturedly.

He twisted his shoulder and shrugged her hand away. "Well, I guess it's about time someone started behaving like a grown-up," he replied caustically, then picked up his pace and walked on ahead.

I was stunned at this uncharacteristically mean reaction, and so was Rachael. She looked at me with a bewildered expression. "What did I do wrong, Darcy? I don't understand."

"You didn't do anything, Hon. I don't know what is wrong with him. Do you, Tom?" I asked, turning toward him.

Tom looked at Mick's back and shook his head. "I've noticed in our interviews that he has started getting a little tense—testy even—with the crew members. We've only been at it for a little more than a day, but I get the feeling he expects to get results immediately."

The morning pretty much went downhill from there. Mick's behavior was outrageous by any standard, not just because it was alien to his normal conduct. From that point on he continued to pout, and his behavior completely ruined the happy mood of the day.

By the time we arrived back on the boardwalk I had decided to go back to the ship with Mick and let the others enjoy the rest of their day. Mick perked up a little and seemed relieved when I suggested that he and I go back and eat in the Whale's Tail buffet restaurant on deck 10. I hoped Rachael would stay behind with Tom, but she insisted on returning with us. Tom said he would have lunch in Cabo by himself.

The tender ride back to the ship was full of tension. Mick didn't say anything at all, and Rachael's anger was apparent from her body language and expression. Looking at her taut mouth and narrowed eyes, I realized I was seeing that unpleasant emotion in her for the first time. It was not hard to imagine I could see my angry expression reflected in her eyes.

24

After saying so long to his travel mates, Tom stepped into No Worry's, a restaurant and bar on the boardwalk. He was agitated about Mick's behavior and just wanted to have a drink and try to settle down. The atmosphere was festive and charming with several tiers of wide planked floors and solid wood pillars setting a nautical tone. Chunky natural wood chairs and tables sat appealingly under bright blue canvas umbrellas, creating a shady relief from the intense sun.

Those spots were inviting, but since he was alone, he opted for a seat at the massive raised bar. Overhead, multi-colored flags with pictures of sea life—turtles, dolphins, seals, and fish—barely fluttered in the weak breeze.

After ordering a Margarita, he picked up a menu and studied it. A burger and bucket of fries sounded pretty good. Now and then he glanced up at the TV suspended from the ceiling just to the left of the bar. News snippets flashed across the screen, and he realized he had no idea what had been going on in the world for the past three days.

Staring out of the open restaurant at the harbor, his thoughts wandered back to Mick's alarming meltdown. It was personally disturbing, but even more worrisome because they would have to work closely together to pull off the delicate interviews.

When he turned back to the menu, a woman had seated herself on the stool next to him. He smiled and nodded politely. "How are you doing?" he said lightly.

"Oh, I'm just great. I've never been here before, and everything is so new and different." She seemed almost child-like in her enthusiasm.

Tom felt a tiny thrill of something . . . excitement maybe and wondered why. While she was talking, he noted that she was quite pretty with soft curly black hair and dark eyes. She had an appealing ethnic look that he could not quite place, and she seemed very relaxed and somehow fresh in olive green cargo shorts and a lacy white blouse. He could not help glancing down to admire her shapely tanned legs and then looking behind her to see who she was with. There didn't seem to be anyone else in the area.

"Are you staying in Cabo on vacation?" he asked.

"Actually, I'm on that big cruise ship over there." She pointed across the harbor toward the *Sea Nymph*, "How about you?"

An odd sensation swept over him as he looked into her eyes. She seemed to be returning his gaze with a strange intensity, and he was experiencing something like déjà vu. He did not know this woman, so he shrugged off the feeling.

He hadn't had a real romantic relationship for years—the whole ten years he worked on the ship to be exact. Now as he approached middle age, he was no great prize in the looks department. Then he recalled Darcy's recent words to the effect that he was looking *cute and sexy* since losing some weight and dressing a little more hip. He had to admit it gave his ego a boost.

"What a coincidence," he laughed, "I'm a passenger on the ship as well."

She pressed her full lips together in a fleeting expression of humor that made Tom's belly flutter. "Oh, are you traveling alone too?" she asked. Well, that answered his question about whom she was with.

"As a matter of fact, I'm on board with friends and mostly for business." He held out his hand. "I'm Tom Smythe."

"Hi Tom, I'm Wendy Stanfield," she replied while firmly shaking his hand. "That sounds interesting. What sort of business are you doing on the ship?"

He hesitated for a moment before responding. "It's a project for the government, looking at um . . . various types of incidents that occur on cruises . . . to passengers, you know?" He was nervous for some reason and wanted to change the subject. He stalled a little by looking down at his menu. "What do you do?" he finally asked, not sure if the question was appropriate.

Wendy tossed her head and beamed. Her whole face seemed to light up, and he realized how pretty she really was. "I'm an interior designer. I have my own small business in Philadelphia and I've had some success recently. I've been very busy but a little stressed. On a whim, I guess, I decided to fly out to L.A. and take the cruise. Now that I'm here, though, I'm feeling just a little uneasy about being alone."

Over a lunch of scrumptious Mexican food, they enjoyed a conversation heavy with small talk and sexual tension. Tom felt elated and confident but was surprised when he realized that most of the afternoon—and four large margaritas—had come and gone.

He paid the tab and they headed down the boardwalk. Somewhere along the way, they decided it would be fun to wade in the surf near land's end, located on the far side of the rocky bluff that towers over the harbor.

On the way into port, Tom had stood at the railing with Mick and Darcy marveling at the singular tall pointed rocks jutting from the ocean floor at the tip of the long narrow peninsula. Why these stark components of the surrounding rock formation seemed so beautiful and mysterious, he could not say . . . only that their singularity appeared to signify a kind of peacefulness.

Not knowing how or even if they could get there on foot, the couple wandered back in the direction of the pier. Then holding hands and laughing conspiratorially, they navigated into a narrow lane running perpendicular to the pier. Serendipitously, they exited the lane at a traffic circle right at the foot of the bluff. Across the way, a steep and narrow driveway wound upward, clearly providing access to colorful condominium complexes they had seen from the ship on their way into the harbor.

A short hike up the driveway brought them to a sign pointing toward the Hotel Soldan, and that seemed like as good a way as any to find a path to the beach. As it turned out, they were able to meander through the resort, mingling with the guests who were eating in outdoor cafes and lounging poolside. Sure enough, the back of the property opened to the beach, and Tom stopped at the edge of the sidewalk to remove his tennis shoes. Wendy slipped out of her sandals, and they plodded through the loose, warm sand down to the water's edge. Walking hand in hand and alone on the beach at high tide, they soon realized it was impossible to go very far because bluff outcroppings extending across the beach and into the water blocked their progress.

As they retraced their steps at the surf's edge, Tom had a moment of unease when he suddenly realized how bizarre this behavior was for him. He quickly buried the thought and said, "Wow, this has turned out to be a much different afternoon than I expected."

"For me also, I am really enjoying this, Tom. Maybe I will see you on the ship."

Tom was definitely tipsy from the alcohol and from this unexpected romantic encounter. If he had been entirely sober he might have thought about the situation a little more, but as it was he quickly asked, "Well, how about dinner tonight, Wendy? What is your assigned dining time?"

"Oh my, I didn't mean . . . well, I guess that would be nice. I have early seating, how about you?"

"Me too, so let's see if the maître d' will switch one of us so we can sit together." Then with little hesitation, he added, "I don't see why you couldn't sit at the table with my three friends and me. I would like you to meet them.

The table is a six-top, but no one else has shown up for dinner." Tom wasn't really considering that such an arrangement might turn out to be permanent, whether he wanted it or not. At the time he was merely feeling a lot looser and more relaxed than he had in recent memory.

25

We had not seen Tom since returning to the ship but assumed we would meet up with him at dinner. Mick, Rachael, and I took the elevator to deck 5 and approached the wide marble-pillared entrance to Mermaids dining room. The setting was relaxing, but the mood was still tense. I had tried to talk to him about his apparent anxiety, but he shrugged me off and told me to just forget it. He hadn't spoken to Rachael, and I hoped the dinner environment would force a conversation.

Our table was located about mid-way through the enormous room of white linen and crystal. As it came within view, I leaned toward Rachael and whispered, "Who is that woman sitting with Tom?"

"I have no idea. I don't think I've seen her before." Turning her face tentatively to Mick, she said "do you see that woman sitting at our table? Who is she?" She obviously wanted to make peace with him.

"No idea," he replied flatly. "Maybe she's just a passenger who has changed her table for some reason. Sometimes people just don't enjoy the company of guests assigned to their table and request to be moved."

I looked more carefully as we approached the table. Tom was sitting next to the attractive dark-haired woman and appeared to be deep in conversation. The feeling was definitely one of familiarity. *What is this about?*

When we arrived, they quickly rose to their feet, and Tom seemed to plaster on a broad but uneasy smile. He gazed into my eyes and seemed to be seeking my approval or understanding for some reason.

Wendy was a young, willowy sort of woman, but judging by the fit of her long elegant black dress, she had a very feminine shape. "Hello Wendy," I offered, and reached over the table to shake her hand. Mick and Rachael followed suit, and we seated ourselves with Mick and me facing them and Rachael on the end.

Wendy sat down and looked across at me. Her dark, sultry eyes opened wide with expectation, and my impression was that she was a very pretty young woman wanting to make a good impression. At the same time, I was experiencing an uneasy sensation. *Please . . . don't tell me I'm having feelings of motherly protectiveness toward Tom.* I had never pictured him with a female partner, and now I thought guiltily that even with his recent improvements, I sort of thought of him like a brother. Of course, I never actually had a brother.

Wendy broke the brief silence. "Oh, I hope you all do not mind my joining you. Tom was very persuasive in his invitation, and I am grateful. I am cruising by myself and haven't had an opportunity to meet many people yet."

That seemed logical, and it indeed was like Tom to be friendly and even sensitive to someone in her position. I relaxed a little, thinking that this was nothing to be concerned about. Still, I wished I could understand what it was that seemed to be annoying me about this seemingly simple situation.

"Wendy and I met at lunch on the boardwalk and sort of hit it off right away," Tom explained. "We took a walk on the beach and had a great afternoon." He turned to look at her and his expression said volumes, in my opinion. *This is interesting. Tom is smitten with her.*

Rachael was asking Wendy what she did for a living, and Mick had leaned back in his chair with a slight scowl as he watched Tom and Wendy interact. This is all we need, I thought, something else to annoy Mick and complicate things.

As it turned out, the meal and dinner talk went well. Wendy seemed quite open and, and I decided my unease stemmed from a silly feeling of protectiveness toward Tom. I also understood that he had come out of his shell and probably was not used to getting so much attention from an attractive woman.

He deserved some happiness, and I was happy for him. Still, I was troubled and didn't know why. As we left Mermaids and headed to the showroom for the evening's entertainment, I thought that I couldn't wait to talk with Mick in private to get his take on the situation.

26

Day 4 – at sea

The thrill of the risky task he was about to undertake had heightened Joe's senses to the point of hyperactivity. He gulped another mouthful from the flask, stuffed it into his coverall pocket, and drew a deep breath to calm his nerves. He looked around outside the crew maintenance elevator to be sure he was not being observed and stepped inside. Keeping his gaze straight ahead, he leaned down to press the button for deck 1.

Thank you, Jesus, for the Internet, he thought as the doors closed. He couldn't have put this plan in motion without it—at least not without calling unwanted attention to himself. It required several months, but he managed to glean all the information he needed about the ship's critical desalination system from the equipment manufacturers' websites and World of Seas online technical descriptions of their vessels. His maintenance crew disguise was working well so far, and he was confident that his detailed knowledge about the steam evaporator equipment and the back-up reverse osmosis system would guarantee success.

Even so, he had to down the better part of a Jim Beam pint before he could actually leave his cabin. He wandered around the ship for another half hour, rethinking his plan and going over his mental checklist before heading for the elevator.

Cruise ships make all their own fresh water using the inexhaustible supply of seawater readily at hand. In this case, two desalination methods produce fifty gallons of fresh water needed each day for each passenger. He decided to target the water systems when he realized that every person onboard was utterly dependent on the ship's ability to produce fresh water for drinking, cooking, and personal hygiene. He chuckled to himself when he thought about the extra suitcase he brought on board filled with plastic bottles of water . . .

exclusively for his own consumption. He knew that if detected, he would appear to be a neurotic passenger with undue suspicion about the ship's water quality.

He was confident in his understanding of the equipment after months of study. The distillation method employs a large gas-fired boiler, which produces steam to evaporate the seawater. The vapor is then condensed into purified fresh water. Distillation removes bacteria and even viruses in the process but uses a lot of energy to produce more than 200,000 gallons of clean water per day—the bulk of the ship's water supply.

To reduce operating costs and establish redundancy, the ship also has a reverse osmosis (RO) desalination system, which produces an additional 80,000 gallons of water a day using half the energy of the distillation method. The ship's RO equipment boasts state-of-the-art semi-permeable membranes that can remove up to 99 percent of dissolved salts and inorganic material from seawater.

Joe learned all about concerns that some seawater microbes and viruses could slip through the membranes, like the Norovirus, which has caused widespread illness on a few cruise ships. Initially, he thought about how delightful it would be to see a ship full of sick passengers and crew. However, he soon realized that the latest technology in stacking membranes used in this ship's RO plant was probably very efficient in filtering out microbes.

Anyway, after studying the physical plant layouts, he decided he was not up to the task of contaminating the input water with a virus, much less the logistical difficulty in obtaining and preserving a bio-hazardous agent. Instead, he decided to concentrate his efforts on carrying out mechanical sabotage of the ship's desalination equipment. Mechanics and electrical engineering, not microscopic organisms, were his forte—he would stick with what he knew.

Stepping out of the elevator, he tried to affect an air of self-confidence as he headed for the metal grate stairway leading down to the kitchen and physical plant. His modest goal was to disrupt the comfort of the passengers for at least a few days. He realized that the ship's real mechanical engineers would detect and repair the damage in a relatively short time, but he intended to make their task as difficult as possible.

Rounding a corner, he entered the enormous galley and strode through the vast sea of stainless steel counters, shelves, and refrigeration units. Suddenly, he was in the throes of extreme anxiety. On an impulse, he quickly stepped behind a six-foot-high bank of gleaming open-back shelves that had been placed eighteen inches from the wall. Hiding like this doesn't make me look like I belong down here, he thought. Peering out between two large cooking oil cans, he pulled the flask from his pocket with a shaking hand and took a long drink just to steady himself. Wiping drops of bourbon from his chin, he told himself it would be his last sip until the job was complete.

He chose this time—3:00 a.m.—because he knew that only a skeleton crew would be on duty, but he would have to finish his work and return topside before the morning shift arrived at 4:00 a.m. to begin breakfast preparation. Of course, there was always the chance that crew members would show up early for work, but he had confidence in the protection afforded by his crew member disguise. Now he realized that no one was in the area, and it was only his nerves making him jumpy. *Get a grip on yourself old man.*

Another minute passed along with a couple of absent-minded sips from his flask. He eased from behind the shelves and continued along the wide center aisle toward the water production plant. Deep in slightly fuzzy thought, he tried to picture the equipment waiting up ahead. While the designs were relatively simple, Joe had studied the science of desalination so he could carry out some tricky and exacting tasks.

Reverse osmosis, first developed in the 1950s is the opposite of the natural phenomenon of osmosis, where water flows through a membrane from a lower to a higher concentration of dissolved solids. The point of RO is to reverse the process so that water flows from a higher concentration—dissolved salts in seawater—to a lower one—fresh water. To achieve this, pressure is applied to the seawater to "push" it through the membrane. Under the right conditions, salt and other organic matter cannot pass through the modern membrane's two ten-millionths of an inch pores, so that mostly pure water flows out of the system.

Joe struggled to get his attention off the basic science and onto his task. Approaching the target equipment, he experienced a rush of adrenaline and satisfaction as he recognized precisely what he'd seen in diagrams and photos. Against the wall, there was the pump, the filter box, and the three six-inch input and output pipes atop one another running behind the unit.

One of the features of the RO equipment is that once it has been set up and turned on, the operation does not require any specialized training or even that an attendant is present. The functions are automatic, and the pump is the only moving part. A built-in cleaning system dramatically reduces the frequency of maintenance, and the housing containing the stacked membranes is easily opened to allow inspection. This latter characteristic was of particular interest to Joe.

Just as he expected, no one was around the equipment this time of the night. Time to get to work, he thought, as he returned the nearly empty flask to his pocket. Abruptly, he stopped and peered along the top of the walls on three sides of the open area, until he was sure the cruise line had not installed security cameras there.

Turning his attention to the tall box that housed the ultra-filter membranes, he quickly loosened the screws holding on the lid and removed it. The stacked layers inside looked deceptively simple, exactly like clear plastic sandwich wrap. They are designed to be tough, but seawater has to be filtered before it passes over them to reduce the quantity of silt. Otherwise, the membranes will get overloaded and fouled.

With a sense of self-righteous indignity toward the cruise line, Joe nodded to himself and removed the tray from his small toolbox. From the bottom, he retrieved an actual plastic sandwich bag, removed the tie, and quickly dumped its contents—about a cup of sand—into the top of the filter box on the side receiving the filtered seawater feed. He knew this would clog the delicate membranes, and greatly reduce the amount of water that could pass through the filter. Even though the thin film polymer is chemically stable and can withstand up to three hundred fifty pounds per square inch of pressure, Joe hoped his little addition to the process would increase the pressure to the breaking point. He closed the lid and tightened the screws.

Moving to the end of the RO module, he found the valves. Peering closely—much too closely—it suddenly registered that his vision was blurred. A spike of panic lodged in his gut as he realized he was leaning on the pump housing in order to remain on his feet. He was in trouble, but there was no time to lose in making his adjustments because the system had an alarm monitor that would alert the crew to an imbalance in the process.

The balance was indeed delicate. Because water naturally passes through the system faster than salt, increasing pressure on the seawater speeds the flow, ensuring that less salt slips through, which is good. However, too much pressure can disrupt the osmotic balance and halt the salt capture altogether, rendering the process useless. Joe finally identified the pressure valve and turned it almost all the way up. Then he located the temperature gauge and pushed it up as well because he knew this would improve the salt diffusion rate, allowing more salt to pass through the filters, which is bad.

He knew these simple changes were reversible, but would significantly reduce the amount of fresh water exiting the system for the time being. Maintenance would require at least a couple of days to clean the sand from the membranes. Maybe if he was lucky, they would have to be replaced—and the ship might not have a supply on board. That thought gave Joe a tremor of excitement.

In a matter of minutes the first alarm would be sounding, so he turned and squinted at the evaporator sitting just thirty feet away. It was located near the

RO unit because both were fed by the same seawater source pipe. As he pushed himself away from the RO pump, a wave of dizziness caused him to lurch sideways, and he fell heavily against the side of the unit. His head bounced off the pump, and he slid to the concrete.

Momentarily dazed and suddenly realizing that he was quite inebriated, he pulled himself to his knees and shook his pounding head. With almost no remaining peripheral vision, he started crawling along the side of the RO unit toward the evaporator. He knew his plan was screwed—as he would be—if he didn't get back on his feet and leave the area now. He could not let himself be caught this soon before he was able to fully implement his plan.

He shook his head again trying to gain some clarity and reached for the side of the filter box to pull himself to a standing position. On his feet, but nauseous and dizzy, he stood for another minute before deciding that he could stay and complete his mission after all. I need one more little drink to steady me and deaden this damn pain in my head, he reasoned, as he weaved his way to the evaporator equipment. At the end of the boiler, he reached for his flask and found that it was empty. Somehow, he resisted the urge to hurtle it across the massive room and shoved it back in his pocket instead.

Blinking several times to clear the fog that was clouding both his eyes and his brain, he squinted down at the flow control valve on the hydraulic pump. He struggled desperately to bring his vision into focus. The valve should be open just a crack to slow the flow of seawater into the boiler. He turned it to the open position. Now too much salt water would flow into the housing too quickly. This would almost certainly contaminate the fine mesh that normally removes moisture from the steam, and in turn, greatly reduce the efficiency of an already expensive operation.

Under normal conditions, the evaporation process requires twice the energy of RO. With the RO unit shut down for maintenance, the ship would have to rely solely on the more expensive process, which would be even more costly due to Joe's adjustments. Of course, maintenance workers would return the valve to its normal position, but the whole system would have to be shut down completely to clean or replace the mesh. That should buy him a few days of satisfying chaos.

Joe was at a standstill and on the verge of passing out as his mind looped continuously on the question of whether he was finished until the sound of approaching footsteps jolted him out of his stupor. He dove behind the boiler and rolled against the white-tiled wall as the first alarm sounded on the RO unit. The footsteps sped up to a run, and a few seconds later a maintenance worker suddenly appeared from a side corridor only a few feet away from the desalination plant.

From his cover, Joe watched both in fear and elation as the worker stared at the flashing red lights on the temperature and pressure valves in disbelief. He grabbed his phone and spoke in rapid heavily accented English that Joe could not follow. The man listened a moment and replied, "Si, entiendo. I will go now." With that, he turned and ran back down the corridor.

Joe wasted no time following him out of the area. He retraced his steps through the kitchen, forcing himself to slow down his pace and willing himself to maintain a straight line. Despite his blurred vision and the throbbing in his head, he smiled and nodded to the first galley workers arriving for their shift and was relieved to find that they looked away and paid no attention to him.

A cute little female crew member approached from the opposite direction, and Joe felt his elation at a job well done instantly turn to arousal. Thank the lord that still works OK, he assured himself. He nodded and gave her his interested look as she quickly passed by. He knew he was home free, but wasted no time returning to his cabin to nurse his headache, relieve the swelling in his groin, and celebrate his success with another pint of Jim Beam.

27

A whole year had crawled by since Plato's death, but Isabel Trindade was still so angry and sad that thoughts of retribution had nearly taken over her life. Dead tired as she was, her sleep had not been at all satisfying ever since that night so long ago when her world had come unhinged. But it was necessary to go about her business, affecting a friendly happy mood, as if the terrible events had never happened.

So she fluffed and cleaned and turned mattresses every day until her body felt as weighty as one of the enormous water buffalos plodding through her grandfather's spice plantation. She smiled at the thought of their mud-packed skin and sad brown eyes. They were domesticated gentle beasts of burden, and lately, her memory of them had become quite acute.

Lying in the narrow bed across from her roommate Terri in their crew cabin on deck 1, she tried to relax by reaching back in time to conjure the magnificent vanilla scent of her lush tropical childhood home. It had been almost a year since she last visited Panaji, the capital of Goa, located on the southern coast of India. She loved and deeply missed her home, nestled in a deep-set inlet on the beautiful warm Arabian Sea.

At the same time, she was grateful to have this job with the cruise line. It was not surprising that World of Seas had many employees from her part of India. After all, Goa is the smallest and richest of the Indian states with a gross domestic product two and a half times that of India as a whole. Its sophisticated blend of Indian and European cultures and religions, and its white-sand beaches and mild climate, draw tourists from all over the world.

Isabel's life had been shaped by the tragic loss of her parents when she was only seven. She had never fully overcome her grief and insecurity, and a feeling of irony related to their deaths. They were killed in a bus accident south of the city at the crossing of Dr. E. Borges and Taleigao Roads, a place Isabel could never bring herself to visit. Her kind and benevolent mother and father had been on their way to the Headquarters of the Salesians of Don Bosco, a Catholic order dedicated to the care of young and poor children, where they planned to make a generous donation. From that horrible day when they left their own poor child behind, her grandfather provided a stable and comfortable life by Goan standards. Then at the age of twenty-two, her life dramatically changed again when she landed the job with World of Seas.

Last September when Isabel first met her co-worker, Plato Des Rameaux, she was immediately intrigued by his outward toughness, which she immediately recognized as a mask obscuring his great inner gentleness. She did not understand why she seemed to be the only one who saw this attractive attribute in poor Plato, but it didn't matter. She quickly came to love him with all her heart and believed he had similar feelings towards her. He became the only person on the ship with whom she felt truly comfortable and secure.

That is why she knew without a doubt that the cruise line had it wrong when they first insisted that Plato killed the cruise director and then threw himself overboard. It didn't matter to her that they found a supposed suicide note in his cabin. She knew that he was innocent and that someone had murdered him and tried to blame him for the cruise director's death.

She suspected the cruise line might be correct with respect to their current theory that her late boss and hotel manager, Suzanne Moretti, killed the crew members. However, she had never heard a discussion of a satisfactory motive and wondered if she might be the only person on the ship who had an inkling of the real situation.

For some time she had felt convinced that the terrible secret Plato entrusted to her just a week before he died had caused his death. She had planned to keep the secret forever to preserve his memory and reputation, but now she knew she had to rid herself of the burden before it crushed her.

Her lowly stateroom attendant position and lack of concrete evidence regarding Plato's death had prevented her from voicing an opinion about what really happened. She knew that this inaction was the source of her anxiety and restlessness. She was losing weight and had a severe bronchial infection, which was not responding to the antibiotics prescribed by the ship's doctor.

She stared at the white corrugated ceiling of what was essentially a wood and plastic-lined shipping container and thought about the conversation she overheard earlier in the day. On a mid-morning break, as she sipped coffee in the crew mess hall and minded her own business, two members of the purser's staff arrived and sat at a table close to her. Maybe she was invisible to them, being a lowly cabin attendant, or perhaps they didn't care if she heard what they were saying about the passengers who had come on board to investigate the highly publicized deaths.

Even if what she heard was right, it was hard to understand why it had taken a whole year for someone to try to determine what happened. She wondered how she would ever be able to find—and speak with—the passenger whose name they had mentioned. She could not consult with members of the crew if she intended to keep her job. But the weight of the secret she carried was fast becoming intolerable, and she knew she would soon have to share it with someone. She just couldn't figure out how she would even be able to identify the man they had talked about, much less get him to take her seriously.

Should she really expose herself and what she knew? After so many months of agonizing over the situation, Isabel was more afraid now than ever, because she realized that at least one other person certainly knew exactly what happened a year ago and might be responsible for all of it. This horrible man could be back on the ship for all she knew, and she sensed that if he knew about her relationship with Plato, she would also be in great danger.

Finally, Isabel checked the bedside clock. It was already 4:00 a.m. and she knew she would not be able to sleep anymore. Her shift began at 6:00 anyway, and she was hungry. She arose and quietly dressed so as not to disturb Terri, then left the cabin and headed toward the crew mess.

As she walked through the kitchen, a maintenance crew member approached from the opposite direction carrying a small toolbox. After glancing his way she quickly averted her eyes. Something about the man startled her and made her feel afraid. As he passed, she noticed that his face was red and puffy and he swaggered as if he'd been drinking. That was hard to believe given that he was in uniform. Nothing would get a crew member fired quicker than being drunk on duty. Still, something was not right about him.

After he passed by, she thought about his cold staring eyes and smirk . . . as if he knew something hateful about her. She shuddered at the thought of his repulsive leer. He seemed a little old to be a maintenance worker. His yellow hair was obviously not a natural color, and that seemed unusual as well. She quickly looked over her shoulder to be sure he was not following her and hurried toward the cantina. She did not recall seeing the man before and hoped she would never see him again.

28

Day 5 – Puerto Vallarta, Mexico

Captain Bentzer sat at his small conference table at the far end of the ship's bridge, about one hundred-thirty feet from the control consoles located at the other end. With him were his second in command, Staff Captain James Early and Chief of Security Roger Ramirez. The captain had placed two first mates, who were navigators, at the helm—which didn't require much effort, since speed and course were wholly automated through the Voyage Management System, GPS, and several other navigational controls. They were in the process of dropping anchor and preparing to lower the lifeboats that would be used as tenders to take passengers ashore.

Bentzer leaned forward with his long slender arms on the table, then reached for the coffee urn and poured his fourth cup of the morning. Too much caffeine, he knew, would give him the jitters but he had to feed his anxiety somehow.

"Half the ship is in near-panicking about the water, ya?" he said, looking from James to Roger and back. It was not a question. "Do you know what we do to minimize?" This was a question with no answer readily forthcoming.

Earlier, the captain made an announcement to the passengers explaining the mechanical problem with the desalination equipment. He assured them it was nothing to be concerned about, except that there would be a short period—perhaps a day—when water would have to be rationed. He said that the ship's engineers and maintenance staff would have the problem repaired within a couple of days.

About two hours later in a second announcement, he dropped the other shoe, telling everyone on board that no showers would be allowed for at least twenty-four hours so they could conserve water for drinking and cooking. In addition, no sheets or towels would be washed today and possibly tomorrow as well. He had tried his best to play down the situation, even attempting to joke that perhaps people should curtail their visits to the gym under the no shower rule. Unfortunately, he was not a man with a knack for humor.

"This is so a minor inconvenience, but many passengers use problems to make more drama than necessary, ya?"

James and Roger glanced at each other, each clearly wanting the other to respond to the boss. Finally, James squared his shoulders and looked at Bentzer. How he wished his old friend, Captain Espen, still commanded the *Sea Nymph* . . . not to mention how much James wished Espen was still alive. Bentzer was capable enough, but he lacked the rapport with passengers and crew that can be critical when things start going wrong.

"There isn't really anything we can do to control how the passengers respond to this emergency beyond what you have already said and done, Dolf. If we supply any more information, it will only make matters worse, in my opinion. Do you agree, Roger?"

"I do. We have to deal with the reality of the sabotage among ourselves. The engineers working on the fix obviously know about it, but we do not want the passengers or any other crew to get even a hint of that, or there really will be panic."

The knowledge that a saboteur was on board was unprecedented for all three officers. Due to this terrorist attack or something of the sort, they had lost the RO unit, and this reduced their fresh water supply by almost a third. The crew was working non-stop to clean out the sand that someone had clearly dumped into the filter membranes. Fortunately, because the equipment automatically shut down as soon as the computer sensed the stress in the system, the membranes did not break.

However, without this relatively low-energy desalination method, the distillation evaporator had to run continuously and the engineers were worried about the drain of energy on the rest of the ship's functions, particularly the three three-phase synchronous motors that turned the propellers, and the six diesel generators supplying electricity for all the ship's needs, including the evaporator.

So reluctantly, the captain gave the order that upon leaving port in about six hours, they would limit their speed to eight knots. At full speed of twenty-four knots, the ship would use over 2,800 gallons of fuel each hour. Slowing down would cut this consumption by half. As a result, they would be very late arriving at their next port. Of course, this would upset the passengers even more, but it was necessary to conserve fuel. "How upset would passengers be if they sit dead in water with no power?" the captain observed sarcastically.

The three men had discussed the recent well-publicized plight of a cruise ship that had foundered and lost power for several days. The negative publicity about the horrendous conditions on board before the passengers were rescued almost ruined that cruise line. World of Seas, particularly the *Sea Nymph*, had all the negative press it could stand in the past year. So managers at the home office in Davie, Florida were clear in telling the captain he must contain the current situation and immediately find and detain the culprit in the ship's quasi-brig.

"The situation would be a lot worse if the flow control valve on the distillation evaporator's hydraulic pump had been turned all the way to open," Roger offered. "For some reason, possibly a mistake, the saboteur turned the valve in the other direction, closing it completely."

"Ya, this would be disaster for sure. Instead of emergency switch turning off pump and water supply, we would have all desalination shut down for repair." The captain shuddered at his own statement. "At least once pump restarted, evaporation went on as normal."

James nodded in agreement and thought about another sensitive issue he wanted to address. In his clipped British accent, he asked, "I wonder if either of you has thought to inform our GAO guests about the attack on our water systems. The FBI is already involved in their effort, and we must report the sabotage to that agency eventually anyway."

Roger stiffened noticeably, and the captain leaned back in his chair, essentially removing himself from the conversation. After staring at the staff captain for a few seconds while he measured his words, Roger replied, "I don't think they can add anything useful. We are capable of conducting our own investigation to determine who did this."

"Of course you and your staff are capable, Roger." James was trying to reassure the sensitive security chief. "It is only . . . well, you were not here a year ago when we had the horrible deaths on our hands. We did not talk to outside authorities as we should have and we lost control before it was over. I just don't want to repeat past mistakes."

"Nothing is getting out of my control…"

"Wait, Roger, I'm just saying the team is on board to investigate crimes committed on cruise ships, and we obviously have a serious one. Perhaps they could be of some help." James pushed his dark curly bangs back off his forehead and looked at the captain for support.

Roger glared across the table at James, and Captain Bentzer leaned forward again. "I will make decision. I will think on what you say, James, and let you know, ya?"

"Good enough, Dolf,"

"And Roger," the captain continued. "I'm sure you thought this, but all security must be more diligent . . . like extra guards on night shifts, ya?"

Roger nodded his agreement, but James knew the security chief was extremely defensive about his position. He was nothing like Tom Smythe who had been a much more objective head of security, and even Tom had dropped the ball when it came to advising outside authorities about problems on the ship. World of Seas managers always emphasized that the number one priority during a cruise is to minimize adverse publicity and maximize the passengers' enjoyment.

29

Rachael and I prepared to go ashore. Naturally, Mick said he was too busy and too tired to leave the ship. At that point, I wasn't sure how much I really cared. I just didn't believe his behavior had anything to do with his physical injuries. He still would not talk about his behavior in Cabo, and I was getting tired of trying to figure him out. He just didn't have much interest in being intimate with me on any level.

I am somewhat introspective, and no one had to tell me that the stress was getting to me. Probably as a consequence, I had increased my usual number of martinis. Last night, even Manuel commented that he was worried about me. "Darcy, has something bad happened again?" he asked when there were no strangers at the bar. "I don't see Mick very much, and you seem . . . different, not happy like before. This makes me sad to see."

"Oh, Manuel," I answered too frankly, "everything is different this time. Mick seems to have lost interest in our relationship, but he won't talk about it. I'm thinking of moving in with Rachael for the rest of the cruise." Even for me, this was a bit too much information to be sharing. He was probably uncomfortable with a passenger talking about such personal issues, but in typical bartender fashion, he rose to the challenge.

"Darcy, it is none of my business, but I got to know Mick a little bit on the last cruise and have talked with him several times now. I don't believe he has lost interest. I see how he looks at you, and it is obvious he is crazy for you."

Sitting to my right, Rachael sipped on a club soda while listening to our exchange. I felt her shift on her stool and thought I detected a quiet scoffing sound. This was unflattering on her part, but I realized she was becoming increasingly skeptical about Mick. On the other hand, I knew she was also worried about me. I resolved then and there to make the most of the cruise for her, despite the underlying tension and sadness.

We left the ship at around 10:00 a.m. and enjoyed another tender ride to the pier. On the way, I explained to her that Puerto Vallarta lies on Bahia Banderas, the second largest natural bay in North America and boasts a hundred miles of coast and beaches. We had decided to spend the morning at the most popular of these, Playa de los Muertos. Onshore, we took a taxi to Olas Atlas—Old Town. We strolled through the historic neighborhood, enjoying the sunshine and checking out the incredible restaurants and shops, and soon enough we arrived at the colorful beachfront bars and cafes.

Following a lane down to the beach, we found hundreds of locals and tourists forming a rainbow of deck chairs and blankets stretching a mile down the coastline. Back a ways from the ocean and the hectic activity at the water's edge, we found an open spot and laid out the large towels we had brought from the ship. We figured, correctly enough, that there would be safety in numbers on the beach.

After spending a long and scorching two hours in the sun, including three runs up to the nearest restaurant for a beer, I was done and insisted on leaving. Rachael is as fair skinned as I am, but she never seems to tire of sunbathing. I don't get it, but maybe it has to do with youth or something to do with her having grown up in tropical climates while traveling all over the world with her parents.

We put our shifts and sandals back on, and I pushed my wide-brimmed yellow straw hat down low on my forehead. Then we went to explore. The town has an interesting mix of modern infrastructure and Old Mexico charm. We even watched a man in blue jeans and light blue work shirt leading a donkey down the sidewalk with its back comically piled high with packages. We soon realized that the man and his *conveyance* were incongruously delivering packages to the numerous modern glass-fronted jewelry stores.

A few streets in from the beach we stopped at a large plaza filled with adorable little girls. It seemed odd until we realized that there was a school at the back of the square, and they were apparently on a lunch or recess break. Several of them enthusiastically pushed their notebooks towards us and shyly asked in precise English, "What is your name?" and "What is your country?" It quickly became apparent that this was an assignment and a contest to see who could acquire the most names. It made me happy to think of these girls being taught to be assertive and engage foreigners in conversation.

As we walked away from the square, a sudden movement on the left startled me. Rachael was walking on my right side, and I swung around with my back to her to see what had caused my momentary sense of alarm. Two men were standing a few feet away at the curb, but it was apparent they had stopped in their tracks when I turned toward them. In fact, they were turning at the same

108

time I was, and they quickly darted around the corner into an alley. One of those familiar chills started down my spine as I watched their backs retreating. I didn't get too good a look at them, except to note that one was fair and tall and the other was shorter and darker.

What was that about? I honestly believed they intended to confront us in some manner, but changed their minds at the last moment. I didn't say anything to Rachael because maybe I had just imagined a threat, and there was no reason to worry her.

I didn't see the two men again, and we thoroughly enjoyed ourselves just wandering around, occasionally stepping into a shop and listening to Mexican rhythms that seemed to come from everywhere at once. Before long we ducked inside a small cheery café to get out of the sun. The walls were painted in red, yellow, and blue with matching checkered and striped table cloths. The air was redolent with baked goods and coffee, so instead of ordering lunch, we opted for espresso and an assortment of appealing and delicious pastries. Rachael was particularly taken by this interlude and wore a wide grin for most of the half hour we spent in that pleasant environment.

To this day, despite how things subsequently turned out, I have a warm memory of that moment in time. Sitting in the quaint Mexican bakery with my daughter, I was able to relax and enjoy watching local residents and tourists going about their business while we sipped extraordinary rich coffee and munched on mouthwatering croissants coated with honey. I thought that I so wanted to come back to this spot with Mick someday.

30

Day 6 – at sea

We were barely moving down the coast of Mexico, and everyone's nerves were on edge about the problem with the ship's desalination system. We didn't really understand any of it and could only trust Captain Dolf when he told us there was no reason for concern.

Rachael and I had skipped our morning workouts since we were not supposed to shower and the thought of trying to take a sponge bath in the cabin's tiny bathroom was unappealing. It was not that big a deal to skip a couple of showers, and the captain said we should be back to normal by tomorrow evening.

This did not stop some of the passengers from being angry and critical of the cruise line. They were especially infuriated about the shortened shore time in Acapulco due to our late arrival. They had expected a particular itinerary and planned—and paid—accordingly, but some early morning shore excursions had already been canceled. All over the ship, we encountered small groups of people bitching about the delay and blaming World of Seas. We were amazed at this rigidity and apparent inability to accept that a mechanical problem could occur on this $550 million highly complex and comfortable state-of-the-art ship.

Mick and I had retired early, and as we lay in bed facing with our arms around each other, I found myself daydreaming about how romantic and erotic our love life used to be. At this point, Mick would be so excited and anxious that he would naturally slip between my thighs and I would blissfully accept his firmness and heat. But that was not what was happening now.

He kissed my forehead and nose, and then my shoulder. "I love you so much, Darcy. You know that, right?"

What could I say? "Yes, I know . . . but it's just so different now. Why don't you want to have sex with me?"

He rolled onto his back and stared at the ceiling. Then he put one arm under his head and sighed. This scene had repeated so many times in the past year I had lost count. He simply could not talk about his feelings, and this was not just a guy thing. One of the characteristics I had most cherished in him was his sensitivity and ability to talk about how he felt.

I tried to change the subject, but couldn't come up with a happy one. "You know, Mick, Rachael's feelings were really hurt the other day in Cabo. Couldn't you talk to her and maybe apologize? She doesn't understand your behavior."

"I know I was out of line, but I was so worried about her and you too. There are so many things that can happen to women in these places. You can't just walk around as if you are back home."

That was bad enough, but then he really astonished me. "I do want to have sex with you," he said softly. "I always do and always will. I don't know what is wrong, but your pressuring me does not help." He didn't even look at me when he said it.

"So asking why you don't want to have sex is putting pressure on you? OK, Mick, I get it. Let me know when you are ready to talk about our relationship. Meanwhile, I'm going to try to sleep." About three hours later I finally succeeded.

31

Day 7 – Acapulco, Mexico

We finally reached Acapulco about midday, five hours later than scheduled. Mick did seem to be trying harder and had been sweet to Rachael and me at breakfast. He still did not say anything about what had happened in Cabo, and again insisted he and Tom were too busy to leave the ship even for a couple of hours. This seemed ridiculous to me, and I'm sure Tom would have liked a break, but Mick would not be swayed, and he and Tom planned to get back to work.

Mick and I had managed to have a cogent conversation about Tom's new friend, Wendy. That brought back wonderful memories of how we used to talk about things back when he was the Mick I met on the first cruise. Anyway, he told me he was really happy for Tom and gleaned there hadn't been anyone special in his life for at least ten years. Apparently, Tom had never been married, and of course, now we knew he had no family either.

I knew Mick was right, and it was ridiculous for me to have any feelings about Tom's love life one way or the other. But I know from years of experience that my intuition is rarely wrong. I just could not shake the uneasy feeling about the relationship. I tried very hard to bury it and go about my business.

"I'm going to meet Tom now," Mick said, as he moved toward the door. "What are you and Rachael going to do today?"

Oh, Oh, is this a loaded question? Please don't start an argument about our plans, I thought. "We will probably check out Acapulco and don't worry, Mick." I reached out to him, and he allowed me to touch his face without flinching. "We'll be very careful. You don't have to worry. Just concentrate on your interviews, OK? Maybe you'll find out something today." I moved in close and kissed his cheek. I didn't think he recoiled, but I couldn't be certain.

I knew that so far none of the crew members they had interviewed knew anything about what went on a year ago. As Tom had suggested, Mick seemed impatient with their process. He just wanted to get the whole thing over with and get off the ship. I was beginning to appreciate how he felt.

Rachael and I now believed that coming along on the cruise was a colossal mistake. She didn't seem to want to cut Mick much slack and told me more than once that I didn't deserve to be mistreated by him. She even made the comment that she could never imagine Brooks behaving the way Mick was.

Talk about a completely upside down situation. Brooks was a terrible husband and had virtually abandoned Rachael and me. No matter how recovered he might be from his alcoholism, he can't erase the past. Ironically, Mick was a wonderful, kind and loving man when we met who appears to be turning into a jerk. I let her comment pass without contradiction because I was very aware of how enamored she was becoming with her biological father. But the fact that she was now trying to compare the two of them, even hinting that I would be better off with Brooks was disconcerting.

Despite all this tension, I was still determined to enjoy the new places we were visiting for the first—and possibly the only—time. So Rachael and I sat together over coffee and talked about what we'd learned about the port from literature the cruise line left in our staterooms.

Acapulco is located on a deep beautiful semi-circular bay about 190 miles from Mexico City. The name means "at the broken reeds" in the native Nahuatl language. It is the largest city in the state of Guerrero and has always been an important port. As early as the eighth century, small dispersed villages had coalesced into larger towns and ceremonial gatherings. The Olmecs were the first to dominate these sites, but a series of other cultures subsequently replaced them, including the Mayans. In the 11th century, precursors of the Aztecs migrated to the area, and by 1486 Acapulco had become part of that empire.

Subsequently, Spanish trade in the Far East gave relatively peaceful Acapulco a prominent position in the economy of Spain and by 1550 galleons were routinely arriving from Asia. Thirty Spanish families moved from Mexico City to establish a permanent base of European residents, and the port soon became extremely important due to its direct trade with the Philippines and its link to Spain, Europe, and Asia.

This lucrative trade route and the luxury items transported also attracted the attention of Dutch and English pirates. In 1615, a Dutch fleet invaded Acapulco and destroyed much of the town before being defeated. The city remained in Spanish hands until the Mexican War of Independence, when José

Maria Morelos y Pavón defeated the Spanish commander, Francisco Parés, and attacked and burned the city.

Like a Phoenix, Acapulco revived itself and became an important port again during the California gold rush with ships stopping on routes to and from Panama. Then in 1920, the Prince of Wales and the future King Edward VIII visited the area and were so impressed they recommended Acapulco as a vacation spot for Europeans, thus beginning its popularity with the elite.

The economy grew with tourism and foreign investments, and in the 1950s it became known as one of Mexico's oldest and most fashionable beach resorts. Millionaires and Hollywood stars like Elizabeth Taylor, John Wayne, Frank Sinatra, and Brigitte Bardot made Acapulco and its nightlife legendary.

Today, Acapulco is home to over 700,000 people, and many of the original expensive hotels have been replaced with new more affordable resorts. Sadly there is also much poverty, and many shantytowns cling precariously to the mountainsides around the city, just tempting a natural disaster to eradicate them, as happened when Hurricane Pauline came ashore in 1997 killing more than 100 residents. Construction of the Ruta del Sol, a road crossing the mountains from Mexico City, has made Acapulco a favorite weekend destination for wealthy Mexicans who now account for most of the city's tourists.

In recent years the Mexican drug war has taken its toll on foreign tourism—people are afraid to travel there with good reason. Rival traffickers fight each other for control of the Guerrero coastal route, which shuttles drugs from South America, and they battle Mexican soldiers who are fighting the cartels.

After realizing the potential for danger in the city, Mick had tried to convince me to stay on the ship with Rachael. He said it was not safe for us to go ashore alone. We definitely took note of the facts, but we were not about to miss out on seeing it. Despite the problems, Acapulco's nightlife is still a main attraction, as is La Quebrada Cliff Divers. The nightlife was not in our cards, so we debated how to spend our one day in the city. We considered sunbathing at one of the many famous beaches, touring mangroves and turtle nesting sites, and visiting San Diego Fort, originally built to protect the town from pirates.

We finally settled on a trip to see the cliff divers, a late lunch on shore, and a tour of the fort on the way back to the ship. We had even decided on a restaurant called Las Brisas, recommended by the ship's guest relations staff. When we were ready to walk off the ship, Mick took a break from the interviews to stand on the deck above us, frowning down with his hands on his hips. What a pain in the ass this was getting to be.

Out on the dock, we quickly arranged reasonable transportation for the day with only minimal haggling over price. During the negotiation, the taxi driver's eyes never left Rachael's face. I thought that was understandable and anyway, his English was passable, and his car was air-conditioned. What more could we ask? Jorge seemed like a good enough guy, but of course, that conclusion was based on nothing more than my gut feeling.

On the way to the cliff, Jorge took us on a scenic route so we could experience the breathtaking views of the harbor and beaches from the top of the bluff. He pointed out several of the glamorous hotels of the 1950s, now just abandoned white stucco buildings with spectacular views. We took numerous pictures and marveled at the lovely postcard-like vistas.

When we arrived at the cliff, the divers were on a break, so we decided to hang around and check out the surrounding area. Jorge promised to wait for us for forty-five minutes and then take us to the restaurant. From the parking lot, we headed down a path to the tourist viewing area. The diving tradition began in the 1930s when young men casually competed against each other to see who could dive from the highest point. Eventually, locals started asking for tips from those coming to see the men, and a formal tourist attraction developed on the site.

We passed the Hotel Plaza Las Glorias/El Mirador, where diners can view the divers from the terrace, and descended a long series of concrete and stone stairs that ran alongside the cliff. People were standing on several landings on the way down—probably because they did not want to have to climb all the way back up. It was difficult to tell where the best place would be for us to view the divers, so we kept going and finally made it all the way to the bottom. We stepped to a railing that appeared to be directly below the dive spot.

I tried to relax and enjoy this once in a lifetime moment with my daughter at my side. Rachael was looking around and chatting about the depth of the water and the height of the cliffs. She shaded her eyes and pointed to a small statue at the top. "There is the shrine to the Virgin of Guadalupe. The divers pray there before they go off the cliff. I wonder if those guys are really that religious or it's just a show for the tourists." She lowered her arm and turned to me. "I read that the divers are professionals and they perform numerous times almost every day. They're sort of considered national heroes."

I couldn't help myself. I laughed out loud and put my arm around her shoulder. "You obviously are my daughter with a skeptical comment like that one."

We had never discussed our life philosophies in depth, and now she looked at me speculatively. "Do you think such things can be genetic . . . your outlook on the world I mean?"

"Who knows, but I do believe some people have inherited some sort of innate desire or need to believe in things based on faith alone . . . and I know I'm not one of them."

"I really know what you mean, Darcy. I could never get into the depth of religion and supernatural beliefs my catholic parents hold so strongly, and I never understood why I saw things so differently."

At that point, the show started, and we watched in awe along with at least a hundred other spectators as the gorgeously fit and tanned divers plunged 120 feet and seemed to barely miss the rocks in the twenty-one-foot wide inlet below. Sure enough, each one knelt to pray and made the sign of the cross before approaching the edge of the cliff. A placard attached to the rail informed us that the inlet is only twelve feet deep so that each dive must be perfectly timed with the ebb and flow of the waves to avoid catastrophe.

When the show was over, we began the long ascent up the stairway surrounded by other tourists. Just as we reached the top, I glanced toward some decorative shrubbery and trees at the edge of the path. Two men were standing partially hidden by the bushes and looking directly at us. They seemed to avert their gaze when I looked at them, and it seemed a little odd since there was no plausible reason for them to be lurking where they were . . . unless maybe they were taking a leak in the bushes . . . *holy shit!* I realized these were the same guys I saw in Puerto Vallarta.

The odds of seeing the same men and having a feeling of being watched in two different cities was highly unlikely. I now knew they had to be among the two thousand passengers on our ship, and I knew I would be looking for them there. From our two encounters, there was no doubt that something wasn't quite right about them. They just didn't look as if they were enjoying a vacation. They were too occupied with doing nothing but hanging about . . . and watching us.

I turned my attention to Rachael as we continued along the path back to the parking lot. As soon as we were in the taxi, I planned to tell her what I'd seen. I glanced back over my shoulder as we chatted about the diving show, but I didn't see the men. As we started looking for our taxi, Rachael turned around, and after a few moments, I felt her stiffen as she grabbed for my hand.

"Darcy, two weird men, are following behind us, and I swear they gave me mean looks when I glanced back at them just now. I think they were sneering and laughing at me. Let's hurry and find Jorge."

I was getting a clear message from the prickling at the base of my spine, which I had already felt too often on this cruise. As we picked up our pace I glanced behind us, and sure enough, there they were, hanging back obviously aware that we had noticed them. One was tall and very blond and the other dark with sort of a Mediterranean look. Yep, the same guys!

For a reason I did not understand, the good-looking blond one gave me a very creepy feeling, even though his companion had a classically more threatening appearance. *What an odd couple.* But they didn't look at all like a couple, and they appeared entirely uneasy and out of place. Their clothing— dress slacks and sport coats—were definitely not typical tourist attire. Something told me they had not come to the cliffs to see the divers.

"Rachael, do you see the taxi anywhere near where Jorge said he would be waiting for us?"

"No, no I don't. Oh, what if he blew us off? We'll have to figure out how to get another ride."

Just as I was about to answer something very strange happened. From behind us came a repetitive plopping sound, and it took a few moments for both of us to realize that someone was throwing rocks from the gravel path onto the ground just in back of us.

"What the hell is going on here?" I grabbed Rachael's arm jogged toward a small group of people standing in the center of the lot about a hundred feet away. Whack! A rock about two inches in diameter bounced off the back of Rachael's thigh.

"Ouch! They hit me," she cried incredulously, rubbing her leg.

I stopped in my tracks and whirled around to face the two men who had been behind us but saw only a family with three teenage children walking about fifty feet back. "What the Hell?" I said again. "Hey," I yelled at the folks, "did you see anyone throwing rocks?"

The husband and wife looked at each other and shrugged. "No entiendo Inglés," he offered as he spread his hands in front of him.

"Shit," I offered back and turned around to check on Rachael. She wasn't there. "Rachael," I screamed, looking around frantically. It seemed like minutes, but I'm sure it was only a few seconds before she responded.

"Darcy, I'm over here." She was standing next to Jorge still massaging the back of her leg. He had a worried expression as he looked around and peered behind his vehicle.

I ran up beside them and screamed. "Get in the car. Get in the car, Rachael." She stepped in and slid across the seat. Jorge jumped in the driver's seat and started to pull forward as I jumped in beside her and slammed the door shut.

Being hit by a rock was not that big a deal in itself I told myself, but the whole weird encounter with the two men had completely frayed my nerves. We were only a week into this trip, and odd things were already happening.

What is it with me and cruises? I reached for Rachael's hand and realized she was trembling.

"Rachael, we're safe now." I eyed the back of Jorge's head and hoped it was true. "How is your leg? Do you think it's serious . . . is the skin broken?"

"It stings, and I know it must be at least bruised, but I don't think there is any blood. What happened, Darcy? Do you think those guys threw rocks at us deliberately?"

"I don't know, but it seemed that way to me. It is such a juvenile thing to do. What could possibly have possessed them to behave that way?" I leaned forward and spoke to Jorge. "Please take us back to the ship now."

32

Back on board, Rachael and I went to eat lunch at the Whale's Tail while we waited to hear from Mick and Tom. We did not want to interrupt them during their interviews but had left a message through the guest relations staff for them to contact us or to come to the buffet.

We found a table for four at the window overlooking the dock. The restaurant's lofty position on deck 10 afforded a pretty good view of the city, although we weren't particularly interested in seeing any more of Acapulco at that point. Rachael sat down gingerly. She had an enormous bruise on the back of her thigh that was already turning black. "I'm so mad at whoever did this to me," she said, wincing in pain. "This will look horrible for the rest of the cruise. I just can't believe we were being targeted. It had to be some crazy person just messing around, right?"

"I just don't know . . ."

"There's no reason for someone to want to hurt us, right Darcy?" Her tone was turning a little frantic.

"Well, no . . . but Rachael, sometimes a stranger—someone who is disturbed—might lash out because of insecurity, envy, resentment, or whatever you want to call it." She played with her napkin and stared at the table. "I can see where you and I might appear to be privileged in many ways. Maybe it was something like that." Even as I suggested this spur of the moment explanation, it wasn't ringing true for me. Having seen the two men watching us from the bushes minutes before the attack—and in Puerto Vallarta—I was convinced the rock throwing was no coincidence. There was nothing about them that suggested they would fit my impromptu rationale.

After a few minutes, Rachael's hunger overcame her discomfort, so she got up and walked over to the closest array of food items. I watched her selecting healthy choices of fruit, vegetables, and cheeses, and thought again about how amazing it was to be here with her—and how totally amazing she was. Just then, I saw Mick and Tom coming through the entrance, and I stood up to wave them over.

"We got your message," Tom said as they sat down at the table. "What happened to your shore excursion? We didn't expect to see you until this evening."

Mick looked at me sheepishly. "Darcy, I'm sorry I was so negative about you leaving the ship. I know it was unreasonable. I'm not sure why I am so worried."

I laughed out loud. "Holy cow, Mick, as it turned out you could not have been more correct. We had a bit of a disconcerting experience at the cliff-diving place." I was not about to let Mick know that I had seen the same men in Puerto Vallarta, and had chosen to leave the ship today anyway. It turned out to be the right decision.

Mick's demeanor immediately changed and I saw the blood drain from his face. "What do you mean? What happened and where is Rachael?" he asked, looking around.

"Look you two," I said, looking directly at Mick, "I'm trying to minimize my concern about this with Rachael. I don't want to upset her any more than she already is. She's getting her food, and she'll be back any minute." I quickly explained what had happened to us. Then I waited a few moments before adding, "She does have quite a large bruise on her leg, but thankfully it is only that."

Tom asked, "what about these two men? Can you describe them and do you think they were Americans?"

I realized I hadn't really thought about their nationality until now. "My sense is, they were Americans, but I can't really say why. Maybe it was their clothes, which didn't seem quite right for the environment, by the way. They were so different from one another that I will have no problem recognizing them if I see them together again. I wonder if they might be passengers."

Mick had been staring at me wide-eyed, and now he leaned over the table, narrowed them, and took my hand. "I knew you should not have gone ashore. I hope you will listen to me next time and do what I say."

Tom's eyes widened as he looked at Mick and then me clearly surprised by Mick's statement. I withdrew my hand and sat back. "You know," I said softly, "that is not really helpful. A moment ago you were apologizing for your behavior. Surely you don't think you had some sort of premonition and knew we would have a problem. I can't believe you really think you should be able to tell me what to do as if I'm a child. I'm sorry, but that's offensive."

120

Tom was plainly uncomfortable and stood up to leave. "I'm going to find Rachael and get something to eat."

Mick continued to glare at me until I got up to follow Tom. *What on earth am I going to do about this situation? Tonight I have to get Mick to talk to me, and one of us has to move out of the cabin.* An eerily familiar feeling settled itself in my gut. Circumstances were getting strangely similar to the events on the first cruise.

33

Las Vegas – that night

The dinner crowd at Ferraro's was lighter than usual. Sidney looked around at the clean white tablecloths and sparkling crystal, newly laid out at the empty tables. She really loved this restaurant. It was conveniently located on Paradise Road just south of the convention center and not far from her condo.

On evenings when she had nothing to do—and there were many—she found herself walking the few blocks to the restaurant and sitting at the bar chatting with other patrons. The place had the warm ambiance that so pleased her when she first moved to Las Vegas before the nightmare began with Paul. It was the undeniably unique family feel in Italian eateries that catered to Vegas locals.

She looked across the table at Brooks and immediately had another undeniable feeling. *I'm really falling in love with him. Lord this is crazy.* Twenty years ago when he was just an asshole tormenting her best friend she had truly hated the guy. Not in a million years would she have believed she could ever be in a relationship with Darcy's ex.

She tried to catch herself before she got too carried away. After all, this wasn't really a relationship . . . yet. For several months Brooks had been inviting her to accompany him for meals and friendly conversation, but he seemed slow to take the next step that seemed so inevitable to her. Meanwhile, she had started picturing a life with him. In fact, other than Brooks she had no social life or romantic outlet.

Divorcing Paul after the years of abuse and emotional withdrawal had obviously been the right move. But now that she was living on her own with money from the settlement, and time to think about her options, her emotions—and her needs—were beginning to reawaken. She had tried to convince herself that Brooks just happened to be there at the time she was most vulnerable and that she needed to move on, but it had not worked. She loved him, and that was all there was to it.

How bizarre this situation was with Darcy still being her best friend and Rachael gaining more of a foothold in Brook's life. *How would I fit into the picture?* Although she had not told Darcy about her friendship with Brooks, she planned to explain it when they returned from the cruise. Why should there be a problem? Darcy moved on long ago, and now she has Mick.

"You certainly seem lost in deep thoughts tonight. Is everything all right?"

"Oh sure, Brooks, I was just thinking about how much I still like this restaurant even though a lot of the Vegas scene has lost its attraction for me. You know what I mean?"

Brooks laughed softly. "Do I ever! The city has really changed, especially in the last ten years, but I think I'm just outgrowing it anyway. I've been considering moving my office and home to another one of my company's cities. I think Denver would be a nice change."

An odd foreboding enveloped Sidney even as she smiled and nodded positively. "Denver would be nice . . . I guess. A lot different from here . . . close to Darcy, um . . . so I guess it would be easier for you to see Rachael when she is visiting there." Sidney clearly saw the odd expression that quickly came and went as Brooks thought about what she was saying.

He paused, obviously weighing his words. "Yeah," he began tentatively. "You know, I haven't shared my feelings about Darcy and Rachael with anyone since we got reunited. Sidney, you know I really appreciate your friendship and companionship, and I feel OK about telling you what is going on. That is to say, Darcy and I will be getting back together before long."

Sidney had grown accustomed to shocking revelations during the years she lived with Paul in constant dread and depression, but nothing had prepared her for this stunning development. Even as she suppressed a wave of nausea and tears that were already beginning to well, she struggled to affect an attitude of detached interest. *How could I have misread what was going on between Darcy and Brooks, and what about Mick?* "Really Brooks? That is very surprising news. I had no inkling."

"Well, it has progressed slowly over the past year since you all came back from the cruise. I have to admit this is something I have wanted for years but didn't know how it could ever happen. Even though I orchestrated you meeting Darcy on the ship, in the end, I really didn't have anything to do with Darcy meeting Rachael."

"I know, Brooks, I was there."

"But Rachael has played a big part in bringing Darcy and me closer because she wants us to be a family . . . and now I think it was meant to be. God really does work in strange ways."

Sidney was dangerously close to either fainting or screaming, and wasn't sure which would be worse. Just when she finally extricated herself from the terrible life she had thought she was stuck with and had found a man she could love, this was happening? The emotions of sadness and disappointment were quickly resolving into cold white anger. How could Darcy lead Mick on the way she was if she planned to get back together with Brooks, and how could she not have said anything about her feelings for him? None of this was making sense, but if Brooks was saying it, it must be so.

Brooks stopped talking and began to worry that he had said too much about his plan. There was really only one obstacle in his way now, and he was sure he would overcome that given just a little more time. Sidney and Darcy are tight though, he thought. Revealing his plans to Sidney might have been a mistake.

He looked at her a little more closely then and realized she was upset. Her pixie-like freckled face had clouded over, and her stunning green eyes shimmered beneath the shiny auburn bangs. He smiled at her and thought about how lovely and desirable she was. If things were different, maybe we could. . . . "What's wrong, Sidney? Are you upset that Darcy and I kept our plans to ourselves for so long?"

"I'm just surprised, Brooks." She pushed her chair back and placed her hand on her stomach. The waves of nausea had not subsided, and she quickly excused herself to visit the restroom. On the way, the tears and mascara finally began to run. She hurried into a stall, grabbed a handful of toilet paper to stifle her sobs, and fought to regain her composure. Five minutes later when she returned to the table, Brooks was in the process of asking a waitress to check on her.

"I was really getting worried. Are you sick?"

"Yes, I guess I am. I don't know what is wrong, but I'd like to go home now."

"Sure, I'll take you home. Will you be all right by yourself?"

"Don't you know I'm used to that now, Brooks?"

As they rode in silence, Sidney's anxiety increased due to the thought that was looping through her brain, which she could not seem to stop. She pictured herself telling Mick about Darcy's deception. Darcy was the best friend she ever had, but she couldn't let herself think about that now that Darcy was suddenly standing in the way of her happiness. She felt confident that Brooks's interest in her had been increasing and that they would already be together if

Darcy had just stuck with Mick. Sidney recalled that on more than one occasion Darcy called Mick the love of her life. *How could she be this selfish? Does she have to take everything for herself?*

34

Day 8 – at sea

Mick was quite sure he heard himself scream. The sound, as well as a sharp spike of anxiety, jolted him awake. *Oh God, not again.* Since Darcy was still sleeping soundly beside him, he knew it must have been a dream. Almost every night now he was awakened by nightmares that he could not quite grasp upon waking.

Earlier in the evening, Darcy confronted him about his behavior, and he apologized again. He was candid in telling her that he did not know what was wrong with him, but without a doubt, he loved her as much as ever. In the end, she agreed to give him a little more time to sort out his feelings. He thought she seemed unwilling to abandon the promise their love held for both of them, and he felt a profound sadness.

At the same time, ever since Sidney's shocking phone call earlier in the day he'd been sliding into an even worse depression, if that was possible. He couldn't really blame Darcy for thinking about going back to her ex-husband. He had to admit that Brooks seemed like an all right guy, especially after the way he helped Tom during his recovery from the scorpion stings, and he and Darcy did have a daughter together. Besides, Brooks was far wealthier than Mick could ever hope to be.

He wanted to confront Darcy about her plans, but that would make it all-the-more real, so he was putting off that confrontation along with a lot more. Anyway, he had repeatedly analyzed Sidney's words and finally concluded that she might just be insecure and jealous or had misunderstood something Brooks said. Mick knew he wasn't the most sensitive guy in the world, but his years of conducting interviews and analyzing the results had given him some insight into the emotions underlying people's verbal communication. It was evident during her call that she wasn't only concerned about Darcy having deceived him. There also seemed to be a personal component to her anxiety over Darcy and Brooks getting back together.

This new development was keeping him awake all right, but ever since boarding the ship his sleep had been intermittent at best. Consequently, he was exhausted during the day and found it increasingly difficult to concentrate on his interviews. Without comment, Tom had started picking up Mick's slack, and although he did not complain, Mick knew it was only a matter of time before they would have to talk about his lack of energy.

He also knew full well that he had lost most of his patience and tolerance with small annoyances. Although he understood this intellectually, he had not been able to control his negative behavior. Even though Rachael was keeping her distance from him, he could not make himself apologize or try to explain his actions. In fact, the damage to his relationship with Rachael was almost as appalling to him as the situation with Darcy. *I only wish I could explain this to myself.*

From experience, he knew he would not be able to go back to sleep for a while. In the windowless pitch-dark cabin, he stumbled out of bed and blindly negotiated around the furniture and across the eight-foot span to the bathroom door. The process was familiar, having now become an almost nightly occurrence. Nonetheless, the experience of seeing exactly the same thing—absolutely nothing—whether his eyes were open or closed was still disconcerting. In the light of the bathroom, he put on his shorts and T-shirt making as little sound as possible, then slipped into his flip-flops and quietly left the cabin. This too had become a routine that he could not explain and could not seem to stop. He made his way up the stairs and contemplated his next sleeping arrangement.

35

I couldn't hold back the tears. Mick leaving our bed in the middle of the night was becoming a habit. He apparently thought I was so fast asleep that I wouldn't realize he was gone. I doubted that even a narcotic could make me sleep that soundly—the martinis certainly had not done the trick.

Clearly, something was wrong with him, and frankly, I thought that maybe something was also wrong with me. It was absolutely counter to my personality and philosophy to be in a situation like this with any man, as Rachael had reminded me more than once. Apparently, he just wasn't the guy I thought he was when we were falling in love on this ship a year ago. And many years ago, I promised myself I would not let any relationship rob me of either my independence or my day-to-day happiness.

The pillow was wet and uncomfortable under my face. I swung my legs over the edge of the bed and felt around until I found the switch for the overhead light. For several nights the same thought had nagged at me. I had been thinking of doing something, but until now had been reluctant to invade Mick's privacy. I pulled on a pair of khaki shorts and a long-sleeved shirt I'd thrown on the sofa before going to bed.

My mind swirled with questions, and my sad mood seemed to worsen as I made my way from our cabin on deck 8 up the stairs to the top of the ship. Since boarding, Mick had grown increasingly distant. He seemed to be slipping back into that mood he was in for months during his recuperation. I was thinking about asking Tom if he was noticing even more of a change in Mick's behavior, but even if that were true, it wouldn't change anything.

I just kept relenting and giving him more time, but now I knew that if he had changed his mind about us and the confinement of the cabin was too much for him, he simply had to face up to it, and we had to make another arrangement. This couldn't go on. I had something to compare it with—the previous cruise with *my Mick*—and this wasn't even close. I knew that tomorrow I would have to take some action even though I had told him we could wait awhile. I guess I'd come to the end of my ability to keep up the pretense.

Emerging from the stairwell, I stepped through the automatic doors into the balmy night. I hated the thought of tracking Mick, but I had to know where he was going on these nocturnal trips. Nothing was going on inside the ship, so this seemed like a logical place to look. Maybe he was just walking around the deck to clear his head. But I knew he typically did not return to the cabin until around five in the morning. I glanced up at the clock over the swimming pool and saw that it was 2:00 a.m. He couldn't be walking for three hours.

In the center of the deserted deck, the pool sparkled in the moonlight. I instinctively looked up and reeled at the rare experience of seeing the cloudless night sky as our ancestors did—without ambient light. I gaped at the thick blanket of stars spreading out to the un-obscured horizon.

It is little wonder that early humans were compelled to invent all manner of supernatural explanations for what I was seeing—and understanding—but they were unable to fathom. *Up there is the origin of and reason for religious belief, and I don't mean "heaven."* I consciously pulled myself back before I really got lost in my philosophical thoughts.

In this peaceful atmosphere, my mood seemed to alter. Maybe I was exaggerating the problem with Mick. It would probably be better if I left him alone and went back to bed. He had told me he loved me every day since we boarded and suddenly that seemed like the most important thing. This flipping back and forth from one mindset to an opposite one was not a good sign. I knew I was beginning to lose perspective. This is what happens to women who stay way too long with an abusive partner.

As I turned to go inside something at the far side of the deck caught my eye, and I stopped to peer through the darkness. Goosebumps rose on my arms when I realized someone was lying on a chaise in the shadows of the overhang. Slowly, I crept in that direction until I saw that it really was Mick, just lying there on his back apparently sleeping. My throat clogged and tears rolled down my face at the incredibly painful realization that Mick preferred a plastic lounge chair to a cozy bed with me in it. My mind did another flip, and I was overwhelmed with bewilderment and anger as I made my way back to the dark, lonely cabin.

36

Day 9 – at sea

The next morning I woke up alone. Mick apparently had not returned in the early morning hours as he usually did. My sadness was overwhelming, and I thought about the words I would use to confront him when I found him. As I was dressing to meet Rachael for breakfast, the phone rang . . . again.

This was just too much. I knew it had to be Brooks despite the three-hour time difference. Apparently, he was an early riser. He had called almost every day about this time with questions about the cruise, and to ask how Rachael and I were doing. Of course, he had called her every day as well. She seemed elated by his attention and gushed with enthusiasm when she described their conversations. I wondered what she might be telling him about my problems with Mick. She was not an indiscrete girl, but she was young and caught up in the relationship with her handsome, wealthy new father whom she had come to adore.

I didn't know what to make of his calls to me. I was uncomfortable talking to him on the general principle that I had come on the cruise with Mick and it seemed somehow disloyal. There didn't seem to be a valid excuse for him to keep calling and although he had not said anything inappropriate, I dreaded the sound of the ringing phone in the morning.

In the last couple of days, however, a new feeling had begun to assert itself. It was the odd curiosity about Brooks that I had experienced when Rachael and I first visited him in Las Vegas . . . and disjointed memories of the few good times we had when we first met. The phone kept on ringing. Maybe it's just Rachael calling to check on me, or it might be Mick, I thought. I lunged across the bed and grabbed the receiver, putting a stop to the annoying sound. "Hello?" I asked tentatively.

"Hello Darcy, how are you this morning?"

I sighed audibly and answered flatly. "Hi Brooks, I'm fine, how are you doing?"

Brooks chuckled and softened his voice. "I have to say I love hearing your voice in the morning. It brings back some pleasant memories."

What? I almost choked and honestly did not know how to respond. "Oh .. . ur . . . OK. Rachael is not here. You can probably catch her in her cabin."

"Come on Darcy, I want to talk with you. I was wondering about something. Do you think when you get home you could come to Vegas to visit for a few days? I would like to spend a little time with you. You know, we could sort of get to know each other again."

This was crazy. I didn't want to be rude, but Brooks was having an effect on me that I didn't even want to think about. I was actually tempted for a moment to say yes. Then I came to my senses, sort of. "Brooks, that wouldn't really be appropriate, would it? Mick and I are moving in together on a more permanent basis after the cruise. We're going down to Marco Island to spend some time at the house he owns there too. Everything is really going well for us, so no, I won't be coming to see you." This sounded lame and insincere, and I was telling a whopper, or maybe what I had said was wishful thinking because right now nothing was going well with Mick.

The line was silent, and I wondered if he had hung up on me. Then it was his turn to sigh into the phone. "Look, Darcy, I get all that, and I'm glad you're resolving your differences, but there are still things I want to say to you. I have to make sure you understand that I am not the person you knew twenty years ago. The drinking and my selfishness ruined the life I had then."

"Stop it, Brooks. It doesn't matter now . . ."

"But it does. I had to start all over, but I never stopped thinking about you and Rachael. I haven't said it before, but I am so sorry. I want to apologize for everything that happened back then."

I had sucked in a huge breath but forgot to exhale. I could not believe what I was hearing. Brooks knew that Mick and I were having problems, and that could only have come from our daughter. I realized just in time that I might actually blackout and sat down heavily on the bed, forcing the air out of my lungs. I was so confused, but I knew I had to end this conversation before I got myself into a kind of trouble I really didn't need on top of everything else.

"Of course I accept your apology. That is ancient history." I tried to sound nonchalant and unconcerned. I doubt it worked. "Oh Brooks, someone is at the door." I lied again. "I'll have to talk to you later. Goodbye." I hung up feeling like a coward on the one hand, but with a deep sense of relief—or something like it—on the other. *Have I been waiting for Brooks to tell me he was sorry all these years?*

131

37

Las Vegas - the same day

Athens Olympia hasn't changed in 15 years, Brooks thought, as he wound his way through the massive casino. Just outside the entrance to Paul's Place, an upscale deli named for the narcissistic owner, he stopped for a moment to collect his thoughts. Then he stepped inside and engaged the cute hostess in some flirtatious small talk. He tried to avoid staring at her artificially pushed-up cleavage and skimpy dress. Instead, he checked out the other patrons as he talked and laughed with her and finally said, "I have a meeting here with Paul right about now. I guess he isn't here yet."

The gal's demeanor instantly changed as she tried to appear a lot more businesslike. "Oh, I'm so sorry, sir. Let me call to see if he's on his way. He gets tied up sometimes." Her look said she might have personal knowledge of this fact.

Brooks was still wondering about that when Paul strode up and enthusiastically shook his hand. "Hi Amy," Paul said lightly patting her forearm. "Can you put Mr. Larkin and me at nine? We'll be talking business, so we need a little privacy."

She smiled and blinked at him a couple of times. "Of course Paul, I'll just be a moment." She gracefully moved out from behind her lectern, obviously trying for a professional look despite her low-cut, high-riding outfit. Paul openly stared at her back-end and long shapely legs as she executed her best model's tuck all the way to a table in the far corner of the room. She spoke briefly to a waiter and then turned and beckoned to them with menus in hand.

Brooks seated himself across from his long-time acquaintance and smiled broadly. "She's a nice piece of work, ha?"

"You don't know the half of it, man." Paul appeared to be in a pretty good mood, but Brooks knew very well how nasty the son of a bitch could become with little provocation. Brooks and Paul went way back in the Vegas community, mainly due to Brooks having supplied all Paul's travel-related needs for years. As CEO of American Travel Corporation, Brooks was not usually involved in a customer's reservations. However, Paul was a special case, as were the tour groups he currently had on the ship. He routinely monitored all of them.

For the past ten years, the two men had maintained a strictly business relationship, except for occasional social events to which they were both invited. During the past year, however, Brooks worked diligently to cultivate a closer friendship with Paul. This was complicated by the fact that Paul knew very well how Brooks manipulated his cruise booking to arrange the shipboard reunion between his wife, Sidney, and Darcy. He seemed to have gotten over his initial anger about that.

Paul was not a man you wanted to cross. He was nothing if not suspicious by nature, and it took a lot of time and patience for Brooks to insert himself into Paul's inner circle and gain his confidence. Even now, Brooks understood that he must be very careful not to appear overly anxious. After the scorpion attack on Tom, he gained an even deeper appreciation for how vicious and unpredictable his *friend* really was.

Eventually, Brooks subtly made it known that he and Paul might have some similar goals. So far he had done well cementing this idea through maintaining contact with his tour group leaders on the ship and with Rachael and Darcy.

Of course, Rachael was an essential part of his life now, and he believed he was convincing Darcy to see things his way. Rachael had been very open during their conversations, telling him all about Mick's behavior and Darcy's unhappiness. He was also well aware that Rachael had her own agenda—albeit an innocent one—to get her biological parents back together. He planned to exploit these facts for his own purposes.

The waiter tentatively approached the table, and in his usual controlling manner, Paul ordered turkey sandwiches with cranberry coleslaw for both of them. Then he turned his attention to Brooks. "So how are things going with our friends on the cruise, any news from there?"

"The ship had some sort of problem with their water system and had to ration water for a couple of days. I take it that it was just an annoyance . . . some sort of mechanical problem. The only other thing . . . Rachael mentioned that she and Darcy had a strange encounter on shore in Acapulco involving two men who scared them." He paused and studied Paul's face. "Apparently, one of them threw a rock that hit Rachael in the leg. That just sounded bizarre, and I didn't think it was anything to worry about." He carefully observed Paul's reaction.

Paul looked up at the waiter who had arrived with their drinks. "Thanks, Kyle. You have club soda for Mr. Larkin, correct?"

"Yes, sir." He placed the glasses on the table. "Will there be anything else, Mr. Denezza?"

"Not for now." Paul answered without even a glance at the waiter who looked relieved and quickly walked away.

Paul nodded to Brooks and picked up his Heineken. "That is an interesting story. Acapulco is a dangerous place, you know, but it sounds like the girl is being a little dramatic. It was probably just a crazy person, and they have left him behind on shore."

"Yeah, she can be a little flaky. She must have gotten that from her mother," Brooks laughed. "Anyway, I don't know much about what is happening with Clayton except that he and Darcy aren't getting along that well."

"Well, of course, I don't know either," Paul answered tentatively, glancing to the side as if he was expecting someone. He turned back and lowered his voice conspiratorially. "The two of them, Mick and Tom? They may have some surprises coming—you never know."

Brooks almost choked on his soda. He picked up his napkin and calmly wiped his mouth then set it down slowly. This was the kind of comment he'd waited months to hear. "Well," he responded, "I wouldn't be too upset if either of them met with some trouble, especially Mick. That bastard rubs me the wrong way if you know what I mean."

Paul made a quick vulgar gesture with his hand accompanied by a lewd grin. "You'd really like to get back in that big blonde's pants, wouldn't you? If only Mick were out of the picture, right, my friend?"

Even Brooks was a little shocked and worked to suppress his disgust. He went through the motions for the rest of the lunch—with no appetite—and was relieved when Paul said he had to get back to his casino operation. He felt slimy just being in Denezza's presence, and after saying so long and shaking hands with the asshole, he almost ran out of the hotel.

As he pulled his Mercedes out of the driveway into the heavy traffic on Las Vegas Boulevard, he pushed the Bluetooth connection on the steering wheel and told the phone to call Grant Murray. He didn't have anything concrete to report, but Paul had finally let down his guard when he suggested a threat of sorts.

38

Manuel was fixing my second martini, and I was trying to think about something other than Mick's problems, this morning's phone call from Brooks, and the two creeps who seemed to be stalking us. I hadn't seen them, but not for lack of looking over my shoulder every other minute. Rachael was off participating in some trivia contest, so I had time to myself. "So, have you heard how everything is at home?" I asked.

"Thanks for asking, Darcy. Yes, the little ones are over the flu, and now everyone is doing OK. I am relieved because it is hard to be so far away when there are troubles at home, you know what I mean?"

"Yes, I know exactly. I just can't imagine the difficulties you and the rest of the crew face in being away from your families for months at a time."

"How is the cruise going for you now? Are things getting better?"

How I wish they were—it's better than the cruise last year I guess, since no one has died so far. I laughed with no mirth whatsoever. "Sure Manuel, things are better. Mick is just working a lot with his interviews, so I have time to spare."

I reached for the drink he was offering and admired his handy-work. Using a frosty pre-chilled glass and shaking the mixture with crushed ice until it was on the verge of freezing made a perfect martini. Manuel knew this was just the way I liked it. *At least something is going right.*

As I sipped somewhat contentedly, staring at the dusky orange sky outside the window, a woman walked up beside me and ordered a scotch and water. She looked around and then settled halfway onto the empty stool. It seemed like an afterthought, or maybe she was just going to lean there while she waited for the drink. She didn't look at me or say anything, and I figured she wanted to be left alone. I couldn't help sizing her up though. She wore a tasteful loose-fitting navy blue sundress and looked to be about five feet four and a little on the plump side.

Maybe she sensed that I was checking her out because suddenly she turned to me and I saw that she was quite attractive with soft brown eyes and the same color hair cut short with wispy curls against her round face. Smiling broadly, she introduced herself. "Hello, how are you doing? I'm Connie Sinclair. I don't think I've seen you around the ship before."

"Hi, I'm Darcy Farthing. I'm doing pretty well, Connie. Would you like to stay and enjoy your drink?"

"Sure, why not. I didn't really have anything going on . . . I'm on the cruise by myself, actually . . . how about you?"

"No, I'm here with my . . . um . . . boyfriend and my daughter, but they are doing their own thing, so I have time to myself. As I looked closer, I could see that she was quite a bit overweight.

As if she had read my mind, she said, "Wow, you appear to be in great shape, Darcy. I've been planning to go to the gym during the cruise because I have to lose some weight and get back into shape myself. I went through a bad break-up with my boyfriend and put on some pounds. Do you exercise on the ship?"

"Yes, almost every day. Maybe I'll run into you at the gym."

"Maybe . . ." She picked up the drink Manuel had set in front of her and took a sip. She smiled at me, leaning back a little as if she was trying to get a better view. "So where are you from?"

"I live in Colorado now, in Colorado Springs, but I might be moving soon."

"You're kidding, what a coincidence. I live in Longmont, the town north of Denver. I moved there from Kansas about five years ago. I'm a travel agent now, and I have a group here on the ship."

"Yeah, what a coincidence," I said, while I waited to see if my intuition was going to try to tell me something about this gal. No message was forthcoming, so I sipped my drink and then another one, and spent the next hour getting to know Connie Sinclair. We actually hit it off pretty well, and by the time Rachael showed up at the bar, we were laughing and joking like old friends.

I introduced my new friend to my daughter, and in just a few minutes the three of us decided to go to the show that was about to start in the main theater. As it turned out, the comedian was marginally funny, but it didn't seem to matter. We had a great time anyway. Wow, am I actually making a friend here? I don't have many of those. I knew I needed a distraction from Mick and my concerns about Brooks. *What the hell, why not go with this and see where it leads since Rachael and Connie also seem to be getting along.*

39

At 1:00 a.m. the inside and outside decks were almost deserted. Melanie Cousins basked in the welcome silence and felt no apprehension as she descended the stairwell from her cabin on deck 7. She was headed for the twenty-four-hour café located all the way forward on deck 4. As many female passengers tended to do when navigating between decks or cabins, Melanie wore only a cotton knee length cover-up over her panties.

Earlier, she had returned to her cabin alone, scrubbed her face, and pulled her thick black hair into a ponytail. Then, for some reason she began to crave freshly squeezed orange juice and decided since it was available just a few decks below, why not have some.

At thirty-nine and newly single, Melanie took great pride in her appearance and made every effort to look younger than her years. Cruising presented an opportunity, and for her, the incentive to walk and exercise daily. So far, she had been relatively successful in resisting the tempting ubiquitous desserts.

Surprisingly, the luxurious mode of travel had proven to be a decent way to meet single men—who were not gay—and presumably had some means. At least they had enough to afford a cruise vacation. She had not realized the number of single—and maybe married—folks who apparently took cruises with the intention of hooking up with someone.

This evening once again, she had partied all night in the Triton lounge and dance club. Steven, a recently divorced fifty-something guy she met earlier in the day while lying by the pool, had turned out to be an acceptable partner. He seemed nice enough, well-groomed and reasonably trim except for a small paunch, so she agreed to see him again. Nothing would come of their little tryst, but she intended to have as much fun as possible.

As she bounced onto the mid-point landing between decks 5 and 4, she suddenly became aware that someone was running heavily down the stairs behind her. She stepped to the side to let them pass, but instead of continuing down the stairs a large man grabbed her around the waist with one arm and clamped his other hand firmly against her mouth.

Caught completely off guard, Melanie could not even form a rational thought. A moment later, instantly thrown into full panic mode, she began kicking furiously and tried to call for help. What happened next was so horrific, overwhelming, and quick, that later she would have difficulty even describing the basic characteristics of her attacker.

He wore a mask and a plain white T-shirt with black pants. All she knew was that he was big and powerful, and was holding a very long knife. When she later tried to recall his voice, it was as if the terror had stripped her memory of any useful details.

Sobbing uncontrollably and choking behind his thick fingers, Melanie was helpless to do anything other than comply with his demand for silence. She knew only that with the knife resting on her throat he had pushed her shift all the way up and yanked her panties off one leg. Then he unzipped and roughly forced her legs apart, all the while pushing the knife edge dangerously into her flesh, and urging her in a hoarse whisper to be quiet.

She turned her head to the side and stared wide-eyed at the carpet's green and red swirls as she tried to calm herself. She knew she could easily die here on this landing, and lacking control over what would happen, she was determined not to give him a reason to become even more violent.

Within seconds he was pushing himself into her. The knife pressed even deeper into her throat as he ejaculated after four powerful and agonizing thrusts. An unmistakable tearing sensation accompanied a grating pain so horrible that she could not stifle a high-pitched squeal. But almost worse than the violation was the nauseating feeling of blood dripping from her neck and trickling between her exposed breasts.

Paralyzed by terror, she stared up at the man now kneeling beside her with his head bent low. His meaning was clear despite the fabric covering his entire face with holes for his eyes and mouth. When he had her full attention, he placed his finger to his lips and shook his head from side-to-side. She nodded vigorously in agreement, and he jumped onto his feet. As quickly as he had appeared, he flew down the stairs and left her alone.

Melanie lay silent in the stairwell, dazed and bleeding and listening, while she waited for the pain to subside. She tried to gather her strength and courage, praying that someone would come to help her. When finally she understood that her attacker was really gone and no one else was coming, the tears came in uncontrollable torrents. Hiccupping large gulps of air between sobs, she hauled herself up against the wall.

Standing still for a minute as best she could on wobbling legs, she tried to breathe deeply to gain some composure. The rape had happened so quickly, and she had been powerless to prevent it. The fact that this happened to her was unbelievable, but that it was on a cruise ship where she had felt safe and secure was astounding. She was shaking violently and in shock, but she knew this could have been much worse. *I am alive, thank God.* Finally, she pulled up her panties, smoothed down her dress and gingerly climbed back up to her cabin. The front of her shift was covered with blood, but the initial flow from the cut on her neck had already subsided to a trickle.

Back in the relative safety of her cabin, she inspected the deep scratch across her neck and seriously considered taking a shower and trying to forget the rape had ever happened. It already seemed surreal, and she knew she was not severely injured. But soon Melanie's anger far outstripped her humiliation. It was bad enough to be a victim, but she'd be damned if she would allow this to happen to someone else if she could help it. She reached for the bedside phone and dialed the operator.

40

Day 10 – at sea

Captain Dolf moved away from the communications console where he had just given his routine morning address to the passengers and turned to Roger Ramirez. "What is happening to my ship? First, an attack on desalination and now you say we have rape reported? Can this be true?"

"I'm afraid it is. The woman is very clear-headed considering what she experienced. She has a cut on her neck from the assailant holding a knife against it while he attacked her. After talking with her, I don't have any question about the validity of her claim. The problem is that she does not even know if this was a passenger or crew member. He wore a mask, and she can't remember anything about his appearance or voice."

"What about cameras?"

"Yes, that is interesting. It looks like the attacker came out of the hallway into the foyer and edged beside the wall, then reached up from under the camera and sprayed the lens with paint. All you can see is an arm and shoulder and then blackness."

The captain sat down slowly and ran his fingers across his close-cropped blond hair. He tapped his fingers on the console a few times as he thought about what his security chief had said. "Do you think there is connection with attack on the water system?"

"I've been thinking about that, myself. In all my years of working on cruise ships, I'm sure I have never seen two serious incidents happen so close together like this. That tells me they might be related and that we might have a very bad guy on board with us."

"You must have something to go with, ya? Something connects the two things—there must be something." His voice rose in pitch with an unmistakable note of anxiety.

Roger had never seen this captain so vulnerable. He was obviously not going to handle the situation very well. Even though these events were unprecedented, it was essential to keep a cool head. Things could be worse . . . and might get a lot worse if they didn't find some clue to the identity of their saboteur and rapist.

"Dolf, we have to remain calm for the passengers' sakes. The rape must not become public knowledge because I'm afraid there will be total panic among the women. Let me continue with this investigation. I will talk to the victim again when she has had time to recover more and see if she can remember anything useful.

The captain leaned forward with his elbows on his knees and looked up at Ramirez. "There is no question now that we talk to the GAO team, ya? It is too much coincidence they investigate crimes, and now we have two. I know how you feel with this, but you go explain everything to them. It is my order, ya?"

Roger knew there was no point in arguing with the captain, but he still did not want to involve the GAO team in the ship's problems. It particularly galled him to have to involve Tom Smythe given the animosity he felt for him. But the security chief was savvy enough to know that if anything else were to happen, God forbid, and they had withheld the information, there could be hell to pay from multiple sources. He did not intend to suffer the same fate as Smythe had a year ago.

41

Early in the morning, Captain Dolf announced to everyone that the desalination equipment had been repaired and everything was back to normal. He told us he had already increased our speed to twenty knots and the weather should remain mild and the waves calm as we proceeded down the coast to Lima, Peru. We were making up time and would arrive at the port early tomorrow morning.

After cruising so slowly for a couple of days, it felt like we were flying over the water. Out on deck 4 just two stories above the ocean I spent twenty minutes feeling the exhilaration of waves rushing alongside and the warm breeze through my loose hair, while I tried to think rationally about things. Anyway, I had decided I needed some time to myself just because a little privacy has always been essential for me. I had to do some soul searching about my problems with Mick . . . since I still hadn't confronted him. I also needed to sort out how I really felt about Brooks.

Since Acapulco, I had actively been looking for the two mysterious men. I hadn't said any more about them to Rachael or Mick, because I wasn't in the mood for histrionics or criticism. But I was getting tired of feeling anxious all the time, and I had decided to talk to Tom about everything as soon as possible. He and Mick were busy with their interviews again today, but we would be meeting for lunch.

So I went back inside and took up residence in a big comfy upholstered chair in a cocktail lounge that would not open for drinks until later in the day. It was relaxing there, and I could look out the window at the ocean and the horizon. In fact, it was so peaceful that I almost nodded off, so it was not surprising that I felt a flutter of annoyance when two young women plopped down in chairs nearby. They were not boisterous or anything, so I quickly checked my attitude and went back to sleepily watching out the window for whales and dolphins.

Suddenly, at the sound of the word "rape" I was drawn to their conversation and obviously had to eavesdrop. "My mother said her name is Melanie and she got raped in the stairwell and then had to go down to the medical facility. The guy cut her with a knife and . . . wow, can you believe it? I thought these ships were safe, but now I'm freaking."

"How come your mom knows about it?"

"Oh, she and Melanie have been playing bingo together, and when she didn't show up for this morning's set, mom went to her cabin. She said Melanie was in there by herself. Can you imagine? She's on the cruise alone."

"Bummer. I for sure won't be going out on deck by myself at night."

I stood and casually walked away. What I heard was so troubling that I wanted to find Rachael right away. There didn't seem to be any reason to doubt what the girl had said—her story was so specific. I thought Rachael was at the pool, so I hurried in that direction.

Out on the pool deck, I squinted in the bright sunlight and went to check her favorite sunbathing spots. I got lucky on the second try. On the upper deck, she was lying on her belly with her long mane flowing over the side of the lounge chair. She looked spectacular in her tan, and white bikini—except for the huge purple and yellow bruise on her leg. After knowing her for a year, I sometimes still pictured the eighteen-month-old child I had last seen. I could not get over how grown up and drop dead gorgeous my daughter became while my life rode an entirely separate but parallel current. I sat down beside her and quietly asked, "Are you asleep, Rachael?"

She rolled over and favored me with a big smile and those eyes. "Hi, Darcy, you don't have your suit on. Don't you want to get some sun?"

I looked down at my blouse and khaki shorts. "Not right now, Hon, but I want to talk to you a minute. I'm afraid something bad has happened, and I need to tell you about it."

Her bright expression immediately dimmed. "What did Mick do now? It bothers me so much to see you unhappy. I'm so mad at him!"

"No no, it has nothing to do with us, but . . . well, don't worry, I know how you feel about Mick." I sat down next to her on the edge of her lounge chair and lowered my voice. "It's that I was sitting inside the ship just now, and I overheard a conversation about a rape that happened last night, apparently in a stairwell. And the woman was stabbed or something."

"Holy shit!" Rachael rarely used bad language, and her face and neck had reddened noticeably. "I mean that is unbelievable. Did they catch the guy?"

"You know, I have no idea, but we are going to find out. If there is a rapist loose on the ship, I want to know about it."

What I was really thinking was that this cruise was getting very scary . . . and after our previous experience, it was unbelievable that violence had occurred on another cruise that we happened to be on. I looked at my watch. "It's almost lunchtime. Do you want to come in and try to meet up with Mick and Tom? I can't wait to tell them about this."

"Absolutely," she said, reaching for her swimsuit cover-up.

42

Mick appeared to be speechless and just kept shaking his head in disbelief. I think it was just too much for him to process in his fragile emotional state. It was one thing to be worried about Rachael and me encountering some imaginary threat on shore, but it was a whole different thing for him to cope with this very real danger to us on the ship. As we learned on the cruise last year, out in the middle of the ocean you are truly a captive of this environment.

Tom pushed himself away from the table. "I have to find out if what you heard is right and if so, whether they caught the guy. I'm going to security to talk with Roger right now. Do you want to come along, Mick? After all, we came on board to look at crimes on ships, and if a rape did occur it will certainly beef up your findings."

I think Tom's comment was intended to lift the mood a little, but it had the opposite effect. Mick scowled at him and answered with a touch of hostility. "Yeah, I'll come along, but you of all people should know better than to make light of something as serious and threatening as this. While I'm thinking about it, what about the two guys who were following you girls? Don't any of you think there could be a connection since we're fairly sure they are passengers?" He stood and leaned with both palms on the table. "And why haven't we seen them around the ship?" He waved his arm around at the room behind him. "If they are innocent, why aren't they here or in the dining room or the pool, or somewhere? They sound as if they would stand out in the crowd."

Tom nodded in agreement. "You're right about all that, Mick. I hadn't thought it through that clearly, yet. Let's go talk to Roger and see what's going on."

One thing I've learned about Tom is that he is your man if there is an emergency or sensitive issue to be diffused. He was practicing on Mick right now, and I was grateful. Everything Mick said was right, though. It didn't make any sense that we hadn't seen those guys around the ship . . . if they were passengers.

After Mick and Tom left, Rachael and I tried to enjoy the rest of our lunch. Somehow, the whole cruise seemed tainted now, and I knew that she was thinking the same thing. What started out as a potentially sweet vacation was turning very sour.

In the past year, there have been many times when Rachael appeared to be thinking exactly the same thing I was—sometimes in a very uncanny way. Now she looked up from her plate and drilled me with her eyes. I tried to drill right back. It was a battle of the big blues.

Finally, she started in. "Darcy, tell me what you really think about everything that is happening—the situation with Mick and those guys and now this rape. I need some reassurance because I'm not enjoying this trip at all and now . . . I'm afraid." Her eyes filled with tears, and it made me think of a multi-shaded watercolor wash of the ocean.

In an instant, I felt an internal switch tug me from the role of friend that I was trying to maintain to that of mom. I scooted my chair around the corner of the table so I could be next to her. She leaned towards me and held out her hand, and my eyes stung as I took it and gently squeezed.

"I know this is scary, Hon. I'm a little freaked out myself, but the first thing is, we don't know what actually happened with the rape story yet. Second, nothing bad has happened to us on the ship, and we haven't even seen those two guys. For all we know they are not even on board." I tried to sound convincing and hoped it would work on me as well.

"You're right. I know I'm overreacting, but this just isn't what I thought it would be like. More than anything else, I think Mick's attitude or behavior or whatever, is bothering me a lot. I talked to Brooks again this morning, and he told me he wants us both to visit him as soon as we get back. He really is so nice and kind. I wish you could see that."

This was not what I needed right now, and it took every ounce of will power I possessed to remain nice and kind myself. I put my arms around her shoulders and gave her a quick hug. "I know the situation with Mick is upsetting, but you will eventually learn that whenever you have a deep attachment in a relationship, things can get complicated. I don't want to give up on Mick just because he has some sort of problem. I wish you could have known him better before—the way he was when we met. Then you would understand. Listen, Rachael, I need you to nurture and enjoy your relationship with Brooks without constantly trying to involve me with him, OK?"

"I get it. You don't have to go into all that again. I know how you feel about him." I could tell she didn't get it at all. What she was getting was defensive.

146

"Hon, I'm not upset or angry with you. I think I sort of understand why you feel so strongly about him, and I have to admit that he does seem to be a completely different person now. Sometimes, though, the world just moves on, and the past has to stay behind."

Rachael shook out her hair and wiped a lone tear from her cheek. She had composed herself, and I hoped she really understood what I was trying to tell her. She stared out the window for a moment then turned and gave me a tiny smile. "I'm sorry. I'm just freaked out over everything, but I'm OK now. Until we hear from Tom and Mick about their talk with security, why don't we go back out to the pool and enjoy the sun? You can read your book if you don't want to sunbathe."

"That sounds wonderful. I'll finish my coffee and join you out there in a few minutes, OK?"

After she left, I looked out at the ocean and sky both shimmering in breathtaking jewel tones . . . like my daughter's eyes. That surface beauty is so deceiving because most things in nature, particularly the sea, are fearsome at their core and can quickly turn hostile. Fear was lurking just beneath my surface as well, but I could not let Rachael see how worried I was. I sincerely hoped she would stop trying to push me towards Brooks because I was having enough trouble holding myself from going in that direction. My explanation to her had been right on—I just needed to heed my own advice.

43

Tom and Mick's meeting with Roger Ramirez was short and to the point. It was apparent that he was giving up information begrudgingly. In fact, he began by acknowledging that he was sharing what was known about the crimes on the ship only because the captain had told him to.

They both knew he harbored resentment toward Tom. He was towing the World of Seas line, blaming Tom for some of the problems last year. And Roger was not happy with Mick for bringing his GAO project on board. At least Tom knew Roger, and at that moment, was a little more put together than Mick was. So Tom asked the questions, and Mick sat back in his chair hearing about half of what was said because he could not keep his mind from wandering back to how badly he was screwing up with Darcy and Rachael.

After curtly acknowledging that there had indeed been a reported rape, Roger became extremely agitated. "What I want to know is how the hell you two even knew about it. We are not telling anyone what happened, and we're keeping the victim's identity a secret."

"Well, I'm sorry to tell you this, Roger, but we know her name is Melanie, and by now I'm sure many other passengers know as well."

Roger looked as if he was going to explode. He stood and bent over the table, and this got Mick's attention. "Hold on Roger, don't get upset with us," he said. "Tom is just telling you what my friend innocently heard two women talking about." Tom leaned back in his chair, and Roger sat back down. "I sympathize with your position, Roger, believe me. I'm sure you are thinking that the captain will be very upset when he finds out the rape is getting to be common knowledge . . . and I say that because you and I know it is inevitable. Once passengers get hold of something like this, it spreads quickly."

Roger nodded in agreement. "You are right, but Ms. Cousins—Melanie—agreed she would not talk about what happened and I naively believed her.

Anyway, the point is we do not even know if the rapist was a crew member or a passenger. I questioned her twice, and she just can't recall many details. The guy wore a mask and only spoke to her in a hoarse whisper." Roger paused and fingered a pen lying on the desk in front of him. "Something else is troubling," he continued. "Before the attack, he sprayed the security camera with paint. This makes me lean toward a crew member."

Tom asked about the injury she sustained, and Roger shrugged. "Just a deep scratch, it didn't even need stitches—just a butterfly bandage, but she said the knife was quite big and looked like a kitchen knife. That worries me too because it also points to a crew member."

"Actually, it would have been almost impossible for a passenger to bring a large knife on board with baggage being X-rayed and all," Mick added.

Roger thought about that. "Anyone can get their hands on one of our kitchen knives if they want to, I suppose. It wouldn't be too difficult up in the buffet."

"It sounds to me like he cut her by accident," Tom said. "If he had meant to kill her or inflict a serious wound he could have. So, at least this doesn't seem to be a homicidal person, for what that is worth. He waited a few seconds to see if Roger had anything else to add, then rose from his seat. "Well, if you don't know anything more, we'll go and let you get back to work." Mick was already part way to the door of Roger's tiny office, really just a glorified cubicle with walls.

"I think you had better sit back down," Roger said quietly. "There is something else I have to tell you."

By the time he finished explaining what had really happened to the desalination equipment, Mick's agitation was evident. "Again, I'm only telling you these details at the captain's order. We're continuing to investigate this incident as well, but so far I'm sorry to say we have no idea who is responsible. The captain wants to know if you have any opinion about any of this. I don't know how you could, but I'm asking."

Mick didn't say anything, and Tom could see how upset he was at this latest development. "We're obviously stunned to hear this," he began. "I mean it's ironic that we are gathering information about crimes, and this ship seems to be a hotbed. It's giving me the same kind of feeling I was having a year ago when things started getting weird on the ship. Is this ship jinxed or something?" Tom said this more to himself than to them.

"Well, do you have anything constructive to say, or not?" Roger was still irritated.

"Only this: If I were you, I would be on the phone to the FBI right now telling them every detail you know about the sabotage and the rape. Forget about trying to save face for World of Seas. Do you want to end up fired like me? Besides that, I hope you tried to gather whatever forensic evidence you could at the site of the rape and from the victim."

Roger shifted uneasily, and the answer was clear. Tom sighed and said gently, "Again, I know something about what you are up against. As security officers, we are not police detectives and serious crimes truly do not occur all that often on ships. My advice to you is to think about anything and everything you can do to gather evidence that an expert might be able to use for identification, even if you cannot." Roger looked dejected and did not respond.

"I would also go down and get as many fingerprints off the desalination equipment as I could find and worry about sorting through them later. Same with . . . I don't suppose you have rape kits on board; I know I never did."

"No, but the doctor checked Ms. Cousins thoroughly and found only the expected injury to her from the rape. Do you have any other advice for me?" Roger asked with an edge of sarcasm.

"As a matter of fact, I do," Mick interrupted. I think you should consider the possibility that the same person is responsible for both crimes just because it seems logical, and not only that but my . . . um, friend and her daughter were bothered twice by two suspicious acting guys, whom they believe are on the ship. One of them threw a rock at her daughter in Acapulco and raised quite a bruise on her leg. Maybe there's a lead there, too."

"What? You can't be serious. With everything else we have to contend with you want me to find two guys who *might* be on the ship and somehow made your girlfriend uncomfortable?"

Mick started to respond, but Tom laid a hand on his arm and gave him a warning look. "Just think about it, Roger, all right?" We'll keep an eye out for the two guys Mick is talking about and let you know if anything else happens, but you have to admit, it could all be connected." Tom and Mick started for the door, but Tom turned back to Roger.

"One last thing, Roger, in my opinion, it will be better to alert the passengers and female crew members about the possible danger, since people are going to find out about it anyway. I hate to say this, but women probably should not wander around the ship alone at night. Talk to the captain about it."

On the way back to the conference center where they were conducting interviews, Tom could see that Mick was not going to be much use. "Why don't you go check on Darcy and Rachael, Mick? I'll continue with the interviews this afternoon, and you take a break. I can tell you are tired anyway. By the way, do you think we should tell Grant Murray about this, regardless of whether the ship chooses to report it?"

"Yes I do, and I don't even want to acknowledge a feeling I'm having that maybe this is related somehow to our problems last year. One thing I have in common with Darcy is, I know there is no such thing as a jinx or curse. Things happen because either people or chance cause them to, and this seems a little much to be happening by chance."

"Yeah, too much is happening here, that's for sure."

44

Tom's annoyance was evident. Wendy wondered if she had done something to upset him because ever since meeting at the Center Bar and then returning to his cabin, he had seemed very distracted. She had been sitting on the foot of the bed, and now she got up and approached him as he sat at the small desk shuffling papers. She put her hands on his shoulders and leaned down to speak directly into his ear. "Is everything OK? You seem not quite yourself."

Tom looked up and spoke to her reflection in the mirror on the wall above the desk. "I'm sorry, Wendy. Some things are bothering me, and I want to talk to you about one of them before we go to dinner. Why don't you sit back down and just let me finish here. It will only be a minute. Then we'll talk, OK?"

"Sure Tom, no problem." She returned to her seat on the bed and sat with her hands folded in her lap. I thought things were going well with us, she thought. *I hope he isn't going to tell me he wants to stop seeing me. That would be bad for me.* Before she had a chance to think much more about it, Tom got up and moved over to sit on the bed beside her.

"Wendy, you know I don't talk about work much, so there are some issues concerning the interviews that have me a bit distracted. I'll try to do better at putting them aside when we're together." Wendy smiled sweetly. *Well, I guess he is not breaking up with me after all.*

He put his arm around her shoulder and pulled her around so that they were eye-to-eye. "Something has happened on the ship and no one—at least not the passengers—are supposed to know about it. Well, a few people do know, so it probably won't be a secret much longer. But when I tell you this . . . um, I want you to promise you will not talk about it with anyone other than Mick, Darcy, and Rachael." He waited for her nod of agreement before continuing.

"Last night a woman passenger was attacked in a stairwell by a man whom they have not identified. The thing is, she was violently raped, and the guy also cut her neck. My impression from talking to the security chief is that they have no clue and nothing to go on. They don't even know if he was a passenger or a crew member."

Wendy grew increasingly nervous as he talked. "Oh, that is really awful and scary. It kind of spoils the cruise in a way because now I'm going to be afraid to go out at night until they catch him."

"That is why I'm talking to you about it. I want you to be very careful and . . . I don't presume to tell you what to do, but I'd feel better if you didn't go out at night unless I'm with you. What do you think about that?"

"Yes, that's fine, Tom. We've been spending most of our evenings together anyway, in case you haven't noticed." She leaned in for a kiss that was quickly reciprocated.

"How long before we have to go to dinner?" he asked a little shyly and waited with an expectant look. This affair or romance or whatever you call it was very new to him. They had been intimate for several days, and Wendy had spent the last two nights in his cabin.

He'd been tremendously apprehensive about having sex for the first time in a long time, but found that everything worked well . . . very well in fact. He had finally realized that it was natural, not really something you had to remember how to do. The relationship was moving fast, but he was convincing himself that Wendy could be right for him. After all, he reasoned, she was charming, beautiful, and smart.

"We have at least forty-five minutes, but I don't really care if we're late."

He chuckled and eased her back onto the bed, stretching out beside her. He kissed her mouth gently and waited to see if she really wanted to make love. He hated being so tentative, but he just did not want to take a chance on doing something wrong. He needn't have been concerned.

She pulled his head down and probed his mouth with her tongue. They kissed passionately for a minute, and Tom reached down to undo his jeans. As soon as he was free, Wendy slipped her hand down the front of his briefs and snaked her fingers around his swollen member, squeezing gently. Tom moaned and began to unbutton her blouse with a bolt of excitement when he realized she was not wearing a bra. As soon as he touched her breasts, she pushed down her shorts and panties and turned her hips toward him.

He gently caressed her nipples and bent his head to kiss them. She rose up and pushed him back onto the bed. On her knees, she straddled him and moved, rubbing herself from side to side. She cried out and leaned down to kiss him letting her hair cascade around his face. "I'm ready, Tom," she whispered. "I want you in me now." She raised her hips and directed him inside with her hand.

Tom was gratified to feel her wetness—the measure of her arousal—as he slid into her tight warmth. He was feeling so much pleasure and contentment that it almost seemed too good to be true. Pushing that thought out of the way, he began moving harder and faster in response to her rhythm and pace. He couldn't help himself as he whispered to her how wonderful this was and that he never wanted it to end.

As seemed to be her pattern, she became out-of-control frantic in her build up to orgasm, burying her head in the pillow to muffle her screams of frustration and pleasure, as she pumped her hips up and down faster and faster. Tom grasped her bottom and kneaded it with both hands in an attempt to help her, as he fought to maintain his own control. Her orgasm triggered his, and they rode it out together.

After a few minutes of lying beside her without talking, Tom abruptly sat up on the edge of the bed. In his hyper-relaxed state, he had just caught himself before he told her he was falling in love along with some other commitment-type expressions of endearment. Recognizing that to do so would be premature, to say the least, he was surprised at the uncharacteristic lack of restraint. He got up and went into the bathroom to take a quick shower.

Wendy smiled to herself as she waited for her turn to rinse off. Sex with Tom was pretty good. She sometimes had difficulty reaching a climax, and so far that had not been the case with him. She rolled onto her side and brought her knees up to her chest, breathing deeply as she thought about the inevitable. *At least that's an added benefit to this relationship.*

45

Day 11 – Lima, Peru

Knowing that someone deliberately damaged the ship's water system was taking a toll on all of us. That, along with the rape and our stalkers had just about pushed Mick over the edge. I was extremely on edge about it too, but I was shocked to realize that Mick seemed utterly unable to cope. How the hell was he going to be able to complete the job he came on board to do?

Our little group, including Wendy and Connie, sat around a table in the Center Bar last night discussing what we should do to increase our personal safety. Of course, Mick said we should not leave the ship this morning, and he and Tom insisted we women should not go about the ship alone at night. The latter seemed like good reasonable advice.

My new friendship with Connie was giving me an avenue for my attention and energy. I was worrying a little less about Mick . . . and Brooks because Connie and I had been participating in some shipboard events during the day, sometimes with Rachael. I was surprised when the miniature golf venue turned out to be a lot of fun, as was the twice-daily trivia contest. I was enjoying myself and started thinking about how rare it was for me to have close female friends. I wondered why I was such a loner.

As usual, it took a while for us to decide among the many possible excursions for our one day in Lima. The ship would not leave port until 7:00 p.m., so we had plenty of time to see several different attractions. Connie said she didn't have any preferences, so Rachael and I attended an onboard lecture to educate ourselves about the city and country, and familiarize ourselves with the shore excursions suggested by the cruise line.

We learned that Lima, the capital of Peru, is among the twenty largest cities in the world with almost ten million people; roughly one-third of the country's population. Francisco Pizarro founded the city in 1535 after his conquest of the Inca Empire. He had come ashore three years earlier armed with a sword in one hand, a cross in the other, and Queen Isabel's royal permission to conquer Peru.

With absolution provided by Dominican priest Vicente de Valverde, Pizarro and his small band of soldiers slain the Incas and captured their king, Atahualpa, for ransom. The ransom was paid in gold, but the Spaniards executed him anyway. Pizarro chose the site for the city on the Pacific coast where the Lurin, Chillon, and Rumac rivers converge, and new settlers soon streamed in from Spain seeking fortunes in the New World.

During the 1600s and 1700s, massive earthquakes repeatedly destroyed Lima, and political and economic turmoil characterized its history even into the present. In the 1820s Simon Bolivar and José de San Martin freed Lima from Spanish rule along with much of South America. Although rich in natural resources and gaining stability, Peru is a developing country, and thousands of the city's residents live in terrible poverty, which we saw firsthand as we rode through the streets.

The three of us left the port in a taxi with a driver who did not speak English but understood where we wanted to go when we pointed to it on the map. I noted the streets we traveled, just in case we had to find our way back to the ship on our own. At this point, I wasn't leaving anything to chance. We drove up Avenida La Marina, turned left on Universitaria, then right on Simon Bolivar to our destination, the Larco Herrera Museum, which houses an extensive collection of Peruvian antiquities. The gently sloping driveway led up to an enchanting eighteenth-century mansion surrounded by beautiful flowering plants. We later found out that the house was built—rather appropriately—on top of a seventh-century pyramid.

According to a large plaque on the wall just inside the door, Archeologist Rafael Larco Herrera founded the museum in 1926 at the age of twenty-five. During his career, he discovered many cultures spanning four thousand years of pre-Columbian history, through his research and excavations along Peru's northern coast. Using his own method, he calculated the age of the artifacts he found based on layers of sand deposited between alternating eighteen to twenty-five year periods of flooding caused by the predictable El Nino phenomenon. On display, was a fantastic array of pottery, jewelry, and household items extracted from tombs in these sandy layers. In fact, today there are forty-five thousand pieces in the collection.

Inside, we spent a couple of hours wandering around the exhibits and entire walls of glass encasing perfectly preserved items. Some of the necklaces and earrings looked as if they could have just come from an Indian market in Santa Fe.

We all opted to visit the room advertised as "optional" that housed the extensive collection of erotic art pottery. Apparently, some visitors to the museum are offended by the existence of this ancient art form and do not want to be exposed to it. The artists captured sexual encounters between people on every shape and type of bowl, jug, and pitcher imaginable. How fascinating that these ancient cultures were so enthralled with the sex act in all its variations, including homosexuality. As we were leaving, we overheard a tour guide explaining to her group that the erotic art was not pornography, but merely this culture's uninhibited depiction of the perfectly natural sex act.

The need to explain this fact seemed like a commentary on our modern attitudes about sexuality. Of course, our myriad hang-ups about human form and function are rooted in the invention of religious taboos regarding sex and nudity, which members of these ancient cultures would probably have found strange. I think we also share the legacy of early European rulers and the Catholic church, which made it their mission to seek out and destroy any native cultures they found in the new world. For better or worse, virtually everything we see and experience in the Americas is influenced by that my way or the highway approach.

After we absorbed all we reasonably could expect to about pre-Columbian art in a short time, we took a break outside and found that the gardens were a relaxing treat. In the lusciously warm sun, we slowly toured the two levels of thick shrubbery and fully blooming flowers including salvias, geraniums, every color of bougainvillea, orchids, and unbelievably bright clumps of trumpet-like flowers described simply as *mermelada*—orange. There was also a bewildering array of cacti. I'd never seen so many different types and colors of flowers successfully planted in such a limited space. On the lower level, we found the gift shop and the Café del Museo with seating on a terrace overlooking the beautiful, well-kept grounds. It was so pleasant that I didn't want to leave.

Although we were getting hungry, we decided to wait a while before we had lunch, and so we took another taxi north to Plaza Mayor, the historical center of the city. We strolled around the square, and at Calles de Bodegones and Los Judios, we crossed over to the lovely colonial yellow stone Cathedral of Lima. With its twin bell towers and twenty-five-foot-high double doors adorned with huge iron lion-head knockers, it was quite an impressive piece of architecture and history.

Perpendicular to the cathedral, the government palace—the current political center of Lima and the city hall—occupies one side of the square. Stoic soldiers with automatic rifles patrolled the area in front its high iron fences and sharp-pointed gates. We weren't put off by this—it made us feel safer.

Just as we were discussing the need to stop and eat, there was an appealing café right in front of us. We made ourselves comfortable at a small outside table in the shade of a balcony above. From there, we watched tourists and residents mingling on the square around an impressive three-tiered fountain.

I had heard other passengers raving about Pisco, a fine liqueur that is Peru's national drink and I had to try one in the form of a Pisco sour. It was refreshing and vaguely reminiscent of a tangy margarita. We nibbled from shared plates of *Aji de gallina*, a spicy chicken dish, and *Pachamanca,* a meat and vegetable stew cooked in an earthenware pot. It was a delightful hour spent in an exotic ambiance.

46

Mick tried to get his mind off Darcy and Rachael being out there somewhere in Lima by themselves. He knew his worries were irrational at some level, but couldn't shake the feeling that something terrible was going to happen to them. Partly as a distraction, he placed a call to his staff in DC to give them a report on how things were going with the work—or not, as the case was.

Eve and Danny insisted they get on the phone together to hear what Mick had to say. He tried to be patient and thought about the need to sound upbeat, while he waited for them to pick up their extensions. "We're so glad to hear from you, Mick," Eve started before Danny could even say hello. "We've gotten a lot of work done on completing steps in the audit plan. The jurisdictions have sent in most of the data already, and from what we've seen there are quite a few cruise crime incidents for us to tabulate. What do you think about us getting started on some draft testimony?"

Mick waited for a beat. "Danny, what do you think about that? Are we really far enough along to write testimony?"

"Well, if Eve wants to start putting something down on paper it's OK with me, but I think we should concentrate on analyzing the data, and of course, we are anxious to hear what you have from your end."

"I'm afraid we haven't found out anything related to the extra-curricular work involving the FBI yet, but the ship has provided the data we requested. Tom has been working with the guest relations and security staffs to obtain all reports of criminal activity on the Sea Nymph in the past year. Some security records exist, but the details are primarily anecdotal. You should know, however, that there have actually been a couple of serious crimes on board during this cruise. Believe me, we'll have those well documented."

"Wow, if it's that easy to have problems I don't know if I ever want to go on a cruise," Eve said.

"The thing is, Eve, serious crimes do happen on ships, but not very frequently. Something about this ship seems to attract problems. I can't explain it. Anyway, I think I'd like to fax you the records we're getting either from the ship or when we get to the next port so you can get started analyzing them. Anything happening there at headquarters I should know about?"

Danny quickly answered. "Not really. Ken comes around every couple of days to check on us . . . I guess to make sure we are working, even without you here to watch us."

Mick laughed. "Yeah, I can imagine that. Keep up the good work, you guys. I'll send the fax as soon as I can, and we'll let you know if anything comes from our interviews."

After that conversation, Mick called Bill Sawyer. After a quick greeting he said, "We haven't found out anything from the interviews yet, but wait till you hear what has happened on this ship."

Bill was amazed to hear about the rape and the sabotage and told Mick he was getting concerned about their safety. "I agree with you that there is something weird about that ship. Who would ever have believed this much could happen in just over a year?"

Then Mick really surprised him. "You think you're worried about us now? Wait till you hear this. Tom talked with Grant Murray this morning to see if there is anything new with his scorpion attack. Grant said they had not found anything on that, but he said something else that was interesting. Apparently, Brooks Larkin, Darcy's ex and an acquaintance of Paul's, told Murray that Paul hinted to him that something might happen to Tom and me here on the ship. It sounds like Brooks is talking to Paul and passing information to Murray. I had no idea such an arrangement existed."

"OK, Mick, this is getting a little hairy. I'll talk to Murray and see how serious he thinks the threat is. After all, Paul is back in Vegas, and he needs to watch his own back since he might be close to being indicted himself. What could he do to you guys there?"

"That is what Tom and I think, too. He was probably just trying to impress Brooks."

"By the way, Buddy, how are you doing? Are you feeling back to your old obnoxious self, and how are Darcy and Rachael?"

Mick came dangerously close to dumping his emotional baggage onto his old friend but caught himself just in time. "I'm fine. There isn't much time for anything but these damn interviews, but Darcy has Rachael and also a girlfriend she met on board to keep her busy. They're all sightseeing today in Lima."

After Mick hung up, he thought about Brooks and Paul from another angle. He could not help but wonder about Darcy's supposed plan to get back together with Brooks. He had not yet asked her about it, but given how she was acting towards him he did not want to believe that Sidney's allegation had any merit. It did make sense that if Darcy was close to Brooks, she would know if he was actively involved in the FBI investigation as an informant or something. *How many secrets can she be keeping?*

Mick and Tom had earlier discussed the possibility that Paul could have something to do with the sabotage or the rape but didn't see how there could be any connection, and anyway, these crimes were not aimed at them personally. So Mick tried to get his mind back onto the task at hand and went to meet Tom.

For the rest of the afternoon, they continued the interviews. A total of three hundred crew members were on the list of housekeeping and cruise director's staffs on the last cruise. At this point, they had worked their way through seventy of them. Mick was still struggling with his own problems and had become wary of the crew members. He found himself flashing back to the previous cruise where they discovered how much of a threat the crew could be.

They were both having a hard time concentrating on their routine questioning, knowing that one of the crew members they were talking with might be a rapist or terrorist. On the other hand, knowing there was at least one criminal on board gave their efforts new meaning.

As the work proceeded, they remained unaware of Isabel Trindade, who was not scheduled to be interviewed until near the end of the cruise. She, however, had thought of little else since the beginning of the cruise. She knew where the interviews were taking place and had been given a day and time for her meeting. However, she thought about presenting herself there sooner, some morning when they were just beginning. Several mornings she started out in that direction but lost her nerve.

Once, she got as far as the interview room but stopped outside when she saw that the door was open and she could hear several male voices inside. With a jolt of anxiety, she realized that one of them was Mr. Ramirez, the chief of security. This confused and frightened her, and she quickly fled back to her cabin. She was intimidated by the security chief and the men from the American government, and fearful that either she would be blamed for something and would lose her job, or the men would laugh at her and not believe what she knew to be true. *Then what would I do?*

47

It was about 1:30 p.m. when we left the café at Plaza Mayor and boarded a city bus for an excursion to Pachacamac, twenty-five miles southeast of the city. These pre-Inca ruins sit in a desert in the Valley of the Lurin River. Structures excavated at the site are believed to have been built as early as 200 AD, but most of the common buildings and temples were constructed much later, between 800 and 1450, by the Huari and later the Ichma cultures. They used the site primarily to worship the *Pacha Kamaq*—Earth Maker—creator god until they were overtaken by the Inca Empire and converted to sun worshippers.

The religious stories surrounding these early cultures are varied, fascinating, and a little familiar. This isn't so surprising since modern religions appear to be based on the same stories that have been retold and embellished over many thousands of years, each new version seeking to make the concepts and miracles seem fresh and believable.

One story holds that Pachacamac made the first man and woman, but forgot to give them food. After the man died, the woman petitioned the god's father, Inti, asking him to make her the mother of all future people. This infuriated Pachacamac, and he tried to kill every child subsequently born to her. However, one of her sons, Wichama, beat-up the god and threw him into the sea, where he eventually gave up the fight and became the god of fish. I thought this story was slightly less believable than Eve being made from Adam's rib after God apparently didn't initially think it was important to make more than one human being.

The Ichma culture eventually joined the Inca Empire, and they built at least five new buildings, including a temple on the main square to worship the sun god. Archeologists have so far discovered seventeen pyramids, but most have suffered heavy damage from the periodic El Nino events.

At the ruins, after reading the many informative brochures and signs around the area, I concluded that the Inca ancestors of some modern Peruvians obviously had a lot going for them. To this day, it is not known how they managed to build megalithic stone fortifications, temples, and entire cities without iron tools or knowledge of the wheel. Their ability to carve massive stones to exacting specifications to ensure structural integrity is mystifying. So is the method they used to transport the stones sometimes up incredibly steep hillsides and hoist them into place since their only draft animal was the llama and they apparently had no mechanical pulley systems.

In addition to their construction skills, the Incas had a prosperous highly structured society with a ruling King and a sun god. Absent any scientific understanding of what the sun is, it would seem a smart and logical choice as something to worship, since it gives life to the planet. Without a written language or currency of any kind, the Incas also achieved a high level of scientific sophistication, performing brain surgery that is a wonder to modern medicine. They bioengineered an amazing variety of food crops, including hybrid corn, squash, potatoes, peanuts, and peppers.

From a biological standpoint, I thought this crop hybridization history was not only fascinating but seemed a particularly meaningful example of how humans have found and lost knowledge over time. To select for desirable traits in the native plants and transform them into new cultivars through the breeding process, the Inca growers must have gained at least a rudimentary understanding of how these traits were passed down from one generation to the next. With no written language they could not easily record these results for posterity.

But in their achievement, they predated the "father of modern genetics," Gregor Mendel, by about eight hundred years. Mendel, an Augustinian monk, was the first to document the fixed laws of heredity and is credited with discovering the pattern and frequency of hereditary factors. For seven years beginning in 1856 he conducted elegantly designed breeding experiments on twenty-nine thousand garden pea plants and painstakingly recorded the systematic inheritance of traits for color, size, position, and texture of different plant parts. He focused on the numerical relationships of traits among progeny and reached a stunning conclusion: Material elements present in the plants undergo segregation and assortment and are passed to offspring, yielding a large number of possible variations. These elements—we now call genes—were not identified until James Watson and Francis Crick discovered DNA in the 1950s.

Ironically, Mendel's discovery of how traits are inherited, which the Incas must have recognized intuitively, was overlooked for forty more years while debate raged over Darwinian theories of acquired characteristics. Likewise, biological, engineering, mathematical, and astronomical advancements made by the ancient Greeks, Egyptians, and Mayans, to name a few, were lost for hundreds of years—possibly some may yet to be rediscovered. Humans have had roughly the same level of intelligence for over fifty thousand years, so it is not surprising that brainy individuals have always figured out how things worked and how to use this knowledge to improve their lives.

This got me to wondering what would have happened if the Spaniards had used their sophisticated written language skills to obtain knowledge from the Incas and other primitive civilizations they conquered, instead of focusing on religious conversion, genocide, and acquisition of riches? I wonder about the total sum of knowledge, and scientific discovery gained and lost, and how much farther along we would be if advancement of acquired knowledge, rather than conforming to religious dogma, had been a priority over the millennia?

I had become somewhat lost in my rhetorical musings, and by the time I pulled myself out of my private thoughts, Rachael and Connie were walking on ahead. I stepped up my pace and considered the surroundings. The entire place seemed to be the same shade of light brown. The building blocks and surrounding land looked the same, due to the lack of precipitation. This area gets just over an inch of rainfall in a year, primarily from early morning drizzle during winter months. Today's residents get water from the rivers flowing from their sources high in the Andes, as did their predecessors.

I caught up with my companions at the foot of the sun temple. We began the climb to the top of the bluff, which was really the top of the excavated temple, after listening to a warning by the bus driver about the hazardous footing and steep incline. He wasn't kidding, and I was grateful for my Colorado acclimation. Many of our fellow tourists gave up midway and never made it to the top. Rachael and I walked up with relative ease, but Connie was clearly out of breath and energy by the time we reached the temple escarpment.

From the top, the river on one side was a green ribbon of foliage cutting through the bare desert. The front side of the temple faced the sea, with a spectacular view of huge islands of sharp rock jutting out of the water not far offshore. When we saw the vistas and the ancient multi-tiered terraces and fortifications that have been excavated so far, we all agreed it was worth the effort.

Clearly, visitors were here at their own risk. There were no walls, guardrails, or ropes to prevent a person from tumbling over the side of the stone terraces, some of which were quite high. This reminded me of the narrow mountain roads back home in Colorado. Visitors from the east coast seem surprised and a little frightened by the hairpin switchbacks with no guardrails—only prudent driving skills—to keep you from plummeting over the side.

We proceeded single file on a path that stretched across the top of the temple. Parts of a low wall had been excavated, and the rectangular cutout sections were reminiscent of the merlons and crenels on medieval castle fortifications. Further along, the stones were arranged in a series of narrow vertical walls, spaced a few feet apart, which might have been a foundation of some sort. The heat was oppressive, but I was so intrigued by the ancient architecture I barely noticed.

Rachael had been very quiet on the climb up and seemed to be deep in thought. As we came to the end of the path, which roughly circumnavigated the top of the temple, she stepped up beside me. "You know, I think I'll leave you two up here and start down to the bottom. I want to read some more of the signs down there describing the other buildings. You two take your time. The bus doesn't leave for another hour."

"That's fine, I'm sure we'll be right along. I wouldn't want to leave Connie up here by herself." She nodded in agreement and picked up her pace. I watched her nimbly navigate along the structure toward the rough-hewn stone steps we climbed to get to the top.

I looked over my shoulder and saw Connie about forty feet back. "Connie, Rachael is going down. Do you want to stay up here much longer?"

"No, just a few more minutes, she answered cheerfully."

I walked to the edge of the wall. Looking over the side, I figured this had to be a twenty-foot drop to the sand and gravel, which then sloped another twenty feet to the bottom of the excavation. The architecture and perfect placement of the stacked rectangular blocks was truly amazing, and the smooth wall fell off vertically below my feet. For a few minutes, I just stood there enjoying the fantastic views with a light breeze blowing through my hair.

All of a sudden I felt that warning twinge . . . again. With a sense of danger that I did not understand, I quickly turned around from the edge of the wall and butted right into Connie. She was standing only a few inches behind me. *What the hell?* I was knocked off balance and began to tumble backward. "No, no," I screamed. To regain my footing, I wildly pin-wheeled my arms, but it was of little use.

In the next second or two, everything changed. I looked into Connie's face and saw something I couldn't believe. Even in my panic, I registered hard squinting eyes and firmly set jaw, with a mouth twisted into a cruel sneer . . . at least that is what I perceived in the portion of a second when I realized she was not trying to help me. She was standing with her arms at her sides, watching me struggle to keep from toppling over the edge.

Then, abruptly, she reached out and grasped my arm. Her feet were planted firmly under her, and her body was rigid. Without thinking, I used her weight as leverage, and thanks to all those core-strengthening planks, I managed to pivot toward her and pull myself upright in a maneuver I could never have imagined, much less planned.

My forward momentum shifted her center of gravity, and before I could react, she flew past me with a squeal of surprise and fell right over the side. All I remember is screaming her name and standing paralyzed with fear and shock on the edge of the wall with my hair falling down around my face, partly obscuring my vision. Then it registered that Connie had rolled down the slope at the bottom of the wall and several people were already running to help. I turned and raced along the top of the temple and down the path as fast as I could, almost falling face first several times on the steep incline.

Three-quarters of the way down, I caught up with Rachael who was descending at a sane pace. "Connie fell over the wall," I yelled as I ran past her."

"What? How could that happen?" she called as she started running after me.

We flew around the structure to the side where Connie had landed, and a crowd of tourists was gathering. Just as we arrived, a woman came out of the group and walked toward us. I recognized her from the bus. "That lady who fell is with you, isn't she?"

"Yes, how is she?" I asked, but we didn't slow down.

"I think she has a broken leg, at least," she said to our backs, "but she is lucky it isn't her neck. She said she was pushed," she yelled after us.

When the words finally registered, I stopped and glanced at Rachael, who was staring at me with a curious expression. "No one pushed her," I snarled.

The woman shrugged and continued in the opposite direction. She called over her shoulder, "I'm going to the office over there to get some help."

"Darcy, what is going on?" Rachael was not moving and clearly wanted an explanation.

"I wish I knew. All I can tell you is that something happened to Connie up there and I think maybe she was thinking about pushing me over the wall, or at least she was going to let me fall." I realized I had begun to shake uncontrollably. Rachael saw the state I was in and moved forward to put her arms around me.

"Why would she do that? I don't understand," she said into my hair.

I tilted my head back to see her better. "Neither do I, but I'm telling you if I wasn't in as good shape as I am and wasn't paying attention, it would be me lying at the bottom of that wall." Terror and shock were already resolving to anger and grief. "She grabbed for me as I was starting to fall and somehow she went over instead. Is it my fault?" I began sobbing into her shoulder, while she awkwardly tried to console me. After about thirty seconds I gained some control and took a step back. I wasn't sure exactly what had happened, but I knew I would never forget that odd hateful look on Connie's face.

"Come on, let's go see how she is," I said, already jogging toward the even bigger crowd that was forming around her.

48

The good news was we got back to the ship before it sailed. Since we were on our own and not on a World of Seas tour, it was not at all clear the captain would have waited for us if we'd been significantly late. The bad news? Now I had one more odd and scary situation to try to deal with, and my stress level almost matched Mick's, which was saying a lot.

By the time we arrived at the pier, I was exhausted. After my initial meltdown at Pachacamac, with Rachael's support, I got it together enough to communicate with the EMTs who had been called in by the ruin's officials. They were obviously anxious to be rid of these silly Americans who had been so careless at their archeological site. I avoided speaking directly to Connie and kept my distance from her, even though she was clearly injured. She remained on the ground, but I could see she was covered with scrapes from her slide down the gravel slope. She was obviously in pain and extremely agitated. I had no problem hearing her sob and wail from my position in the center of the crowd surrounding her. I didn't trust myself to keep it together, so Rachael pushed through and went to comfort her until professional help arrived.

While the ambulance driver and his two technicians seemed competent, they did not speak English. Luckily, a couple of our fellow tourists were able to help with translation. The bottom line was that Connie was damn lucky. After carefully evaluating her condition, the medics splinted her right leg, gently placed her on a backboard, and loaded her into their ambulance, which frankly looked as if the Incas might have used it themselves.

The driver gave us a choice between the Instituto Nacional de Enfermedades Neoplasicas, thankfully referred to as Inen, a large public hospital about fifteen miles away that apparently specialized in cancer treatment; or the Clinica Anglo Americana, a British and American private facility that was a little farther up the coast, but sounded a whole lot better.

Rachael and I arranged with the Pachacamac staff for private transportation by limousine and followed the ambulance up to San Isidro, one of forty-three Lima districts.

This was obviously a high-end tourist area and beach resort, with many American hotel chains. We passed the Radisson and found the small neat modern-looking clinic tucked in between older buildings on Cavenecia just northwest of Ovala Gutierrez circle and park. The limo driver dropped us off, and we entered through the front door, while Connie was taken around to the back. Inside, the English speaking medical staff assured us they had state-of-the-art diagnostic equipment and would be happy to check Connie, just as soon as we paid the receptionist. We dug through Connie's purse and found a credit card, which we were pleased to hand over.

The X-ray of her leg revealed a hairline crack in the fibula, the small bone on the outside of the calf. The technician said this type of injury is similar to a stress fracture and is often seen in sports injuries, resulting from a sharp hit or twisting motion. Thankfully, the tibia—the main weight-bearing bone—appeared to be okay. She had no spinal damage that they could discern, but her back was definitely sprained. They cautioned that it would be at least several weeks before she would be able to walk normally.

She cried intermittently with yelps of pain as the very young cute doctor with a British accent cleaned the scrapes that virtually covered her arms and back, that is everywhere her revealing sundress did not. Then he applied an antibacterial salve mixed with a topical anesthetic. After he fitted her with a removable walking cast and gave instructions about removing it only to shower, he was ready to send us on our way.

"Wait a minute," I said to him outside the examining room, "we're on a cruise ship docked up at the Callao seaport—what is that, about 30 miles north of here? How will we transport her, and how will the ship's doctors know about her condition and everything you have done here?"

He studied me for a minute and then looked—with a comical double-take—at Rachael standing beside me. I think it was the first time he'd noticed us since he began concentrating on Connie. His face broke into a wide grin. "How do you do, I am Doctor Albert Atkinson." He shook both our hands enthusiastically. "I see your problem," he said thoughtfully. "It so happens I am off duty in another half an hour's time. If you want, I'll take the three of you back to Callao in my motor . . . well, with your friend in the back with her leg elevated it will be a little crowded . . . if you wouldn't mind too much. I'll be pleased to speak with the ship's physician when we get there." As an afterthought, he added, "I live a short distance up the coast from here in any event."

I could have kissed him and almost did. Then we saw his car. It was the oddest and ugliest vehicle I had ever seen—an old Italian Fiat Multipla, he explained. There were three individual seats across the front and back of the boxy compact, an interior design I had never seen before. Thankfully, the pain medication he had given Connie made her very drowsy, so she was compliant with the plan and dozed during most of the forty-minute trip.

The drive north along the coast was interesting, to say the least, with Rachael jammed in next to "Al" and me against the door. I was very nervous about Connie's condition, but the doctor didn't seem too concerned. He was more interested in pointing out local attractions, especially when the route took us up Avenue Costanera along the gorgeous beachfront. Al pretty much ignored me and blatantly flirted with Rachael the entire time. It was beyond a doubt the most bizarre car ride I'd ever had.

When we arrived at the pier, Al kept his word and spoke to one of the ship's doctors for about 10 minutes. He also handed over the X-ray of her leg and a record of everything they had done for her. He insisted on exchanging email addresses with Rachael and drove away just as the medical staff pushed Connie onto the ship in a wheelchair.

The ship's doctor kept her for observation for about two hours. After giving her a heating pad for her back and a prescription muscle relaxer and some Percocet—oxycodone with Tylenol, he suggested some exercises she could start doing for her back in about three days. There wasn't much else he could do for her. His advice was to stay put and order food from room service for a couple of days while her back muscles straightened themselves out. Then they wheeled her to the cabin.

Mick, Tom, and Wendy joined Rachael and me at The Whale's Tail, and I was eating as if I had just been rescued from a desert island. When I tried to explain to them what happened in those few seconds with Connie on top of the temple, I found it very difficult to convey what I felt at the time. Finally, I pushed away from the table and started to get up. "I guess I realize I'm going to have to go to talk with her. I can't reconcile what she did, but it happened so fast that I'm having doubts about my own perceptions."

Mick got up too and reached for my hand. He brought it up to his chest in both of his. "Let me go with you, Darcy. I know from past experience that your perceptions are excellent, and if she did try to hurt you, maybe you shouldn't go to see her alone." He stared into my eyes and spoke in a voice that was gentle and empathetic.

I couldn't believe it. This was my Mick, the Mick I fell in love with. *Where have you been?* "Thanks, thank you so much, I would like your support. Let's wait until later this evening after she has a chance to rest, and then we'll check to see how she is. If it seems appropriate, I'll ask for her version."

I looked down at Rachael and saw her puzzled expression. It occurred to me that she had rarely seen Mick interact with me in this calm supportive manner. Then Tom caught my eye, and there was no mistaking his expression. He knew exactly how I was feeling.

49

After knocking twice, I was about to suggest we leave, assuming Connie was asleep or couldn't get to the door. "We should have called before we came down here," I said to Mick. Just then, the door opened slowly, and Connie peered out.

She was obviously groggy. I noted she had changed into a loose-fitting long-sleeved white cotton dress. "I was just lying down watching TV," she said with a sad head shake and a deep sigh.

I tried to smile at her even though my heart wasn't in it. "Can we come in and talk to you?" I asked.

I thought she was going to send us away, but after a few seconds, she opened the door wider and hobbled back to the bed. After she painfully settled herself against several pillows including arranging one under her cast, she turned the sound down with the remote and just stared at me.

After a couple of awkward seconds, I said, "I'm so sorry about your injuries. Connie, I would never want anything to happen like this, and it is really upsetting. I'm just glad you weren't hurt worse. You easily could have been with that terrible fall."

"This feels bad enough, but I guess you're right." She didn't say anything else, and Mick shifted uneasily. We were still standing beside the bed since she had not invited us to sit, and we couldn't anyway because the small sofa was covered with clothes.

Finally, I decided to go ahead with what I wanted to say. "Can you please tell me what you think happened up there?" Just before she answered, I could swear I saw a fleeting glimpse of that expression I saw up on the temple. Before I could think much about it, she looked pensively at Mick for a moment and then started talking to me for the first time since her fall.

"I don't know what happened. One second I was standing there worrying that you were going to fall over backward. The next thing I knew, I was tumbling down the embankment." She looked away as if to collect her thoughts and then turned back to me.

She quickly averted her eyes again, and in a voice barely above a whisper, she added, "I sort of felt like I was pulled or pushed over the side."

Mick stiffened beside me, and I reached down to grab his hand. I didn't want him to make this worse than it already was. "OK Connie, I have to tell you that I had a similar feeling. Why were you standing so close behind me when I turned around? That is what got me off balance to begin with."

"I don't really know what you mean. You're my friend, and I just walked up to see what you were looking at. I didn't know I wasn't supposed to get close to you." She sounded defensive, and couldn't maintain eye contact with me for long. Then she gave Mick a peculiar look.

Oh God, could I have misread Connie's interest in me? Is she a lesbian and wanted to get up close and personal, believing I would reciprocate? There had never been any other sign of that possibility, so I tried to dismiss the notion. I said how sorry I was again and told her to call me if she needed anything at all. Mick mumbled his condolences, and we left her alone.

"Darcy," Mick started as soon as we walked away from her door. "There is something funny about her. I can't quite explain it, but she seemed sort of . . . furtive, for lack of a better word. I didn't like her insinuating that you pushed her. And that is what she did because there was nobody else around, right?"

"I guess so, but I'm feeling partly responsible now. She doesn't seem to be angry with me, and maybe she's as confused as I am about the . . . accident."

I didn't intend for Mick to know that I was now feeling almost entirely responsible for her injuries. She startled me when I turned around, and I over-reacted. She obviously tried to grab me so I wouldn't fall, and I must have misread her expression. It was probably just a look of panic. I could tell that Mick would not agree with this assessment, and I just did not want to ruin the good feeling I was having about him right then.

We decided to go to our cabin and rest for a little while before meeting Tom and Wendy in the Center Bar. Once we were settled on the bed, for lack of other comfortable seating, Mick looked at me with a sort of sheepish expression. His dark wavy bangs had grown a little longer than usual, and it made him look even sexier. "Can we talk for a few minutes about all the things that have been happening on this trip?"

"Sure Mick, have you learned something new?"

"Well, sort of. Nothing has come from the interviews yet, and security hasn't identified the rapist or the person who damaged the desalination equipment. By the way, I assume you did not have any encounter with the two stalker guys in Lima."

"Oh, I'd almost forgotten. No, if they were around, they were careful. I didn't see them. I haven't seen them on the ship either, and I have been looking."

"Well, here's the new wrinkle in this whole thing."

I listened, dumbfounded, as Mick explained about Grant Murray's relationship with Brooks and what he had revealed about Paul. When he was finished, he looked intensely into my eyes—something that brought a rush of pleasant memories. "So, can you come up with any reason why Brooks would be involved with Murray and possibly acting as an informant?"

"None whatsoever, but we know that Brooks manipulated Paul's booking on the cruise last year, as he did mine, and they go back a lot of years in the Vegas community. But I'm scared about what Paul might be planning to do to you and Tom. Have the two of you come up with any ideas . . . and could any of the stuff that happened on the ship be related to Paul?"

"No, actually we can't think of a way Paul could do anything to us here on the ship, and the other things that happened don't have anything directly to do with us, anyway."

We were sitting side by side with our backs against the pillows and Mick suddenly drew up his knees and shifted his weight around so that his body was facing me. "I wish things could be the way they used to be between us," he said sadly. "I know it's mostly my fault, but I don't really understand it."

Mick was clearly worried—and had seemed so for a while—but this was different. More personal in that he seemed to be trying to ask me something without stating it. "Mick, part of the problem is that we used to be able to talk about everything, and now so much of what you think and feel is hidden. I just don't know how to help you, or us for that matter."

He leaned in and kissed me in a very intimate way that he seldom did anymore. His hand was on my breast before I knew it, that old feeling of heat and excitement flowed down my body, and I was instantly damp with anticipation. "Oh Mick, that feels so good." I should have stopped there. "Why can't we be really together and intimate like we were before?"

He tilted his head back and looked into my eyes again, this time with an odd questioning look that I didn't understand. "Really? Are you sure that's what you want, or do you have some other plan?"

What the hell is he talking about? I suddenly pictured myself hanging on a yoyo string waiting for the next bounce. "Yes, of course, that is how I feel, but now the mood is spoiled . . . again, isn't it Mick?"

50

Day 12 – at sea

Lori Bannon happily primped in front of the mirror in her stateroom, as she prepared to join her parents for dinner. She felt so grateful to them for allowing her to have her own cabin. Finally, at age eighteen, after many happy family cruises, they had decided she was responsible enough. Maybe they're looking forward to their privacy as well, she thought, as she fiddled with a large gold hoop earring that wasn't quite hanging straight. This thought would never have occurred to her before she matured. Now she could sort of see her parents as ordinary people. She was feeling quite grown up as she sipped the half glass of white wine her dad—in the cabin next door—said she could have.

"You're not really breaking any laws," he told her, "since we're in international waters."

She picked up her brush and pulled it through her long brunette hair a few strokes, then stepped back to assess her appearance. The skimpy halter top and shorts were sexy, particularly on her voluptuous frame, but all the girls on the ship dressed the same way. Completing her makeup with a second layer of mascara, she thought about how wonderful this trip had become, and about Nate McAlpine, a young man from Scotland, who was also traveling with his parents. She almost blushed at herself as she thought about the hot and heavy sex they had already shared in her cabin—since he did not have one of his own. One night when his folks were attending the late-night ballroom dance venue, he dared to stay with her until 2:00 a.m. She was full of excitement over these risky exhilarating encounters. *But if Dad finds out, I'll be dead!*

Nate was so adorable, and his accent alone was enough to make her hot. She peered closely at herself as she applied the bright pink bubblegum-flavored lipstick that Nate loved. Lori jumped at a sharp knock on her door but knew it was only her mom and dad coming to pick her up.

As she turned the handle and began to pull the door open, a strange man wearing a ski mask forced it all the way back to the wall with his arm and rushed in, slamming it behind him. She hadn't had time to react, and when she finally gasped with alarm, a large sweaty hand quickly covered her mouth. She began to retch even as she tried to scream.

Before she knew what was happening, the big man had thrown her down on the bed. As he climbed on top of her, without thinking, she reached up and tried to pull his mask off. In the instant before he slapped her face really hard, causing her teeth to crunch together and her eyes to sting, she glimpsed a portion of the bottom of his face and ear. Panic-stricken, she kicked as hard as she could, bucking to throw him off her, but he was too strong. Only after he hit her face several times—the final blow with a closed fist—and showed her a long kitchen knife, did she manage to calm down.

She was on the edge of consciousness when he pulled down her shorts and forced himself into her. *Daddy, please help me!* Lori had never been hit in her entire life, much less physically attacked, and suddenly she did not feel at all grown up. The man was hurting her so badly, and it was nothing like her pleasant and exciting encounters with Nate. Her last thought as she slipped away, was that she would never have sex with Nate or anyone else ever again.

51

Day 13 – at sea

Last evening, virtually everyone on the ship heard the *alpha alpha alpha* alert, which is the sea-faring code for a medical emergency. Wild speculation among the passengers was short-lived because the few crew members who knew what had happened began to spill their information to other crew members and passengers. There had been another rape.

Tom met with Roger Ramirez to get the facts and was disheartened to learn that they still had no clue about the perpetrator. All Roger knew was that they appeared to have a serial rapist on board, even though the descriptions given by the two women did not precisely match. Tom did not think this was unusual since severe trauma often interferes with the formation of accurate memories.

Lori reported her impression of a powerful fair-skinned man with light-colored hair in his thirties or forties. He wore a white T-shirt and jeans, and she had no way of telling whether the man was a passenger or a crew member. The girl was so traumatized that the ship's doctor heavily sedated her and her parents were, according to Roger, *ready to tear the ship apart.*

Captain Dolf also called a meeting with Tom and Mick to discuss the attacks. His distress was evident, as he asked them if there was anything else his security team could be doing. "They are completely capable, you know? It is only this has never happened before, ya? We have called the FBI in Miami, our first port in States, but we are on our own until then."

Tom assured the captain that Roger was doing everything possible, but short of interviewing all four thousand people on board, the only thing they could do is collect all the physical evidence possible. He tactfully suggested that since the ship did not have formal rape kits onboard, the medical staff should be sure to carefully examine the victim and obtain any forensic evidence that exists.

"Ya, I know this. I will talk with Doctor Friesen and make sure they do all they can."

Tom and Mick looked at each other and were both thinking the same thing. Chances are the girl has already showered, and any potential DNA from the rapist is probably gone. Before they left the meeting, Tom told the captain that he should keep in mind that they were neither FBI nor police and could not formally help with the investigation, other than to give an opinion if asked. Aside from that, all the events on this cruise would become part of their findings in the GAO/FBI investigation.

As they headed back to their interview room, Mick could not suppress his conflicting thoughts. While these crimes were horrendous, they would add a lot of weight to his eventual results—which would help to convince the Congress to act on drafting legislation regarding cruise ship crime.

52

Later that evening, Joe stretched out on his bed and smiled as he sipped almost continuously from his bottle, like a suckling infant drawing sustenance and comfort. Everyone on board was talking about the rapes, and no one had any idea who was responsible . . . all the women are scared shitless, he thought, as they should be. He reached down and vigorously rubbed his crotch with his open palm, squirming with arousal and anticipation. It's about time, he thought, as he got up and started to assemble his tools.

As usual, he was drunk and only partially in control of his actions. That didn't matter though. He would carry out his plan in its entirety or die trying. As he had hoped, almost everyone on the ship was rattled, and World of Seas managers had to know by now that they were in deep doo-doo. He hauled himself up and prepared for his mission. Swaying a little, he struggled to buckle the heavy tool belt around his waist and had to put his hand against the wall to keep from falling over. The sea must be getting a little rough, he told himself.

He had decided to step up his efforts to cause chaos aboard the ship. Since his attempt to put the desalination process out of commission had not entirely worked as he intended, he decided to use his engineering knowledge to try to sabotage the ship's electrical system.

Around 3:00 a.m., he made his way to the crew stairway dressed in his maintenance coveralls, feeling confident and secure. So far, none of the maintenance workers or any other crew members had taken notice of him. Even so, he would be relieved to complete this job and not have to push his luck any farther. He noticed that security had stepped up surveillance at different times of the day, and he would scrub his mission if he found any guards posted in the area where he was heading.

Down in the belly of the ship, he gazed at the power plant comprised of six cylindrical generators that produce electricity to run everything on the ship. He blinked a few times and shook his head, trying to improve his vision. The setup looked somewhat like the schematics he had studied online. The main switchboard, enclosed in metal, draws power from the generators to supply electricity for all other uses. Most of the energy is shuttled to motors attached to the three engine propellers, with air conditioning the next most significant usage.

This sophisticated electrical control system includes an automated monitoring function to collect data from all the various components. From these data, information is recorded about all system characteristics, primarily to plan maintenance schedules. A line of computer monitors displays multiple settings based on automated analyses. Much of the time there is no need for a person to watch the monitors, particularly at this hour. As he looked around, he was elated to see that no one was there. He would have to hurry just the same.

Joe unzipped his coveralls down to the waist and wiped sweat from his forehead while continuing to assess his surroundings. An engine room tends to be hot and must be continuously cooled to ensure that overheating does not cause an electrical fire hazard—the most feared of all shipboard catastrophes. Typically, if a short circuit develops in onboard wiring, the high current flows can generate enough heat to melt cables, which can burst into flames.

The ship had over-current protection, including circuit breakers, intended to prevent a fire hazard. The breakers act as a major switch in case of an emergency, and this was fine with Joe because he had no desire to be onboard a ship that was in flames. He merely wanted to disrupt the electrical system enough to cause a power outage lasting several days.

He also knew about the emergency power supply or standby system that would supply power to essential uses in the case of a primary power failure. However, essential use did not include significant lighting in cabin areas or any more than the most basic kitchen requirements.

Blearily, Joe walked over to stand next to one of the waist-high, tube-shaped engine cylinders and peered across the room at the five large white air conditioning units. Although he had seen pictures of similar engine room setups, he was not fully prepared for the size of the machinery and the level of automation.

He was so deep in concentration that he almost failed to hear the voices. He jumped behind the engine and squatted down just as three crew members entered the plant. Joe watched, fascinated, as they made a circuit of the equipment and glanced at each monitor, laughing and joking. Their inspection lasted for five minutes, and then they left the way they had come. He let another two minutes pass before slipping out of his hiding place. He leaned against the engine cowling, while he treated himself to a gulp from his flask.

His gaze fell on the ballast tanks, which hold an amount of water to compensate for the weight of fuel as it is used. It is the weight of the fuel and the massive engines in the bottom of the ship that keep it upright—like a child's weighted punching-bag toy that always rights itself. Joe marveled over the engineering of this bottom heavy design. It is the reason the ship can roll forty-five degrees and right itself with only twenty-nine feet of hull beneath the surface.

He knew there was nothing he could do to the ballast tanks themselves and also realized that the entire electrical system was completely computerized . . . beyond his level of knowledge. His only options were to disrupt the electronic connections between the engines and the computers and destroy the breaker switches. He retrieved his flask once again and drank deeply while looking around one more time. *Yes, that is what I'll do.*

The main breaker that could be used to shut down the entire system in an emergency was on the wall in plain view. Lesser breakers were locked in a box with a heavy chain and padlock. These switches could be rendered useless using the small hammer he'd brought along, but first, he would have to get into the box. He pulled a set of bolt cutters from his belt and began to cut the lock. Unfortunately, he was so drunk by this time that his attempts to break open the box bordered on the pathetic.

Just as he was beginning to make a little headway cutting through the lock, he fell sideways against a generator and slid to the floor. This falling down on the job was becoming a pattern. He lay sprawled on the floor, suddenly thinking about what he would do next, utterly unaware that he'd been unconscious for about twenty minutes. He'd been awakened by the sound of more voices.

Two members of the crew who were scheduled to perform some routine maintenance entered the engine room and rapidly approached his position. As soon as they saw Joe, they assumed he was a fellow crew member who had too much to drink. "What do we have here?" one of them said, elbowing his companion. "Hey, you there, you'd better get back to your bunk before a supervisor sees you."

They were reluctant to get a co-worker into trouble—more than likely fired, but as they moved on to the other end of the room, one of the men glanced to the side and was stunned to see the partially severed lock and bolt cutters on the floor below it. "Hey, what the hell is going on?" He looked over at Joe and stepped up his pace.

Joe had staggered to his feet and was already starting to run out of the engine room. Still unsteady and bleary-eyed, he just managed to make it around a corner and directly into a women's restroom. The two crew members were close behind but did not see where Joe went and ran on past. In the bathroom, he quickly pulled off the coveralls and stuffed them in the trash can. After peeking out the door to make sure no one was around, he left and ran up the steps to the first location where passengers were allowed—deck 2. It required every bit of his remaining will power to stay calm and upright while mingling with the regular passengers. Meanwhile, the two crew members went directly to security to report what they had seen, including an excellent description of their saboteur.

53

Day 14 - Arica, Chile

When we arrived at Arica, the northernmost city in Chile—just twelve miles from Peru—Mick finally offered to go ashore with me. I couldn't believe it, and part of me just wanted to enjoy a day with him. The other part thought this would be an excellent opportunity to talk to him about what was going on—or not—between us. As it happened, most of our conversation centered on the astounding events of this cruise—the rapes, the sabotage attempts, and the two stalkers we assumed were still lurking somewhere.

We went ashore alone because Connie was still confined to her room, and I told Rachael that I wanted to spend some time alone with Mick. The situation with Connie was so scary and troubling that on top of everything else, I was just trying not to think about it.

Roger called Tom earlier in the morning to tell him about the report by the two maintenance workers regarding a strange crew member they believed was trying to damage the ship's electrical system. As we proceeded to the gangway to leave the ship, I asked Mick about it. "So, you were saying earlier that they now have a description of the guy. Wouldn't they know who he is if he's a crew member?"

"According to Roger, the guys who saw him said he was an older guy with longish blond hair, wearing maintenance coveralls, but neither of them recognized him. They also said he appeared to be drunk. They can pull up pictures of all the crew members to see if they can find him. I think they're working on that right now."

I thought about that for a minute. "The only link that makes sense among the different events is that one of the guys who bothered Rachael and me had sort of long blond hair, and didn't you say the girl who was raped said her attacker was blond? So I guess the logical question now is could one man be responsible for everything?"

"There is still nothing to make me believe that other than speculation linking strange events together."

All of it seemed unbelievable to us, and I guess talking about these odd occurrences, in light of the terrible violence we experienced on the first cruise, somehow made us feel closer—for a little while, at least.

The local atmosphere was warm and sunny, and so far our moods seemed to match the weather. I thought Mick looked terrific in his dark blue shorts and white linen shirt left open to mid-chest. He seemed more relaxed for a change, and I was trying for the same feeling as I soaked in the local ambiance and history.

We were strolling down the pier in the shadow of Morro de Arica, the black rock formation that towers over the harbor. The site is a national monument of the fighting there between Chile and Peru during the Pacific War of 1880. Actually, this port has been a center for shipping silver and other valuable ores, and mining supplies since 1570, but is now a developing beach resort.

The first inhabitants of the area, as early as 6000 BC, are thought to have been the Chinchorros, primarily fishermen, but best known for their practice of mummification using a different process than the Egyptians and predating them by many centuries. Many cultures called this area home, including the Tihuanaco and Inca Empire. The Mapuche tribe later dominated, and they managed to fight off both the Incas and the Spaniards until finally falling to the Spanish Crown in 1550.

A lot of fighting ensued into the 1800s between the Chileans and Spaniards, and between Chilean loyalists and separatists. After Chile won its freedom from Spain, an Irish-born patriot, Bernardo O'Higgins, became the country's first president. Political and economic turmoil continued into modern times, but in 1973 General Augusto Pinochet toppled the socialist government. From then on, especially with the final return to democracy in 1990, the political climate became increasingly stable. Chile has now transformed itself into a market economy.

At the end of the pier, we exited the gate onto Maximo Lira, a two-lane road that parallels the shore. A traffic cop stationed at the intersection for the safety of tourists directed us across to an outdoor market. It extended from the sidewalk up a short pedestrian street to the pink and white San Marcos Cathedral. This famous landmark was initially designed by Gustave Eiffel—of Eiffel Tower fame—but was rebuilt in 1888 following a devastating earthquake.

We spent a pleasant hour slowly perusing the artisans' booths and checking out the local textile and pottery goods. I couldn't help myself; I had to buy a cute pair of thong-type sandals with a colorful traditional alpaca design on the straps. Then after a quick self-tour of the lovely cathedral, we headed north down Francisco Bolognesi to the little city center.

After wandering around the shopping area a while, we walked about a block down a side street and found a nearly empty restaurant obviously catering to locals. No one appeared to speak English, so after drinking another pisco sour while Mick sipped a Corona, I decided this would be as good a time as any to talk to him.

I reached across the table and put my hand lightly on top of his. "Mick, I want to tell you something serious about us. It's very sad, but even though this is pleasant, I just don't think I can go on the way we are. Mick's smile faded, and he slowly withdrew his hand from under mine. He leaned back and turned his head to gaze up the street with a look that was difficult to interpret.

"OK, I see you have already disengaged. See, this is what I mean, Mick. So what I want to say is I think I'm going to move out of our cabin and in with Rachael for the rest of the cruise." His eyes slowly panned back, and he nodded his head in apparent agreement. This was going to be easier than I thought, but that made it all the sadder.

"That makes sense," he said softly. "You don't have to pretend anymore. I'm sure you will be surprised to know that I'm very aware of your plan to get back together with Brooks."

This was the last thing I expected to hear, and it caught me so off guard that I just sat there staring at him in disbelief. For some reason, his words made me very angry in a way I had not even felt up to that point. I practically yelled at him, drawing stares from the few other patrons. "Are you trying to read my mind now? Well, you're not very good at it. I'm not doing any such thing, but why would you even think that?" By the time I finished, I was spluttering with frustration.

"Come on Darcy, Sydney told me all about it. Brooks told her he was getting back together with you."

I almost fell off my rickety little chair. "What? Why would she say such a ridiculous thing? That makes no sense, and why are you talking to Sydney anyway?"

"She called me just to give me a heads up, so I wouldn't keep making a fool of myself while you're playing your little game with Brooks and me at the same time."

His words hit hard—virtually knocking the wind out of me—and it took a minute to process what he had said. Sidney was my best friend, and after all that had happened with us, I couldn't fathom why she would do such a thing. Something about this seemed familiar, and it nagged at the corner of my mind, but I couldn't bring it forward. The spooky feeling I had was that somehow the secret thoughts I was having about Brooks had become common knowledge.

"That is unbelievable," I finally managed. "I have to tell you, Mick, your lack of interest in me has made me wonder about Brooks. He does seem to have changed, and he certainly has made it clear that he wants a second chance with me . . ."

"I knew it had to be true, I just didn't want to believe you could be so deceitful."

"Oh, for God's sake. As I was saying, I have not mentioned this to anyone and definitely have not decided to go back to him . . . Mick, don't you know how much I love you?"

He drew his long legs up under the table and looked across at me with a forlorn expression. I thought he suddenly looked about ten years older. Finally, he shook his head and looked away at the traffic. It struck me then how despondent he was. He seemed to be on the verge of tears.

"Mick, look at me! I asked you a question. Don't you know how much I love you?"

His moist eyes slowly raised to meet mine. "I love you more than I thought I would ever love anyone after my wife died. I want to believe you, but I know I have been in a bad mood for a long time, and I wouldn't blame you or be surprised if you were done with me."

"A bad mood . . . is that what you call it? Mick, you've been a whole different person, and I am just plain tired of it if you can't tell me what is wrong. That is why I'm offering to move out of the cabin. At least maybe you'll be able to stay in your bed and get some sleep if I'm not there." I heard the note of sarcasm, but I didn't care.

There had to be an explanation for the apparent link between Brooks and Sidney and her call to Mick. I tried to imagine the two of them together in order to form some sort of theory. Then in a flash, as they say, I recalled Sidney's secretive comments to me about having found someone she wanted to have a romantic relationship with. *Oh! That has to be it.* She only mentioned it that one time outside the FBI building in Vegas, but my gut told me I was right.

But if she and Brooks are dating, which is bizarre to begin with, why would Brooks tell her that he and I are getting back together? And if they are not dating, what possible motive would she have to call Mick and inform on me?

My whirling thoughts were making me dizzy, but I looked into Mick's eyes, and they began to slow.

"Mick, you are my best friend, or at least I want you to be. Right now I have an idea, and you are the only one I can share it with. What Sidney told you is completely bogus, but I have a strong suspicion that she is in a relationship with Brooks, or wants to be. That has to have something to do with what she told you."

Mick seemed to slump in his chair with a release of tension. "I have to admit, at first I wondered if maybe something like that was going on, too. I just couldn't figure out why she would be so concerned about me, you know? I thought maybe she had some other agenda."

After the little heart-to-heart, I figured our situation might improve, since Mick had been agonizing over his conversation with Sidney for quite a while. When he asked me to reconsider moving out of the cabin and promised once again to try to overcome his depression or whatever it was, I just couldn't refuse. *OK, I only hope this isn't sending me back to first base.*

54

It was way too soon to try something else under the circumstances, but Joe's behavior had slipped out of his control. Since nothing had happened since he was cagey enough to escape last night's adventure, he figured he was home free. He'd been staggering around the ship drinking and seething about his lost daughter and had just settled down at a corner table near one of the cocktail lounges. He was also struggling with his almost uncontrollable urges and was having difficulty focusing on the task he had decided to undertake this evening. It would be his last opportunity to carry out the mission, and he must not fail again.

This time, he had come up with a simple yet ingenious plan. This one was well within his ability to pull off as long as there were no crew members around to see what he was doing. Frustrated beyond measure, Joe could not keep his mind from slipping back to his liaisons with the prostitutes he routinely visited back home. He also couldn't help his preoccupation with the unholy women running all over the ship wearing next to nothing. Taking one of them now would be easy. All he had to do was find a secluded spot, and one would come along eventually.

Squinting across the room, he wondered if he was seeing double. He shook his head and ran his beefy hand across his eyes. Two of the most gorgeous women he had ever seen were sitting at the bar, and they looked almost exactly alike, right down to sundresses in similar shades of yellow. Maybe they're twins, he thought, but as he watched he realized that one was older than the other—sisters then, or even mother and daughter.

A few minutes later, he got up from his table, paused a few seconds to get his balance, and slowly approached the bar. He casually slipped onto a stool, leaving three empty ones between himself and the women. The bartender immediately threw down a cocktail napkin and asked for his drink order.

"Jim Beam please, my man." Joe smiled genially. He knew he cut a fine figure for an older guy and would be able to impress these bimbos, especially the older one. They were even more attractive up close, and though they did not look in his direction, he was aroused just thinking about getting lost in all that long blonde hair.

Manuel did not like the looks of this guy. He was obviously already drunk and certainly didn't need another. He especially did not like the way he was looking at Darcy and Rachael. The guy was even giving him the creeps, and that was saying a lot. He poured the man's drink and took his card key to charge it to his room.

Suddenly, Manuel was leaning over the bar very close to Darcy's face, and she frowned as she turned away from Rachael to look at him. "What is it Manuel, is something wrong?"

"Please, Darcy, you must be careful when you leave here. I don't like the way that passenger looks." He tilted his head slightly toward Joe. "And I don't like the way he looks at the two of you. I can tell he is very drunk, and I won't serve him a second drink."

"Thanks, Manuel. We'll be careful. We haven't been straying too far from your bar and our cabins in the evening unless Mick is with us because of the rapes."

"That is very good. I myself am feeling suspicious of men I see around the ship, like this one." He gave the same head tilt.

After he backed away, Darcy looked at Rachael and then they both turned to look at the man sitting down the bar from them. Darcy turned away quickly and caught her breath. "Rachael," she whispered, "I see what Manuel is saying. That guy is sort of blond although it looks like a dye job and he wouldn't be that bad looking if he weren't so weathered. But there is something off about him. Holy shit! He could even be the one they almost caught in the engine room, but no . . . this guy is a passenger."

"Let's go see if Mick and Tom and Wendy want to do something with us. I feel uncomfortable staying here now."

As soon as Darcy finished her martini, they slid off their stools and started to leave. They were about to walk away when Joe decided to make his move.

"Hello, young ladies. Isn't it a nice evening? Won't you allow me to buy you another drink?" He smiled, showing them his whole set of not-so-white teeth.

Manuel immediately moved up to stand in front of Joe. The guy was slurring so badly he was almost comical. Darcy looked at Joe and shuddered then glanced at Manuel and nodded. She took Rachael's hand and answered with her back turned as they walked away. "Thanks, but we have had enough for one night."

Joe swiveled back toward the bar and drained his glass. "Fucking bitches think they're too good for me," he said half under his breath, but not quiet enough. Manuel heard him loud and clear.

55

Somehow Joe managed to pace himself somewhat until midnight when he weaved his way to the cabin and changed into his replacement uniform from the laundry. That ass-hole bartender refused to serve him any more drinks, which had caused him to make several trips to the cabin during the evening just to keep his buzz on. Screw him and all the rest of them. Tomorrow they'll be singing a different tune, he said to himself, chuckling.

Beginning around half past midnight, Joe started a circuit of the sixty-five sliding glass doors leading to the outside decks, beginning with those in areas he believed would be deserted at that time of night. At each door, he pulled the wires out of the assembly on the electronic sensor that caused the doors to open when a person stepped in front of the beam. Then for good measure, he unscrewed the cover on the small black box attached to the wall near the ceiling that housed the electrical components and made his own adjustments using a screwdriver and small hammer.

He planned to take the entire night to disable every door leading outside the ship. He had hit on this brilliant scheme when he noticed how upset passengers became when they happened onto just one door that was out of order. He could not wait to see the reaction in the morning when none of the doors worked. He laughed heartily just at the thought of the panic that would ensue.

Shortly before 3:00 a.m., Joe was thinking that he might have to make a detour to his cabin to refill his flask. So far, he had disabled twenty doors but was disappointed that it was taking so long. He thought the work was improving with each door, though, and once he quenched his thirst, he would move a lot faster.

The monotonous nature of the task was wearing on him, and he had become increasingly careless and noisy. He was standing on a small folding stool, which he had stolen from an outside deck earlier in the day after the worker who was using it walked away. The door he was currently working on was far aft on the starboard side of deck 5—the right side if you are facing forward. Consequently, the outside deck extended forward almost the entire length of the ship. Unfortunately, Joe did not realize that there were heavily used crew stairways at the back of the ship on nearly every deck, and one of them was just around the corner from his current position.

Oblivious to his surroundings, he tried to concentrate on lining up his screwdriver in one hand to hit the end of it with his hammer to smash the tiny components in the electrical box. He did not hear the man and woman who happened to be security guards chatting as they came out of the stairwell and into the foyer next to him.

The woman turned toward Joe and initially smiled at a fellow crew member having to work in the middle of the night. Immediately, she had a feeling that something did not look right about this worker. She wasn't sure if it was his disheveled looks—the weird stringy blond hair and his age—or the realization that a sliding door was not something the maintenance staff had to repair during the night. She turned to her partner and saw his perplexed expression. He was already moving toward the corner where Joe was teetering on his stool with an exaggerated expression of concentration.

"Hey, come down from there for a minute." The guard's deep voice startled Joe and caused him to sway from side to side a couple of times before falling backward with his arms flailing helplessly in the air. He wasn't hurt from the short fall, and the two officers dragged him up and propped him against the wall. He could barely stand.

They had planned merely to verify what he was doing, but as soon as they realized how intoxicated he was, they hauled him into the nearby elevator and descended to deck 4. Joe tried to resist, telling himself that all he had to do was shake them off and run like hell again. His attempt was somewhat feeble, and it was only a bit of a struggle for the two officers to get him to the security office at the center of the ship. By the time they arrived, Joe had pretty much exhausted all attempts at escape. They seated him in a small room, and the female officer stood outside the door until Roger Ramirez arrived.

56

Day 15– at sea

Tom approached his old office behind the guest relations counter and thought again about how odd this reunion had become. With each new problem on the ship, Roger had become a little less defensive and more cooperative. He might be a bit arrogant but he's not stupid, Tom thought. He would be smart to learn from what happened to me under somewhat similar circumstances. The captain was becoming increasingly angry and bewildered by the crimes on this sailing, and of course, it was all coming down on Roger.

Tom had long-ago recovered from the shock of being fired by World of Seas, and he was able to take a somewhat philosophical view of the current situation. Now, he was just intrigued by Roger's call asking him to come to his office as soon as possible. He assumed there had been some sort of break in either the sabotage or rape cases . . . at least he hoped there had not been another incident. Roger's door was open, so he knocked lightly on the doorframe.

"Come on in and sit down, Tom. Do you want some coffee?" Coffee pots, like irons and other such appliances, were forbidden in individual rooms and offices due to the fire hazard, but no one had ever complained about the pot that was almost always turned on in security.

"Sure, I'll have a cup. It's early." Tom wondered why Roger was suddenly acting so friendly towards him. "You must have found out something significant."

Roger opened his desk drawer and pulled out a mug. He wiped it out with a tissue and reached over to his side credenza to pour a cup for Tom.

"Just black is fine," Tom said, reaching across the desk for it.

Roger sat back and sipped his coffee. "I have something all right, and it will be of great interest to you. In fact, I believe this will blow you . . . and your travel companions . . . away."

"You have my attention, what is it?" If he hadn't known better, he would have thought that the ordinarily all-business security chief was actually relishing imparting whatever news he had.

"The saboteur struck again last night . . ." Roger began.

"Oh, crap. I was hoping there had not been another problem."

". . . But we caught him." Roger raised his left hand to prevent Tom from speaking, while he picked up a piece of paper with his right. He turned the paper over to reveal a photo and handed it to Tom. "Do you know him?"

Tom glanced at Roger questioningly, then looked closely at the rough and rather sad-looking blond man in the picture wearing the white coveralls of the maintenance crew. Tom realized that Roger thought perhaps he would know who the man was so he tried to search his memory but came up empty. He handed the photo back. "No, I'm afraid I don't recognize him, should I?"

"His name is Joe Moretti." Roger watched Tom's face, waiting for the name to sink in and after about twenty seconds he was rewarded with a dawning look of amazement.

"Oh my God, Suzanne's father? Are you saying Suzanne Moretti's father also works for the cruise line?"

Roger laughed. "Not quite, he's a passenger who's been posing as a maintenance worker to pull off his twisted revenge plot against World of Seas. He's obviously a drunk, and he's such a mess I'm surprised he got away with as much as he did. Last night a couple of our officers caught him at it again and easily subdued him. But first, he managed to put a bunch of the sliding doors leading to the outside decks out of commission."

Tom's thoughts were swirling around the previous cruise and their horrendous encounters with Suzanne, and her subsequent incarceration and death in Valparaiso. "This is unbelievable. Have you been able to find out what he was thinking or what he thought he could get out of damaging the ship?"

"It seems that World of Seas informed him of Suzanne's mental breakdown and murderous rampage in a phone call and then he received a letter from the state department telling him she had died. He said he could not stand having his beautiful, intelligent, and deeply religious daughter accused of murdering several people and attempting to murder several more. Those were his exact words."

"That sounds rough—the way it was done."

"I'm reading between the lines here, but I think he was already unstable, at least an alcoholic, and Suzanne's behavior and death pushed him over the edge.

As I said before, he just wanted vengeance—revenge against the cruise line. He blames World of Seas. In his mind, they killed her."

"Where is he? I'd really like to talk with him."

"I thought you might, and I don't have any problem with that. The only thing left hanging is whether Moretti committed the rapes. He sort of matches the description given by the second victim, and he does seem a little perverted, but he categorically denies that he did it. We're holding him here in the brig."

"How ironic, since that is where we kept Suzanne that last night on the way to Valparaiso."

Tom left to see if Mick wanted to join him when he talked with Moretti. When he met up with Mick, Darcy, and Rachael in the buffet, he couldn't help but add a dramatic flair as he explained this astounding development.

Mick and Darcy stared across the table at him in disbelief. "Do you mean that Suzanne's hatred for us has followed us onto this cruise as well?" Darcy asked.

Tom shook his head. "No, I would not look at it that way. Joe Moretti doesn't know any of us. All he was told was that Suzanne went crazy and killed people. I'm sure he must have seen some of the media coverage over the past year, but he was probably only focused on the cruise line that hired his daughter and then allowed her to die. I have a feeling we are going to find that he has not been sane or sober for the past year."

Finally Mick found his voice. Suzanne had nearly killed him, and he'd tried to put her out of his mind for the past year. "I assume you are right, Tom, that we don't have anything to do with him being on the ship. I'm trying to get my head around this and can only speculate that the Moretti's are one crazy family . . . and yes, I guess I'd like to come with you to talk to him."

"OK, Mick. By the way, I think Roger hopes Joe Moretti committed the rapes as well, so everything will be tied up neatly for him. He said Joe admits to the sabotage efforts but absolutely denies the rapes, so I think he is hoping we can somehow get him to admit to them."

Tom and Mick left the restaurant as soon as they finished eating. Back at security, Roger escorted them to the small holding room and left them alone with Joe. After six hours to get sober, Joe's initially docile demeanor had deteriorated to belligerence. He was hung over and much in need of a drink.

After ten minutes of trying to talk rationally to him, Mick and Tom knew they would not get any more information than Roger had. Tom phrased the question of the rapes directly. "Look, Joe, you might as well admit to the whole thing because you know it will come out. I don't know if you are aware of this, but there is some DNA evidence from the rapist that will eventually be analyzed. Did you rape those two women, Joe?"

"Get out of here and leave me alone." He was shouting. "I didn't rape nobody, not that I couldn't have easy enough. You can't get me for that." He put his face into his hands and leaned forward. "Fuck ya'all. I'm in trouble for wanting to avenge my poor Suzanne when any father would'a done the same." He rubbed his face and licked his cracked lips. Then he seemed to remember that Tom and Mick were still there. He turned his eyes to the ceiling. "She should'a listened to me and Jesus and stayed a home, then she' wouldn'ta been punished and none of this would'a happened," he mumbled into his palms."

He lowered his hands and stared across at them with wet bloodshot eyes. Suddenly, he brought his fist down on the table with a crash. "I need a god damned drink," he shouted.

As they left security and proceeded to their interview room, Mick asked Tom what he thought about Joe. "It seems logical that he could be the rapist, but you know, I don't think he had it together enough to do it, how about you?"

"I agree, but Roger wants to believe he did, so I don't think he will put much more effort into finding someone else. I hope he doesn't end up regretting that decision."

Part Three

The Rapist et al.

57

Day 16 – Valparaiso, Chile

Another sea day passed, and Mick did seem to have flipped into his trying-harder mode. We had made love a couple of times, and he clearly enjoyed it, as did I. Something about our bodies and the way we fit together seemed to approach perfection. We climaxed together, which was normal for us . . . when we had sex at all, that is. Still, the passion and intimacy we had known before just wasn't quite there.

Since clearing the air about Brooks, things were a little better between us. I was still confused and angry about Sydney having called Mick. I wanted to call her but thought I should wait until I wasn't quite so upset.

After about ten days on the cruise, I finally came to the end of my tolerance for Brooks's phone calls and told him not to call me anymore. I appeased him by saying that I would talk with him at length after the cruise. Now I knew I would never consider going back to him, and I intended to make that crystal clear.

We were all hoping that Joe Moretti was in fact the rapist and that all the problems on board had been resolved. Of course, we still had no idea who the two stalkers were, but nothing else had happened, and I was ready to chalk it up to some kind of misunderstanding. I was feeling the same way about Connie. She was feeling a little better and behaving normally, even spending time up on deck with us. It seemed she was of the same mind . . . we should just try to put the *accident* behind us and move on. Today, Rachael stayed on board with her, and they planned to sunbathe at the pool, taking advantage of the quiet atmosphere while most people would be off the ship.

I could tell that Mick was frustrated over the lack of results from the interviews. I wanted to help him, so last night while we were making love, I exacted a promise from him to go ashore with me and take a break from the work. Anyway, Tom was going ashore with Wendy, but said he intended to do some work while in Valparaiso as well.

They had quite the little romance going, and she had all but moved into his cabin. She joined us for dinner almost every night and seemed really to care for Tom. We hardly saw her during the day, and I assumed she had found activities she liked to participate in. I had decided to be happy for him, but there was something about her that still troubled me. I didn't know what it was, so I kept telling myself I was way too protective of him because he once seemed emotionally vulnerable.

This morning, when the ship pulled up to the dock, we all stood at the railing up on deck 14 to enjoy the view of the port area. One of the fascinating things about "Valpo" are the old funicular lifts—boxes on rails—that climb the steep hillside, transporting people to the upper parts of the city. We watched them move slowly up and down the ancient-looking tracks. The array of brightly colored buildings and beautiful old mansions sitting here and there on the hillside among the more modern structures were also interesting and beautiful in their own way.

Valparaiso, lying mid-way along the Chilean coast, was founded in 1536 by Juan de Saavedra, who named it for his hometown in Spain. The port became a critical trading and naval base for the Spanish armada. Numerous foreigners invaded the city and it was finally destroyed by Sir Frances Drake in 1578. Following Chilean independence, Valparaiso became an important stopover for ships traveling around Cape Horn. Things changed dramatically in 1906 when an earthquake demolished much of the port. Then the opening of the Panama Canal greatly decreased its popularity because ships had a much faster way to travel from the Pacific to the Atlantic.

This city held extremely unpleasant memories for us because it is where the previous cruise ended and Mick almost died. So at the suggestion of some fellow passengers we decided to spend the morning in Vina del Mar, sometimes called Chile's Riviera. It is a premier beach resort about five miles north of Valparaiso and has been an exclusive residential area for Chile's wealthy citizens since the 1870s. Even the President of Chile has a summer home there.

Vina certainly lived up to its reputation. It was lovely and there was no poverty evident in this community. We spent a very pleasant morning wandering around the outdoor flea market and near-by gardens surrounding an old colonial mansion. We were standing on the sidewalk admiring the landmark flower clock made entirely of blooms that someone constantly refreshes and changes with the seasons, while we tried to decide where to go next.

I looked around at the luxury apartments and condos lining the busy street and caught my breath when I saw those same two men standing on the sidewalk. They were directly across the street and did not seem to have noticed us. Grabbing Mick's arm, I whispered, "don't turn around too quickly, but I'm sure those same two guys are over there on the other side of the street."

"You're kidding," he said, as he slowly turned to look in the direction I was indicating. "Where?"

"They were right there. Sort of between those parked cars. Now I don't see them."

He looked at me dubiously. "Oh no, please don't act like I'm making them up. They were there. I'm not saying they are following us, but I know it was them."

"OK, I believe you." Mick put his hands on my shoulders. "But they don't seem to be posing much of a threat. They have to be from our ship, but they're probably just tourists like us, only a little strange."

I wasn't at all sure about that and kept looking over my shoulder for the rest of the day. I couldn't help but wonder if the reason they were keeping a low profile was because Mick was with me instead of Rachael.

58

Tom and Wendy were in the old part of the port city, within sight of the *Sea Nymph* looming in her slip alongside the pier. Tom's reason for going ashore in addition to spending time with Wendy was to visit the justice center at Plaza Sotomayor. At the back of the square, he stood on the steps leading to the massive grey building, the impressive colonial Intendencía—the government house—which is now the seat of the Admiralty. Looking across the square, he assessed the nondescript building housing the police department. He simply could not come back to Valparaiso without trying to talk with the police chief about what happened to Suzanne during her incarceration in his jail. He'd never quite accepted the explanation about her suicide.

Wendy agreed to wander around the neighborhood and wait while Tom conducted his business. He called ahead and fully expected Chief Thomás Contreras to be expecting him. He was not disappointed and was pleasantly surprised to find that Contreras spoke passable English. Unfortunately, a common language did not help Tom obtain the information he was seeking. He asked many pointed questions about Suzanne's last days, particularly probing to see what, if anything, she had said. He especially hoped she revealed something about her relationship with Paul that would be incriminating.

Contreras seemed evasive and obviously was not enjoying the conversation. "She did not speak much at all and said nothing of importance. She only would say sometimes, when will someone come for me? But no one came . . . and then she . . . was gone," he said sadly." In parting, the chief added somberly, "You talked me into taking her off your hands, Mr. Smythe, but this did not turn out well for me. I did not like such a terrible thing as her suicide to happen in my jail."

Tom left with a bad feeling about Chief Contreras's explanations, which lacked specificity, to say the least. He hoped that speaking in person would make a difference, but it was essentially the same as when he talked to him by phone almost a year ago. Contreras was not willing to provide details about what happened to Suzanne. More important was the question of why the chief was so guarded. It could only mean that he needed to protect himself. This was a dead end and a closed door. The U.S. government was not inclined to delve into the matter any further. They accepted her death as a suicide, but Tom still wasn't convinced. Finally, he decided he'd done all he could concerning Suzanne and would try to stop worrying about it.

He arrived at their prearranged meeting place and looked around for Wendy. "You look deep in thought. Was your meeting successful?" she said from behind him.

He turned and gave her a hug. "Not really, but it doesn't matter. Let's look around a little before we go back to the ship."

They held hands and walked, checking out the small businesses crammed together, lining every street. Some tourists were about, but the farther they walked, the more they encountered mostly local families who appeared to be running errands, walking dogs, or accompanying children. They stopped at Plaza Cochrane to take pictures. It was a medium-sized round of concrete at Serrano and Clave streets with a defunct fountain in the center. Like much of the old port area, it seemed somewhat neglected with dog feces and trash strewn underfoot. This was undoubtedly indicative of most areas that did not specialize in tourism.

As they began to backtrack toward the pier, Wendy noticed a sign pointing to *Escalera de la Muerta*. "Look, Tom, there are those famous stairs of death. I read that thirty-two people have died falling down them, but most of them were drunk. Let's go check it out."

They rounded a corner, and there were the cement stairs leading to the upper part of the city. At the base of the steps, they stood looking up. "These are crazy steep and how many steps are there?" Tom asked, staring up to the barely discernable top.

"I think there are about 160, but there are a few landings on the way up so you can stop and rest if need be. Let's climb them." Wendy had already started up the steps next to the wall. "The only thing is I hate to touch this railing. It has to be filthy."

"I agree. Can you climb all the way up without holding on?"

"I don't see why not, and I have to say I'm glad I wore athletic shoes rather than sandals."

The metal pipe railing was on the left side of the steps against a high wall colorfully painted with pink, blue, green, and yellow birds, fish, and other indistinguishable images—graffiti that could pass for art. All around the city they had noticed many walls and buildings covered with this type of embellishment. "I wonder who paints all these murals and pictures?" Tom asked rhetorically as he started up the steps behind Wendy, walking close to the wall, but not touching anything.

The steps were extraordinarily shallow and steep, and Tom's feet hung over them by several inches. Soon enough he realized he was stumbling a little every couple of steps because his toe would catch the leading edge. Trying to watch his feet at the same time, he looked over to see how Wendy was doing.

She was climbing to his right on the opposite side of the eight-foot-wide stairs. Next to her was a lower wall that appeared to be part of a home with overhanging trees. No one else was braving the stairs, and Tom was beginning to wonder why he was doing it. *Is it to impress Wendy?*

On the way up, Wendy stopped several times to catch her breath. She considered herself to be in pretty good condition, but her thighs were burning from the exertion. Preoccupied with the effort of putting one foot up in front of the other without tripping, her mind was taking its own independent course.

She thought about why she came on the cruise to begin with. She'd been avoiding facing her personal situation ever since meeting Tom. Now she considered how this situation was putting her in an untenable position. She had to take responsibility for what was happening to her life, but it was so hard. All she could really feel was the same overwhelming terror she endured for several months before deciding to take the trip.

Once they made it to the top, it took a minute for them to catch their breath. After looking around the non-descript Plazuela Electurio Remirez, they walked across the street to the only thing that appeared to be of any interest. In front of a small house was a stone monument with a man's picture embossed on a black plaque. The date of April 6, 1944 was the only legible piece of information. The rest was in Spanish and worn away from the weather. "Could he be the one who built the stairs?" Tom wondered out loud.

When Wendy did not reply he turned around and saw that she was already heading back to the top of the steps. He called to her, "do you want to go back down right away? We could walk around up here a little if you want." He looked around him at the quiet residential street and realized there didn't seem to be much to see.

"I'm ready to go back down. It was just something to say we did—climbing the stairs of death," she answered, waving her arm toward the steps. Approaching the top and starting to descend, she moved over to the right next to the painted wall and slowed her pace so that Tom could pass her.

He stepped carefully knowing that she was right behind him, which made him a little self-conscious. He did not want to appear too tentative, but the steps seemed even steeper looking at them from the top down. It appeared to be a never-ending almost vertical trek. *Why was it necessary to make these stairs so steep?* He caught himself thinking about the thirty-two people who had not made it down alive and immediately pushed the thought away.

Wendy moved a little to the left and positioned herself directly behind Tom who was just two steps below her. He really is a nice guy, she thought, looking at the back of his head. *If only things could be different.* Could Tom help her—save her from the mess she was in? *Could we make a life together?* Then she thought about her work and her associates and the terrible mistakes she had already made; the box she was in with no way out.

Without much in the way of forethought, she raised her arms and bent them at the elbows turning her palms toward Tom's back. When she glanced behind her, she lost her balance and almost fell over on top of him. As she caught herself, the butterflies already in residence in her gut took flight, and she was momentarily afraid she might vomit. She breathed deeply and let out all the air as she peered around Tom to see if anyone was on their way up. She closed her mind to everything except that moment and flexed her shoulders.

Tom was carefully descending but began to experience slight vertigo from watching his feet. He gasped and quickly stepped about two feet to the right grabbing for the railing. He was thinking that germs on his hands would be infinitely better than taking a header down the steps. Tom's movement startled Wendy and brought her out of her trance-like state. She grabbed for Tom to stop her forward momentum and screamed as she came up with only a handful of his T-shirt. She stumbled down two steps, and Tom grabbed her around the waist, quickly pulling her down to a sitting position beside him.

"That was close, Wendy! You almost went down head first." Tom was breathing hard and trying to suppress his panic. Holy shit, it really had been close, and he didn't really know why—it had happened so quickly.

Wendy sat with her head down between her knees and tried to get control of herself. After about a minute she looked up with tears in her eyes. "Thank you, Tom. You saved my life. They stood up, and he held her against his chest for a minute.

"It's OK now. A close call, but everything is OK." Clearly, he was trying to convince himself. He realized he was shaking all over and wondered if that little shock had taken a year or two off his life. "Hold on to the railing now—to hell with the germs."

As she carefully put one foot in front of the other with her hand on the railing and Tom on the other side silently holding her elbow and watching his feet, she wondered if this could be fate. Maybe she was meant to be with Tom after all. But by the time they reached the bottom she realized it was just carelessness or a random event. *It just means I am back to plan A.*

59

Day 17 – at sea

Everyone, particularly Mick, had avoided talking about the fact that Suzanne had made her move against them on the previous cruise after they sailed through the Chilean Fjords and approached Valparaiso from the south. That time, they traveled from East to West around Cape Horn—in the opposite direction as now. On shore, Mick had enjoyed the port with little discomfort, but now they were back on the ship moving away from the port again heading south toward the beautiful but frigid fjords.

Early in the morning, he awoke actually screaming, and Darcy tried to comfort him. At first, he seemed glad that she was there, but as soon as he calmed down and realized he'd been dreaming he quickly pushed her away.

At least he was in their bed and not up on the deck. His primary feeling was embarrassment over his lack of control, which seemed like a terrible weakness. "I wish I knew what I was dreaming that caused me to be so upset," he said. "I never can remember." Those were about the last civil words he spoke. Just when they both hoped things were getting better, Mick was aware that he was becoming increasingly anxious, and told himself and Darcy that it would be better if she left him alone.

After breakfast, she still suggested the two of them go for a short walk around the outside deck to get some air. Mick reluctantly agreed, but as soon as they went outside, he reacted poorly. She felt him tense up and begin to shake. He would not walk anywhere near the railing.

"OK, Mick. Let's just go back inside. This seems like torture for you. How do you feel?"

He veered toward the door and rushed in ahead of her. "Haven't I told you repeatedly that I don't know what is wrong, so I don't know how I feel, do you get that, Darcy?" His irritable tone left no doubt that something was seriously wrong. Mick was increasingly emotionally distant, and his level of hostility was worse than ever . . . so soon after he seemed to be getting better. Ever since returning to the ship in Valparaiso he had irrationally blamed her for everything that went wrong, even minor unimportant things. Once they were back inside, rather than upset him even more, she decided to stay away from him for the rest of the day and evening.

During their interviews, he was irritable with Tom as well and gave up on the work at about two-thirty. "We're not getting anywhere, and I'm not feeling good, so I'm going to lie down," he said, as he rushed out the door. Tom didn't mind having to work alone, but he had been watching Mick closely because the deterioration in his mood was undeniable and worrisome. He considered going after Mick to try to talk to him but decided to wait until later in the evening.

When Tom finished up for the day, he went to find Darcy. She was sitting with Rachael at a table in the Center Bar. "Hi, you two. How was your day?" He pulled up a chair and sat down between them smiling broadly at Rachael.

"We're OK, but Tom, we're anxious about Mick . . . well, at least I am," Darcy said. "Have you noticed anything about his mood?"

Rachael looked over at Darcy with a sad expression. "I do care about Mick. I just don't like to see you so unhappy."

Tom patted Rachael's hand. "I sure have noticed. Mick is really struggling, and I'm more worried about him than ever. In fact, I'm going to find him and try to stick close tonight whether he wants me to or not."

"Thanks, Tom. That makes me feel better. I just wish I could understand what the hell is wrong with him after all this time. Whatever is going on with him, it's definitely getting worse."

"I know, and I have some ideas about that, but let me try to talk with him tonight and then I'll tell you what I'm thinking."

60

Why haven't I been able to see things this clearly before? This is obviously where it was supposed to end. That must be why I haven't been able to move on and I guess it's why I'm back here. Darcy doesn't need the grief I'm causing her and I can't stand feeling like this any longer. Losing Beth and mom and dad, and then being hurt so badly—I'll never be back to normal, not after this much time has passed. I'm supposed to be all healed and everyone I care about now is fine . . . no, they're not fine so long as I'm pulling them down with me.

Mick's thoughts seemed clear one moment and disjointed the next. Every ounce of his mental strength had been required just to walk up to the railing. Now he was peering down at the waves rushing by two stories below. He'd been standing on deck 4 for at least fifteen minutes trying to think about what he should do to take care of his problems. Without much thought, he gripped the top of the railing and placed one foot up on the middle horizontal bar. He took in his surroundings and realized this was the exact spot where he watched in horror as Suzanne attacked Sydney and Darcy and then turned her weapon on him.

He looked down at his hands clenched around the wood cap of the top rail and studied the gate that was built into the railing below. He knew its purpose was to allow passengers to exit into lifeboats in case of an emergency. For the first time since the attack, he had a clear memory of the gate swinging open and the panic and desperation he experienced at that moment. Darcy and Sidney down on the deck, then the knife . . . *stop! You've resisted thinking about it for a year. Don't start now. The helplessness, fear . . . the anger . . . too much. It's too much.*

Mick tried to block out everything else as he stared down into the black water and thought about how numbingly cold it must be. Again, without consciously thinking about it he shifted his weight to the foot that was resting on the horizontal bar and slowly raised his other foot off the deck. He straightened his arms and hoisted himself up so that the top rail lay against his thighs. His arms were shaking with tension and fear. But he held his position and contemplated the strangely inviting unseen depths as the waves smacked against the hull. He could almost feel the weight and endlessness of the deep quiet that seemed to be closing around him—and the cold. He'd never before experienced such utter loneliness. *Of course, it's because I am alone . . . completely alone . . . even when Darcy is with me.*

He couldn't see the water any longer because tears had filled his eyes and were spilling—flowing actually—down his face and soaking his shirt. He could hear sobbing, but it sounded as if it were far off, maybe even in another dimension or a childhood memory.

Slowly, he brought one leg up and over the rail so that he was straddling it, still grasping with both hands. His knuckles were white and painful and his entire body quaked from the cold wind blowing up from the water.

"No Mick, this is not happening, not on my watch." The calm matter-of-fact voice seemed to come from the same dimension as the sobbing, which he could barely hear over the sound of the wind. He knew he'd imagined that someone spoke to him.

He leaned farther out and was suddenly sure of what he was supposed to do. He relaxed the leg muscles that held him to the railing and bent further over the water. As he floated out on his forward momentum, suddenly two strong hands grabbed his shoulders and pulled him toward the deck. He lost his precarious balance and fell backwards into Tom's arms. They both tumbled onto the deck, and Tom grunted as Mick landed partly on top of him.

Mick lay on his back with his arm covering his eyes, and cried. Tom knelt beside him. "It's all right now. Trust me, Buddy, you really will be OK." He had a fleeting thought that this was the second time in as many days that he had pulled someone from the brink of disaster.

Tom had looked for Mick all over the ship and then on a hunch, went to the one place that held so much significance for all of them. As soon as he saw Mick up on railing, he knew his mounting suspicions were correct. Under normal circumstances Mick did not have a self-destructive personality. He really was ill, and knowing about the things Mick had endured over the past few years, Tom believed that he was suffering from Posttraumatic Stress Disorder. That was the only reasonable explanation for his depressed behavior and acute anxiety . . . and now this.

Tom knew something about PTSD from his time as a cop on the streets of L.A, where he witnessed grown victims of child abuse, accident and crime victims, veterans of the gulf wars, and even first responders, struggle with the symptoms. He'd wondered about this for several weeks, but hadn't felt confident enough to say anything about it.

One of the characteristics of Mick's condition was the very fact that he could not discuss what happened here on the deck a year ago. But once Darcy shared a little of her worry about Mick's loss of intimacy and his irritability with her, Tom knew his amateur diagnosis had to be correct.

He knew well that anyone exposed to trauma could develop this disorder. Mick surely had suffered more than enough with the double shock of his own near death and his helplessness watching Suzanne attack Darcy while being powerless to help her. All this while still recovering from the deaths of his wife and parents.

Mick sat up on the deck. He was exhausted and ashamed, and just wanted to get away to be by himself. But strangely, he also felt calm in a way he hadn't experienced for a very long time. He looked at Tom and shook his head. "I don't think I'll be OK. Look how fucked up I am. Crying like a damn baby and . . . he looked at the railing where he had almost ended his life. . . . and what did I almost do, Tom?"

Tom put his arm around Mick and helped him up. "Come on, let's go inside and warm up. You're freezing. They entered the ship and Tom steered Mick into the elevator and up to Tom's cabin. Once inside, he poured Mick a glass of water and convinced him to take a shower. He handed him a pair of his own shorts and a T-shirt to put on, and then called room service. Twenty minutes later they were sipping hot coffee and eating burgers and fries. Mick was relaxing on the sofa while Tom sat on the edge of the bed.

"Feeling any better?"

"I guess so, but I'm obviously completely losing it." Mick looked imploringly at Tom. "What the hell is wrong with me?"

"PTSD, I believe. Ever hear of it?"

"Of course, but that's what combat veterans get."

"No Mick. It is what many people who suffer all kinds of trauma get."

Mick thought about that as he dipped his French fry into a pile of catsup and stuffed it in his mouth. "OK, maybe. I can't believe what I've put Darcy through and how tough it has been just to function." He looked up at Tom and hesitated.

"What is it? It will be good if you get it all out. You haven't really talked to anyone about how you feel about the attack as far as I know."

"How do people get over this?"

"Here is what I know. The disorder is an emotional numbing that can cause a person to lose interest in things or feel detached from life. They might have disturbing dreams and trouble controlling their feelings, like anger and hostility or . . . like being suicidal. Does anything sound familiar?"

"I guess." He was studying the carpet.

"Anyway, there is medication, but I think the most important thing is to get some help—therapy. Even without that, I know it will help you to talk about what you're feeling, just to the extent you feel comfortable. But Mick, please, you have to get professional help when you get home. This is something you can get over and I hope you will start by explaining it to Darcy. You are lucky to have a woman who is so smart and kind. She will help you."

They finished their meal, and Mick got up to leave. He put out his hand, and Tom shook it. "I think I'll owe you a debt of gratitude for life. I'm really scared to think what I would have done if you hadn't come along when you did."

"I'm just glad I was there. It goes without saying that the best way you can repay me is to accept help and do whatever it takes to get well."

61

Mick took his time returning to the cabin. He was trying to sort out his thoughts about what had happened and especially Tom's advice. One thing was right for sure. He needed to have a serious conversation with Darcy. *If I'd been better able to look inside myself before and open up a little, maybe we wouldn't have lost what we had.* He had to admit though that nothing had changed that much . . .

he was still anxious and confused. Maybe if he didn't put it off too long, he could at least explain about tonight. With a leap of faith, he assumed Tom was right in saying that she would be able to help.

Darcy was wondering if Mick was all right and whether Tom had been able to talk with him when the lock turned, and the door slowly opened. She was sitting on the bed propped against pillows watching an animated movie about penguins . . . well, not actually engaged in it, just nervously passing the time.

She watched Mick come through the door and instantly knew something was wrong. He was wearing different clothes and carrying his shirt and pants. "Are those Tom's clothes?" she asked nervously. "What happened, did you fall in the pool?"

"I took a shower." Mick threw his dirty clothes on the couch and stood at the foot of the bed looking at her sadly. She turned off the TV, swung her legs over the side and went to stand in front of him. Her arms went around his waist, and she looked up, trying to read something from his eyes. "I'm so sorry, Mick, I can see that something else has happened and I'm afraid to hear what it is."

Mick kissed her cheek and slipped out of her hold. He pushed the pile of clothes aside and sat on the couch looking up at her. "Yes, it's something important and telling you about it might be the most difficult thing I've ever done."

She sank down beside him and took his hand in both of hers. "I have a feeling this is personal . . . Not another problem on the ship. Do you want a glass of wine or something?"

"No, I'm fine. I ate dinner with Tom." Mick's face suddenly became a window through which his pain and anxiety were obvious, and she was stunned at the sudden transparency. She knew at that moment that he'd been hiding something behind a mask of sorts that had now been stripped away. She squeezed his hand tighter. "I'm listening Mick. I love you, and whatever you have to tell me, it will be all right."

As Mick described as best he could the events of the evening, and Tom's suggestions about PTSD, Darcy's thoughts crystallized into one clear judgment: *I should have put this together myself because it seems so obvious now. Tom has to be right, and now we'll find a way to help him.*

When his story was finished, he withdrew his hand and sat back staring straight ahead at the bathroom door because there was nothing else to look at. She remained quiet, and in a little while, he turned to her. "Darcy, I thought about killing myself tonight. It is so hard to admit to something that I would never have believed I would be capable of. If Tom had not been there, I think there is a real possibility I would have done it."

"I don't know that you really would have, but I'm glad he was there. What he told you sounds right to me too. What are you going to do?"

"I don't think there is any way around it. I need to get some professional help when we get home." He put his arms around her and gently kissed her lips. Then he slid his hands down her arms and held her hands as he leaned away from her. "I hope you will still be with me in DC because I really need you, Darcy."

"You're a brilliant guy, Mick, and that is one of the things I love so much about you. You're not the type to let this get the best of you now that you know what is going on." She was feeling a closeness with him that transcended their romantic involvement. "You remember what I told you about my life twenty years ago?"

"You mean with Brooks and Rachael. Of course, I remember."

"Well, you know how my therapist pulled me away from the brink and taught me how to compartmentalize my memories so I could function normally. Maybe this is sort of similar. Anyway, of course, I'll be with you as long as you need me . . . and Mick, I am right here when you do really need and want me."

62

Day 18 – Chilean Fiords

No matter what else was going on with this cruise and plenty was, I had no doubt that Mick would eventually get better and we would get our lives back on track. Hopefully, I wasn't being too optimistic. I was relieved to finally have a plausible answer. That is what I was thinking when I sought out Tom to thank him for saving Mick for me. Between all the events of a year ago and now this, I knew there was a bond of friendship and affection between the three of us that would never be lost.

While Mick and Tom continued with their work, the ship continued down the coast of Chile and through the fjords, which were still as startlingly beautiful and forbidding as when we last saw them. Rachael, Connie, and I had spent a few hours outside taking pictures and marveling over the scenery and the sparking white-blue glaciers spilling down the craggy hills into the narrow channel. Of course, being a tour guide Connie had been here before, but I enjoyed watching Rachael's first reaction to this stark untouched landscape so close to *the end of the world*.

As if I wasn't trying to juggle multiple plates already, later that afternoon I finally came to understand all about Connie Sinclair. Rachael had returned to her cabin to take a nap while Connie and I visited the Center Bar. Unfortunately, I consumed one too many martinis and was definitely tipsy. Maybe I let myself go due to my feeling of relief now that we had a handle on Mick's situation—I don't know—but it didn't help me cope with what happened next.

I was still blaming myself for Connie's accident—that is what I convinced myself it had been. While Manuel busied himself preparing for his evening crowd, I found myself apologizing to her once again. "I'm so glad you're getting better so quickly," I offered. "It's amazing to me how well you can walk around in that cast. Does it still hurt?"

"No, actually I can't really feel it, but I have to keep it on most of the time for a few weeks. My back is actually worse than my leg, but that's getting better every day too. I'm fine, Darcy, don't worry yourself about me. What do you say we go out and get some fresh air before it gets completely dark?"

I was game for just about anything at that point. "Sure, why not. I could use a little exercise since I haven't been to the gym in a couple of days."

We zipped up our jackets and headed out to the deck. The sky presented a fantastic display of gold, peach, pink, and pearly grey stratus clouds above the horizon, where the sun was beginning its quick descent behind the mountains. We were heading toward the wider Strait of Magellan and would soon be out of the narrow channel. I was feeling good, partly from the vodka, as we strolled around the deck with our hands in our pockets breathing in the crisp totally unpolluted air.

As we approached the bow, the sun disappeared and left us instantly enveloped in darkness. We came around the corner next to a short set of steps that led up to a large deck with curved sides that followed the contour of the front of the ship. From there you could look over the railing at the bow cutting through the water five or six stories below.

Mick and I had come out to this quiet spot many nights during our cruises just because there were no lights, not many people went there in the dark, and it provided an incredible view of the night sky. I'd never been here when it was so cold though.

I followed Connie up the steps and forward to the front of the ship. She leaned over the railing and just stayed there watching the ocean. I stepped up beside her just as she turned around and I followed her line of sight up to the bridge, extending across the length of the ship about five decks above us. The windows across the front were well lit, but by that time, she and I were standing in almost complete darkness below.

The clouds had entirely covered the moon, and I shivered in the chilly air as she turned back to me. From less than two feet away there was just enough light for me to see something that made me freeze in place and not from the cold—she was looking at me with the same hateful expression I had seen at the top of the temple.

"What is it, Connie? Why are you looking at me that way?" I instinctively started backing away from the railing, but she snaked her hand out in a flash and grabbed my arm . . . just like last time.

"Don't go. I want to share something with you."

The words were normal, but her tone and facial expression were anything but. She was threatening me in a way that I could not understand, but I knew I had to get away from her. My impression at the temple had been correct—Connie wanted to do me harm, and I couldn't imagine why. "I am going," I said, as I turned away from her and tried to shrug her hand off my arm.

She slammed her body against me smashing my stomach against the railing. With both hands, she pushed on my back so that I was leaning out over the water and hissed into my ear, "How dare you try to steal him away from me. You had your chance, and now he is mine. Do you understand?"

"Who?" I gasped, trying to twist around to face her. "Who are you talking about? Do you mean Mick? That's crazy." Poor choice of words, I realized a little too late. Rage completely overtook any reason she still possessed. She exhaled a loud shrill scream, and despite her back injury and the cast on her leg, she bent down and pushed her shoulder under my butt. She was going to try to lift me up and over the railing. I knew there was no way this was going to work for her.

With that thought, I felt my feet rise off the deck. Shit! I pushed back with all my strength and twisted around to face her. She wasn't nearly strong or agile enough to launch me over the side, but she had given it a good try. She screamed again and lashed out with her fists, pummeling me and then grabbing a fistful of my hair.

I caught her hand and tried to pry her fingers loose, but she kneed me in the stomach and scratched at my face with her free hand, while she pulled me down to the deck by my hair. Before I knew what was happening, we were rolling around punching and scratching each other—it was a real cat fight.

"You can't have him, you selfish bitch," she screamed. You had your chance twenty years ago. Now Brooks is mine. How dare you!"

"What? Stop it, Connie, let me go," I shouted. "Stop fighting. I don't want Brooks. Why would you think that? Calm down and talk to me."

I thought a huge patch of hair was being ripped out of my scalp. Her grip did not loosen, and my head was pounding. I stopped pulling away and held her free hand while pressing my body against hers. She struggled to free herself, but I was the clear winner in the stamina department. She finally ran out of steam and relaxed. So did I and we both rolled over onto our hands and knees. I quickly stood up and staggered to the railing. Leaning with my back against it, I bent over with my hands on my knees gulping huge breaths of frigid air that stung all the way down, while I kept one eye on her.

As she struggled to get to her feet, I went to stand over her. "Connie, how do you know Brooks and why the hell would you think I want him? Haven't you seen me with Mick during this whole cruise?"

"Don't try to pretend that you're not leading Brooks on . . ." She was panting and could barely speak. "I know you're making him think you two can get back together, just like he has always hoped."

I was astounded, and then I thought about Sydney. Sadly, there were only two names on my short list of female friends, and what, they are both in a relationship with my ex-husband? I couldn't even think straight, and my head hurt like hell. At least Connie seemed calmer now, and I relaxed a little. "Connie, who are you really and how do you know Brooks?"

She stared at me and shook her head, then shifted around to a sitting position and wrapped her arms around her knees. "I really am a travel agent, but I don't live in Colorado," she admitted. "I work for Brooks, and he and I have had a relationship for several years until you came back into his life."

She had raised her voice again, and I was surprised that she could sustain the anger after the effort she had expended on our fight. How could I not have seen a connection between her being on the ship with a travel group and Brooks's company also having groups on board? Am I that desperate for friends? I looked back down and realized that she was crying. Tears rolled down her face as she looked up at me with a pitiful expression.

"You can have your pick of men, why do you have to go after Brooks?"

"I swear to you, Connie, I am not doing that. I don't care what Brooks has said to you . . . and others, I am happy with Mick and will never go back to my ex-husband." I couldn't believe she had tried to kill me over Brooks—she was so confused and enraged that surely she hadn't consciously thought to get rid of me permanently.

"You attacked me, and could easily have killed me in Lima. I ought to report you to security, and I have to think about that, but I know you need help and I'll definitely tell Brooks about this. Now, why don't you go back to your cabin and stay the hell away from me for the rest of the cruise."

She stood up and glared at me for a few seconds, but apparently changed her mind about whatever she was about to say. She turned and slowly limped away into the night.

63

Day 19 – Strait of Magellan

We were cutting across the bottom of the continent, on a more sheltered route than the one we would eventually take around the tip. The Strait of Magellan would take us to Ushuaia, Argentina, which is advertised as the southern-most town in the world. Meanwhile, the weather was reasonably mild, but the air was still crisp. I had agonized over whether I should even tell Mick and Rachael about Connie. I hated to add to Mick's problems, but in the end, I decided to sit down with both of them, and Tom, to explain the whole thing. We all met for an early breakfast that turned out to be a little more interesting than the three of them expected.

I held Mick's hand the whole time I was explaining what had happened and was prepared to react if I felt him becoming agitated. He was shocked and angry as were Rachael and Tom, but he handled it surprisingly well.

Tom suggested we tell Roger Ramirez about her and I knew we should, but I had already decided not to get her involved with security, which would mean all of us eventually being detained by the FBI.

He frowned when I explained how I felt. "I don't agree with that decision, Darcy. He ought to be told he has yet another unbalanced passenger on board. Besides, you are playing this down. She really could have killed you at those ruins . . . you would not have been as lucky as she was if you had fallen over backward."

"I know that Tom, but I don't think she will be a threat to me anymore and certainly is not a threat to other passengers. She obviously needs some help. What I am going to do, however, is call Brooks to tell him exactly what his employee did and why. Look, Tom, if you feel you need to do something about this, you could call him as well."

Rachael had been quiet so far, but now she spoke up. "Surely, Brooks had no idea about how Connie felt. He would never have intentionally hurt someone that way." She looked hesitantly at Mick and then naturally decided to say what she was thinking. "I think Connie was right about Brooks wanting to get back with you, Darcy. That doesn't surprise me at all. But he couldn't be involved with anyone else. Connie had to have imagined his interest in her."

Yeah, and did Sidney imagine it too? Mick looked at me, and I knew he was thinking the same thing. Of course, this was wishful thinking on my girl's part. She just could not see Brooks in anything but a positive light.

Tom suggested I let him make the first call to Brooks so there would be no question about what had happened. They were friends, after all, and Tom had a lot of credibility with him. After Brooks helped Tom with the scorpion attack, they became even closer. I knew this situation was upsetting him, so I agreed with his plan, and he left to make the call.

Then Mick did something characteristic of the man I first fell in love with. He turned to Rachael who was sitting next to him and offered his charming award-winning smile. "I want to tell you something, Rachael, but first I want to apologize for anything I've done to hurt you or make you sad. I know it's hard to understand, but I've been having kind of a hard time, and I let it affect the way I treated you. I'm very sorry."

Before she could respond, he explained briefly—leaving out the details of his meltdown out on the deck—what he now believed was happening to him. As she listened intently, I saw her attitude toward him shifting. When he was finished, she put her hand on his arm and said, "I knew something had to be wrong, and Darcy tried to tell me that, but I guess I have some issues myself."

Mick figured she was talking about her desire to see her biological parents back together and he let it pass. "I want you to know that Darcy and I want to do everything we can to help you succeed with whatever you want to do, just like your mom and dad do." He picked up her hand and shifted in his seat to face her directly. "We really hope you will come to DC and go to school. We can get a bigger place, or we'll get you an apartment if you would rather be on your own. I just want you to know that I want us to be a family . . . Well, a second family for you of course. And, you'll be able to visit Brooks whenever you want, OK?"

I knew Rachael well enough to understand that this was precisely the right thing for him to say. She would be charmed by him just as I was, and similar to what Brooks had managed as well. Besides, Mick was offering her the proverbial cake to eat and to keep.

64

"Hi Tom, how's it going?" Brooks shifted the phone and glanced at the bedside clock. A wave of apprehension flowed through him. "It's awful early here. Is everything OK?"

"Actually no, it isn't. I have to tell you something disturbing that has been going on for a while here, but we just figured it out last night."

"Rachael? Is there a problem with Rachael?" he croaked.

"No, it isn't Rachael. She's fine.

Brooks sat up on the edge of the bed and ran his fingers through his hair, trying to prepare himself to hear something terrible because he knew his friend would not have called him, essentially in the middle of the night, otherwise. "Go ahead, Tom."

Brooks could not believe what Tom was saying about his employee and friend. They often flirted, and she was very attentive whenever they were together. But he had no idea she was so enamored with him and especially that she could have done something like this—trying to hurt Darcy—because of him. He had truly believed they were on the same page during the times he asked her out for cocktails or dinner and then took her back to his apartment for casual sex. There was no insinuation that their relationship was anything more than that. He didn't know that Connie had been injured . . . She didn't even mention it during phone calls about their onboard travel group.

When Tom finished explaining everything, Brooks asked "Is she really all right, Tom? Is Darcy really OK? I can't believe any of this."

"She's fine, but Connie was under the impression that you and Darcy were getting back together and apparently that is what set her off so you can imagine how Darcy feels."

"I swear there is no reason for Connie to have assumed she and I had anything serious going on. Oh man, I'll have to take some action against her—I hope nothing formal though . . . she must be crazy."

Brooks thought about the times he talked more openly than maybe he should have about Darcy and his desire to have her and Rachael back in his life. He thought he was talking with a friend at the time and had no idea the impact his words were having on Connie. He couldn't believe how unaware he'd been and cringed internally at the realization of the pain he'd inadvertently caused.

Tom was still talking. "Brooks, I'm wondering why Connie would have thought that about you and Darcy. She and Mick are very much together, and that should have been obvious to Connie from the day she and Darcy met. It is clear now that their meeting was no accident and Connie knew very well who Darcy was. She had to have gotten the information about Darcy being on the cruise from you."

"You're right. I talked a lot about Darcy and Rachael going on the cruise, but I had no idea Connie had . . . feelings about me . . . or the kind of anger toward Darcy you are describing. The more I'm thinking about this, the worse I feel about my part in it. Tom, I can't imagine what I would do if anything happened to Darcy or my daughter."

That evening when she thought she had calmed down sufficiently, Darcy called Brooks, but the conversation did not go well. In response to his denial about having a relationship with Connie, she lost control and attacked him, saying that she wondered if he sent Connie to take her out of the picture so he could have full access to Rachael. She was furious, but even before all the words were out, she knew it didn't make any sense.

"Darcy, how can you believe such a thing? You know how I feel about you. Didn't I ask you to come to Vegas so we can try to renew our relationship? I think it goes without saying how much I love Rachael and want her to be a big part of my life as well."

"OK, Brooks, maybe you didn't send her to hurt me intentionally, but tell me this; what about Sidney? What have you led her to believe about us? Are you aware that she called Mick and basically told him that you and I were getting back together?" I was ranting. "Don't you know how much she cares about you? How many women are you stringing along and hurting . . . I'm counting three of us so far." I stopped to breathe.

"Darcy, I . . ."

"No, Brooks. You're a selfish asshole just like you always were and I'd better not ever find out that you are also pretending to care about Rachael in order to manipulate me."

Brooks was overwhelmed with Darcy's anger and with thoughts about his conversation with Sidney. He recalled how upset or ill she had become the day he told her his plan to get Darcy back, and he knew he had made it sound as if Darcy was in agreement. "Sidney and I have dated," he said quietly, "and I like her very much, but it's not the same as how I feel about you."

"Just dating, ha? Like it was with Connie? You are a complete fool. Unlike Connie, she is a very stable wonderful woman and she obviously cares a lot about you . . . for some reason. Listen carefully, Brooks. Get a grip and think about what you're doing and what you might be throwing away. I will never come back to you, and you have to move on." Darcy was furious and knew this tirade had been building for a long time. "Sidney is my best friend. How could you be hurting her now just the way you hurt me years ago?"

After the call, Brooks sat at his desk in his downtown office and stared out the window at the distant strip hotels shimmering in the mid-day sun. He put his head down on the desk and thought about Darcy's stinging words. Forcing himself to confront how he might have led Connie on, much worse was what he'd done to Sidney. Insensitive—that is what he'd been he now realized.

Darcy was right. He had been selfish, but it was due to his long-standing plan to reunite with his family, which had all but consumed him. He was utterly oblivious to the effect his words and actions had on Connie and Sidney. Was it really possible Darcy would never come back to him? He had lived for that dream so long he scarcely knew how to think about other options. Had he convinced himself that it was possible, with no basis in fact whatsoever?

As puffy cumulus clouds shaded the sun and the light changed dramatically, he pondered his life and how he evolved from an irresponsible alcoholic to a successful businessman. He knew his metamorphosis had been possible only because of Rachael—the desire to be a good father and somehow correct the damage he'd done to his family. Now he was beginning to understand that the opportunity to be the father he wanted to be was within his reach, but Darcy might never be in that picture. *Will I ever be able to let go of that part of the dream? Maybe it's an obsession.*

He couldn't resolve that question yet, but his thoughts unexpectedly turned back to Sidney. They hadn't spoken since the day she had gotten so upset with him at the restaurant. Now he wondered if he was overlooking something else that was precious. Is it too late to make amends there as well?

65

Day 20 – Ushuaia, Argentina

We stayed on the ship when it docked in Ushuaia. The weather had changed dramatically, and it was pouring rain. Despite the freezing cold, a surprising number of passengers left anyway to spend the day on shore. Mick and I had toured the town at *el fin de mundo*—the end of the world—on the previous cruise, so I wasn't too upset about staying onboard. Rachael didn't express much interest in going ashore either, primarily because of the weather.

Mick and Tom were still talking to crew members, so Rachael and I enjoyed a leisurely lunch and then decided to see a movie in the little theater down on deck 2. We didn't even check to see what was playing. It didn't really matter because we were just passing the time. I was trying to get my mind off the encounter with Connie and what I should do about her. Meanwhile, we hadn't heard of anyone else being attacked, and we figured Joe Moretti must be the rapist after all. All we needed now was for Mick and Tom to find out something to help with the case against Paul Denezza.

With so many passengers on shore, the ship seemed very quiet, almost deserted. We were on our way down the stairs to the theater with Rachael in front leading the way. "I can't wait to see what film is showing. I've never been to a theater without knowing what I was going to see," she laughed over her shoulder.

"I guess I haven't either." We arrived at the foyer outside the theater, and the marquee on the wall just outside the entrance announced that we would be seeing the 1984 film, *Romancing the Stone*. All I could think of was the opening scene that had always stayed with me, which was interesting now that I thought about it, given my new writing career. Kathleen Turner's character, a lonely author, named Joan Wilder, has just finished a romance novel. She is in tears over the emotional ending she has written and has been so preoccupied with it that she has run out of groceries, including tissues and cat food. She opens a can of tuna and gives it to her cat.

"It's kind of old, but I always liked that movie. Is it OK with you?" I asked.

"Sure, I don't think I've ever seen it."

We walked behind the wall that formed an entrance with two aisles at either end and sat down three rows from the back of the seventy-five seat theater. The movie started, and soon we were engrossed in it. We were the only ones there, but about mid-way through I heard someone come in and sit down behind us.

We had each brought a bottle of water and Rachael had finished hers. She leaned over and said, "Darcy I'm going out to the ladies room. I'll be right back."

I nodded as she stepped across me to the aisle. Thirty seconds later, I thought I heard her voice, and then I definitely heard some sort of commotion. I jumped to my feet and ran out just in time to see Rachael standing at the bottom of the stairs holding on to the handrail, and looking up with a frightened expression.

There didn't seem to be anyone else around. "What's the matter, Rachael?"

She turned to me, and when I saw how pale and shaky she looked, I pulled her into my arms. "What happened?"

"It was those two guys again. They were sitting in the back of the theater, and they followed me when I left. They rushed me and sort of pushed me aside . . . and . . ."

"What, Rachael? What did they do?" I was feeling some panic myself.

". . . One of them, the taller one, grabbed me as he went by." She started to cry and buried her head in my shoulder.

"What do you mean? How did he grab you? Tell me what happened. They're gone now."

"He grabbed my breast as he passed me and it hurt, I mean it was no accidental brush." She continued to sob all the way back to her cabin. I needed to stay with her, but I also wanted to talk to Mick and Tom. After a few minutes, I realized we had to call security and report what had happened.

"How do you feel about doing that?" I asked her when she had regained some of her composure.

"Yes, I think we should have made more of an issue about those guys before. They are harassing us, Darcy. Why are they doing this?" The tears started again, and I was about as angry as I could ever remember being—at least since the horror of the last cruise.

I grabbed for the phone and called security. I wasn't playing around and pretty much demanded to speak with Roger Ramirez. About five minutes later he called back. We had not met, but I'd heard a lot about him from Mick and Tom.

I introduced myself and explained our connection. While attempting to repress the rage I was feeling, I explained the attack outside the theater giving as detailed a description as I could. "These guys were undoubtedly passengers—not crew members," I insisted. "This is not the first time we've had a problem with them. We saw them watching us on shore too." I started to tell him about what happened in Acapulco, but he stopped me and said that Mick had already mentioned the rock-throwing incident.

He promised to look into the problem, but since we did not know who they were among three thousand passengers, there wasn't a lot he could do. He was sympathetic, but all he could offer was, "If you see them again, stay clear but go to the nearest house phone and call us. Maybe we can get someone there quickly enough to catch them." He paused a moment to think. "The only other option would be for you to come to security and look through pictures of all the male passengers to see if anyone looks familiar. Uh, the problem is, we have no way to search by age or any other parameters except citizenship. That might be helpful if you think they're Americans."

"I think they might be. Let me talk to Tom and see what he thinks, and we'll get back to you about looking through pictures of passengers."

Rachael sat on the bed with a forlorn expression as I hung up the phone. "I wouldn't mind looking through a bunch of pictures if it will tell us who those creeps are. I don't think I even want to leave the cabin until I go to visit my parents in Buenos Aires."

"Oh honey, I am so sorry this is happening. I just can't explain how unbelievable it is that we are having all these problems. We had no reason to think this cruise would be anything but a pleasant vacation." I sat down beside her on the bed and put my arm around her shoulder. "I'll say one thing for sure. I'll never set foot on another cruise ship."

"Me either." She fell onto her side and drew up her knees. "I think I'll see if I can take a nap now. I just want to forget about that awful man grabbing me like that." She closed her eyes. I sat on the couch feeling completely helpless and watched the tears trickle down my beautiful girl's cheeks.

I was thinking that we should never have brought her along with us. Somehow, we should have known there could be repercussions after what happened last time . . . but how could these men have anything to do with what happened on the first cruise? It didn't make any sense, but something else did, and it was scaring the hell out of me. After what happened today it was evident that whatever their motive and plan, Rachael was their target.

66

Day 21 – at sea

Late at night after the ship sailed passed Horn Island and rounded the tip of the continent, someone died onboard. Everyone heard the emergency alert during the night, and by morning many passengers already knew about it from conversations with crew members who they knew well from previous cruises.

When Tom and Mick began hearing the rumors they immediately went to ask Roger about it. They wanted to talk to him about the latest incident with the stalkers and Rachael anyway. They found him consumed with paperwork and trying to prepare for a briefing with the captain. His impatience was obvious, but he asked them to sit down anyway.

"Yes, we had a death onboard last night, but I guess you already knew that." I would have contacted you anyway, but first I need to get past the initial reports and briefings . . . you know what I mean, Tom."

"I completely understand. Was there something about the incident we should know?"

"Believe it or not, we think the deceased woman was attacked on the deck, possibly with the intent of sexual assault."

"Oh no," Mick said.

"But it looks as if she died from some sort of natural occurrence like a heart attack or aneurysm. Apparently, we don't have any witnesses because once the sun set it was too cold for most passengers to be outside."

Tom leaned across the desk. "How do you know it was an attack?"

"The condition of the body indicates there was a struggle, but she doesn't seem to have any life-threatening injuries. Of course, we won't know for sure about her medical condition or the cause of death until we have an autopsy when we get to Florida."

"I guess that removes any thought about Joe Moretti being the rapist, not that I believed he was," Tom said.

"That is one of my biggest problems this morning. The captain was relying on the fact that we had caught both the saboteur and the rapist."

Tom knew Roger had played a big part in planting that idea, but he decided not to pursue it. "Is there any chance I could take a look at the body?"

"Yeah sure, I don't have any reason not to let you."

"Will you report what happened outside of the cruise line?" Mick asked him.

Ramirez actually chuckled. "Are you kidding? With everything else that has happened and you guys on board to investigate crimes on the ship, at this point how could we not? I've already called the FBI in Miami and told them we have yet another thing for them to look at when we dock. I think it's safe to say they are a little dubious about this ship of ours, given all the problems we've had." He shook his head. "The captain is about to have an aneurysm himself."

He gave Tom a sheepish look and added, "Before you ask, yes we swept the deck for any forensics and looked closely at the body. We didn't find anything. She must have died before the attacker could leave any evidence."

"So you think it is the same guy who raped the other women?" Mick asked.

"That would seem logical. Even on this ship, I don't think we could have two would-be rapists. Anyway, the FBI will also come on board to interview Melanie and Lori, who both happen to be staying on the ship all the way to the U.S. Joe Moretti will be turned over to them as well." Then Roger surprised Tom. As he rose from his chair, he said, "Tom, I have to say that I'm getting a better appreciation for what you went through last year, but right now I have to get ready to brief the captain."

Tom stood too, preparing to leave, but faced Roger as he came around his desk. "We know you're busy, but what do you think about the two men that are following Mick's friend, Darcy, and her daughter? We told you about this before, and now there has been a fairly overt move—an assault by the sound of it—to frighten the girl. Does it occur to you that one of them might be your rapist?"

"No, that had not occurred to me. If I were you, I would encourage the ladies to come and spend some time looking at our pictures of the passengers as I suggested."

"We talked about it, and Darcy and Rachael will call your office later today and arrange to do that. Maybe you could leave word with your staff."

"Yes, I'll do that. I don't see how your friends can fail to identify the two men eventually. It will just take some time to go through at least a thousand pictures unless they find them early in the process."

After Roger explained where the latest attack happened, Mick and Tom left him to his preparations and went to the site. They were both surprised and pleased to find that tape had been stretched across the deck in both directions to keep people from walking on the crime scene.

Mick looked around. "You know they're reporting to the FBI and worrying about evidence because we are on the ship. Otherwise, I doubt they would be this diligent."

"You're probably right, but I sure hate to admit it."

Mick was embarrassed that he had made this comment to Tom, who had been the one not reporting crimes on the ship a year ago. He had become so accustomed to interacting as colleagues and friends that he had forgotten the problems they had with each other back then. "I'm sorry, Tom, that was uncalled for."

"Don't worry. I understand exactly where you're coming from."

They looked carefully around the deck for several minutes. Then Tom walked to the wall and leaned over the tape. He ducked under it and took one giant stride, then reached down to retrieve a tiny piece of white paper. "This could be something the attacker dropped during a struggle," he said, as he stepped back outside the tape and held it out for Mick to see.

He had barely caught it between his thumb and forefinger, and he reached into his pants pocket to retrieve a small plastic bag. Mick raised an eyebrow. "Do you always carry evidence bags with you?"

As Tom shook the scrap into the bag, he laughed. "Only since the cruise last year; there could be DNA on this, but who knows whose? I'll give it to Roger."

Then they went to the cold storage area to look at the body. There were two inhabitants, and the quasi-morgue only had accommodations for three. It would be highly unusual for more people than that to die on one cruise. The remains of the very elderly man was of no interest to them, and they turned their attention to the woman.

She'd been attractive with long dark brown hair and appeared to be in her thirties. As soon as Tom saw her, he knew Roger was correct. Extensive bruising on her face and arms indicated she had fought with someone. "Some of these bruises could be the result of having fallen on her face if she suffered a heart attack," Tom said, "but others don't seem to fit with that scenario." No external injury appeared to be fatal as Roger had indicated, but something happened to this woman beyond a natural medical event.

"You know, Mick, I have a strong suspicion that Roger is right about this being the work of the rapist. I don't believe the guy intended or expected her death and I suspect this incident will end his little spree.

67

Day 24 – at sea

During the three-day journey north toward Buenos Aires, Tom and Mick were making good progress working their way through the interviews. They were concerned about the men who had been bothering Darcy and Rachael and anxious for an identification. The women had spent a total of five hours over the past two days at the security office looking through pictures, but so far had not recognized them. Hopefully, today they would have more luck.

Because the ship's computer system was not intended to display images of passengers in this manner, one of the security staff had to sit with them and bring up each person's record, which had proven to be tedious. Tom was frustrated by this but knew from his own experience how slow the system was.

Rachael insisted on returning to her cabin after they finished at security and planned to stay there until it was time to meet everyone for dinner. Mick hated to admit it, but he thought that might be for the best. He felt a little better, but it was very upsetting for him to see how frightened and worried she was, along with Darcy.

At three o'clock Tom looked up to welcome his next interviewee and was immediately struck by the panicked look on the face of the pretty Indian girl. While her eyes darted around the room and her hands shook visibly, he glanced at his notes, then stood and pulled out a chair for her, offering a friendly smile. "How do you do, Isabel, my name is Tom, and I want to thank you for coming to talk with me." Her discomfort was obvious and he wanted to put her at ease. He had talked to a few crew members who seemed intimidated by having to speak with the American government men. It was true that Isabel was both intimidated and frightened but also relieved to finally be able to tell her story. She sat down and looked up at him. Then quickly averted her eyes, looking down at her lap.

"Isabel, we have a few questions to ask you about the cruise a year ago, when you were onboard working for Suzanne Moretti. Do you remember that time?"

She was surprised by the question since she had been able to think of little else since then. She drew a deep breath sat up a little straighter and began to speak softly.

As the story of Plato's relationship with Paul and Suzanne, and Isabel's short-lived romance with him tumbled out, she could not help but cry. She had rehearsed what she would say many times and pushed on before she lost her courage. "Plato was a good person, and someone killed him. He would never kill himself. Mr. Denezza was a nasty man who made Plato agree to do things because, well, Plato wanted money for us to be able to have a better life. At first, he told me only that he would get a lot of money from the wealthy passenger from Las Vegas, Nevada, and wanted me to quit the cruise line and go with him when he left the ship. He said he thought the man and Ms. Moretti were having an affair, but at first I did not believe this because Ms. Moretti was the captain's wife. But then Plato changed his mind and didn't want to do anything bad to Mr. Denezza's wife. He was so scared because the man threatened him."

Isabel was breathless by the time she finished her speech. She looked at her lap and wiped tears from her face. "I know he just wanted to do the right thing at the end." When she looked back up at Tom, she was bewildered by his broad smile, which seemed so out of place with her sad story.

Tom felt a twinge of compassion and tried to put her at ease. "Thank you. You've provided the information we came on board to find. I wish we had scheduled your interview sooner. You can't imagine how important this is. I am very sorry about what happened to your friend. Also, I'm afraid we will need to get more details from you about everything Plato told you. Now I have to tell you something, and I hope it won't be too upsetting."

Isabel could not imagine what could be worse than what happened a year ago and then having to come here and tell the story to this important man, whom she didn't even know if she could trust. She stared back at him wordlessly and wiped a stray tear from her cheek.

"Your country has a justice system where people are brought to trial for their crimes in a court with a judge and jury panel. We have a similar way in the United States. Isabel, you are a crucial witness who knows that Mr. Denezza hired crew members, including Plato, to kill his wife. We want to make sure he pays for his crime, and you will probably have to testify at his trial."

Isabel just stared and waited for him to continue. Suddenly the impact of his words hit her, and she shifted uneasily in her chair. "But a trial would be in the United States. I would not be there to do this."

He smiled gently. "We would take you there and provide whatever you need. You would stay in a nice hotel in Las Vegas, and then after you testify, we would bring you back to the ship, or take you wherever you want to go. This is necessary, or he will get away with what he did to Plato.

She had never considered the possibility of traveling to America. This idea was just as frightening as everything else that had happened. She thought about what Tom had said and finally sat up straighter and looked him in the eye. "I am very afraid to do this, but I understand how it works . . . It is necessary to tell this story at a trial. I will try to do this if you will be there with me?" She lowered her eyes to her lap again, clearly embarrassed.

"Don't worry, it will all work out fine, and I think you will enjoy visiting my country, although Las Vegas is different than the rest of the U.S. I will make sure I am with you for the trip if that makes it easier for you."

After she left, Tom walked to the folding partition that divided the room in half and peeked around the unfastened edge. Mick was finishing up his interview, so Tom stepped in and walked to the front of the room still smiling broadly.

Mick knew the moment he looked at Tom that he'd found out something useful and after hearing Isabel's story he was elated. They decided to call special agent Grant Murray in the morning to tell him the good news. Mick was visibly relieved, and Tom knew that having found what they had come for would help his friend in more ways than one.

It was late afternoon in DC, and Mick caught Eve and Danny just as they were getting ready to leave for the day. After he got both of them on the line, he began to explain that he was going to give them a summary of the case study, including the crimes that have been committed on the ship. Eve quickly interjected, "Oh Mick, I wanted to tell you that I have drafted an outline for the testimony and . . ."

Danny interrupted her. "There isn't even enough data yet to make that worthwhile."

"That isn't true Danny; you haven't even seen what I've done with it . . ."

"Hey, stop it you two. This is an expensive call, and I want to give you information. You can get on with your competition later." Mick's annoyance was evident.

When silence followed his rebuke, he continued. "Look, you can begin drafting the case study. I'll let you two decide how to divide up the work, but this is a priority because we have everything we need for it. I'll be emailing you my notes, Danny, along with the final records from the ship's log.

Our message should be that there have been X number of incidents reported by passengers during the study period. You'll use the survey data for that. This ship is typical of large cruise ships, and a virtual crime spree has taken place here during our study."

He recapped the sabotage and physical attacks that had occurred during the sailing, and Eve repeated her comment that she would never set foot on a cruise ship.

Danny sounded elated, "What a story we have to tell. That will get their attention—meaning the Congress."

"Let's hope so because the problem with crimes on ships is apparently worse than we thought.

68

It wasn't so much that Isabel thought the man was not worthy of her trust. She only knew that she was more frightened now than at any time during the past year. Up until a few minutes ago, no one in the world had any inkling about her relationship with Plato or the burden of knowledge she had been carrying. Now the American man knew all about it, and this did not make her feel secure. She thought she would feel a sense of relief once she talked with him, but that was not the case at all.

Worse, she had promised to take a journey that was far outside her feeling of comfort and she was already having second thoughts about that. She believed the friendly man, Mr. Smythe, was sincere when he promised to take care of her, but she could not shake a feeling of foreboding now that someone else knew her secret.

These thoughts were troubling, but she was due to begin her shift and would have to put her concerns aside so she could concentrate on her job. She left the conference center after the interview and hurried along the cement hallway toward the crew stairwell. Her work section consisted of guest rooms from 6020 through 6035, and she was due up there in five minutes. Her assistant would already be assembling their cleaning supplies and gathering up towels and ice buckets.

As she began to climb the stairs, a man walked up behind her and grabbed for her arm. He caught only the sleeve of her uniform jacket, and she was able to shake him off. A cry for help went unheard because no one else was around. With nowhere else to go, Isabel turned and ran up the stairway. He started after her, but tripped on the bottom step and lost some momentum. Although only four steps ahead, this allowed her to make it to deck 3. After running out of the stairwell, she raced down the broad aisle past the photography studio and the gentlemen's cigar bar.

Glancing over her shoulder, she was horrified to see the ugly dark-haired man about twenty feet behind and gaining on her. She tried to run faster, but it was no use. He easily caught her and threw her up against the wall, pushing his belly in against her chest. He placed one big hand against the wall above her head. Everything about him was huge, and although he was not overly tall, he still towered over tiny Isabel. She couldn't breathe properly and felt as if he would crush the life out of her. What have I done, she wondered? Her mind went to her beloved home in Goa, and then to poor Plato and how her life had become so intolerable . . . and now this.

The man quickly looked around to make sure they were alone, then leaned his face down close to hers and whispered. She scrunched her eyes closed and tried to block out his foul sweaty odor, but she managed to listen. After about thirty seconds he leaned back and she opened her eyes. He was appraising her with an evil smirk, "Do you understand?" he asked in a low growling tone.

She fought to overcome her fear, knowing that he did not intend to hurt her . . . right now. She slowly nodded. "Yes, I understand." He nodded back and lifted his body off her. After staring at her menacingly for a few more seconds, he turned and jogged away.

Isabel ran down the deck about fifty feet and darted through a crew-only door and into a work area reserved for kitchen employees. Several workers stared at her as she ran past them with tears streaming down her face. At the back of the room she jumped into the elevator, a glorified dumb waiter, used to transport carts of food and dishes up to the Whales Tail. Sobbing, she hit the button for deck 4 and struggled to catch her breath.

She raced around the end of the guest relations desk, down the short hallway, and pounded on the door to the security office. After stumbling in, she leaned on the desk and waited for her chest to stop heaving. She was very afraid of the big passenger, but her sense of duty told her that she must report this violent man.

Isabel's worst fears were confirmed when the only security staff member on duty discounted her report. Of course, Isabel did not say anything about her conversation with Mr. Smythe—too many people already knew about that—and she did not trust the security staff any more than she did the Americans.

She was at the bottom of the crew hierarchy and had little credibility; while the security staff, on the other hand, were near the top. The stout dark-skinned female guard seemed to find humor in Isabel's story. She looked down on tiny Isabel and laughed. "You probably imagine that a passenger would have any interest in you one way or the other. You really ought to stay away from the guests. The only place you are supposed to be on the ship, other than the crew quarters, is your assigned cabin section."

This haughty woman refused to believe that a man chased her down and grabbed her and Isabel was too intimidated to argue. She knew she could never trust any of the people in authority, including Mr. Smythe. A trip to the United States was out of the question. She left and ran to the elevator and then to the safety of her crew workroom on deck 6.

69

Day 25 – Buenos Aires, Argentina

Tom and Wendy left the ship early in the morning to spend the day in Buenos Aires. I figured Tom was feeling better than at any time during the cruise, now that the primary reason for him being along had been satisfied. He and Mick would finish the interview process in case another crew member had information, but he told us he thought Isabel's testimony would be enough to convict Paul of conspiracy to commit murder and murder for hire. He was confident Murray would agree, and he and Mick had decided to wait until later to make the call to Vegas.

I decided to stay on the ship with Mick, while Rachael went to visit her parents at their home in the upscale Palermo Chico neighborhood, where her father worked at the U.S. consulate. She and I had looked at pictures of three-quarters of the male passengers and had not seen anyone who looked like either of the two men. Today I planned to spend more time on the task.

As Rachael was leaving to meet the car her father was sending for her, I called Marianne Alosa. "I'm staying on the ship, Marianne. I hope you have a pleasant visit with Rachael. She can't wait to get home to see you. I'm sure she will be telling you all about this, but just to give you a heads up; she is now talking favorably about checking out Georgetown or George Washington Universities. They both have outstanding rowing programs."

"That is good news. Her Olympic dream is still alive."

"I know, and I'm planning to move to DC, so Mick and I will be able to look out for her if one of the schools works out. I believe we can get the application process started during the two weeks she plans to spend with us after we get home."

"That is good news, Darcy, for Rachael and for you and Mick. We miss her terribly, but Ray and I know that Kenya is not going to offer her the opportunities she wants and deserves." Marianne paused, and I could sense her ambivalence. "Of course every parent has to go through the letting go process at some point. We are fortunate that you will be with her since we can't be close by."

Afterward, I could not help but marvel over this relationship with Rachael's adoptive parents. They are good people, and I was overwhelmed with gratitude for the way they raised Rachael, and for the ease they demonstrated in bringing me into their family. It was truly amazing but also had its awkwardness. I intentionally did not mention anything to Marianne about the negative aspects of the cruise, including the strange encounters with the two men. Rachael asked me not to tell her parents about it and to let her share whatever she was comfortable with. I was only marginally OK with this approach, but I reluctantly agreed.

70

Late in the afternoon, Rachael returned to the ship in a melancholy mood and went straight to her cabin. The visit with her parents had been wonderful, but she hated to leave knowing that her time with them was short and therefore precious. If she moved to DC and enrolled in college when they moved to Africa, she knew she would not see them very often over the next few years.

When she realized someone was knocking she had been deep in thought about her family and future. She knew it had to be Darcy, so she quickly opened the cabin door. A man wearing a mask pushed the door wider and strode into the room. Before she could react, he pulled a knife from his pants pocket and turned the point toward her face. His head was covered by black wool, but there was no doubt about who he was—the rapist.

He quickly slammed the door shut. Rachael backed away from him and stopped abruptly when she hit the foot of the bed, all the while transfixed by the sight of the knife he was waving in front of her. Her heart felt as if it would jump out of her chest, and try as she might, she could not overcome an attack of rising panic. She was hyperventilating and choking on her own breath when he placed his hand on her chest and roughly shoved her down into a sitting position.

Looking up at him wide-eyed she leaned back on her elbows and tried to formulate some words, but couldn't speak through the sobs and hiccupping. He laughed at her dilemma from behind the mask and pointed the knife at her throat, motioning for her to lie down on the bed.

Through her terror, a couple of thoughts stood out with total clarity. *He's going to rape me . . . I'm a virgin. This cannot be my first . . .* She found her voice in the form of a high-pitched scream, which could easily have been heard out in the corridor or in one of the next-door cabins, except that no one was there.

"The man slapped her across the mouth, and she immediately quieted. Wide-eyed and terrified, with a tiny trickle of blood oozing from the corner of her stinging lip, all she could do was stare at him. The slap had interrupted her panic attack, and she looked closely at him for the first time. At the bottom of the mask several strands of blond hair poked out, and she knew this had to be the man who grabbed her near the theater. He was very muscular, and she wondered if she would be able to fight him. Then she looked down at the knife, dangerously close to her neck and the panic returned.

He laughed again, shoved her down onto her back and unzipped his black trousers. With the knife still at her throat, he pushed the pink sundress up over her hips revealing white lace panties.

She squirmed backward on the bed desperate to distance herself from him. He grabbed her ankle and pulled sharply, causing a spike of pain to shoot up her leg. He dragged her back down to the foot of the bed and waved the knife in front of her again. Then with a slow, deliberate motion he moved it slowly down her torso letting it hover above her crotch. He plainly gestured for her to spread her legs and she squealed, shaking her head and looking frantically around the cabin for something that could save her.

His movement brought her eyes back to him. He had drawn his swollen penis out of his pants and was roughly pulling her leg to the side. Rachael's eyes widened at the sight of him. Added to her panic was a wave of anger she had never felt in her entire life. She kicked at him with her free leg and was rewarded with another slap. Tears welled up and slid down her cheeks. She shook her head to clear her vision and finally found her voice.

"Please don't do this to me. I'll do anything else you want, but don't try to rape me." She knew she was pathetic, but also knew she would have to fight him. She did not want to think about how that would probably end, but she could not just let this happen, and she could not take her eyes off his enormous member. "No! Not like this . . . please," she cried.

As he lowered himself between her legs with the knifepoint now close to puncturing her neck, his other hand was busy roughly trying to open her. The moment she felt his hand and hard flesh against her she went crazy. With a full-throated scream, she shot to a sitting position, grabbing for his face. Before he could pull away, she shoved her hand under the mask and ripped him with her long nails.

He yelled and yanked her hand away. Just as he retaliated by pushing the blade against her neck, she pushed her arms down between their bodies. He was not expecting the strength in her powerful shoulders, and she was able to throw him off balance. He fell to her right, but as she tried to roll away, he lashed out and sliced her forearm. She looked down at the spurt of blood quickly soaking the bed. "No," she cried, understanding that this was not a superficial wound.

He barely glanced at the spreading blood pool, jumped up, and ran to the door. When he darted into the corridor, Rachael ran to the bathroom, grabbed a hand towel, and pressed it against her arm. It didn't do any good—blood saturated it within a few seconds. She strode to the open door and looked up and down the corridor, but he was nowhere in sight. Shock and terror finally took their toll, and the adrenaline subsided as she leaned against the doorframe. A terrible pain reached her consciousness, and she doubled over and cried out. Large drops of blood fell from beneath the wet towel onto the rug. *I have to get to the phone.* As she turned to go back into the cabin, the walls began to spin. Dizzy and nauseous, and unable to stand any longer, she fell to her knees and then onto her side against the open door.

On the edge of consciousness, she thought she heard someone calling her name. Then she remembered the horrible man and what he had almost done to her. *At least I stopped him in time.*

Darcy sprinted to her daughter and knelt down. "Rachael, Rachael, can you hear me?" *Oh shit! All this blood.* She jumped up and ran to the bedside phone to call for help. After the operator assured her help was on the way, she returned to Rachael and applied as much pressure as she could against the four-inch bone-deep gash. "Rachael, what the hell happened to you?"

71

Mick and Tom arrived at the medical facility amidships on deck 2. As they hurried inside Tom looked over at Mick's distraught expression. "You don't remember being in here after you were stabbed, do you?"

"No, I was out of it the whole time, but this is hitting pretty close to home, Tom. I'm scared about whatever the hell has happened. The message I got just said it was urgent."

They had run through the ship from the conference center and did not slow their pace as they flew into the waiting room. They could see Darcy's back through the open door leading to the examining rooms. She was leaning protectively over a body lying on a gurney.

Mick ran up behind her. "Darcy, what's going on?" When he looked down at Rachael's deathly pale face and the large blood stain on the sheet he nearly collapsed. Tom came up beside him, and Darcy straightened and turned to them. Her expression reminded Tom of the way she looked a year ago sitting beside Mick's gurney in this same room.

Mick put his arms around her and looked down at Rachael again. Now he could see that she was breathing steadily and he groaned with relief. "What happened?"

"I'm still not sure exactly what happened, but she has a very deep laceration on her arm that nicked the artery." With a quivering hand, she smoothed a wrinkle in the sheet that covered Rachael up to her chin. Mick removed his arms from around her and took her hand in both of his. "She bled a lot, but she's all stitched up, and the doctor said it should heal in a couple of weeks." She clutched Mick's arm with shaking hands. "Oh God, she was attacked and maybe raped."

Darcy was clearly near to collapsing herself, and Mick and Tom held her elbows to make sure she didn't topple. She stood still for a few seconds with her eyes closed before continuing. "She woke up for a little while and said something about a man with a mask, and that she stopped him before he could do it to her. I think that is what she said anyway."

Just then the doctor appeared with a bottle of valium and handed it to Darcy. These will help if the arm is too painful, or . . . just if she's having trouble coping.

Tom spoke quietly to him. "Was she raped?"

"As far as I can tell there was no penetration, but her mucosa are somewhat inflamed, and she obviously fought with someone. That is a very nasty knife wound." He nodded toward Rachael. "Chief Ramirez told me to be sure to check for any forensics on her." He shook his head. "We're not set up for that, but I did look closely and did not find any hairs or ejaculate. I took a swab anyway. If it was a rape, I believe it was an aborted attempt. Miss Alosa will be awake before long, and she will have to tell us what happened to her."

Twenty minutes later Rachael began to stir, and they all gathered around her again. She opened her eyes and looked up, eventually focusing on Darcy. Tears rolled down her cheeks. Darcy placed her palm against Rachael's wet, puffy, face. "Are you in pain, Rachael?"

"Only a little, but oh, oh no, I can't believe what happened. That awful blond man tried to rape me. I fought him and . . . owe!" She had tried to raise her arm.

"It's OK. You have a deep cut, and the doctor has stitched it. It will heal just fine, and your arm will be back to normal. Rachael, are you sure the man who attacked you was the same one who grabbed you at the theater?"

"Not positive, but yes, I think it was him."

Tom and Mick exchanged a look. Tom said, "I cannot believe the same guy who attacked the woman on the deck would risk another assault. I would have sworn that would not be the case."

Rachael looked up at Mick. "You might be able to recognize him by the scratches on his face. I got him with my nails." Mick leaned down and kissed Rachael's forehead. "We'll find him now for sure. You did well to fight him off. Try not to worry, Rachael." He didn't know what else to say, so he turned and walked toward the door.

Tom had a quiet word with the doctor and then followed Mick out into the corridor. Mick said, "Thankfully it looks as if she'll be all right, but this is so bad on so many levels. She could have been killed and probably should not have resisted. She is so much like Darcy it's scary." He leaned against the wall next to the entrance and looked at his feet. "Darcy will blame herself for this, I can tell you that for sure, and what about Ray and Marianne?" He looked sadly at Tom "How will we ever be able to explain how we let this happen to their daughter? I never should have brought Darcy and Rachael with us on this job. What was I thinking?"

"Mick, stop and listen to me. Don't let this set you back. There is no way we could have anticipated any of these things happening, and the odds of encountering any crime or violence on this cruise were astronomical, to begin with. Hey, don't forget I worked on this ship for ten years with very few serious incidents in all that time . . . until last year."

"Come on, Tom. The odds are way outside the universe of chance. You know the link has to be us. I don't know how, but all of this has to be related to last year's cruise even if indirectly like with Joe Moretti trying to avenge Suzanne."

Tom was already walking away. He began shaking his head. "Come on, I want to talk to Roger. He has to understand how serious this is and now he has to find those two guys. I guess it's possible that one or both of them are responsible for all the attacks. Anyway, the doctor is going to scrape Rachael's nails and then we will have DNA from one of the bastards.

72

Day 26 – at sea

"We cannot stand for you to stay on the ship or go to DC with Darcy. You are going to fly home from your next port, Montevideo. I will arrange a flight for you to come home."

"But Dad . . ."

"Rachael, don't argue. You are going to move with us to Kenya, and we'll figure out something as far as school goes." Ray Alosa had never barked orders at his daughter before.

The earlier phone call from Darcy had shocked the hell out of him, and Marianne was so upset she was physically ill. Darcy had tried to explain the situation with the two men on the ship who had apparently been watching them and the attacks on other women during the cruise.

Afterward, he had railed at her. "You did not protect my daughter. You are irresponsible, and frankly, you seem to attract trouble. We should have realized it was a mistake to put our trust in you."

Rachael knew how upset he was with Darcy and she also knew she needed time to think about whether she should let this horrible thing influence important decisions about her future. "Dad, please calm down. I really am fine. I have a cut on my arm, and I went through a very scary situation. That is all. I need to talk to mom and reassure her. And I know you are both angry with Darcy, but none of it is her fault, and she and Mick have done everything they could to take care of me."

After she talked with Marianne at length, assuring her that she really was all right and that the attack had been random and could have happened to anyone, she spoke with Ray again. "Dad, please don't be mad at me, but I'm not sure I want to come back home right away. We will be in Montevideo tomorrow, and that is too soon for me. This just happened yesterday. I need a little time to rest and think about what I want to do, OK? I promise I'll call every day and tell you guys how I am and what is happening here. The cruise will be over in three days anyway."

Ray reluctantly agreed, but Rachael had never seen him so angry. She knew that the comfortable relationship between her parents and her birth mother had been damaged and wondered if it could ever be repaired. She also knew very well that she had not been entirely truthful with her mom and that was also a first. The attack had not been random. It was apparent to her as it was to her travel companions that the rock-throwing stalking rapists had been after her from the beginning.

73

After the stressful conversation with Ray, I had to force myself to phone Brooks. As it turned out, that call was even worse. However, later when I thought about it, I realized that I had finally cleared the air with him and maybe it wasn't so bad after all.

Calmly, I tried to explain the attack on Rachael, but he went nuts and wouldn't let me finish. Even after Rachael got on the phone to let him know she was OK, he was still beside himself.

Back on the line, I listened to him berate me. "It's unbelievable to me now that I encouraged her to go with you and Mick. You took her into some kind of dangerous situation that you should have expected after your last cruise experience."

"Brooks, you have travel groups in this supposedly dangerous environment, as you did on the cruise a year ago. Let's not forget your role in what happened then. Speaking of that, what exactly is your relationship with Paul and what do you know about what he is up to?"

"Paul might still be responsible for what is happening there. Don't you understand how dangerous he is?"

"Are you two friends? We know you got some information from him and passed it along to agent Murray. How is it that you are so tight with him?"

Brooks almost exploded. "Don't you try to transfer responsibility for any of this onto me. I'm not there, and if I were, Rachael would be safe. Just so you know, I have been helping Murray by using my long-time acquaintance with Paul." He yelled at me, "You are the one who is supposed to be taking care of my daughter."

That did it! For a year, I had been trying to be civil and friendly to Brooks for Rachael's sake, but suddenly all my old anger bubbled up and out. "Your daughter? How dare you! I might not be the best example of a mother, but you never cared about her or paid any attention to her when it counted. You abandoned us, and you were pleased to give her up at the time."

My heart was pounding, and I felt as if I had run a marathon. Thankfully, Mick had taken Rachael back to her cabin, so that neither of them heard my tirade. Brooks took his time in responding. I guess he was trying to regain his composure too.

"You are absolutely right, Darcy. What we both did to Rachael can never be forgiven. I know very well what a terrible husband and father I was, and I've suffered every day since I gained my sobriety because of it. I am scared to death of losing her again and, well, I've been clear about my feelings for you." He suddenly lowered his voice as if it took great effort to calm down. "I'm sorry. I know you must have been trying to take care of her, but it's hard to be here and not be able to do anything about this."

"Fine Brooks, let's just forget it. This whole business with you and Paul, and Connie and Sidney is so complicated and confusing to me. I told you before, you need to stop living in the past and realize you can't go back. I understand your protectiveness of Rachael is partly due to guilt—I feel some of that too—but she got along just fine without us for eighteen years, didn't she?"

After that uncomfortable conversation, I lay down on the bed and tried to pull myself together. I wanted to be there for Rachael to give her whatever support she needed. I knew she had rejected Ray's demand that she leave us and that warmed my heart. Maybe she didn't place too much blame on me, but I was making up for it with what I was heaping on myself.

I had to face the fact that Rachael would not be in this situation if she had continued her normal happy existence with her wonderful parents and exciting life in the diplomatic community. That is, if she had never met me she would not be caught up in this investigation and the trauma of the cruise, not to mention the complexity that meeting Brooks and me has brought to her life.

I knew Ray was overwrought, but also that he was fundamentally right. I was beginning to think I did not know how to be a good mother. In hindsight, I could see that when things started going south on the cruise—so to speak—I should have left the ship and taken Rachael back to Colorado.

Some soul searching was in order, so I allowed in some unwelcome introspection. Maybe I'm fooling myself to think I can make up for all those lost years. I'm the same person I always was, and I was the world's worst parent, having done the unthinkable. Brooks and I should step back and get out of Rachael's life. We are only confusing her, and we have accidentally exposed her to danger. She was very nearly raped and could have been killed. I have to talk her into flying home to Buenos Aires. Ray is right. She belongs with her parents. No matter how much I love her, I will never be good for her. Isn't what I told Brooks just as true for me? I can't make up for the past. Besides, it will take all my energy to help Mick once we get home. It will be much better for everyone if she goes back to Ray and Marianne.

Rolling over onto my stomach with my arms folded under my face, the old longing ache returned. It was a constant through all those years when I believed I would never see Rachael again. Having to give her up a second time would be unbearable, but it's not fair for her to be torn between her parents and Brooks and me.

My thoughts were riding a very dark current, but my logic seemed reasonable. We'd been through so many unbelievable life-changing events in the past year, and I'd asked myself many times how it could be. Could there really be something pulling strings in the world after all? If there is an intelligent force working on a micro level—as in deliberately bringing Rachael back to me—then existence would be far more frightening than I ever imagined. Everything would still be out of our control, but that would be far worse than being subject to randomness—blood-chilling in fact. It would be far better to be at the mercy of chaos, where at least we have a chance of bringing order to life than to be manipulated by something for its own unknown purpose. Sadly, based on the reality of the world, I see no reason to assume that purpose would be benevolent.

As is sometimes necessary, I struggled to pull myself back into the real world. There was wetness under my cheek, and when I looked over at the clock, I was surprised to see how late it was. I had to find Mick, and Rachael of course, to make sure they were all right. We had to decide where we would eat dinner. It might be best to stay in one of our cabins and have a little party, rather than go out in public.

I was regaining a tenuous grip on my emotions as I left the cabin. My practical nature couldn't stay subverted for long, no matter how much self-pity tried. Logically, none of the violence on this sailing was any of our faults, and I was doing the best I knew how to take care of my girl.

74

Day 27 - Montevideo, Uruguay

Mick wanted to go ashore with me in Montevideo. He said he realized that for a long time he had not been taking care of me in more ways than one. He felt that I needed him to be strong, especially after the trauma of Rachael's attack, and with his new-found introspection, he wanted to try to do better. It sort of sounded like the old Mick talking.

Rachael stayed on the ship and planned to remain in her cabin. Except that, at some point, Roger was going to send a security guard to escort her to look at the remaining pictures, and take her back to the cabin when she was finished. I had only had a chance to look at a few more yesterday with no luck. Rachael said that before the day was out, she would find her attacker unless the men had somehow avoided having their pictures taken when they boarded or had dramatically altered their appearance.

Tom and Wendy were going ashore and planned to spend part of the day with us. Tom confided in me that he was beginning to feel anxious about the end of the cruise. He knew he had strong feelings for Wendy and he didn't know what would happen when they had to go their separate ways. This was so reminiscent of the way Mick and I felt on the previous cruise.

In the morning we all toured the Puerto Del Mercado, an exciting group of shops, street vendors, galleries, and restaurants, located less than a block from the end of the pier. To get there, we walked about a mile from the ship and crossed Franklin D. Roosevelt, a broad avenue running parallel to the coast. I was worried about Rachael, and it was difficult to relax, but Mick was making a special effort to be attentive to me, so I tried to match it.

We strolled along holding hands and checking the leather goods, jewelry displays, and street art. Then we entered the enormous indoor barbeque restaurant and shopping mall. The amount of food being cooked and served, primarily meat, chicken, and seafood was astounding. The building was already so full of tourists that there was no place to sit in the restaurant areas or at the long communal tables. We spent about a half hour wandering through the little stores and enjoying the ambiance. Then we decided to split up for a couple of hours and then meet at the entrance to the market on the corner of Yacaré and Perez Castellano.

Tom and Wendy opted for a bus tour of the downtown area, and we decided to take a self-guided walking tour of the major attractions within a couple of miles of the port. Mick and I really enjoyed Montevideo—for a while. It was one of the places we said we would like to revisit someday.

As South American countries go, Uruguay has a healthy economy and a relatively high standard of living. The country's social services are the best on the continent, and one and a half million people—over half the population of the country—live in the capital city. This was not always the case, and the country has a long history of military rule, unrest, and political instability.

The Spaniards held Montevideo as a military stronghold until 1825 when an exiled military officer, Jose Gervasio Artigas, brought the country to the end of a long struggle for independence. Civil war and dictatorships soon followed as well as long-standing economic problems due to financial pressures on a welfare state with few natural resources. Stability did not come until 1985 with the return to civilian rule.

The center of the city was surprisingly clean and modern with a charming combination of colonial and art deco architecture. We wandered in and out of public buildings and a beautiful old theater. Among the many pieces of information and statistics we picked up along the way, I was particularly intrigued by the results of a recent survey of the city's populace, in which sixty percent claimed to be atheists.

Another interesting and possibly tangential fact was that almost everyone goes to college. In Uruguay's system the education is free, but beginning five years after graduation, everyone pays a small annual fee back to the state for their entire working lives. Consequently, Uruguay has one of the highest literacy and education rates in the world. This sounded like socialism at its best.

The time passed quickly, as usual, and we started working our way back toward the port to meet Tom and Wendy. We had wandered a few blocks north of the central part of the city and didn't think twice about traversing streets that were primarily residential as we aimed in the general direction of the port. As we neared the waterfront, the buildings became sparse and a little more run down. Some were empty and boarded up.

We had just crossed Piedras Street, one block from the water, and turned down a somewhat deserted diagonal side street to take a shortcut in the direction of the pier. Deep in conversation and more or less in our own world, we were not nearly as alert to our surroundings as we should have been. Literally out of nowhere, someone grabbed me from behind and tried to pull my purse strap off my shoulder. I was aware that a second person was assaulting Mick, but I was busy fighting to keep hold of my bag. I whirled around and kicked at my assailant, while I pulled on the strap with all my might. I wasn't about to let some street punk get my belongings.

The notion that this was a simple mugging was short-lived. To my right about fifteen feet away I saw that Mick was involved in basic hand-to-hand combat. This wasn't about theft. That was when I actually looked at my attacker and gasped. It was the blond half of our stalker pair. Still pulling on the strap of my purse, I managed to land a kick to his shin, and he momentarily released his grip.

Just then, I saw Mick throw an impressive punch that landed on the other guy's jaw and knocked him cold. The blond tried to leave me to help his friend, but I jumped on his back and grabbed a handful of his jaw-length hair. He was trying to shake me off but still moved toward where Mick was standing over the unconscious attacker. I kicked at the back of his legs and managed to hold on.

The full realization dawned on me that these really were our stalkers and the guy I was riding was the one who accosted Rachael. I was horrified, but before I could think of what to do, he dove at Mick, and I lost my grip and slid to the pavement. I started yelling at him to get the hell away from us. Before Mick could react, the man pulled out a knife and rushed him.

All I could do was scream. *Another knife! Not again!* I don't think I even had a cogent thought about why we were being attacked, only that Mick was about to get stabbed again. I stood there in shock watching him fight for control of the weapon—probably the same one that cut Rachael. I regained some control of myself and moved in closer to the action. I'm not sure what I intended to do, but I knew that Mick was fighting for his life—and mine. I couldn't just stand back and watch.

I could not stop screaming, and Tom later said he heard me from two streets away. He and Wendy raced around the corner of an abandoned warehouse and Tom immediately jumped into the struggle. Wendy stood beside me with an odd mesmerized expression as she watched the battle. With two against one, it should have been over quickly, but the blond body-builder type guy would not give up. He swung his fist and caught Mick in the throat. Mick fell to the pavement like a rock holding his neck and gagging, and I ran to help him.

When I looked up at Tom, he had his hand around the blond's wrist and was wrestling him for the knife. It was terrifying. Mick wasn't able to help, and

I felt frozen in place watching helplessly while Tom struggled for control of the blade.

Wendy approached to within eight feet of them and observed intently. Almost in slow motion, I saw the guy turn to look at her, and in the next instant, it was over. He was down on the pavement with blood spurting from a hole in his chest. It was horrible. He moaned twice, and that was it. He was dead.

Tom was covered in blood but did not appear to be injured. He stood staring at the body, his chest heaving, with an unreadable expression. The dead silence was broken by a piercing wail. Wendy had become hysterical, and that was perfectly understandable. But instead of running to Tom, she got on her knees beside the dead guy and peered closely at his face. What the hell are you doing? I thought. Tom stared at her while she sobbed over the body.

Mick slowly sat up still rubbing his neck and coughing, but sprang to his feet as soon as he comprehended the scene. Just then, our other attacker whom we had momentarily forgotten started to come around. Wendy jumped to her feet and stepped back. Tom and Mick hauled him up and pinned his arms behind him. He was big, but mainly he had a mean face with a large nose, black slicked back hair, and dark pinpoints for eyes, and . . . two red welts running down his cheek. We were all in shock, but Wendy was inconsolable. I knew that Tom had to be wondering what was going on with her. I sure was.

Someone had heard the fight and called the local police. An older model cruiser screeched around the corner and careened to a halt right in front of us. Two burly cops got out took one look at the blood and drew their weapons. One of them started talking on his radio, and it was obvious he was calling for an ambulance. We looked at one another, and our communal thoughts were obvious. These cops probably did not speak English, and we would have a difficult time explaining all of this. We could not afford to be delayed in the city with the ship scheduled to leave in a few hours. Tom and Mick let go of their prisoner, and we started to run.

The surprise factor plus the two guys we left behind—one dead—gave us a head start. Only one of the cops took off after us. By our appearance, there was no doubt that we were tourists and they weren't about to shoot us—at least we hoped not. We assumed they would think the guy we had been holding had killed the other one . . . at least until he was able to make them understand otherwise.

We cut down the diagonal street to Perez Castellano and entered the mercado from the back side. Drawing plenty of open-mouthed stares, we ran between the vendor stalls toward the front entrance closely followed by the cop repeatedly yelling the word stop! He knew that much English at least. We didn't comply. We just kept running and dashed between the traffic on Franklin D. Roosevelt, then continued up the pier. The cop didn't catch up to us until we had almost made it to the bottom of the gangway. Soon enough, his partner showed up in the patrol car with our live assailant in the back seat.

While we tried to catch our breath, both of the cops grabbed Tom, since he was the one covered in blood, and started to haul him away. We waved our identification cards at the two security guards who were checking passengers back onto the ship, and they ran down the gangway to help us.

A rapid conversation in Spanish ensued, and then everything stopped while we waited for Roger Ramirez. He arrived about five minutes later. By now, a small crowd of passengers had assembled, and Tom's bloody appearance was causing quite a stir. Roger spoke briefly to the officers in Spanish. Then he turned to Tom and asked him to explain what really happened.

Roger had learned that based on the story told by our dark stalker, the cops thought the dead guy was a tourist and we had attacked him for some unknown reason. After Roger explained to them that all of us, including the dead guy, were *Sea Nymph* passengers, and that the two men were also wanted for crimes they committed on the ship, the cops decided they wanted nothing to do with it. However, they still insisted that Tom would have to be arrested and charged with murder. *What?*

While the cops pulled their passenger out of the car, Roger told us that by requesting Tom's arrest, they thought they were covering themselves with their superiors. With a rather dramatic flourish, he placed Tom in custody. While one of the guards held Tom's arm, Roger turned to the other prisoner and said, "Please turn around, Mr. Marone, with your hands behind you. Another guard slipped on handcuffs and took him away. We all looked questioningly at Roger, and incongruously he winked at us. "His name is Georgie Marone—Rachael found their pictures."

Then he spoke with the cops at length about the body, which had been taken to a city morgue. They agreed to return it to the ship within the next three hours. Tom assured them this was a wholly American—and cruise line—matter, and U.S. authorities would thoroughly investigate the matter.

75

Mick accompanied Roger while he transported both his prisoners to the brig. He locked up Marone first and turned to Tom. "Look, I have to try to explain all this to the captain. He will undoubtedly speak with local authorities before we leave. We're in their jurisdiction after all, and they could change their minds about how this is going to be handled, so it's tricky." Tom nodded knowingly but remained quiet. "Since I promised I would arrest you, you will have to be confined until we get to international waters. Just go to your cabin and give me your word; you'll stay there."

Tom laughed. "I would probably have done the same thing when I had your job, Roger. Sure, I'll stay under lock. First, tell us who these guys are and what happened with Rachael.

"Like I said, she came down here to look at pictures, and after about ten minutes she found the dead guy. His name is Lance McKenna. Then Georgie here popped up because they are sharing a cabin."

Mick scoffed, "Those two big guys in one cabin? That must have been fun."

"It's a small suite, so not as bad as you might think. There is one thing that will interest you." He seemed to wait for effect and lowered his voice. "They are both from Las Vegas."

Tom and Mick looked at each other, and a wide grin appeared on Mick's face. "Gee, I wonder who is paying for their suite?" he asked rhetorically.

As Tom was leaving to return to his cabin, he turned to Roger, "Just don't forget about me, and meanwhile, why don't you and Mick talk to Marone and see if you can find out what the hell this is all about.

A few minutes later Roger went to speak with Captain Bentzer, and Mick sat down to have a chat with the prisoner. The guy was big and mean-looking, but the death of his friend and the predicament he realized he was in had turned him somewhat meek.

He readily confessed to being an old friend of Paul's from high school and said he had done various jobs for him over the years. Lance McKenna was a dealer at Athens Olympia and also a longtime friend of Paul's. "I can't believe he's dead. Paul will go nuts when he finds out, and my life won't be worth crap."

Georgie was nervous but obviously wanted to minimize his own culpability. When Mick asked about the rapes on board, he readily answered, "We don't know nothing about that, except . . . Lance did go after the Alosa girl. He got really carried away and out of control. I tried to stop him from doing that, but he wouldn't listen. He thought it was funny because it would just look like the other rapes."

"Come on, Georgie, you don't think I'm buying that, do you? How did you get those welts on your face?"

"I swear it's the truth." His hand went to his cheek. "Oh that, I'd forgotten about it. Lance did it. I'm tellin ya, the guy went over the edge. We got into a fight about him doing stuff that wasn't part of the deal." He jumped up and began to pace the small room. Pushing a meaty hand through his thick black hair and shaking his head, he looked at Mick. "Christ, why the hell did I agree to this? I don't know anything about the other rapes, and I'm almost positive Lance didn't either."

He came back to stand at the opposite side of the table and stared down at Mick. "You gotta believe me, I didn't bargain for any real violence." He seemed to consider whether to continue as he sat down in his chair. "Look, the truth is Paul sent us to make Ms. Farthing and her daughter so uncomfortable and scared that they would want to leave the cruise and maybe you would go too."

Mick studied his face. "Georgie, that is lame. You might have been having some fun at their expense, but that can't be why Paul sent you. What else was he paying you for?"

"Paul just wanted to make sure you wouldn't find out anything about him that could hurt him, ya know? We were talking to him every day—telling him what was going on."

"What do you mean, going on with what?"

Georgie leaned back and stared at Mick. "I swear, Lance just decided to help himself to the Alosa girl. I didn't have nothing to do with it, and I don't know about nothing else."

Mick leaned over the table and poked him in the chest. "Never mind that," he shouted, "tell me the reason Paul hired you two."

Georgie jumped back in his seat and almost tipped over backward. "We were just supposed to get you and Smythe to leave the cruise before you found out anything."

"How would you know whether we found out anything about Paul?"

Georgie shook his head again. "Why the fuck did I agree to this? I'm screwed. Why couldn't Lance have stuck to the plan and kept his pecker in his pants?"

Mick yelled at him again. "What was the plan, asshole?"

He gave Mick a sullen look and tapped his fingers on the table, cocking his head to the side. "I was mainly along for the ride. McKenna was the one with the arrangement with Paul. I shoulda known better."

"I'm losing patience here, Georgie. If that's true, you can help yourself by telling us their plan."

"We mainly kept our distance from all of you—from everyone on the ship—but we heard all your interviews with the crew members. We were waiting to see if anyone would say anything about Paul. If that happened, Lance was supposed to take care of it."

For a moment Mick thought he had not heard correctly. "What do you mean, you heard us, how?"

"You'll find them in the cabin anyway so I might as well tell you. Paul set us up with these super-sensitive listening devices so we could hear all your conversations through the walls."

Mick was amazed. "You mean to tell me you have been able to hear our personal and business conversations the whole time?"

"Yeah, pretty much. We carried these ah . . . electro-acoustic receivers," he boasted as if Mick should be impressed. "They're black boxes only about this big." He held his thumb and forefinger about four inches apart. "Paul said they're used for finding bombs and shit because they pick up sound vibrations even through concrete. But I spose they're illegal as hell for what he was doin. We just set up in the next room or in the corridor and could hear everthin, no problem."

Mick was shocked to think this had been going on without their having any idea. "So, you know we never found out anything."

Georgie laughed. "Yeah, nice try smart guy. I'm afraid we heard everthin that Trindade girl said, and she wouldn't a been no threat to Paul. I made sure she's too scared to ever tell anyone that story again."

"What? What did you do to her, you bastard?"

"Naw, I just put the fear a God into her. She's OK. I figured that'd be enough for Paul, but Lance wanted to do somethin else to her . . . he didn't get a chance.

"That had better be true."

He folded his hands on the table and affected a forlorn expression. "Paul will cut off my balls when he finds out we blew this job. He and Lance are pretty tight, so that'll make it even worse. I knew we shouldn't confront you and the broad on shore. That was all McKenna's idea, and I didn't know he had a knife. I thought he was just gunna to scare ya."

Mick was incredulous. This guy isn't the smartest tool I've ever come across, he thought. "Hey Georgie, don't you have a clue that Paul is now the least of your worries?"

Mick left Marone locked in the room. When he was finally able to contact Roger, he asked to meet him back in security so that he could witness and verify the confession. After the prisoner repeated everything to Roger, Mick noted that he did not deviate from his original story: Basically, they were sent to spy on Mick and Tom with electronic equipment; McKenna attacked Rachael but not the other women; and Marone had not hurt anyone, except during the final attack on shore, which was McKenna's idea. Mick pushed a pad of paper and a pen across the table to him. "Write it all down and sign it."

By the time it was over, the prisoner was shedding a few crocodile tears—mostly over having been caught, but he was also congratulating himself for keeping one loose end to himself—*the other job.*

Later that evening after they entered international waters Roger released Tom. After hearing about the confession, the captain agreed that Tom acted in self-defense and the cruise line would take no action against him. He would have to give his account of the incident to the FBI of course.

With the assistance of a phone call from a Spanish-speaking World of Seas manager in Davie, Florida to the Montevideo police chief, the captain also convinced the local authorities that they did not want the headache that would result from trying to handle this cruise ship debacle.

After Mick described the details of Marone's statement, Tom could not wait to call Murray. It was late afternoon in Vegas, and the conversation made Murray's day and more. Tom noted that the ordinarily no-nonsense agent seemed uncharacteristically ecstatic. Murray assured him that this news would put Paul away for a long time, maybe forever, and they might not even need testimony from the Trindade girl. She would be their back-up just in case Paul's attorneys managed to somehow discredit or eliminate Marone's confession.

Murray said he would arrange with headquarters for the U.S. Marshals to meet the ship in Miami to take Marone back to Vegas, and would arrange for transport of McKenna's body as well. "I'll take great pleasure in arranging for an arrest warrant for Denezza. I'm sure he'll be wondering why he isn't hearing from his thugs on the ship, and I can't wait to see his face when we take him. I'll be there in person for that."

"For now, the DC and Miami FBI will be investigating the two rapes and the woman's suspicious death and of course Joe Moretti's antics. None of that seems to have anything to do with Paul unless McKenna really did attack the other women."

"We might get some DNA evidence to pan out, but if not, I guess it's possible we'll never know . . . just like so many other crimes committed on cruise ships," Tom said. "That's a statement I never thought I'd hear myself make. I guess any remnant of my loyalty to World of Seas and the cruise industry must be long gone."

76

Day 28 – at sea

Tom made it his practice to keep his romance with Wendy entirely apart from his work. He never discussed the interviews with her, even when she subtly asked about them a few times. At this point, he was trying to deal with his ambivalent feelings about McKenna's death. Despite his law enforcement background, having killed the man weighed heavily. Other than that, everything seemed to have come together neatly, and he was trying to completely relax for the first time. He still believed he should maintain confidentiality concerning the work until he and Mick were able to complete their documentation of the crimes.

Wendy had poured them each a glass of wine, and now she was sitting at the desk-vanity preparing for bed. The day had been pleasant, and Tom even spent time with her at the pool, which he had never done before. Everything seemed fine—the same as always only Tom was a little more subdued. She looked up at his reflection in the mirror as he stood a few feet behind her, watching. She had to find out what he was thinking so she chose her words carefully.

"You must be so relieved to have caught those men, well, except for the death. I was so scared when you were fighting with him, and then all that blood was horrible. Everything is OK now, right?"

Tom had been thinking all day about what he wanted to ask her and now seemed a good time since she had broached the subject. "Yes, it's a relief to finally have the information we were looking for." He came around to stand beside her. "Wendy, I want to ask you something. Had you seen Lance McKenna around the ship? I just wondered if you knew him from somewhere?"

"No, Tom. How would I?"

"We all noticed the way you reacted when he . . . when I stabbed him. It was like you had some connection."

"I had never seen a person die before. I guess it must have really affected me. That's all, Tom."

Tom wanted to accept what she said. He knew he had fallen into a relationship with her that held deep meaning for him and he believed she felt the same way. Still, his powers of observation had not entirely failed him. Cringing inwardly, Tom realized he did not fully believe what she had just said with such apparent sincerity. It was possible she was so sensitive that she would react to a stranger's death in that manner, but he also knew that Darcy and Mick had noticed her behavior and thought it was off somehow.

She finished brushing her hair and got up. Without speaking, she carried her glass, her reading glasses, and a book to her side of the bed. She placed them on the small nightstand then turned down the covers, looking up at him suggestively. "I'm so tired, Tom, aren't you? The sun was so hot out there, it wore me out." She sat on the edge of the bed and opened the little drawer in the nightstand about three inches. She placed her glasses inside but did not close it all the way.

Tom stripped off his clothes down to his briefs and went to his side of the bed. He smiled down at her as he reached to switch off the overhead lights. The darkened room glowed with a soft yellow aura from the low-wattage light above the vanity. Wendy's thick almost-black hair glistened where it fell around her face. His breath caught when she smiled and held out her hand for him to join her.

He was troubled by their earlier conversation, but he was determined to put it aside for now. The cruise was almost over, and he wanted to show how much he cared and wanted to be with her. As if reading his mind, she rolled onto her side to face him and whispered, "I can't believe the cruise will be over in two days. The time has gone so fast, hasn't it?" She closed her eyes and sighed. "There isn't much time left for anything."

He faced her with his head tilted back so that he could see her more clearly—without the blurry near-vision of middle age. On many evenings he had enjoyed removing her thin, short nightie like the one she was wearing now. He put his hand on her rounded hip and rubbed gently along the silky fabric.

"I have been thinking about what will happen with us when we get home," he said and held his breath waiting for her reply.

"What is meant to be will be. I know it sounds trite, but I have to believe that."

This was not a definitive declaration of her feelings for him, but he thought perhaps it went without saying. Yes, if their romance was meant to be, as surely it was, everything would fall into place—like it has for Mick and Darcy, he thought.

Wendy's thoughts were racing down an entirely different path. She had put this moment off for weeks and could no longer wait. *Yes, some things really do have to turn out as they are intended, even if we have doubts.*

Tom leaned up on one elbow and began the familiar process of pulling her nightie off over her head with one hand, while he caressed her belly and breasts with the other. With his eyes closed, he brought his mouth to her nipple and flicked with his tongue in the manner he had learned she loved. He felt her shift position and knew that she was pulling the garment off the back of her head and dropping it onto the floor.

But in the back of his mind, he knew something did not feel quite right. She had leaned so far away from him that he lost contact with her body. Just as he opened his eyes, she raised her arm and brought it down hard against his upper thigh. "What the hell." He jerked his leg to the side and looked down in total disbelief.

A hypodermic needle was embedded there, its plunger still at the top position. He reached for it, but she was faster. She jumped on top of him and positioned her leg so that he could not reach the needle, then reached around behind to finish the injection process. Her hand came down on the plunger just as Tom raised his body off the bed and threw her to the side.

He felt another jab and the needle came away in her hand. She threw it across the room, and neither of them saw it hit the wall and fall down behind the couch. In a panic, realizing that she had injected him with something, he grabbed her shoulders and shook her violently. "What did you do, what did you give me, some kind of drug?" He could not fathom what had just happened, or why.

She could not get away from him, so she merely knelt on the bed, her head hanging down onto her chest. Tom stood up at the side of the bed and looked down on the shining waves draped around her face. He was breathing deeply and waiting for some reaction to whatever had been in the syringe. A light-headed feeling slowly manifested. Grabbing her chin and forcing her to look up at him, what he saw there was unexpected. Her hard expression did not convey remorse, sadness, or even anger. In that instant, Tom knew that she was something and someone far different from what she pretended to be.

His chest felt as though it was cracking. With tears stinging his eyes he struggled to gain some composure in the silence of the cabin. Then very quietly he asked, "What was in the needle, Wendy?"

She continued to stare at him with a frightening alien expression, then sighed deeply, and her composure gave way. "It's not Wendy, Tom. It's Lilith—Lilith Schrom. Even as she tossed her head defiantly, tears streamed down her cheeks.

Never in his life had Tom experienced anything close to this shock and disbelief. She lied about her name, was all he could think. Then the connection came. "My God, you are the researcher that Darcy found out about . . . the Death Stalker research. He felt the blood drain from his face and he put his hand down to his thigh as he started to collapse onto the bed. He yelled at her. "You injected me with venom? Are you crazy? Oh my God." He had turned his back on her to reach for the phone when Lilith hit him over the head with the bedside lamp.

She got up and quickly dressed. She was in a daze and only knew she had to get out of the room before Tom woke up—if he woke up. *But where will I go?* She could not believe her plans had fallen so short. Paul would kill her if she did not complete this job. She looked at Tom. He should be dying, but he was lying quietly and breathing steadily with only a welt rising on the top of his head.

Lilith frantically searched for the syringe she had brought onto the ship in an insulin kit and stored in her cabin's mini-fridge. She had to know if Tom had received the full dose of the serum she had concocted from scorpion venom, but she knew the answer. The amount planned for him would have caused almost immediate death. She looked everywhere but could not find her weapon.

Tom groaned and started to pull himself up from the floor. She looked around again and then stared at him. As he slowly sat on the bed and turned his head to the side to look at her, she knew. Not only had she failed to inject the venom, but she had been caught, and nothing short of a trip over the side of the ship would save her from Paul or prison.

Five minutes later, still frightened but subdued, Lilith held a cold, wet towel against Tom's head. At first, she had sobbed uncontrollably and repeatedly said she was sorry, but that was over along with everything else. Her explanation seemed believable about how surprised she was to learn that Paul also sent Lance and the other man on the cruise. She knew Lance from the casino gambling tables but said she'd never before seen Marone.

She also told him about her gambling addiction, and about how Paul had been able to force her to be his weapon against Tom. Tears ran down her face again. "I have fought so hard on the ship to stay away from the casino, but during the day I have gone there and . . ." She sobbed into her hands. " . . . I've lost so much more money."

A knock on the door brought Tom to his feet. His emotions were flat, and his head was still pounding when he opened the door and peered sheepishly at Roger.

Lilith rolled over onto her side and cried softly. Tom looked at her and said, "Can we just take her card key and put a hasp on the outside? Let her stay here instead of going to the brig?"

After having maintenance secure her inside the cabin, Tom went with Roger to security and provided more details about who she was and why she had attacked him. Then he said, "What I want right now, Roger, is to talk to Marone again."

At first, he denied any knowledge of Paul's other plan, but Tom and Roger pressed him and pointed out that his situation could only be helped by cooperation.

"Yeah, OK, Paul told Lance to get rid of Schrom after she did the other thing. I wasn't part of that deal." He looked up at Tom. "Hey man, I'm glad she didn't get it done. I guess she waited too long or didn't have the guts when it came down to it."

After they left, Georgie concentrated on turning what he had told them into the whole truth in his mind. No one except Paul knew that he had hired both of them to throw Lilith over the side as soon as she eliminated Smythe. Now Paul was screwed, and Lance was an idiot who had gotten what he deserved. It had been just plain stupid to take that knife on shore.

No one knew, or ever would know, about the rapes—Lance hadn't even figured it out. The thought of that puss raping anyone was hilarious. Paul had assured them that the inept security staff on the ship would not know how to handle serious problems, especially once Smythe was out of the picture. True enough, the ship had turned out to be a great place to play out his fantasies. But why, he wondered, had that Schrom bitch waited so long to try and get rid of Smythe?

Georgie knew he had done everything possible to make sure the blame for almost everything would fall on McKenna. He congratulated himself once again, this time for having the foresight to toss his blond wig, spray paint, and ski mask over the side. What a fantastic brainstorm it had been to buy that equipment in a shop in Puerto Vallarta—on a whim—figuring they might come in handy if he needed to soothe his urges and avoid blame for his resulting actions.

77

January 15, 2009 - Washington, DC

We flew from Rio to DC, and the trip home was thankfully uneventful, but the emotional atmosphere was highly charged. Poor Tom was literally going through a grieving process over Wendy . . . Lilith. I knew all along that something didn't seem right about her, but I suppressed my concerns because Tom liked her so much. I understood very well that I would have been entirely undone by guilt if she had succeeded in killing him. If only there had been a picture of her in the research literature, I thought, I would have recognized her.

As it turned out, Roger called Tom while we were waiting to board our flight to tell him that the stateroom attendant found the hypodermic while she was vacuuming the cabin after Lilith was taken off the ship. The syringe was full, and apparently, none of the venom reached Tom's system. He was preserving the evidence for the FBI. The bureau was undoubtedly going to be busy when the ship docked in Miami.

Mick confided in me during the long plane ride that he thought he had made a breakthrough of sorts. "I don't know if I can explain it. I think the act of protecting you—fighting for you on the street in Montevideo—somehow canceled out some of my feelings of guilt and helplessness about the attack last year. I wasn't thinking about the danger to myself." He took my hand and held it in his lap with both of his. "I only thought that I had to take care of you." He squeezed my hand a little tighter and grinned. "I love you so much, sweetheart, and I know I will forever."

This was like the happy ending of a fairy tale. There had been so many ups and downs over the past year that as long as he was acting and talking like the Mick I first met, I didn't care how he rationalized it. I knew he still had a long way to go.

Rachael came home with us as planned, and she and I were staying at the condo in Tenleytown. We'd been back only a few days, but I was already helping her make appointments with the colleges. We hoped they would be able to meet with her during the two weeks before she flew home to Buenos Aires—possibly for the last time. She would return to DC to begin school in the spring.

But I was secretly worried about her. She seemed uncharacteristically quiet and even a little irritable. Ironically, I was thinking that my girl would benefit from the same kind of trauma counseling Mick was arranging for himself. The trouble was, she refused to discuss it with me. In fact, she laughed and said she was happy to be applying for school and that she felt fine. "I had practically forgotten about the attempted rape until you mentioned it," she said with a completely straight face.

Yeah, right! Her parents still wanted her to return to Argentina and then move to Africa with them, but she had refused. It occurred to me that Rachael wouldn't do anything anyone wanted her to do.

When she left for Buenos Aires, I planned to return to Colorado to finish moving out of my patio home. I would eventually sell it but had decided to wait until the real estate market improved. I would place my larger furnishings in storage and just wasn't sure how long they would be there.

For the foreseeable future, Mick was going to be very busy with his team, analyzing data and writing their report to Congress. Bill's staff was waiting for GAO's results so they could finish drafting their legislation. I was learning a lot about this process and finding it fascinating. It appealed to my scientific and analytical curiosity. Of course, I was currently unemployed, except for having somehow reinvented myself as an author. I was already making notes for my next book.

78

March 1, 2009

Mick had been seeing a counselor for five weeks and seemed to be doing OK. He said it was helping him, but I wondered if he had already done a lot of the healing by himself. My joy over having our loving, intimate life back was indescribable. Apparently, Mick is the man of my dreams after all. Rachael's situation was another thing entirely. Despite her initial attempt at normalcy, she had become increasingly depressed, and neither Mick nor I had been able to convince her to seek help.

She returned to Argentina as planned to see her parents before their transfer to Kenya. I only talked to her once right after she arrived home and it was clear that Ray and Marianne were exerting a lot of pressure on her to stay with them. They were afraid for her, and how could I blame them? It was a shock when Rachael told me flatly that she had not decided whether she would go with them or come back to us. I was convinced she was leaning toward moving with them even though she did not want to live in Africa. I was beginning to worry I might never see her again.

I took a risk then and asked to speak with Marianne. I was surprised she would even talk to me but relieved because I had to tell her how strongly we felt that Rachael should get some professional help to deal with the trauma of the attack. Marianne did not think Rachael would have any problems now that she was home with them. To my dismay, she said, "God will help her heal. He is all she needs in addition to Ray and me." There was nothing I could say to that. To myself, I couldn't help wondering about how many people seemed to have more faith than common sense.

The saddest thing was that Rachael seemed genuinely to love Georgetown University and Bill had assured her the school would accept her with his recommendation. However, he was very clear that he would not exert any influence unless she was positive about what she wanted to do. That was the crux of her struggle—torn between the potential of college life with her beloved rowing sport and her parents' desire and influence. We were waiting to see what she would do.

79

April 15, 2009 - Las Vegas, Nevada

Brooks had done his share of soul-searching during the past fifteen years and had just completed another round. For the past six weeks, he had turned most of his management responsibilities for American Travel Corporation over to his vice president for operations so that he could devote some time to himself and his issues. Far from being a needy individual, he had demonstrated great strength of character in overcoming his addiction.

So it was not surprising that he was mightily worried about his new temptation to fall off the sobriety wagon. Two times since his combative conversation with Darcy, he came dangerously close to taking a drink. He had believed that part of his life was behind him, but the stress and sadness of the realizations now facing him were exacting a heavy toll. He attended two AA meetings, for the first time in years, and believed he'd found renewed strength and faith to help him stay sober.

Finally, he wrapped his mind around the fact that Darcy was not going to be a part of his life, other than being Rachael's mother. The next step had been even harder for him. After years of looking in only one direction, he finally faced the many possible routes his life could take. He realized he was not really in love with Darcy as he had convinced himself. Now he understood that he'd been trying to revisit the past, believing that if they were together, he could assuage his guilt over his previous outrageous behavior toward her and his daughter.

Connie returned from the cruise literally a broken woman. She had come into the office several times, and he couldn't help but notice that she was gaining weight. Again, due to his guilt over somehow having misled her— although he still did not grasp exactly what he had done that was so wrong— he could not fire her. At this moment, she was sitting in the chair in front of his desk, and he was trying to figure out how to talk to her without making things worse. "How are your leg and back, Connie? Are you healing up OK?"

The embarrassment over her misguided actions and now being called to Brooks's office were almost more than she could handle. At the same time, she was still full of anger at him for misleading her. She could not look him in the eye, so she let her gaze wander around the beautifully appointed office, which she had helped him decorate. "I'm getting better. My back aches a lot, but I'm sure it will heal eventually."

"I don't want to add to your problems, but I think you know that I'm aware of everything that went on between you and Darcy on the cruise." Connie shifted in her chair and looked out the window, her eyes glistening with a combination of sadness and rage.

"Anyway, I want you to know how sorry I am for whatever I did or said that caused this to happen. I also want to say that I know now there is no chance of my getting back into a relationship with Darcy. I was fooling myself about that and . . . wanting it to happen had pretty much taken over my life and my senses." Surprised at this confession, she turned her eyes back to him. "So Connie, I understand how a person can be sure of something and then find out they are mistaken. What I want to tell you . . . if you decide you want to stay on with ATC, you and I will have a completely professional relationship."

She stared at him. She'd expected he was going to fire her, and she couldn't believe this was the same man she had known for five years. Something had changed, making him more direct and open. Brooks was still talking. "If you do stay in your position, as a stipulation, you will have to agree to get some counseling. I'm pretty sure you have some anger and jealousy issues to work out."

So he thinks he knows what is best for me. Whatever the case, I can't afford to be out of work now. "I agree to that, if it's what you want."

"If you don't follow through with that . . . well . . . I hate to have to say this, but what you did to Darcy was a crime, and you might still have to pay."

So, a threat too. She nodded in agreement and shifted uneasily in her seat. It was clear that she did not want to spend any more time in his presence, so he concluded the meeting, and she left.

After the door closed quietly, he sat soaking in the silence. He glanced to the south at his beloved view of the strip shimmering in the sunlight. Tiny rainbows reflecting off thousands of glass panes brought a smile, but he wondered if he had done the right thing with Connie. Leaning back in his high-backed desk chair, he studied the ceiling for a few moments, then shot forward and grabbed the phone. Something else had been on his mind a lot lately. He'd held off contacting Sidney until now, but he was ready to face her.

He pushed the speed dial number for her cell and listened to it ring. Just as he thought her message would kick in, she picked up. "Hello Brooks, it's been quite a while. How've you been?"

"I haven't been doing very well, actually. Sidney, are you aware of the things that happened on the cruise with Darcy and my employee?"

"Yes, of course, Darcy filled me in on all of it. It sounds like she is fortunate she was not more seriously injured or killed. I can't imagine how you must feel about your employee having done that."

Using Paul's predicament as an opportunity to break the ice, Sidney had called Darcy during the previous week. At first, there was awkwardness between them, but their friendship had come too far for it to disintegrate now. She apologized to Darcy for overreacting with her phone call to Mick on the ship. "I don't know what I was thinking. I should have questioned Brooks more about what he said about you two instead of getting so upset, and I should have trusted you."

Darcy then described her last phone conversation with Brooks, and afterward, they both agreed to put the whole episode in the past. Of course, Darcy was also relieved that Paul would soon be out of the picture. Sidney asked, "Doesn't it all seem so pointless? His life is over and all because he wanted to make sure I didn't get his money. I'll bet even Paul can't understand how everything escalated so far out of control."

Sidney turned her attention back to the current call. "You know Brooks, because of you and our relationship I did a terrible thing too, and I'm really ashamed of myself."

"No! Don't say anything about it. You are not the one who is guilty here. Please, Sidney, I've thought about this a lot, and there is just one thing I want. If you can possibly agree, I'm asking for us to go to dinner tonight, or if you're busy, whenever you can. I know it isn't possible to pretend that things that happened didn't, but maybe we can sort of take it slow and start over. What do you think?

Sidney had also been thinking a lot about the situation with Brooks. After her conversation with Darcy, she knew he had been a little unbalanced to think he would get her back in his life. In response to his craziness, she had done something just as misguided with her call to Mick. She thought under the circumstances that maybe she and Brooks could both start over in a way. She still had strong feelings for him—that she knew for sure.

"I don't have any plans for tonight. Why don't you pick me up and we'll decide where to go to eat. But Brooks, my opinion is that we should talk about what happened between us and why."

80

May 5, 2009 – Washington, DC

"OK, both of you give me updates on where you are with your sections of the report." Mick reached across to the front of the desk and picked up the documents Eve and Danny had brought to the meeting. He thumbed through the draft report and then laid it aside and looked up at them expectantly.

Danny looked at Eve to make sure she wasn't going to jump in first with some off-the-wall comment, then began his presentation. "One of our messages seems pretty clear, and we can document it without any problem. That is the section on incidents of sexual assault and rape on cruise ships. Those are the most often reported crimes. We obtained data for 2008 for three major cruise lines with ships sailing out of ports in Florida, Texas, and California. These data were compiled from local law enforcement agencies, cruise line records, and ship's logs."

"From this fairly complete body of information we can say that in 2008 during 140 days of cruising, there were a total of seventy-two sexual assaults and rapes and fifty-one robberies. For the four million passengers on the ships during that time, our statistician calculated a rate of fifty-seven assaults per one hundred thousand passengers. It's a complicated formula to get there, but the point is that the number is higher than the rate for the entire U.S. for any year, not just 2008." He shrugged and looked down at his notes. "We'll have a lot of footnotes explaining various aspects of the analyses and statistical significance of the results of course." He paused to see if Mick had any questions.

"Sounds good so far, keep going, Danny."

"OK, the cruise lines say they have data showing it is safer to be on a ship than on land, but our findings contradict that. We have determined that there were no special circumstances that would make 2008 an atypical year. Besides, we have results from other private sector studies of crime on cruise ships over the past ten years, and they all have comparable results."

"The bottom line is there doesn't seem to be much that security on a ship can do to safeguard passengers under current conditions, especially in private areas. There are so many opportunities for these assaults to happen in the confined space of a ship at sea and we also found that many of the rapes were allegedly perpetrated by crew members against guests. The incidents occurred in many locations on the ships, but mostly in passenger cabins."

"So during 2008, there were four cases of passengers or crew members who went missing while at sea. It is relatively easy for a person who is drunk or otherwise incapacitated to get carried away and fall overboard, and that accounts for some disappearances. Others might be suicides. When you add the violent nature of some individuals, it is little wonder that people have disappeared or been assaulted on cruise ships. That's about it, Mick."

Mick was pleased with what their analyses were showing. "Good job, Danny. You'll need to refine your language some, and we just have to be careful about how we address the *Sea Nymph* case study. You know, almost everything that happened while we were on the ship was about vengeance of one kind or another, not random crime. Mostly it was Paul Denezza trying to cover himself and get back at us for interfering with his plans on the first cruise. He invited a lot of violence and madness when he hired people to do his bidding."

Mick leaned forward and sighed. I guess the good news is that by the time we make this public, his fate should be decided, and our part in it can be discussed openly at the hearings."

Next, it was Eve's turn to impress the boss. She sat up a little straighter and smoothed out her skirt. "OK, Mick, we have put together recommendations for the Congress to act on, but the jurisdictional problems remain when ships are in international waters. Outside the twelve-mile limit, there are no reporting requirements. Another big problem is that victims have limited access to police and medical care. Even onshore jurisdiction can be a serious problem, depending on the country. Our report will not have specific solutions for these problems, but here are the recommendations to Congress I've come up with for the report." She breathed deeply and began reading from the draft of her report sections.

- *Install higher guardrails, more deck cameras, and peepholes in cabin doors*
- *improve transparency in reporting crimes at sea, including establishing a structure between the cruise industry and the FBI, and requiring ships to maintain records of all deaths, alleged crimes, and passenger and crew complaints*

- *require ships to carry rape kits and have trained sexual assault specialists onboard*
- *implement education and training, for certain crew members, in crime prevention and detection, and evidence collection and preservation*
- *improve screening of cruise ship employment applicants to identify those with histories of violent or sexual crimes.*

"We also think that specific well-established law enforcement practices should be applied to the cruise ship environment, like limiting access to crime scenes, using protective clothing to prevent contamination of the scene, photographing all aspects of the crime, and making sure sexual assault victims are not allowed to eat, drink, shower, or brush their teeth prior to being examined." She sat back and waited for Mick's response.

"OK, that sounds good. I'll look at your draft in depth and give you my comments. Thanks to both of you. I don't see any problem with Senator Sawyer being able to draft legislation with this information. Eve, I know he would also like to somehow address the problem you described with lack of jurisdiction in international waters."

81

July 3, 2009 – Marco Island, Florida

I ran my hand over the brown speckled marble and watched a ray of sunlight sparkle off the specks of garnet. Rising off my stool to see out the picture window, I craned my neck to see the water's edge at the bottom of the sloped lawn. No manatees in sight. I still could not get used to the idea that the usually elusive animals would come right up to the little wooden dock at the back of Mick's property.

Then I looked back at my manuscript on the screen before me and thought again about how grateful I was to have this peaceful environment in which to write. And to escape from the public uproar and media attention due to the unlikely events of our two cruises. I was also finding that this lovely Florida-style home, which Mick's parents had left him, was an inspirational place for me to write.

I closed the laptop and got up to get a glass of ice water. As I was closing the refrigerator, Mick came up behind me, and his arms encircled my shoulders. I turned into him and waited for that familiar and welcome look straight into my eyes and seemingly through me.

"Are you still thinking about Rachael?" he asked, pulling me in close.

I had been so troubled about her, and I was still trying to come to terms with having found and now seemingly lost my daughter again. She had gone to Africa with her parents after all, and last we heard she had entered a government-sponsored counseling program to deal with the feelings left behind from her attack. I figured she would also be addressing everything that happened in her life over the past year and a half. Brooks and I were a big part of it, and now I realized how overwhelmed she must have been. She just had not been able to resist Ray and Marianne's pull on her, and I thought that maybe she needed to experience her familiar family environment for a while after everything she's been through.

"I was thinking, Mick," I said into the wonderful scent of his neck, "I have a feeling Rachael probably sought counseling only because Marianne didn't want her to. When I talked with her last night, she acted as if she's in limbo and has no plan to return to the States." Mick affectionately rubbed my back. "I'm just so sad and at odds with the way things turned out."

"I know it isn't what we expected," he said gently, "but she's young and she knows where you are. Give her a little time. She isn't forgetting about you, and nothing can change the fact that now you know her and where she is." He kissed my cheek and turned to walk toward the living room. Over his shoulder, he said, "by the way, I just got off the phone myself with Bill. His staff is finishing up the legislation on cruise ship safety." He's naming it the Rachael Alosa Act."

"Oh Mick, how wonderful, at least I think it is. How do you think Ray and Marianne will react?" I followed him out of the kitchen.

"They already have. Bill talked with them before he made the decision. He and the Alosas have been close friends for so many years that he knows how they will react to things and you know how much he cares for Rachael."

"Yes, I get the feeling she's like the daughter he never had."

"There's nothing but respect in the decision to name the legislation after her." We had reached the sofa and plopped down together, and Mick immediately stretched his legs out on the coffee table. "Anyway, Bill says the hearings are scheduled for next month in conjunction with the issuance of our report . . . so I'll be testifying for the GAO." He looked at me and frowned. "You haven't said yet whether you will come to DC with me or stay here."

"I'll probably go with you, sweetie. I can write at the condo as well as here. This is so great; will it be good for your career?"

"Actually, this whole cruise ship crime issue and our report have become such a hot topic that if all goes well and the bill is passed, it will be perfect for me. They say the president is in favor of this type of legislation and won't have a problem signing it." He was silent a moment then he picked up my hand and brought it to his lips, sending a thrill all the way down . . . "You get a lot of the credit too," he said between kisses on my knuckles, "because your first book and the anticipation for your next one has drawn so much attention to the subject."

"Isn't it strange that both of us are benefiting from all the madness and violence?"

He shrugged. "I've thought about that. I don't know what to say other than I feel as if we earned it. By the way, Bill faxed me some portions of the speech he'll give when he introduces the legislation. His Senate International Relations Committee is co-sponsoring the bill with the Committee on Government Reform. Do you want to hear some of what he's going to say?"

"Of course."

He put his legs down and reached for a document from the table. I looked over his shoulder as he read.

"Each year eleven million people travel on cruise ships. We can't allow confusion over jurisdiction to endanger the lives of Americans who enjoy this mode of travel. Criminals must be held accountable for their crimes at sea, just as they are on land. We commend the GAO for its unique approach to studying this issue. The data on specific crimes, some of which GAO staff witnessed first-hand, are invaluable in supporting this measure . . ."

"Bill said the House Committee that oversees International Relations is sponsoring a similar bill, and there isn't much doubt that they will both pass, be combined, and reach the president's desk." We leaned back, and Mick held my hand. He had become so much more romantic—the way he was when we started out and I was hoping it would last.

"Oh, and apparently, a very influential lobbying organization called International Cruise Safety, led by the father of a woman who disappeared from a cruise ship, has given its full support to the legislation, and Bill said some law firms will be there to testify because they were hired to represent cruise ship victims or their families." He turned his body toward me. "Listen to this, one of them will say their research found that out of 190 complaints of sexual assault on cruise ships during a five year period, not one perpetrator was prosecuted. That should pretty much seal the deal for us."

"That is great news for your study. Can I come and sit in the gallery when you testify?"

"Absolutely, I'll ask Bill to get you a pass."

Mick had been commuting between DC and Marco every other week, and since his return two days ago we had both been engrossed in our separate work. We hadn't had much opportunity to talk, and this seemed like a good time to catch up.

Both of us were relieved about Paul's impending trial. Murray called to tell us that the government expected an easy conviction for his scheme to kill Sidney. Once it's over Paul will spend the rest of his life in prison, most likely at the U.S. penitentiary in Florence, Colorado also known as super-max. Georgie Marone had become an eager witness for the government in return for some leniency in his own pending case.

Murray told us the prosecutor videotaped Isabel Trindade's testimony and she might not have to appear in person. Our previous depositions will also be introduced. They mostly concerned Suzanne's role in the plot, which was tangential to Paul's case. Sidney will have to testify in person, but she's prepared and will be able to handle it. Paul will also stand trial separately for his additional crimes; sending McKenna, Marone, and Schrom to menace and possibly kill passengers on the recent cruise. Again, Marone will be a star witness.

With respect to the crime scenes on the ship, the limited evidence collected revealed only one useful DNA sample—Marone's—from the swab taken from Rachael's fingernails. His plan to blame McKenna for everything fell apart once the evidence linked him to that attack. As a result, he will likely spend a lot of time in prison, albeit a reduced sentence in exchange for his testimony against Paul.

Seemingly, Paul Denezza and his cohorts had counted on there being no competent investigation or collection of evidence on the ship. He might have been correct in this assumption, had Tom not been there to insist on at least some forensic data collection. In fact, no one will probably ever know what happened to the woman who died of a heart attack after being assaulted on the deck, since no evidence was found linking that crime to Marone or anyone else.

Tom was keeping us informed about the World of Seas case against Joe Moretti, initially handled by the North Miami FBI Field Office. They had moved him to Armor Correctional facility, a prison hospital in Miami, to undergo some sort of treatment for alcoholism. He was in a lot more trouble than he probably ever imagined, and I could only wonder what his state of mind must be now that he was sober and awaiting his fate. The Department of Homeland Security in Miramar, Florida had an effort underway to establish jurisdiction for his crimes, at least concerning the eighteen hundred Americans onboard. Evidently, the government wanted to charge him with terrorism. His sabotage attempts had all taken place in international waters so once again the jurisdictional issues would be complicated.

Meanwhile, Lilith was living in the Las Vegas jail at federal expense and without bail and was about to stand trial for her attacks on Tom. Since she was an Israeli citizen, the U.S. could decide to deport her following her sentencing. The Israeli government does not have any extradition agreement with the U.S., but in this case, they have expressed interest in exchanging her for a U.S. citizen being held in one of their prisons. They apparently consider Dr. Schrom to be a valuable asset.

Tom was not looking forward to her trial where he would have to testify and was keeping a low profile while he struggled to come to terms with her deception. He found an apartment in Marco only about a mile from us, and we were getting together for dinners when Mick was in town. A few nights ago, Tom revealed that he was mostly upset about how vulnerable he had been—

so easily taken in by her. How long would it be, I wondered before he would be able to trust his instincts about women?

He was also trying to find a job in a terrible economy, and because of his age, security guard positions at condominium and townhome complexes were the only offers he had received. Mick had been asking around at the state and federal law enforcement agencies he worked with to see if he could find or create an opening for him. We hoped something would work with that because Tom has so much to offer.

Mick and I had been sitting on the couch for about a half hour talking about all these issues when my cell phone rang. I didn't recognize the number and hoped it wasn't a member of the press who had managed to track me down. "Hello? I answered tentatively."

"Hey Darcy, it's great to hear your voice. Are you and Mick recovering from your latest cruise adventure, or should we say nightmare?"

I put my hand over the phone. "It's Don and Charlie calling from home in Seattle," I whispered. "It's great to hear from you guys too. Mick is here with me at his house on Marco Island. We were just talking about all the aftermath from the past year. What a coincidence that you should call now.

"Maybe more than you think, Darcy." Charlie chuckled and then waited for a beat. "Wait till you hear why we're calling." I recognized an air of excitement in his voice that was puzzling. They were both on the line now and obviously struggling with which one of them was going to give me their news.

"OK," Don said after a short pause, "I'm elected. Darcy, our sweet daughter Penelope will celebrate her eighth birthday in February of 2011, and we have decided to take her on her first cruise to celebrate. We are going to Australia and then back across the Pacific. And well, we want you and Mick to come with us."

I started laughing out loud, and Mick gave me a curious look. "I love you guys, but I can't begin to tell you all the reasons why I never want to set foot on a cruise ship again."

Mick raised an eyebrow. "What is it?" he whispered.

I held up a finger while I listened to Don and Charlie tell me how many cruises they had been on where nothing out of the ordinary happened. Charlie got serious then. "We almost died on that first cruise with you, and it hasn't stopped us from cruising. What we are proposing is a year and a half in the future, Darcy. You will change your mind."

Don chimed in, "It will be a fabulous trip." I could picture his hand-in-the-air gesture. "You know we would never put our darling Penelope in danger."

After I disconnected, Mick and I just stared at each other. He had gotten the gist of the conversation, and after I filled him in, we both burst out laughing. "Can you believe that?" I asked.

"Well, they are right about it being a ways in the future, sweetie. Who knows, maybe we will change our minds. I suppose it could be the best cure for us—a completely different cruise in another part of the world—a happy, uneventful vacation. You know what they say about getting back on the horse . . . besides, there's no way lightning would strike a third time."

CPSIA information can be obtained
at www.ICGtesting.com
Printed in the USA
LVHW042206281019
635548LV00002B/256